THE DUKE'S AGENT

An early fan of Georgette Heyer's Regency romances, Rebecca Jenkins began collecting diaries and journals from Georgian England as a child. Her passion for the period led her to study history at Somerville College, Oxford, from where she went on to become an accomplished journalist and broadcaster. *The Duke's Agent* is her first novel. She lives in County Durham.

Also by Rebecca Jenkins

THE DUKE'S AGENT

Rebecca Jenkins

Quercus

Published in Great Britain in 2008 by Quercus
This paperback edition first published in 2009 by

Quercus
21 Bloomsbury Square
London
WC1A 2NS

Originally published in 1997 by Richard Cohen Books.

A CIP catalogue record for this book is available
from the British Library.

ISBN 978 1 84724 788 9

10 9 8 7 6 5 4 3 2 1

Printed and bound in Great Britain by Clays Ltd, St Ives Plc.

THE DUKE'S AGENT

CHAPTER ONE

It was early evening in late July. The vast sky was brushed with clouds. Pinks intermixed with soft blues and dim charcoal all hung against a luminous satin ground. A rider plodded along the path that ran through the wide expanse of wheat grass spreading out to the horizon. Both man and horse bore themselves with that air of detached resignation common to travellers who know it is a steady pace that goes the distance. The road crept up a broad flank of land then dropped towards a squat manor house tucked away in a dell. At the shoulder of the rise the rider checked his horse. Straightening his back and rubbing the aching muscle at his neck he sat contemplating the scene before him.

Along the sweep of the road every leaf and blade stood out as the sun painted it with exquisite definition. The house was old. The light acted on its bricks like linseed oil rubbed on fine wood, illuminating them with a ruddy glow that seemed to come from within. Five yew trees stood before the house. When they were planted their severe, dense lines had no doubt been a fashionable elegance, but with the years they had grown proud until their height overbore the house, blocking its mullioned windows. There was an air of abandoned shabbiness about the place, and the treacle light flooding over the valley touched the scene with mystery.

'No one home, eh, Walcheren?' said the man, patting the neck of his horse. The big bay raised his head a few inches from the grass, his attention fixed elsewhere. The man sighed and collected the animal, forcing its head up from its feed. 'Onward, old friend, there's a way to go yet.'

The iron gates were rusted back against their posts and weeds overran the gravel carriage circle. The house seemed to huddle over the yard. The stranger could not make up his mind whether the atmosphere was threatening or merely truculent. He halloed twice but no response broke the watchful stillness of the place.

'Quite forces a man to talk to himself,' he remarked and swung a booted foot over the animal's head to dismount. The horse, used to this unconventional descent, stood calmly, content to be abandoned.

The man standing looking up at the house was of medium height. He dressed in the fashion of a gentleman, nothing shabby, nothing flash, nothing very remarkable. He was the kind of man you might pass on the street and not notice unless your eyes happened to alight on his face. It bore examination, gaining in interest the closer you looked. Blue-grey eyes remarkably bright against tanned skin, in contrast to his hair which was the colour of ripening wheat. A straight nose, and lean cheeks marked out with strong parallel lines. A reserved, watchful face.

The studded oak door that sheltered under a stone vault was formidable, but on inspection proved to stand a little open. The stranger advanced into a hall where the light from the windows barely seeped in. His skin sensed damp. He called out, his voice falling dead on the air. The empty house was alive with a dull hum which seemed the audible embodiment of the stench of rotting things that thickened the air. A cramped staircase curved up to the left. As his eyes were adjusting to the lack of light it was the buzz of the flies that drew his attention. A large dog lay sprawled at the foot of the stairs, its bared fangs a dull gleam in the rictus of death. The lupine head lolled, part severed from the heaped body. The blood that had pumped from its dying flesh had dried to a sticky stain that heaved with blue flies.

Holding a handkerchief to his face, the man took stock of his surroundings. To the right was a low doorway. He crossed to it, his firm step ringing out cleanly on the stone flags. The doorway led into a large, oblong room looking out over gardens to the rear of the house. Through high old windows he caught a glimpse of an ancient parterre clogged with weeds. Heavy tapestries covered the walls. One was half torn away; the tattered remainder hung askew, dangling perilously from a rusty nail. The remains of a wood fire, a few days old perhaps, stirred in the draught. The mantel above the fireplace was blackened with smoke.

The stranger contemplated the comfortable wing chair that stood by the cold hearth, newspapers strewn about it. He flicked up the corner of one. It was folded back to the central section bearing the despatches from the war and reports of the prices at the London Corn Exchange. It was easy to imagine some person perusing them there of a night. His booted foot dislodged a square brown bottle from a pile that lay half-concealed behind a log basket. It lolled heavily on to its side, the noise making him start. All around was the debris of a male, solitary life – a discarded glove, a scuffed riding crop, a rack of pipes and a near-empty tobacco jar with a cracked lid.

There was nothing to interest him here. The stranger continued his search. He came to a room that had been a library, though there was little more left now than the ghost of the books that once filled its shelves. A small collection bore signs of use. With a gloved hand he tipped their spines one by one towards the light. A *Young Farmer's Calendar*, Tull and Miller on tillage. A handbill floated free from between pages. It extolled the virtues of a Complete Guide to Landlords, Tenants and Lodgers – '*being a methodical Arrangement of the whole law respecting the taking or letting of Lands, Houses, or Apartments*'. He returned the sheet to its place. The remaining books were mostly a collection of sporting volumes. He struck his hands together to rid his gloves of dust.

Whereas the rest of the house was greatly neglected, the disarray in this room was more systematic. A chair lay on its back and the desk that stood in the window had been disembowelled. Its drawers lay about it in a sea of trampled and torn paper. The stranger's manner grew alert, his interest focused on the desk. He righted the chair and set to sifting the debris of paper. During his search he abstracted a few sheets which he folded up and put in his coat. After a while he stood a moment, scanning the room. He drew up a pair of library steps and made a swift and efficient search of the higher shelves and other crannies where something might have been overlooked. At last he gave up. The shadows were pressing in on the room, the sun near setting.

Brushing a cobweb off his coat, he retraced his steps to the front yard. His horse, who had wandered off in search of fresher grass, trotted up at his master's appearance as if glad of the company.

'Rum set-up, old boy,' the stranger commented, rubbing the animal's velvet nose. 'Our man's housekeeping left something to be desired. Dirty camp, rotten unit, d'you think?'

The gelding merely tossed his head, eager to be gone. The man laughed and, mounting once more, turned the animal out of the gate. Passing through a plantation of large-leaved limes and oaks below the house, they picked up a winding track marked by a small white boulder bearing the words 'Woolbridge, 2 miles'.

The high grasses and dropping ground soon hid the house from view. The rider took a deep breath of the fragrant air. The track skirted a hay-field, then inclined sharply downwards into an old wood clothing the steep banks of a gorge that channelled a fast-moving stream. A quaint bridge spanned the water, on the far side of which was a little house of dressed grey stone. Since there was no grand house in sight for which it might crown a perspective, the rider guessed it had been built as a fashionable eye-catcher by some landscape-improver of the last generation. The tea-house had an elegantly wrought-iron balcony that overhung the gorge, an ideal place to set up an easel, he thought. The setting was dramatic. The mellow stone bridge, the white falling away of precipitous rocks, the rushing torrent below, the over-arching trees with trailing green boughs – there was enough interest and composition to delight any admirer of the picturesque.

'Fair makes the heart leap up,' murmured the traveller. The horse danced a step or two, tossing his head against the reins. 'Walcheren, you have no eye,' his master told him. 'Never fear, I know there is no time to take a sketch – more's the pity.'

Casting a final appreciative look over his shoulder, the man spurred his horse at a trot on into the wood.

The dying sun was not strong enough to penetrate the forest. The light filtered in grey-green as he rode along the track. Tree stumps loomed over the path, grotesque outlines textured with obscene funguses growing liver-spotted and luminous. Through the tangle of branches the powerful presence of the brown water made itself felt as it tumbled over white square slabs of rock below. The dwindling path grew slick with clay mud. The horse whinnied nervously, his hooves sliding on the treacherous surface. The rider began to doubt that this could be the right path.

Ezekiel Duffin hung his weight on a branch and slithered down the bank. He was tired. His boots pinched and his attention was fixed on reaching the sheep hut where he planned to spend the night. He would build a fire, free his bruised feet and spend the evening working at the leather of his boots with the ball of goose fat he kept in his knapsack. His stomach rumbled and he adjusted the rush bag that hung under his long coat. The two trout that rested there would make a fine supper. Cheered by the thought, he made a clicking noise to his dog and cut through the undergrowth towards the old track that ran down by the river.

There was a crashing sound, as if a large and none too sure-footed deer or stag bounded through the undergrowth, and a figure propelled himself on to the path almost directly under the horse's hooves. Walcheren rose up in fright on his hind legs, his eyes rolling.

'God save me!' Duffin cried, throwing up his arms to protect his head.

'Reason would be a better aid. What the devil do you mean jumping out like that?' cursed the rider as he struggled to calm his mount.

A yellow dog was barking and dashing about between the horse's feet. Walcheren reared up again, stretching every sinew to bolt away from this terrifying place. The rider wrenched him around in a circle to distract him from this purpose. He shouted at the man to get the dog away. The large bay, whipping about with unexpected speed, struck the man from the narrow path.

His arms flailing, Ezekiel Duffin snatched vainly around him for something to stop his fall. The treacherous undergrowth gave way under his bulk and he rolled down the bank into the river, a branch knocking his head with a glancing blow as he fell. He came to rest with the upper half of his body on land, but his legs lost their purchase. The vast weight of water pressed sleek and brawny about them, willing him to join the river's course. Duffin cast his strong arms about the freezing surface of the rock. Buffeted by the immense load of the water, his lower body swung out into the stream. On the bank, his dog ran backwards and forwards, barking uncontrollably.

'Shut your yap, ya daft bugger,' Duffin mumbled irritably through his haze.

The rider regained control of his mount and, anchoring him to a branch, moved swiftly down the bank calling out, 'Hold fast. I'm on my way.'

'I'm holding,' responded the poacher in a dour tone. What did the fool think he'd be doing? he muttered to himself, aggrieved.

A strong grip took hold of his wrists and the rider dragged Duffin on to the rocky ground. Duffin clambered to his feet, shaking himself like a large bear. He batted a not unfriendly hand at his dog, which leapt up at him whimpering with relief.

'Hold your peace, Bob, bloody animal.' He accepted the proffered arm, and the stranger helped to haul his stocky figure back up to the path. 'Well now, sir, I don't rightly know whether to thank you or curse you – you and your horse. Mind you, fine one, he is,' he said admiring the handsome Cleveland bay, his polished oak coat set off by black legs, mane and tail. Ezekiel put up a confident hand to the horse's neck. Walcheren dropped his head to have his nose rubbed. 'Well, no harm done, eh? And I beg your pardon, boy, for startling you so,' he told the horse. 'But you gave me a bit of a frit, too. That you did.'

The rider climbed back down the bank and returned with Duffin's rush bag which had broken loose in his fall. The nose of a trout peeped coyly out through a gap in the weave. Duffin's eyes grew wary. His rescuer was a gentleman, that was clear.

'You're new in these parts, sir. Passing through?'

'I'm on my way to Woolbridge. Am I on the right road? Though road would seem an extravagant term for this blasted track.' The gentleman swatted at an insect that pitched its high whine into his ear. 'This is yours, I believe.' He handed over the bag and leant down briefly to acknowledge the dog,

Bob, who was making overtures of friendship at his knee. 'Fresh trout make a good dish for a hungry man,' he commented blandly.

He swung himself up on to his bay, gathering the reins. Duffin stepped back from the horse's head. His dark face broke into a crooked smile.

'This track's not much used these days, but it'll take you to Woolbridge, given time. You've not much longer in the wood. Hurry and I'd reckon you'll make the bridge before sundown.'

'I'd best be gone then.' The gentleman hesitated. 'May I make some reparation?' He made as if to take money from his purse, but stopped at Duffin's dismissive wave.

'I'm in no need of charity, your honour. It was an accident pure and simple. No harm done.'

He looked about him and spotted a shape stuck in a branch to the side of the cut made by his recent descent. 'I even see me hat. Well now, God is gracious!'

'Good evening to you. I hope you make a warm fire soon and dry those clothes,' the gentleman called after him as he set off.

'Aye, I will, never fear,' came the reply.

Glancing back, the rider saw the poacher's stocky figure stepping cautiously through the undergrowth to retrieve his hat, followed by his yellow mongrel.

The man had not misled him. The green vault of trees soon began to open out. The woods thinned and the path climbed up to a wide plateau of newly enclosed common. The fledgling hedgerows and fresh-cut fencing wobbled across the land, as if uncertain of their permanence. In the cut below, the river broadened, growing more civilised in measure with the taming of its banks. Its surface composed itself to a glassy smoothness and there, as the river bent, was Woolbridge, a market town of some five thousand souls.

At last he approached the ancient bridge. Across it, the town sprawled before him in the setting sun. Down stream the river was stained purple, red and ochre with the dye from the woollen works at the water's edge. The houses clotted together around yards in growing density along the alleyways threaded around the mills and tanning pits that scarred the lower town.

The mud rose up the gelding's legs as they passed through the cramped alleys of the working quarter. The stench from the tanning yards and the rotting sewage in the sinks between the tenements made it an unhealthy place. No one lingered there unless they had to. The buildings piling up the hill grew better spaced. The street broadened and began to show elements of graciousness as it approached the brow of the hill. It was here, beyond the market place, that the leading citizens of Woolbridge had their dwellings, fine stone houses built on plots spiralling out about the parish church, whose medieval tower crested the town.

The lamps were being lit outside the houses as the rider turned his tired horse into the stable yard of the Queen's Head. Standing opposite the church at the junction of the main eastern and southern roads into Woolbridge, this was the town's finest hostelry. Here Jasper Bedlington, innkeeper, was honoured to cater to the gentry (Fine Assembly Rooms – Dances held twice a month in the Winter Season). The postboy had just brought the papers from the posting house at Greta Bridge, so the front parlour was unexpectedly busy. Captain Adams had that moment arrived to collect his copy of the *Newcastle Courant* and was making conversation with Mr Gilbert, the surgeon, who, on the same pretext, had come to take a glass of wine in company.

Captain Adams, a well-preserved man of fifty or so, had retired from a line regiment some years previously. He liked to cultivate the air of a bluff, no-nonsense soldier, though his contemporaries in the regiment might have told you that he was a quiet sort of fellow when in the King's service. Mr Gilbert was a leading citizen of the town. A surgeon by training, he was a man of means and only practised occasionally when particularly desired, or when he felt the need to demonstrate the lesser talents of Dr Phitts, the town's other medical man, who was forced to doctor for a living.

Having prevailed upon Mr Gilbert to keep him company with a glass of port, Captain Adams arranged himself by the parlour fire, settling his stiff leg on a wooden stool.

'So I hear His Grace the Duke is sending some fellow to investigate that Crotter's affairs, eh?'

Mr Gilbert, a discreet man, contented himself with lifting a knowing eyebrow across the top of his glass.

Captain Adams snorted and rubbed his leg. 'Never was a death more providential, I'd say!' He took a draught and speculated how far old Gilbert would open up. The man liked to play at piety like a canting Methodist but underneath it all he was as fond of gossip as any. 'Potter discovered him, they tell me.'

'It was he who brought the corpse into town,' replied Mr Gilbert carefully. One of his many contributions to the life of the community of Woolbridge was to serve as medical authority on the few occasions when cause of death needed to be ascertained. 'He'd been dead a day or two – his heart stopped as he sat in front of his fire. May the Lord have mercy on his soul and may the lesson remind us all of the precious gift of life.'

Captain Adams did not quite see the connection. From his point of view Crotter had died. The precious gift of life had proved something of a jilt to him – but he was not going to quarrel.

'There was no one to miss him, I suppose,' he observed.

Mr Gilbert flinched a little at the Captain's robust lack of proper sentiment in the face of death. The bluff soldier gazed into the fire.

'Never would have servants about the place. The man lived like a pig.'

'Captain! Captain!' the surgeon protested. 'We should not speak so of the dead! It is true that Mr Crotter perhaps lacked the domestic felicity such as you and I gain from the blessed married state, but ...'

'Crotter needed a wife, you say?' cut in Adams. 'Well, not any more. Ha!' The Captain marked his humour with a self-congratulatory tap on the arm of his chair. 'Another glass, sir?'

Mr Gilbert was diverted from replying by a commotion as the stableboy came in search of the innkeeper. A gentleman visitor had just arrived in the yard. Woolbridge was not unused to visitors. It did not lie far off the post road, but between fairs and market days travellers of the better sort were uncommon. Adams and his companion craned their necks to look down the passage to see who the stranger might be.

A gentleman of thirty or thereabouts entered the parlour. He wore a neat sort of riding dress, and Captain Adams fancied he had something of a military look. He was casting about for some pretext to engage the newcomer in conversation when Jasper Bedlington bustled in from the tap. He was a barrel-shaped man with receding hair that had left him with a monkish tonsure above a boyish face.

'Mr Jarrett, sir? Why, we had given you up for tonight. There was but one piece of luggage brought up from the posting road quite a hour ago, and no sign of your manservant. It'll take but a moment to ready your room, sir.'

'I had business on the way, so I rode over from York. My man is indisposed and is to follow in a day or two,' replied Mr Jarrett. He had a deep, calm voice. 'Are there any messages left for me?'

The innkeeper cast an appreciative eye over his visitor; he liked a proper gentleman. 'Now I am glad you mentioned

that, sir, for there was a boy who came over from Sir Thomas
up at Oakdene Hall. Let me see.' Mr Bedlington wiped his
hands thoughtfully on his apron and turned to roar over
his shoulder. 'Polly! Here, Polly! Where did you put that
note the boy brought for Mr Jarrett, my love? My wife, sir,
God bless her,' he explained, turning back to the traveller, a
surprisingly coy blush staining his rosy cheeks.

Mistress Polly blew into the front parlour, a jolly-looking
woman of formidable size.

'Now Jasper, my pet, you know you put it yourself in a
safe place and never gave it to me.' She twinkled engagingly
at Mr Jarrett and inserted her bulk behind the bar. 'I rather
think you put it by Mr Raistrick's special reserve. Aye and
here it is!' She returned with a piece of cream paper folded
under a seal which she presented to the visitor with an energetic bob curtsey.

Mr Jarrett, feeling that such friendly service required that
his kindly hosts should be rewarded with the satisfaction of
their obvious curiosity, gravely broke the seal and read the
contents.

'But how kind, I am invited to tea tomorrow afternoon,'
he informed the company.

The couple before him beamed, as if genuinely happy at
their visitor's good fortune.

'Our boy, Jack, will be pleased to show you the way to the
house, sir. It's not far. And what time would that be, sir?'
asked Mrs Bedlington, poised to go and arrange matters.

'Three in the afternoon?' ventured Mr Jarrett.

'Capital. That's all arranged then,' said his host, striking
his hands together as if to seal a bargain. Then, wreathed in
smiles, Mr Bedlington proceeded to shepherd his guest up
the stairs to his best room.

'Jarrett, eh?' said Captain Adams, as the innkeeper and
his charge disappeared. 'But he's a youngish man. That's
unexpected.' Then, noticing his companion was looking

bemused, he picked up his paper and tapped a section with a broad finger. Mr Gilbert's eyes scanned an advertisement for Barclay's Asthmatic Candy, 'for many Years been proved a most effectual Preservative from the ill effects of Fogs and DAMP AIR'. He looked up at the Captain perplexed.

'No, no, man! The announcement, there!' insisted Adams. Then Mr Gilbert saw it:

NOTICE

The Duke of Penrith announces an AUDIT following the recent demise of James Crotter, Steward. All tenants residing in the County of Durham and the North Riding of Yorkshire are required to attend at the Queen's Head, Woolbridge, on the first Thursday and Friday of August next.

F.R. Jarrett Esq.
July 27, 1811

CHAPTER TWO

He had slept well. His thirty years of life had given him experience of all sorts of shelters, from shattered Portuguese chapels to West Indian palm huts, and he was pleased to find his bed free of fleas and the room to himself. Despite his recent months of inaction Jarrett found it difficult to fall out of the habit formed on patrol of rising at half past two in the morning. When not occupied in active service, the custom left a man with many extra hours to fill. This Sunday he disposed of his first waking hours by ordering his thoughts and impressions on to paper. That done, he sharpened his pen afresh and began a letter. Mrs Bedlington's cherished grandmother clock was striking five below as he signed it. Fanning out the few papers he had culled from his search of the old library on the table before him, he checked through what he had written. He folded up two closely written sheets in his letter, addressed and sealed it.

He got up, stretching his stiff back. Outwardly the wound in his side had healed to a long puckered welt, but inwardly it still ached on a morning. He opened the casement and leant out to look over the tumbled roofs. There was a comforting homeliness to the scene before him. Thin trails of smoke drifted up as hearths were rekindled. These roofs sheltered hundreds of human souls whose entire lives were encompassed by this place. His imagination stretched out for a moment to comprehend what that must be like – to belong so wholly to one place; to live your life from cradle to grave known to all your neighbours. His fingers strayed to the slim plait of golden hair he wore about one strong brown wrist. He tucked it back beneath his shirt cuff. Much as he might appreciate the virtues of a settled life, he knew himself incapable of sustaining them in his own person. He was destined to be a wanderer from birth. He pulled his mind back to his present task.

The inhabitants of the Queen's Head began to stir. Mrs Bedlington, her hair still in papers, was scolding the maid, Molly, out of her warm bed to stoke the kitchen fire. Master Jasper stood before his piece of glass humming an air as he stropped his razor rhythmically against a leather strap. In the stables the horses fidgeted, their ears twitching to catch the sounds of Matt, the stableboy, coming with his pails of feed.

Jarrett sat at his window with a sketch book on his knee. Across the street stood the church. Under his swift fingers a pencil impression appeared. The Norman tower with its worn stones. A side view of the porch over the west door. The wicket gate overgrown with a romantic twist of dog-rose. A little man in a dusty black hat too large for his head came bustling down the street and opened the wicket gate. His outline with its preposterous hat took shape on the paper. Two more men arrived from behind the church and entered the tower. The bells began to ring across the roofs of Woolbridge.

There was a knock on the door and Mrs Bedlington entered, looking flustered in her best Sunday silk.

'Is there anything you might be wanting, Mr Jarrett, sir? Before we go to divine service, that is – it being the Lord's Day.'

'No. No, I thank you,' Jarrett replied, hurriedly putting his sketch aside. 'I shall be attending there myself.'

From below the innkeeper called up, 'I'm gone, Polly!'

'Indeed, my love; we shall follow directly,' his wife shouted back, before recollecting herself. 'My husband is music master, sir,' she explained apologetically. 'Keeps them all in order in the gallery. Always likes to be there early.'

Through the casement Jarrett saw Mr Bedlington hurry across the street bearing a large crumhorn. He watched him negotiate his way carefully through the wicket gate.

'Well, if you've no need of anything, sir, I'll be off. The maids, you know, sir. Those girls would be late for their own funeral I shouldn't wonder if they weren't harried.' With this observation Mrs Bedlington closed the door briskly behind her, pausing on the other side of the thin wall to bellow up the attic stairs: 'Molly Dade! No amount of preening 'll make you better than you are in the eyes of the Lord – you come down here directly, girl!'

Jarrett shrugged himself into his coat, picking up his hat and a Malacca cane. He caught a glimpse of himself in the glass as he passed. 'Fine enough for the provinces,' he murmured to his reflection. He was leaning down to polish a smudge from one hessian boot when he remembered the letter. He picked it up from the table and slid it into his coat. It was better not left lying about. Settling his hat on his head with a smart tap, Mr Jarrett set off for church swinging his cane.

The street below was clogged with gigs and carriages as the worthies of Woolbridge arrived for the service. St John's church stood on a hill. To the north it fronted the road. To the south its graveyard fell away behind the church, its oak-bordered boundary giving on to the Desmenes, the open common land that marked the town's eastern edge. Snaking up the hill came a patchy line of the lesser folk among the Reverend Prattman's congregation. Tenant farmers with their sturdy wives, and the lumbering lads, their farm workers, straggling behind them as they eyed the girls, serving girls from the merchants' and tradesmen's houses who giggled together in knots. Weavers with their thin-faced apprentices, shopkeepers and small traders, they all walked up through the graveyard, stopping to greet acquaintances on the paths under the oaks.

These two sides of Woolbridge, the carriage kind and the stout ordinary folk, met and mixed at the west door where the Reverend Prattman presided. He towered above his people, tall and hearty in his clerical wig and wide-winged black gown, flinging out his massive hands in welcome. He was the benign epitome of the Established Church, embracing in his range of responses the whole people of his parish. He greeted the rough sallies of the farmers with loud appreciative barks of laughter; he bent over the delicate Mrs Gilbert, the surgeon's wife, with gentle attention; he directed his clerk and bell-ringers while swapping a Cambridge jest with a retired parson colleague from his old college.

The number of eyes that looked studiously away as he met them made Jarrett aware that he was the principal object of speculation that morning among the carriage trade. The blatant attention annoyed him. He set off on a circuit of the church to while away the few minutes before the service began.

The southern wall of the chancel revealed plain, elegant Norman lines. He was admiring a thirteenth-century clerestory window to the left of a low hammer-headed door when he heard sounds of female voices advancing up the steep path. From behind a fine coffin tomb he saw a party of girls approaching.

His first impression of her, as she lifted her skirts to climb the hill, was of a slim ankle accentuated in a fresh white stocking. She had delicate feet, neatly shod in black shoes decorated with a bright square buckle. On his first full view of her his immediate association was with a canvas by de Goya he had seen in Spain – inappropriate perhaps for an English setting, for it was of the painter's mistress reclining naked on a sofa. This girl had the same sensuous black curls, luminous skin and air of seductive mischief. He found the source of his impression hard to pin down, but her movements were redolent with it. A certain confidence. The bold openness with which her dark eyes cast about the world. Here was a subject for an artist's pencil!

'Now then, Sal, have you had a token from your soldier boy?'

The black-haired girl turned. The question came on an ill-natured note and she paused. 'What's it to you, Prudence Miller? Have you so few followers of your own that you have to ask after others'?'

The circle of accompanying girls laughed, half-uneasy, half-eager, their eyes wide in anticipation. Prudence Miller, a solid, bonny girl with a ruddy complexion, advanced to confront the black-haired Sal.

'At least mine ain't married!'

Jarrett could not see Sal's face but he was near certain she stiffened.

'And of who are we speaking, Miss Prudence?' Sal managed to speak the name so as to convey a wealth of contempt.

'Your soldier boy's back, Sal. He's married his sergeant's daughter, Sal, and the sergeant he's taken the Swan Inn on the bridge right here in Woolbridge. What say you to that?'

As Sal seemed to lack a ready answer to this, the floodgates of Miss Miller's resentment broke.

'All these years you've been telling us Will Roberts'd be back to make an honest woman of you, while you've been flittin' round our men acting like no honest girl would. And now he's back and married another. What do you say to that, Sal?'

There was a particular stillness to the pause that followed. Then in a half-singing voice, an echo of a child's taunt, Sal responded:

'Fa-la-la; there are plenty of fish in the sea, Prudence

Miller.' With a swing of her skirts she turned on one graceful foot and walked off, calling casually over her shoulder,
'You comin', Maggie?'

A little girl with bad skin and blue pop eyes detached herself from the audience and hurried round-shouldered after
her friend.

A party of men came clumping up the hill, diverting the
girls. Hands went to waists, drawing attention to curved
hips; shawls and hair were twitched and lips bitten red.

'You mind you keep to your tune this mornin', Harry
Nidd,' counselled Prudence saucily to a tow-haired youth
with a broken nose.

'You keep to yours and he'll see you at Lovers' Leap one
of these days, Prudence Miller,' called back Harry's companion, a sandy-haired man with sharp features.

'You keep your sauce to yourself, Joe Walton,' retorted
Prudence, blushing at the general laughter as Joe swiftly
countered, 'There's many a girl likes my sauce, Prudence
Miller.'

The singers filed into the church through the door in
the chancel wall. Jarrett, conscious that the service must
be about to begin, made for the path that led to the west
door. As he passed, Sal and Prudence were picking up where
they had left off. Sal seemed to be getting the better of the
engagement. Her head was held high and her manner lofty,
while her opponent stood red-faced, her arms akimbo.

'I've no need of your men, Prudence Miller. I have one
much finer than you'll ever have hope of – a gentleman!'

'A gentleman! What gentleman would ever walk out with
the likes of you!'

'You don't know him, but you'll hear of him before you're
much older, you see if you don't.'

Prudence was not convinced. 'A gentleman!' she scoffed.

'Aye, a fine gentleman!' Catching sight of Jarrett, Sal
jerked her head towards him. 'As fine as that one there.'

She turned and smiled directly at him. Jarrett looked straight into those bold, dark eyes. She had remarkably large pupils that made her eyes seem almost black. He found himself smiling at her. He touched his hat and, with a brief nod of acknowledgement, continued on his way.

As he rounded the corner a compact, military-looking man with a high colour and receding hair accosted him. 'Captain Adams, sir,' he said, thrusting a chubby hand towards him. 'And you are Mr Jarrett, the Duke's new agent?'

'In a manner of speaking,' replied Jarrett, shaking his hand.

'Thought so. Saw you at the inn as you arrived.' Captain Adams smiled and rocked his cane as it rested on the ground as if his stock of conversation was drying up. 'Glad to meet you. Capital. Church?' He said, gesturing towards the doorway into which most of the congregation had now disappeared. 'Come sit with the lady wife and me.'

'That is most kind,' replied Jarrett. 'I will be glad to.'

They entered the building and he caught a whiff of the charnel house.

'Recent burial,' explained Captain Adams, sensing his companion's reaction. He indicated disturbed earth at the back of the north transept. 'But you'll know about that. Going to be a plaque or some such. Subscription and all that.'

Jarrett surveyed Mr Crotter's final resting place. 'Who buried him?' he enquired. 'I understood Mr Crotter had no family in Woolbridge.'

'I believe Sir Thomas saw to it,' replied Captain Adams, after pondering the question a moment. 'Wouldn't do to have the fellow lying about in this heat!' he added jovially. 'My wife, sir.'

Jarrett found himself bowing to Mrs Adams, a broad-beamed capable-looking woman, and her pale daughters. As the ladies were taking their time to arrange themselves he stood to one side in the aisle looking about the building. Towards the front of the church various degrees of box pews were arranged, each assigned to a particular prosperous household. Benches filled the spaces where the servants and ordinary folk sat. Above, to the left of the chancel, Mr Bedlington and his motley collection of musicians were tuning up in the gallery. The singers sprawled about, waiting. The young man who had bandied words with Prudence was hanging over the rail conversing with Sal, who sat below on a bench looking demure and mischievous at the same time. Jarrett glimpsed Prudence Miller's impotent fury and felt pity for her. She was no match for Sal. His fingers itched to capture the scene – 'The Country Service: a rural vignette'.

The little man in the over-large hat trotted up the gallery steps. 'Music master,' he commanded, 'the parson would remind the singers that they are not to sing the responses!' Then, looking to neither left nor right through an accompaniment of jeers from the singers, the clerk scurried back down the stairs.

Henrietta Lonsdale entered the church half a step in front of her aunt. It had been a trying morning. She had known it would be from the moment her aunt's voice had wavered out to arrest her progress as she passed the bedroom door on her way downstairs to breakfast. The words were not material; it was their tone – that pathetic, cajoling, invalidish note her aunt assumed when she wanted to be petted. Henrietta was a dutiful niece to her widowed aunt. She prayed regularly and quite sincerely for God's assistance in granting her patience and a better temper, but the carriage ride that morning had been frosty. Aunt Lonsdale's mood had lightened a little on arrival at church. They had been greeted at the carriage door by Mrs Bedford who had hardly allowed them time to set foot to ground, so eager was she to share the excitement over the Duke of Penrith's new agent.

Henrietta lifted her eyebrows a little at all the fuss. She knew perfectly well that Aunt Lonsdale considered Amelia Bedford a vulgar sort of woman, but the Duke's agent was too choice a morsel for her to be particular about the provenance of the gossip. Henrietta surveyed the man blocking the aisle. So this was the new agent. His clothes were remarkably well cut but they hung slightly loose as if he had lost weight in sickness he had yet to regain. She noted, nonetheless, that he had a good leg. She followed the line of his gaze. Gawping at Sally Grundy, was he? A pity his manners did not match his tailoring.

Jarrett heard a musical voice speak behind him.

'If you will permit, sir.'

He turned to let by two latecomers. A youngish lady near his height, well dressed, with an elegant face and direct grey eyes nodded to him. She was accompanied by what he took to be an aunt or some such female relation: a middle-aged woman with a thin, pampered face and mournful look that reminded him of the expression dogs assume when begging for food at table. The grey eyes of the younger woman met his as they passed and he was surprised to catch a trace of derision in them. He looked after her. The lady carried herself remarkably well. Perhaps he had imagined her disdain.

The Squire, Sir Thomas of Oakdene Hall, advanced in procession with his household down the aisle to settle in his family pew. His outdoor servants arranged themselves with much scraping of wood and jangling of spurs on stone in the benches behind. The Reverend Prattman advanced to his desk and the service began.

It was not much different from most country services. The Reverend Prattman had a strong, clear voice and the decency to keep his sermon short. The singers, disregarding the clerk's instructions, sang the responses lustily, causing the parson to sulk. Glancing to his right, Jarrett saw that his lady critic too had noticed the parson's pout. For a brief moment their eyes met with shared amusement. Then she recollected her dignity and gave him her profile. With a jolt he remembered where he was and his role as Duke's agent. When a man wore regimentals the ladies were not so cold. He shrugged off the rebuff as he rose for 'O for a thousand tongues to sing', to the accompaniment of a strong beat from the side-drum. Jarrett, who had a decent light baritone voice, found himself enjoying the hymn along with the rest of the congregation. The musicians entered into their task with spirit, rendering the sacred tune in a sort of merry jig. The lady to his right had a tuneful soprano and he amused himself composing harmonies against it. Whatever my lady critic's opinion of him their voices blended well.

The service ended and Captain Adams parted from Mr Jarrett with repeated assurances that they would be sure to see one another again that afternoon over tea at Sir Thomas's. As the agent crossed the street returning to his inn, the lady with the critical eyes was settling her aunt in their carriage. The elder lady lifted an eyebrow in the direction of Jarrett's neatly dressed figure.

'He is a well-looking man, to be sure,' Mrs Lonsdale commented vaguely.

'Hmmm,' responded Henrietta, preoccupied with fixing the rug about her aunt's knees just as she liked it. The black-haired Sal passed down the street, swinging her hips, framed between two of the young singers from the gallery. Distracted, Miss Lonsdale spoke her thoughts aloud.

'He in turn seems to find Sally Grundy well-looking enough. He was watching her through half the service.'

'My dear, never!' exclaimed her aunt, growing quite animated. 'Oh my love, did you hear? Will Roberts, Joe Roberts the carpenter's son, is come back from the militia in Ireland. It seems he has taken the opportunity to better himself and has married his sergeant's daughter.' Mrs Lonsdale's face reflected a smug smile as she patted the rug more closely about her. 'I would not have thought him so sensible – he is well free of the slut.'

'Perhaps not,' returned Henrietta, thankful her aunt had not fixed on the impropriety of her comment, 'if she were to call him before the magistrate on a breach of promise.'

'The hussy would not be so bold!'

'Sally Grundy, aunt? Why boldness is her very trademark.' Rueful amusement crossed Henrietta Lonsdale's face and she added quietly, 'Somehow I cannot help but like her for it.'

'Fie, Henrietta, you are ridiculous!' her aunt told her.

Under the guidance of Master Jack, the innkeeper's twelve-year-old son, Jarrett found his way to Oakdene Hall. He was ushered into the Blue Drawing Room as the clock struck three. Sir Thomas crossed the wide expanse of carpet and polished boards to greet his guest.

'Ah, this must be Mr Jarrett. Welcome, sir, welcome to Oakdene Hall.'

'I must thank you, Sir Thomas, for your invitation. It was most gracious.'

'Nonsense, nonsense. I received word of your coming. And how did you leave my dear friend, the Duke? Dear me, 'tis many a year since I saw him last.'

'He goes on as well as can be expected, sir, for a man in his condition; he is no longer young.'

Sir Thomas seemed to bend a little more under his own years, and his eyes behind his round glasses looked melancholy.

'Ah yes; tempus fugit, tempus fugit – for us all, eh?' He shook off his thoughts and asked, 'But what of this sad affair?'

'As to that, Sir Thomas, may I present His Grace's compliments and thank you for the trouble you have taken on his behalf. I understand it was you who saw to the burial of the unfortunate Crotter.'

Sir Thomas waved aside all thanks. 'No matter. No matter. A man is a poor creature if he cannot be of service to his friends.'

'His Grace is most fortunate in his friendships, sir.' Jarrett paused. 'I would not trouble you at this time, Sir Thomas, but may I call on you again – on business?'

Sir Thomas was an old friend of the Duke's. And yet Jarrett sensed a certain reluctance in his host at his request, as if he disliked to hear of troublesome things.

'Ah yes, business. How do you find matters?'

'I fear I am all at sea as yet, sir. Mr Crotter seems to have been an indifferent book-keeper.'

'What will you do?' The old man asked the question while looking off, smiling and bowing to some guests across the room.

'There are yet some days left before the audit, Sir Thomas. It provides opportunity for me to ride about and see how things stand on the farms.'

'A bad business.' Sir Thomas gazed down at his feet and paused. When he spoke again it was in a reluctant voice. 'Crotter was much on his own and greatly trusted. I hope there is no villainy in the matter. Your presence – so swiftly; your connection to the family ...' He peered up at Jarrett over his spectacles.

It was the look of such a timid, foolish creature that Jarrett's protective instincts were aroused. 'I do not suspect it, Sir Thomas,' he replied more confidently than he meant. 'More likely an aversion to book-keeping; nothing that cannot be remedied. And as to the family – no one knows me here; in Woolbridge I am no more than the Duke's agent. Let me remain so for the present, if you will. A little anonymity may prove my best assistance in uncovering the true state of affairs – at least until Charles is able to join me.'

Sir Thomas was transparently more than happy to be relieved of the burden of referring to so sensitive a subject as

Mr Jarrett's particular relationship to the Duke's family. 'Of course. Discretion. Absolutely as you wish.'

Jarrett smoothed over his host's embarrassment. 'I must add that Charles, too, sends his compliments. He had hoped to accompany me, but the Duke's affairs have detained him in York.'

Sir Thomas, who only dimly recalled Charles, Marquess of Earewith, the Duke's eldest son, as a short boy in knee breeches, smiled vaguely. 'Well, good. I fear I must make a journey away from home in the next few days, but Tuesday – shall we say a week this Tuesday, in the forenoon?'

Jarrett had hoped for an earlier interview but Sir Thomas's attention had already moved on.

'And see, here is Captain Adams wishing to speak with you. I believe you are acquainted?'

Captain Adams drew near with his wife on one arm, and on the other a lady Jarrett had glimpsed at a distance that morning at church. She was a short plump woman with brassy hair who dressed in a florid, fashionable way. She brought to his mind a figure representing 'a lady of the town' in some over-coloured popular print. This lady was introduced as Mrs Amelia Bedford, the wife of a carpet-manufacturer in the neighbourhood. She gave Jarrett a cold, brief nod, swiftly transferring her attention to her host.

'Oh, Sir Thomas,' she cried, laying one plump white hand on the baronet's arm and looking up into his face with a flutter of eyelashes. 'Such a pleasant gathering! But I do not see our friend, Justice Raistrick; is he not here?'

Jarrett sensed a distinct hush fall among the other members of the circle before Sir Thomas responded in a distracted manner, 'Mr Raistrick? Otherwise engaged, I believe. Ah, I beg pardon, I must leave you.' In response to a servant's signal, Sir Thomas detached himself from the group.

'Fie, Amelia!' scolded Mrs Adams in a penetrating whisper. 'You know very well that man is not received in this house.'

The door opened and Sir Thomas handed in an extra-ordinary creature – a frail, shuffling figure who might have been of normal height but for a freak of nature that had doubled her forward upon herself under the mighty weight of a giant hump. Two thin arms trailed loose, like unwieldy ropes ending in filigree monkey's paws. The eyes in the face mask that tilted out to the world under the overhanging hump of flesh and bone were vacant – nothing within look-ing at nothing without. Sir Thomas settled this thing in a chair, fussed over it, rearranging a trailing shawl to disguise the indecent arms, and was summoned away to tend to some new arrivals.

The circle somehow melted away. Captain Adams drew off to seek some gentleman's opinion about a militia matter. Mrs Adams and Mrs Bedford sat in uncomfortable silence a moment, before Mrs Bedford leapt up with an over-exuberant show of enthusiasm, crying, 'Oh, Maria! There is such a lovely timepiece over the mantel there – do come let us look at it.'

Dragging her stoic companion behind her, she made for the far end of the room. There she proceeded to make conversation in dumb show before a very ordinary carriage clock. She fluttered her shawl about her, throwing out animated gestures as if she was on the stage, all the while casting nervous glances back towards the old lady who sat in isolation amid a group of empty chairs.

Abandoned in his corner Jarrett could not forbear examin-ing this apparition. Suddenly, as if a person darted forward to fill an empty doorway, the rheumy eyes focused. Jarrett found himself fixed by a look charged with mischief and one eye winked. 'I should like some tea.' The voice was papery but authoritative and perfectly clear.

'I shall fetch some, madam,' he responded, springing to his feet, glad for an excuse to cover his confusion.

He returned to find his companion transformed. She had

somehow collected up her limbs, and the slanted face peeped out almost roguishly from under her hump.

'He should not have made me come,' she stated with a fierce bob of her head in the direction of the inoffensive baronet. 'Make conversation with these chuckleheads! Pshaw! Chuckleheads!' she repeated with relish. 'I stand no nonsense. Did ye see Amelia Bedford? Her father sold pigmeat and still she gives herself airs. Can't abide lunatics – give her the goosebumps.' The old lady gave Jarrett a wicked smile and leaning towards him confided: 'Can't do a thing about me, though; I'm kin to *Sir* Thomas and he has £8,000 a year. Ha!' She gave a snort of amusement. She tipped her tea dextrously from the patterned cup into the deep saucer and sipped it delicately. 'So you're come from the Duke, eh? About time the booby paid attention to his affairs. That Crotter was a bad lot.' She pursed her lips. For an instant Jarrett wondered whether her sharp nose and pointed chin might meet. He decided evasion was the best policy.

'Crotter. Sad affair. He died of a heart attack, I hear. Most unexpected.'

Faded blue eyes challenged him with liquid intelligence, forcing him to drink some of the insipid tea so that he might look away.

'Pfft!' She tossed her head and gazed stonily away from him.

'I beg pardon, ma'am, we have not been introduced,' he said, in an effort to bridge the silence. 'My name is Jarrett; Frederick Raif Jarrett. I fear I do not have the pleasure of knowing your name ...'

'Lady Catherine Gilling,' she replied haughtily, adding snappishly: 'I know who you are. I am not a simpleton, young man!'

At that moment his singing partner from the church, the lady with the direct grey eyes, entered the room behind her aunt. She was above average height for a woman, and though not a beauty she had what the polite world calls countenance. The old witch had so unsettled him he heard himself ask, 'I beg pardon, ma'am, but who might those ladies be – the ones who have just come in? I think I saw them at church.'

Lady Catherine was diverted from her sulks.

'Ha! You mean my young friend Henrietta,' she stated. Jarrett, startled by her uncomfortable clear-sightedness, was appalled to see her snap her fingers to attract Henrietta's attention, confirming the action with an imperious, 'Here. Come. I want you here, child!'

The lady took this summons in good grace. She crossed the room to lean over Lady Catherine and kiss her wizened cheek.

'Miss Henrietta Lonsdale, may I have leave to present to you Mr Frederick Jarrett. He's come from the Duke, you know.' With this mischievous introduction Lady Catherine wriggled back in her chair, and composed herself as if she was about to watch a play. As Lady Catherine's chosen puppet Miss Lonsdale proved wilful. With a graceful incline of her head she acknowledged the introduction, following it with a swift, sweet smile in which Jarrett hoped he detected good will. She turned back to Lady Catherine.

'I am indeed pleased to meet Mr Jarrett, but, Lady Catherine, I must go pay my respects to Sir Thomas; we have just this moment arrived and he will think me very odd.'

'Fiddlesticks, girl! Stay here. If only for the pleasure of seeing your aunt fret at the sight of you in such unsuitable company.'

'Lady Catherine!' Henrietta's startled response betrayed her thoughts. 'You go too far!' In her embarrassment Miss Lonsdale shed some of her poise. Jarrett realised she was probably younger than he had first thought. He was amused.

At least the old lady did not dissemble like the ordinary run of drawing room hypocrites.

'Fear not, ma'am. I am not a man to take offence at honesty. It is clear that many here are uneasy at my presence.'

'The ninnies can't place you,' interjected Lady Catherine. 'They must always know where to place a stranger or it quite unsettles their stomachs. Ninnies!' The little woman rocked back and forwards in derision.

Jarrett found himself overcome by a vision of the old lady as Humpty-Dumpty in some old print and he had to pretend to cough before he laughed. He was not fast enough for Lady Catherine.

'Find me amusing, eh?' she said fiercely. Jarrett looked straight at her, catching a fleeting glimpse of the depth of misery pent up in her eyes.

'An unfortunate association in my mind, ma'am,' he said as honestly as he could.

All at once the fire was gone and she half-smiled. 'Unfortunate association,' she repeated. She nodded with her whole body. 'Apt.' She looked up appealingly at Henrietta. 'Don't you think, my dear?'

'You must be tired, Lady Catherine,' Henrietta said, her manner betraying her affection for the old woman.

'Not tired; tedious. These people.' She waved a thin, wrinkled paw at the assembly. 'I shall go to my room,' she announced and scrambled off her chair. A servant appeared to help her. A few feet away the old lady turned and addressed Jarrett. 'You'll do, young man. If you need help – and you may – ask me. He's no good,' she said with a half-fierce, half-loving toss of her head in the direction of her kinsman, Sir Thomas. 'A booby. But I am no simpleton.' With that statement she made her exit.

They were left standing in silence in an oasis of polished boards. Henrietta surveyed the agent. His blue eyes were very bright against his sun-darkened skin; it gave him quite the buccaneering look. He caught her watching him and smiled. The expression transformed his face with an unexpected gentleness.

'I do not know why Lady Catherine thinks you may need assistance, sir.' Now why on earth had she said that? It was most inappropriate. Henrietta was flustered. It seemed important to justify her friend to this stranger. 'For all her eccentricities she speaks only the truth.'

Jarrett considered his companion's attractions. They were considerable – the more so when her poise was softened by confusion. He watched her mouth frame its words with care.

'Lady Catherine *is* no simpleton, you know – and an excellent friend.'

Back at the Queen's Head the tap and parlour were full of customers. Meeting Mr Bedlington at the foot of the stairs, Jarrett asked when the post left from Greta Bridge.

'The letters to the North go at seven in the morning each day and to the South at four o'clock,' the innkeeper answered. 'Might there be a letter you want taken, sir?'

Jarrett felt a familiar tightening sensation at the back of his head and shoulders; the sense of being watched. The whole tap could overhear them. He looked about the room, but every group seemed deep in their own conversation.

'No, not as yet, I thank you. I shall doubtless be riding out that way myself in the next day or so.'

Mr Bedlington hurried off towards the parlour.

Jarrett found his room stuffy and he opened the window. He was feeling confined and restless. Towns were well enough but he preferred open spaces. Out at the manor he might pursue his investigations relatively free from prying eyes. In these small towns the gossips picked over your every step. He came to a decision and went in search of Mrs Bedlington. He found her in the kitchen nook basting fowls.

Her fleshy face was an alarming shade of puce and sweat ran off her cheeks.

'Such company we have tonight, Mr Jarrett!' she exclaimed. 'There's the Box Society up for its quarterly dinner and, as luck would have it, a recruiting party's just arrived from Gainford – and all demanding to be fed. And me shorthanded.'

'In that case, Mistress B, let me relieve you of one burden at least. I shall move out to the manor. I find no hardship in sleeping rough and there is much to be done there.'

For a moment Mrs Bedlington seemed likely to be offended at the desertion of her favourite guest, but as the officer with the recruiting party had just sent word that he was in need of a room she was soon reconciled. Within the hour Jarrett was riding Walcheren out of the stable yard.

He left Woolbridge by the eastern road, the way he should have come the night before. He had crossed a toll bridge that stood below the ruins of an old abbey when he noticed the mouth of the path he had mistakenly taken on his arrival. He had a notion to see what it looked like in full daylight, so he turned Walcheren down into the wood.

The river path was pleasant by sunlight. The river gleamed pewter between its white rocks. There was a flash of exquisite blue, highlighted by a dab of orange, and he caught a delightful view of a kingfisher as it darted over the surface of the water. The track was much overgrown and Jarrett debated with himself as he rode the merits of setting some men to clear it. The horse climbed the incline, leaving the river behind. Just as they were mounting the brow of the hill, as the trees grew wider spaced, Jarrett caught a whiff of tobacco smoke. A yellow dog ran into the path and barked.

'Hold your peace, Bob, you know him,' said a voice. And there, sitting at his ease on a log, smoking his pipe, was the poacher.

CHAPTER THREE

Duffin removed his pipe deliberately from his mouth. 'Fine evening again, sir,' he commented.

'And a fine prospect, too,' responded Jarrett appreciatively. The man had chosen a spot at the mouth of a gap in the trees. An alder and a graceful willow framed a broad sweeping turn of the river below. With a flash of a white breast, a swallow skimmed over the golden water, catching flies in the lazy summer air.

Duffin drew contentedly on his pipe. 'Aye,' he agreed.

'I trust I find you recovered from our unfortunate encounter of last night?'

'You find me dry, sir.'

The burly man leant down to knock out his pipe on the stump. He was hatless and his hair short. It stuck out in a mat of bristly spikes all over his square, bullish skull. 'Ezekiel Duffin's my name; countryman,' he said gruffly. 'And this here is Bob.' The yellow dog sat on its haunches panting slightly, his pointed ears pricked up and a lively look of expectation in his eyes. He was a mongrel that seemed to have reverted to plain hound. Jarrett reflected he had seen his ancestor once among images of Egyptian hunting dogs in a collection of antiquities he had visited in London.

The younger man nodded in a friendly fashion. 'Jarrett,' he said cheerfully. 'My name is Frederick Jarrett. I am staying at the manor up the track here.'

Duffin was watching the swallow through narrowed eyes. Following the curves the bird carved through the air below, he scarcely acknowledged the introduction, but nodded to himself as if confirming something. Jarrett became aware that the sharp eyes had returned to him.

'Back from soldiering, are you?' Duffin asked abruptly.

'I am in His Majesty's service, yes.'

'Household Cavalry maybe?' The tone of the question seemed to imply that Duffin made certain assumptions about gentlemen who took up service in such a regiment. 'You handle the beast well,' he added grudgingly, as if to soften the question.

Jarrett laughed. 'Do I look as if I've just stepped off a gingerbread field day? No. Light Dragoons, the 16th. Lately in Portugal – though I had some years with the 68th Regiment of Foot in the West Indies.' He smiled engagingly. 'Are you an old soldier yourself?'

'Me? We-ell, happen I did a spell once. Didn't take to it.' Duffin stood, thrusting his pipe into a deep pocket, and picked up his pack. He slid a wry glance at the rider above him. 'Didn't reckon you got that dark complexion these parts. Portugal, you say?'

'Aye – and Spain.'

'Invalided out?'

'On leave – an unlucky chance. But I am sound enough now.' Jarrett gathered up the reins to move on.

'I'll walk a ways with you, sir,' volunteered Duffin unexpectedly. 'If you've no objection.'

'None in the world,' responded Jarrett. 'Glad of the company.'

The dog Bob foraged before them, in search of rabbits and other potentially interesting creatures. He frequently disappeared from sight, re-emerging at intervals to check on the progress of his master. They passed the folly, crossing the stone bridge, and on through the fields. As they approached the outer edge of the plantation the roofs of the old manor house peeped up above the trees.

'Did you know the previous tenant of this place, Mr Duffin?'

'Me? Crotter?' The poacher snorted. 'Not to speak to.'

'But you passed this way many times?'

Duffin shrugged his pack into a more comfortable position. 'In the summer, I reckon,' he answered in an off-hand manner.

Jarrett glanced down at the man below him. He had an idea and he wondered how his new-found acquaintance might take it.

'If you have no urgent business,' he ventured, 'I wonder if you might assist me at the house. There are some tasks to be done – I would be grateful for the aid of a strong back. I have not had time to engage any men as yet. It would take no more than an hour or so. Paid work, of course,' he added.

Ezekiel stopped in the path and examined the face above him. Jarrett gazed calmly back. Humour warmed Duffin's pebble-grey eyes. He shot out a large and none too clean hand, a smile transforming his dour features.

'Aye, why not?'

Jarrett clasped the proffered fingers and they shook hands formally.

'Can always do with a few shillings,' Duffin remarked as they set off again.

'Shillings, Mr Duffin? The price of labour is steep in these parts.'

'Nay. Quality's to be paid for. As you'd know, being a gentleman.'

The men fell silent as they approached the abandoned manor. A miasma of decay clung about the entrance, un-settling the horses. The dog too crowded closer to his master, making little whimpering noises in his throat.

'Even been a gravedigger, Duffin? As you can smell, there is a corpse to dispose of,' said Jarrett as he swung off his horse.

'He was a good dog, that one,' returned Duffin, unperturbed. 'Fearsome beast but a good watch dog.'

Jarrett looked sharply at the man, his hand stayed above the latch, but Duffin was turned away instructing his dog to stay outside.

'Creatures don't like to see their own kind in decay. Alike with men in that, I reckon,' Ezekiel observed philosophically.

Seemingly unaware of his companion's surprise, the poacher was keen to set to the task at hand. 'We'd best bustle, sir,' he prompted, 'he's ripe enough. There'll be implements in one of them byres if some varmint's not carried them off.' With that he walked off towards one of the outhouses in the manner of a man who knows where he is going.

True to his word, he returned in a few minutes with two spades and a piece of sacking. It was unpleasant work. The stench that had collected in the pent-up space of the hall had physical force. The decay was well advanced and the flies in no mind to be disturbed. What with the rank, sweet stink and the swarming insects there was not a breath of clean air to be had. Both men worked swiftly and silently, handkerchiefs tied about their mouths. They bundled the remains of the hound on to the sack and carried it out into the yard. There they buried it between yew trees.

'So you've been here before, Duffin,' challenged Jarrett as soon as the outdoor air permitted conversation.

Duffin paused as he balanced a heavy load of soil on his spade and tipped it into the hole with a grunt. 'As I said, I pass this way now and then. That dog would bark. We knew one another but he'd bark whenever a body passed.'

'How was it you knew it was the dog we had to bury?' Jarrett pressed him.

Duffin was busy with his spade and did not look at him. He was no fool, Jarrett was ever more certain of that.

'Passed by and he didn't bark no more. You and I know that smell – and they took Crotter to the church days back,' he ended with a sly grin. 'That'll do,' he said, putting the spade aside and picking up his coat.

'Come in and we'll see if there is any refreshment to be had,' said Jarrett, retrieving his own coat and discarded cravat. 'Perhaps you may show me where it is kept,' he added over his shoulder.

'No, sir. Mr Crotter didn't invite the likes of me to drink with him,' responded the poacher blandly.

Jarrett decided to try the frontal assault.

'Do you know what happened here, Duffin?' he asked as they entered the house. Watching the man, he sensed, with some amusement, that he was taken aback at the directness of the question, almost as if the younger man were not playing the game by the proper rules. Duffin retreated into a know-nothing truculence.

'Why would I? It was none of my doing,' he said. It seemed that the poacher was more offended at the thought of being accused as a dog-killer than of housebreaking. 'I'd have no need to cut his throat – a good dog like that. I'd sooner cut a man's.'

'I beg your pardon, Mr Duffin,' Jarrett soothed him. 'I do not mean to accuse you. I merely wondered whether, being so familiar with these parts, you had not seen something of the men who broke in here and did this. Come, there must be something to wet a man's throat somewhere in this god-forsaken place. I saw bottles enough in the other room on my first visit.' He led the way to the oblong room he had examined the day before. Duffin followed, nursing his affronted honour.

Looking about him, Jarrett resolved that no manner of tidying or housekeeping would reconcile him to living in that house. The gloom of the room seemed to enter his bones. It did not bear any sense of threat, but rather a stifling melancholy, salted with damp. Opening a sturdy corner cupboard, he discovered a couple of bottles of decent brandy.

There was a chink of glass on glass behind him and he turned to see Duffin adjusting his knapsack. Jarrett's eyes made a swift inventory of the room. The chair by the fireplace and the newspapers strewn about it were undisturbed. Then he noticed that the pile of square bottles that had stood behind the log basket was considerably diminished. Duffin followed the direction of his host's gaze.

'There's a woman as'll pay a farthing a piece for those down on Fish Lane,' he commented airily.

'What, Duffin, would you steal?'

The poacher bridled. 'Steal, your honour? I never steal. Stealing is taking from honest men. I only pick up what's not wanted. You might call it foraging, being a military man.'

Jarrett laughed. 'You're welcome to them, Duffin. Only say – have you foraged here before? At the time the dog died perhaps?'

Duffin's features set into familiar dour lines. 'If you've no need of anything more, your honour, I'll take me due and be on me way. Bob'll be a-frettin' and a-wanderin' if I don't see to him.'

Jarrett seemed unaffected by this rebuff. A bottle of brandy in each hand, he strode across the room. 'So be it, Duffin. But stay and take a glass with me before you go.' He headed out of the room towards the library. 'Maybe you can advise me on another mystery. We'll have to make do,' said Jarrett, passing Ezekiel a bottle as he fell in behind him, 'no glasses.'

In the library Jarrett stood with his back to the window looking about the room.

'Now what do you fancy could be missing?' he asked.

'What might you be looking for?'

'Ledgers? Books a man might set his figures down in. No. Anything. They must have come for something.' He spoke as if to himself but he watched Duffin as he said it. The man gave no reaction.

'He was a warm man but not so as you'd know in his dress,' commented Duffin, looking about the shabby room in disgust. 'Never had a thing about him worth a shilling. Must have all gone on drink.' He sniffed piously and took a pull at the bottle in his hand. Jarrett, who was crouched over the confusion around the desk, looked up. The poacher, it was clear, had a hard head. Jarrett closed his teeth against the mouth of his own bottle to hold the liquor back.

'What, he had nothing – no fobs, or watches, or …'

'Aye,' Duffin interrupted him. 'He had a watch. Fancy thing, imported from foreign parts.' In answer to Jarrett's unspoken question, the poacher elaborated. 'Reason I recollect is it broke. Aye, some time back now. And he made a fearful to-do about hows Nathan Binks was not craftsman enough to have care of it. Binks was grieved, he was – griped at the ole tap for days, he did.'

'Nathan Binks?'

'Watchmaker on t'market. We sometimes partakes in the same establishment.'

Jarrett contemplated the pieces of the desk. 'A man might keep valuables in his bureau.' He turned over a fragment of a drawer idly. 'What manner of watch was it?'

'How would I know?' responded Duffin roughly. 'It was fine and foreign, that's all. He had this habit of pulling it out when he was talking, just to show what a big man he was.' Duffin stuck out his gut and parodied a self-important man consulting his watch.

Jarrett smiled. He stirred the debris of the desk with the toe of one boot. 'Well, it is not here now.'

Duffin was gazing about the room with an expression of mournful disgust, his bottle clasped to his broad chest. ''Tis a powerful drear place. Haunted, I shouldn't wonder.'

'By Crotter maybe, do you think?' asked Jarrett lightly. 'I should like to encounter his shade. I have a question or two to put to the gentleman.' He stood up. 'Ah well, I suspect I shall not have the pleasure. Crotter is dead and buried, but a pretty puzzle he has left us.'

The whole room was dank. The high windows with their mullions reminded Jarrett of a prison. Outside the glorious evening was spreading its colours across the sky.

'I will not live in this house,' declared Jarrett, more to himself than the company, but none the less Duffin nodded in dour approval. 'The little house down by the river, the folly – it is deserted, I think?'

'None lives there to my knowledge – 'cept maybe an hoot owl.'

'Excellent. That will serve my needs. I shall set up there. I must be getting old,' Jarrett said as he led the way out of the room. 'Bivouacking under the stars no longer holds the charm it did. Now I confess I prefer a roof over my head – but not one such as this. Here I should likely find myself wandering the halls at night with a bit of chain hoping for some ghostly company.'

The little tea-house Jarrett had passed on his arrival was solidly built and the roof mostly watertight. None of the gentry had visited it for some years. The square room with its balcony was barren save for a few abandoned pieces – an elegant spindle-legged table that had seen better days, two chairs and an ancient carved wooden chest empty but for dust and a nest of earwigs.

Duffin, who showed no inclination to be on his way, helped Jarrett forage some straw and other essentials from the old manor house. His knowledge of the place and its contents convinced Jarrett that he had been a frequent visitor there. A rough lean-to at the back of the folly provided just enough stabling for his horse. After little more than an hour Jarrett found himself at his new door, sweeping the last of the debris from the floor. Behind him the hearth was cleared, his bedroll was laid out on a mattress of straw and his other belongings neatly stowed in or around the chest. Beyond the balcony the river kept up a constant musical sound. Jarrett contemplated the scene with a guilty thrill. He could anticipate Charles's exasperation at such gypsy behaviour. But after all, his valet Tiplady had abandoned him after their unfortunate quarrel in York. The Lord alone knew how long it would take his servant to mend his temper and follow him to Woolbridge.

While scouting behind the lines around Caldas da Rainha that February Captain Jarrett had been careless enough to suffer a direct cut from a French sabre during a skirmish with a party of dragoons. As chance would have it, it had been the Frenchman's guts that had spilled to join with the Portuguese dust. Captain Jarrett's men had pulled him from that field alive but his wound had festered. He might have died in the military hospital at Lisbon but that his friend Captain Cocks, on his way back home on family business, finding him lying there in his blood and delirium, had elected to convey his brother officer to London along with some despatches he carried. Jarrett had woken to find himself at Ravensworth. As his strength crept back the countless petty oppressions that accompanied civilised life increasingly weighed on his spirits. By setting up camp in this charming spot he could snatch a breathing space. His valet Tiplady, with his disapproving sniffs and petty rules of propriety, would reappear all too soon to drag him back into the confines of a proper gentleman's existence.

Duffin had found a new spot to smoke his pipe just above the bridge. Below, huge fragments of stone were strewn across the breadth of the river as if some giant had thrown down bits of a puzzle in a rage. Between the boulders the water dazzled with rainbow lights in the setting sun. Jarrett came out of the folly carrying two fishing rods and set off down towards the river. He paused to look up and down the stretch of water. He took something out of the bag slung about his waist and began to prepare his line. Duffin ambled over.

'Trout?' he asked.

Jarrett gave an affirmative grunt. Gripping his rod under his arm to free one hand, he paused in his task to pass the other rod to the poacher who took it without a word. As the two men disappeared into the summer foliage of the steep bank the countryman's voice drifted up.

'A mite of feather from a blackbird's wing caught up with a twist of yella silk round a body of fox ear down – that's the best of a summer's night. There's not a trout tha's not been tempted by a bit of fox down dressed up right.'

It was midnight and the stars were vivid in a clear sky. Duffin and Jarrett lay stretched out about a brisk fire. Plump trout were skewered over the flames on a spit contrived out of a musket's ramrod and two green boughs that steamed and spat in the heat. Duffin chuckled as he gazed into the flickering light, a bottle cradled in his arms.

'Poaching with the Duke's man,' he said. The notion clearly gave him great satisfaction. 'No need to watch for the keeper.' He laughed again. 'His face'd be a proper picture.'

In the shadows beyond the flames Jarrett was sketching. He glanced up to grin briefly in recognition of the joke.

'Not that Dickon Pace'd ever creep up on the likes o' me.' Duffin shook his head. 'Oh, no. Ox-footed bugger.' His face plainly reflected his low opinion of the Duke's gamekeeper. ''Tis like half a troop of beasts a coming through t' wood to hear him. Have to be half deaf or daft not to take heed.' He drank deep to confirm this statement before leaning forward to take a slice of trout on the blade of a wicked looking knife. 'They's ready,' he announced through a mouthful of pink flesh.

Jarrett put his sketch aside and picked a trout off the fire. He looked preoccupied. 'Who the devil would take those books!' he exclaimed in irritation. 'If only Crotter had disappeared there might have been reason to it, but there he is dead and buried in the church.'

Duffin was busy extracting fine bones from his mouth with grimy fingers. He watched Jarrett put aside his fish absent-mindedly and pick up the paper again.

'Tha' making a map?' he asked.

'A map?' Jarrett looked up, surprised. 'Oh, no.' He glanced at his sketch and then leant across to hand it to the man. 'It is yours if you like it. Take it – with my compliments.'

Duffin tilted the paper towards the fire. In the red light he saw a pencil sketch of himself, Ezekiel Duffin, fishing in his long coat on the rocks down by the river. He could make out the very spot. A place they called Friar's Cast. He was intent on his taut fishing line and Bob was there, plain as day. The dog's back haunches were half-crouched, and his ears pricked forward, as if he were about to bark. Just as he did that first moment when a fresh caught fish broke through the surface of the water. 'Tha's Bob!' he exclaimed. Then embarrassed by this show of emotion, Duffin reined in his enthusiasm. ''Tis like,' he said shortly. Jarrett could see he was pleased. The poacher folded the paper with great care and stowed it in between layers of coats at his breast. He cleared his throat and wiped his mouth with the back of his fingers. Jarrett busied himself with his trout to give Duffin a moment to regain his composure.

'I sees him in the lane.' Duffin lay back from the flames, his face in shadow. Jarrett was still. The trout was uncomfortably hot and it burnt his fingers. 'His kind are of the town but he was in the lane after dark. Knew it had to be mischief.' There was movement in the shadows and the sounds of Duffin fortifying himself from his bottle. 'I was in t' wood a-minding me traps and the dog was barking and barking. Then he stopped – all of a sudden.' Duffin paused. 'So I went up, didn't I,' he said aggressively, as if Jarrett had challenged him. 'Poxy fool! None of my affair,' he scolded himself.

In the darkness Jarrett had put aside his uneaten fish. He lay stretched out, his back supported against a stump. His arms were folded across his chest, the shape of his white shirt gleaming in the darkness.

'So I's goes up to t' hall, don't I? Mother was ever a-saying – Ezekiel, you must be shoving your nose into other folks' business. She weren't wrong.' He fell silent, contemplating his mother's words in the flames.

'What did you see, Duffin?'

The other man started. He looked bemused. The drink was beginning to take effect.

'At the old manor,' Jarrett prompted him in a low voice, 'what did you see there?'

'I looked in window. Into that room. Crotter were asleep by fire and the other varmint was standing and cursing over him, but he never moved. Just slept, peaceful like.'

'Then what happened?'

'He went off. It were dark. No moon. And cold, though it were summer. Then he came back a-carrying.'

'What was he carrying? Could it have been the books, the ledgers?'

'Could be.'

Jarrett tried to recall the details of the oblong room. He remembered the blackened fireplace. 'Did the man try to burn the books?' he asked on a flash of inspiration.

The question appeared to amuse Duffin. 'He tried. God's truth. He did try. He was piling up the wood and looking about him for things to make fire burn hot. Even tore down one of them bits o' cloth a hanging on t' wall and put that on. Didn't do him no good. Poxy fool. Leather bound,' he explained.

'So the books would not burn up?' asked Jarrett. 'What did he do with the remains?'

'How would I know? None of my affair. Left him to it.'
Duffin gazed into the fire. He hugged the near empty bottle
to his chest as if he were cold. 'A right bugger, that one.'

'You knew the man, Duffin.' Jarrett's words were a statement rather than a question. In the shadows he barely caught
Duffin's nod of assent. 'Who was the man, Duffin, tell me.'

The poacher shook his head earnestly. 'You don't want to
be knowing that. Leave it be.'

Jarrett leant forward, showing his face in the firelight.
'Duffin, you and I are old soldiers,' he coaxed. 'I can hold
my own with the most desperate of characters. A man has
a right to know his enemy. If you knew the villain, tell
me.'

The fire had sunk to a reddish glow between them. For
a frustrating moment Jarrett thought his companion had
drifted off into a drunken stupor.

'The Tallyman. They call him the Tallyman.'

'And how would I know him, this Tallyman?' Jarrett
asked softly. 'What manner of man is he?'

Duffin was reluctant to answer so direct a question.
He sank down into his coats, as if drawing away from its
demand. At last, he conceded that his companion was not
going to be put off.

'Great tall fellow; yella hair; cribbage-faced,' he growled.
'Used to be at sea, they say. You'd know if you crossed his
path.'

'And who does he serve, this Tallyman?'

'Does mischief for all kinds, so long as they pay.'

'So – for hire, is he?'

'Wouldn't call him particular in anything save preserving
his hide,' snorted the poacher. 'Not one to cross, that 'un – a
proper shite-fire,' he added gloomily.

'And where might I find this bell-swagger? There must be
a place to seek him if he is a man who hires out.'

It took Jarrett some persistent coaxing before Duffin

would admit to knowledge of any of the Tallyman's haunts. The rogue clearly had a formidable reputation.

'There's an alehouse,' he told Jarrett at last. 'A house of call for the rivermen down on the water. Innkeeper goes by the name of Lumpin' Jack.'

'Lumping Jack?' Jarrett was inclined to think that the poacher was spinning him a yarn, but the man was owlishly in earnest.

'Aye. Lumpin' Jack – he's a great lump of a man and his wife's as big. Tallyman and him are thick. Bad place. You don't want to be going there after lamps are lit.'

'So the Tallyman can be found at Lumping Jack's alehouse?' repeated Jarrett.

'Lumpin' Jack'll take messages.' Duffin was impatient with such innocence of the ways of villains. 'Tallyman moves about. Never in same place twice. But you don't want to be going down there!' Duffin was fierce in his advice. 'Leave it be. You've better things to do than get your throat cut and your carcass slid in water down by the sluice.'

Jarrett was touched by his concern. 'Duffin, I will have a care, but I, too, cannot help sticking my nose into curious business. I have a taste for mysteries. I cannot help myself.'

'There's curiosity and there's foolishness,' responded Duffin severely. 'Men who stays alive know that.'

It was the dead grey hours before the summer dawn. The acrid wood smoke drifted low over the ground in the chill air. The dog Bob, who had been sleeping by the fire, sat up as Duffin lumbered to his feet. 'There's no telling you,' said the poacher in disgust. 'I'm off to me snares.' He gathered his belongings in stately silence, slipping the remains of a cooling trout into his pocket.

Jarrett was sorry they were parting in such ill humour. 'Good night,' he called after him, as Duffin stumped off into the greying darkness. 'I hope to see you when you pass this way again.'

46

The poacher's stocky outline paused halfway down the bank below the bridge. Duffin's voice came clear through the pre-dawn stillness. 'The house goes under the sign of the Three Pots,' it said. 'And you'll see me again – if you live,' he ended lugubriously.

The pale pre-dawn light was filtering through the windows as Jarrett returned to the folly. He lit the fire and blew out the remains of a single candle that guttered on the table, then slung his crumpled coat over a chair. The motion recalled the disapproving features of the valet he had left behind in Yorkshire.

'Why, Master Jarrett, Mr Tiplady would never forgive you treating a good coat like that,' he mocked himself aloud. He took up the garment to brush it half-heartedly. A paper, dislodged from an inner pocket, tumbled to the floor. It was a torn part of a sheet he had gathered from Crotter's library and overlooked. It seemed to be part of a document written in some sort of legal language. From his recollection of the Latin drilled into him at school, one or two of the legal phrases did not quite ring true.

He opened the double window-doors and stepped out on to the balcony to examine the smudged paper. Amid the wherebys and whereofs it appeared to be a portion of an alehouse licence for a place called the Moorcock, at Fiddler's Croft. There was a tenant farm of the Duke's that went by that name if he was not mistaken. The signature on the bottom of the paper was partially torn off but Jarrett could make out the letters and words: '-tter, agent to the D-.'

'By what right were you granting alehouse licences, Mr Crotter? You were no magistrate,' Jarrett said softly. 'And I wonder how much you were getting by it?' he mused. Above, the last stars flickered, as elusive as time. They offered him no answer.

CHAPTER FOUR

The Duke of Penrith, old and ailing over the last few years, had not kept abreast of his affairs as he should. Jarrett wasted a few moments cursing himself for setting off so hurriedly on this adventure. He had been so restless, so eager to be off doing something, that he had departed without adequate preparation. His Grace had been in one of his choicest vacillating and complaining moods, and Jarrett had found it so impossible to keep his temper with him in that condition that he had taken the first excuse to get away. It was too late to turn back now. He would have to make do. Among the few papers the Duke had managed to scrape together Jarrett traced the hill farm called Fiddler's Croft. It lay a few miles up the dale from Woolbridge in an isolated spot. It was one of the new farms brought into existence by the Enclosure Acts of the last generation. In the list written out in a spidery black hand the tenant was given as one Samuel Gibbs, a sheep-farmer who laid the occasional crop of oats.

The new day dawned bright and clear as Jarrett set off on Walcheren following the broad track that wound up the dale. As he should have anticipated, the Duke's maps were old and the distances imperfectly surveyed, but by mid-morning he came within sight of a clump of buildings that formed Fiddler's Croft. According to the recent steward's returns – the unfortunate Mr Crotter's – Samuel Gibbs was a model tenant. He had been granted a rent rebate in the previous year for improvements which included a fine new stone barn, and likewise a sheepfold. As with all the Duke's leases, the tenant had agreed to plant six oak, ash and alder trees for 'the better maintaining of the house, hedges etc. in sufficient and tenantable repair' for every year of his eighteen-year tenancy. On paper Mr Gibbs was an exemplary tenant. Plain sight told a different story.

The farm Jarrett surveyed from the furrowed track had fallen on evil times. There was not a tree or sapling to be seen in the bowl of fell that lay below him; nor was there any sign of a fine new barn. There was a sheepfold of sorts. A piece of dry stone walling began bravely enough but petered out in a pile of stone before it had even turned one corner, as if the builder had lost interest in the project. He had finished the enclosure by cobbling together a rough fence of pickets. Looking about him, Jarrett could see no immediate purpose for it. There was but one lone sheep in sight, and that stood so far off as to be scarcely distinguishable. If anyone here dealt in sheep, Jarrett thought, the animals would be unlikely to be their own property.

A dishevelled house stood amid this clutter. A few hens scrabbled about the midden heap before the door and a gaunt pony, harnessed to a gig, waited in the yard. There was no other sign of movement or human presence at the height of this summer's morning. On the track leading to the farm stood a gibbet on which a sign hung, shifting in the breeze. Jarrett reached into his saddle bag and fetched out a neat telescope. Its magnifying power brought the sign into focus. Through cracked layers of brown varnish he could just make out the outline of a plump game bird. The Moorcock.

Jarrett dismounted and unrolled a battered greatcoat from behind his saddle. He shrouded himself in this disreputable garment, turning up the heavy collar to shadow his face. It draped about him with all the familiar comfort of an old friend that had seen him through many a long march. Picking up a handful of dirt he rubbed a little on his face to remedy the excessive cleanliness of his appearance and rubbed a little more on his boots. He took out his pistols, loaded them and stuck them in the deep pockets of his greatcoat. Ruffling his hair with a quick hand, Jarrett remounted and rode boldly down towards the Moorcock.

He flung open the slatted door and stepped in. The light that filtered through the tiny windows was supplemented by a meagre oil lamp. The grease in the lamp and the dung burning in the hearth contributed their foul qualities to the airlessness of the low-ceilinged room. The nook to the side of the cavernous hearth was occupied by an ill-favoured man who was laid out like a corpse, head tilted back and hands folded across his stomach. His chest moved as resonant snores bubbled out through his slack mouth. Three men were grouped around a table, a domino game set before them among a clutter of pots and spilled ale. Another man, thickset, with arms like slabs of beef, balanced on a chair tipped up against the wall watching the game.

The thickset man's legs hit the floor with a sturdy thud. He set his meaty forearms on his thighs ready to spring up and confront the intruder. He was a man accustomed to his bulk gaining him respect. He weighed up the stranger and decided he had no need to get up as yet.

'What?' he demanded. He had a low forehead and dull eyes.

The three disreputable-looking characters around the table leant back from their game, as if marginally interested in the action. The newcomer was not particularly broad or tall, but he had a lean, spare look that might mean trouble.

He did not flinch or falter at this greeting. He surveyed the room blankly, strode to an unoccupied table, sat on a chair with his back to the wall and laid a pistol on the tabletop under his hand.

'You sell ale here, Beggar-maker, or is that sign a picture of your ma?'

Jarrett's voice had changed. He congratulated himself on a creditable imitation of a rogue who had once served under him when he was a young lieutenant – Long Tom, the hardest man in the division (but the sweetest singer you could wish to hear, when he was well oiled).

He seemed to have made the desired impression. Belligerence waned in the thickset man's eyes to be replaced by a certain wariness. He got up. His movements betrayed a body that had run to soft fat and he wheezed as he moved. He fetched a pitcher of ale and a mug and set them before Jarrett.

'That'll be a penny,' he said. His eyes skirted round the pistol and he took care not to crowd the visitor.

Jarrett sensed the man's uncertainty. So far so good. He hoped he would be able to see the charade through. He looked into the pale eyes staring down at him. The man was thinking. It was clearly a painful process. Curiosity and caution jostled in his expression. He wiped a corner of the table with his filthy blue apron. 'Travellin'?' he asked with a comical pretence of casualness.

Jarrett kept his face a wooden mask and returned a hard look through narrowed eyes. He lifted the mug to his lips with his free hand and drank deliberately.

'Come far?' the alehouse-keeper persisted.

Jarrett set down his mug with effect. 'The coast,' he said at last, with a jerk of his head in the general direction of the east coast. Long Tom, he recalled, when in his most bullying mood, had always been short in his speech, relying on hard stares and significant pauses for effect. The technique appeared to be working with this bumpkin. Behind his mask Jarrett was beginning to find the brevity of their conversation absurd. If the pauses became any heavier he was afraid his levity might break out and give him away.

He took another swig of the cloudy ale. The curved grip of the pistol felt cool and firm under his hand. 'I'm looking for a man,' he said. 'They call him the Tallyman.'

It was an arrow shot at venture, but it struck home. The big man looked away and stepped back from the table.

'None here by that name,' he said too fast. He turned and stumped back to his chair by the far wall.

'This is the Moorcock?' Jarrett sent his voice cutting across the room. The three players were hunched over their dominoes, blocking him out with their turned backs. The alehouse-keeper's bulk seemed to have deflated in his chair, pricked by the very mention of the Tallyman's name. He barely answered Jarrett's jeering question with a jerky nod and turned away to stare at the frozen game. 'And you don't know no Tallyman?'

Silence spread thick between them, torn only by the snores of the drunkard asleep by the hearth. Jarrett was losing his audience. He picked up the pistol and contemplated it ostentatiously. 'Fancy piece, this,' he said in a voice loaded with meaning. 'Mighty accurate. But has a temper all its own – that she does. You wouldn't credit it.' He sketched a graceful flourish with the weapon. 'Sometimes – she just goes off!'

Four pairs of eyes were fixed on the slim blue barrel. He had their attention. 'Catches me quite unawares sometimes,' Jarrett finished and held them with a hard stare.

The pause that followed seemed unaccountably long. He was laying it on as thick as a travelling player performing melodrama in a country barn. The image came uncomfortably close; he had the sinking feeling he was about to get the bird. One of the players, a small man with hollow eyes and grey cheeks, pushed over a domino with an audible click on the wooden table. 'Tallyman and he's of a piece. They's welcome to each other,' he mumbled. He tossed his head defensively in the direction of his companions and said in a rush, as if to forestall their objections, 'Tallyman don't call here but once a season to collect. His lay's in town, down on the river – at the sign of the Three Pots. That's all we know here. Wouldn't want to know more.'

A performer could not wish for a better exit line. Jarrett finished his ale. He bowed mockingly to the company and backed – as gracefully as he could – out through the door, the pistol held loosely before him. He rode off slowly, with a swagger, as he imagined a confederate of the Tallyman might. Reaching the road he put his spurs to the big bay. As he cantered off, he laughed out loud. 'Perhaps Mrs Siddons would care for a new leading man, eh, Walcheren? I could hardly believe they would buy that bill of goods – but they did, they did.'

Out of sight of the Moorcock he reined the bay back into a walk as he stripped off the warm coat and stowed his pistols in the saddle bags. 'So what have we learnt, old friend?' he asked aloud, rubbing at the dirt on his face with a handkerchief. 'One, Crotter was not behaving as a decent steward ought – letting a good farm go for a thieves' alehouse – sheep rustlers, I'll wager; and even writing them out licences.' He paused. Walcheren's ears twitched as his eye caught sight of a tempting bit of foliage. Jarrett's strong hands mechanically pulled the horse's head back from the bush. 'Now why would he do that? Why issue licences when any half-wit knows only a magistrate has the right?' Walcheren was dawdling again. He kicked him on. 'These peasants must be easily parted from their money. Two, this Tallyman fellow was in the roguery somewhere. But in what fashion?' he mused.

Jarrett's blue-grey eyes gazed out over the summer scenery, his attention turned inwards. The bay horse took advantage of the slackened reins to snatch a bite. Then another. 'A partner or agent? Is there some other villain in the business? According to Duffin's account, Crotter was dead when this Tallyman took the books, and this bully hardly sounds like a reading cove – what think you, old friend?'

Jarrett looked down to note that they had halted. Walcheren, leaving his master to his discourse, was absorbed in consuming grass. He hauled the horse's head up and spurred him on.

'There is nothing for it, we shall have to seek out this Tallyman and ask him,' he said, and energy surged through his veins at the prospect of the hunt ahead.

Two dams blocked the river at each end of the bend in which the town of Woolbridge sprawled. The dams fed the mill races that powered the wheels and machinery of the cloth mills and carpet factories at the water's edge. Flat-bottomed boats and wherries slid across the smooth water above and below the bridge as the rivermen ferried raw materials and finished goods to and from the factory docks on the town banks. As Walcheren's shod hooves echoed on the stone of the ancient bridge the scene was alive with activity. There were bargees with bright red kerchiefs tied about their throats. Bare-chested, their muscles gleamed with sweat as they lifted bales of wool on to the landings. A group of boys splashed in the dye-stained shallows, deepening the grimy hue of their skin in patches until they appeared piebald.

There was work in the town and a purposeful hum about the place. The grinding and thudding of the machinery throbbed out from the woollen mills. The rivermen joked and called to one another and swore above the rush of the water.

The streets clinging to the side of the steep hill had not been broad to begin with. Over time they had become encrusted with poor shacks, stalls and lean-tos that cramped the way. Jarrett and Walcheren had to jostle past the other users of the street. The respectable working man walking about his business; the rag and bone man with his basket on his back crying out his trade; the woman who took in laundry selling gin from her half-door while she gossiped with an acquaintance. About her stall lean, ragged fellows loitered drinking at mid-day. They bore the sullen, explosive air of the young and energetic who find themselves at a loose end.

The street wound about and swallowed up all sense of direction. Little alleyways filtered off between the jumble of wood and masonry, signs and stalls and washing hung between window and window across the narrow street. It was not going to be easy finding the house that went under the sign of the Three Pots. Many of these alehouses were merely a poor basement room in some tenement. Jarrett began to think he would need to find a guide. He was loath to ask directions. Despite the bustle he could sense that he was in a close-knit community. The gin-seller and her gossip were weighing him up and he felt the eyes of the group of drinkers fixing on him. They were already half-cut and he had no desire to be drawn into some brawl for their amusement. He kicked Walcheren on as if he knew where he was going, following along the line of the river as best he could.

To his left Jarrett glimpsed the river down a slip that led to a small landing. Two rivermen had just left their craft and were coming up the lane.

'G'day, Tobias,' one greeted the other. 'And how's thee, man?'

'I'm to the Three Pots,' replied his friend. 'Bloody Thorndike's played me false and I'm looking for another load.'

'I'll walk with you. I'm mighty dry. Good drinking weather, this,' laughed the man, wiping the sweat from his face with his folded shirt. He slung the garment across his bare neck as they strode past Walcheren, scarcely giving the rider a glance. His luck was in today! Allowing a decent space to extend between them, Jarrett set off to follow the two men.

The Three Pots stood at the end of a short alley. It was a shabby, half-timbered house, standing hard up against the high wall of a tanning yard. To the far side and behind the building the deep waters of the river swirled on their way to the lower dam. Jarrett could see why Duffin might warn against visiting the place after dark. The street was a quiet dead end. Those people who hurried past the mouth of the alley kept their eyes to themselves, and the tenement opposite showed no signs of life at its mean windows. The door to the house stood open. Jarrett did not like leaving Walcheren unattended in such a place, but he had come so far it seemed foolish not to go in. He dismounted and followed the rivermen through the dark passage.

The room into which he emerged was unexpectedly spacious. His two guides were over by the bar and Tobias was speaking to a coltish youth wrapped in an apron, who was writing in a large book laid open on the counter.

'Tobias Hind,' Jarrett heard the man say. 'I'll take any load.'

'There's nothing in right now,' replied the youth as he wrote in a painstaking hand. 'Mr Bedford's just brought in a load of dye. That's why there's nowt in. You've but missed it by an hour. But Mr Pickering's expecting wool. He may send down at any time. Have a glass while you're waiting,' he consoled, with the smooth solicitude of the salesman.

Jarrett caught the youth's eye. The barman gestured to the newcomer with an abrupt jerk of the head that he should wait and turned to draw a pitcher of ale with practised ease. He handed the pitcher to a lad of six or seven. 'You take that to Mrs Riley down on Fish Lane,' he directed. The lad walked carefully out of the shop and the youth yelled after him, 'Mind you come straight back with the money or I'll flay ya!'

The youth poured a mug of ale and brought it over to Jarrett without being asked.

'Is this Lumping Jack's house?'

The barman nodded. He had a watchful, guarded face.

'Is he here?'

The youth busied himself collecting up some dirty pots. 'Lumpin' Jack and his missus are gone to Darlington. They'll not be back this day or next, I'd reckon,' he said.

'As it happens, my business is not with him. I am looking for one they call the Tallyman. I may have work for him. I was directed to ask for him here.' Jarrett slid a silver coin across the table, keeping his fingers resting lightly on it.

The youth's eyes flickered and he looked the stranger up and down. 'What kind of work?' he asked.

'My business, not yours,' answered Jarrett, pulling back his hand to leave the coin in plain view. The youth wiped the table and picked up the mugs. The coin was gone.

'Not been in a while,' he said. 'I heard word he'd gone to the coast. Might be in Friday night. Can't tell you more.' He moved off to deal with some new customers. As the interview was clearly at an end, Jarrett finished his ale and left.

Retrieving Walcheren who was standing forlorn looking out over the water, it occurred to Jarrett that he had not eaten since the night before. The thought of Mrs Bedlington's boiled ham drew him to retrace his steps and make his way up the hill towards the Queen's Head.

Mrs Bedlington greeted him with exuberance, as if they had not just parted the day before. 'Why, Mr Jarrett!' she cried with coquettish pleasure. 'You have come to pay us a visit! You must be famished, poor man,' she fussed. 'No one to have care of you in that horrid old manor. You just sit there and I'll fetch you a nice bit of ham and green peas, fresh picked this morning.' She turned to catch sight of her maid in the act of kneeling down, a pail beside her. 'Molly! Not with water, you silly slut! It's a dry rub with sand for boards, as you well know if you'd but take a moment to reflect, girl!' Driving the unfortunate maid before her, Mistress Polly bustled away to the kitchen.

Jarrett found himself the sole occupier of the little parlour. The sun streamed through the windows and he took pleasure in the room's calm after the crowded alleys of the river quarter. The tap through the passage past the stairs was quiet that afternoon. One or two regular customers could be heard drinking and exchanging the occasional subdued remark.

There was a clatter outside and a medley of hoots and cries, and a boisterous group of young men roiled into the tap like a pack of young wolves. They bore all the marks of being on a spree; doing every alehouse in town by the sounds of them, thought Jarrett. He could only see a small wedge of the room beyond the passage, but the sounds carried clearly. There were shouts of, 'Bar! Bar! Where's the tapster?'

'Why wait for him? We can draw our own,' said another.

This presumptuous suggestion was countered by the arrival of Jasper Bedlington. He spoke with the cheerful, nononsense authority of the professional innkeeper. 'What's this? What's this? Well, well – Will Roberts and friends. Celebrating your return from Ireland, my boy? You'll be glad to be rid of your red coat I'll be bound, eh, Will? You put that down, Nat Broom. I can draw me own ale, I'll thank you. So you're all here, eh? Does your Nancy know you're not at your loom, Harry Aitken? She'll not relish the sight of you half seas over on a Monday afternoon. And Joe Walton, too. There you are. I'll take the money now, if you please; you're like to forget later on, the way you're headed.'

Chastened by this treatment, the group settled down. There was a tone to their voices Jarrett had come to recognise from his time as an officer. He had heard it frequently enough when the lads broke loose for a spree. They were entering that phase of intoxication when young men's excited energies balance on the cusp between exuberance and violence. The innkeeper retired into the background. The voice Jarrett overheard had more than a little of the boisterous boy smarting from a telling off by the school master.

'That's right, Harry – what will your Nancy say? And as

for you, Will Roberts, your sergeant'll be on to you – half cut in the middle of the day.'

'Aye, a proper man's full cut or nothing, that's his philosophy,' replied Will.

'So Sergeant Tolley's hoist the blue flag at the Swan, has he? And how is it living with your sergeant, Will? I've heard of marrying the service but, by heck boy! And they say he's a proper bastard.'

'Didn't marry him.' Will sounded like an even-tempered sort.

'Oh aye?' The words were a jibe. 'Way I hear it, marry his daughter and you get him on your back for life. You're either a fool or a brave bugger, Will Roberts – whatever the skirt's condition.'

'Have another beer and quit riling him, Nat,' intervened another voice. 'You always must be stirring.'

Nat laughed and drank some more. 'What's this about Black-Eyed Sal, then?' he started off again. 'I heard word she's talking about a breach of promise – you slighting her to marry another. That's a court matter, that is. You'd best lie low a while, man. That piece is mad enough for anything.'

'Sal's not a bad lass.' Will's voice was placating.

Jarrett had a picture in his mind of an easy-going, pleasant sort of fellow. He shifted in his seat to try and get a glimpse of the speakers through the passage. He could just see the edge of the group. There were perhaps five or six young men in their early twenties. Nat Broom was a wiry, dark-haired man, tense and quick. One to keep your eye on if he was under your command. Unreliable; the kind who bore grudges. The peacemaker who intervened was Harry Aitken, the weaver. He had the most married look of the three. His dress was cleaner than the rest and all his buttons were firmly fixed.

Will Roberts was a country Adonis. So this was the suitor who had slighted Sal. They would have made a striking couple, yet to Jarrett's mind the boy he saw before him would have been vastly outmatched by the black-haired witch he had encountered in the churchyard. Will Roberts was tall and clean limbed. Curly chestnut hair fell over a broad forehead. He had a sleepy, handsome face with a straight, clean-cut nose and full lips. Thinking of Sal's bright, mischievous face, Jarrett could imagine that she might be piqued to have lost so handsome a swain, but somehow he could not believe she would have chosen such a biddable boy to match her fire. And yet, women were a mysterious sex.

'I'd not mind having Sal after me!' chipped in a voice.

'You're not married, Joe, and you don't have a bugger like the sergeant for a father-in-law,' chimed in Nat Broom. The envious kind, that one, thought Jarrett; a troublemaker. 'Never fret, Will lad,' Nat went on. 'Old Tolley'll see her off. Even Black-Eyed Sal is no match for the sergeant. How the likes o' him ever got fixed with a wife and daughter, the Lord alone knows. I can't see him living under the cat's foot.'

Mistress Polly emerged from her kitchen bearing a loaded tray. She seemed unsurprised to catch her favourite customer eavesdropping.

'The lads aren't disturbing you, Mr Jarrett?' she asked, setting the dishes before him. 'Will Roberts and Harry Aitken are good boys but that Nat Broom's a troublemaker to my mind,' she said, succinctly summing up Jarrett's own impression. 'He gets them all fired up at times. Never you mind, sir. You get this inside you, and then I've an apricot pie just out of the oven.'

The pie was good. And to please Mrs Bedlington he ate two pieces. It was nearly three by the time he finished and Jarrett was feeling the need to take some exercise. 'Did you get your letter taken to the post, Mr Jarrett?' enquired the innkeeper as he cleared away the plates.

The letter! It had gone clean out of his mind. Sunday morning seemed a week ago, so much had happened in the last day and night. Jarrett felt inside his coat pocket. The letter was safely lodged there. He drew it out. 'As you see, I have it still.'

The innkeeper glimpsed the direction written on it in a bold, flowing hand: *The Most Hon. the Marquess of Earewith, to await collection at the Red Lion, York.*

'Would you like me to send the stableboy to the post at Greta Bridge, sir? There is time to ride over on a good horse. The York Mail is due at four.'

'Thank you, but I have a fancy to take it myself. I could do with the exercise. My compliments to Mistress Polly; her fare is excellent.'

The innkeeper bobbed his head in acknowledgement, a pleased blush colouring his round face. 'Thank you, sir. My Polly prides herself on her apricot pie. You can't miss the way. Just turn left out of the yard and follow the road over the toll bridge by the old abbey. It's not above three miles.'

Some time later Jarrett was riding up the dusty road towards Greta Bridge. The post road ran along a ridge, and the lane leading to it from Woolbridge was steep in parts. He was negotiating a rise that passed by the edge of a wooded area in a semi-reverie, dazzled by the hot sunshine, when his senses jolted him into a sudden awareness of danger.

There was a half-human roar and two stocky figures burst out of the bushes, arms raised. One wielded a stout stick, the other a long hammer of the sort lead miners use. By force of habit his sword hand moved to his sabre hilt before consciousness of the lack of weight reminded him of his civilian dress. Jarrett's battle-honed instincts clicked into action. In a detached, objective part of his brain, he noted the swiftness of his reactions with a mild sense of surprise. Dodge the blow. Parry with a clumsy kick of a boot hampered by the stirrup. Now rear the horse up – pray he would not balk.

No. Good fellow. Walcheren reared up on command, flailing out with shod hooves.

The exhilaration of violence flared within him. Months of inaction had not dulled his stark pleasure in the economy of movement of a professional fighter. Not that these were particularly expert opponents. They were clumsy – alehouse sluggers. They swung at him together, blocking and jostling one another in their ragged attempts to get at him. The old campaigner in him wanted to chide them for bad tactics.

Walcheren too was demonstrating he had not forgotten his old tricks. In response to his master's pressure, the bay rose up again, flinging out his forelegs to land a hearty blow under the chin of the shorter of the two assailants. The man stumbled to one knee, stunned. Jarrett pulled the horse around in a tight circle. The long hammer slid past his right shoulder as he turned, numbing one side of his back. This was getting hot. Struggling to control the nervous animal, he felt behind him in his saddle bag. Every sinew was strained with the effort required to keep control of his mount. He shifted his weight as the animal bucked to one side. For a sickening moment his balance gave way and he began to slide out of the saddle. If he was thrown he did not fancy his chances with these two. With a massive effort that pulsed a tearing pain through his old wound he regained his seat. The horse spun round leaving his back exposed for a moment to the burly man with the hammer.

The smaller man's fall had winded him and he stood back a little from the fray. The taller of the two advanced towards Jarrett. He was big and brawny. Under the brim of his hat his eyes had the fixed, blank look of battle madness. Jarrett's heightened senses noted the pallor of the man's skin under the grime. His assailant came in for the kill, swinging the heavy hammer with unstoppable force.

Jarrett wrestled the pistol free of the saddle bag, levelled it and fired in one smooth action. The horse reared as the sound reverberated. The hammer hit Jarrett's thigh with a sickening thud and his leg went dead. The big man faltered. The hammer slid to the ground and he put his hand to his shoulder, a confused look on his face – almost like a child waking from a heavy sleep. Jarrett's mind was crystal clear, every sense stretched taut. He took advantage of the pause to back Walcheren a pace or two. He dropped the useless pistol and snatched its twin from its resting place.

At the sight of this second weapon his attackers decided to retreat. They scuttled, half bent over, into the scrub and fled down the steep bank in the direction of the river. It was too steep for the horse to follow. Reaction was setting in and Jarrett felt bone-weary. He did not even try to give chase. As the two villains dropped away from him he caught the fragment of an exchange between them.

'What about the paper?' the smaller of the two asked.

'What about our skins!' snarled his companion, moving clumsily as he clutched his wounded shoulder.

'He'll not like it.'

'Bugger him,' came the stout reply and the pair vanished into the wood.

He was alone once more. Walcheren's breath came hard and loud through flared nostrils. He soothed the animal, running a gloved hand over the satin neck. 'Easy now, easy, old fellow.' The bay gave his black mane a fierce shake, stared out into middle distance a moment then dropped his head and began to snatch at the long grass. 'Go to it, friend; there's nothing like a mouthful to recruit the nerves.'

He winced as he tested his leg. It throbbed with a deep, dull ache that communicated jabs of pain through the network of his bones at the slightest movement. Gingerly he inspected his thigh where the hammer had struck. The bone appeared to be whole, although under the distracting mask of pain it was hard to tell. Jarrett wiggled his toes experimentally within his boot. Lightning pain shot up the limb but everything seemed to be functioning. His discarded pistol lay on the ground a few feet away from his hat.

'There's nothing for it, you'd better fetch them,' he encouraged himself aloud. 'One, two, three ...'

Next time, he told himself, as he stood uncertainly on his good leg, shaking and sweating, he would remember to swing his weight to the other side when dismounting. The sudden violent exertion had set his old wound aching in counter-protest to his leg. At times like this a man might be glad there was no one to see him. He clung unashamedly to the saddle a while, drawing deep breaths as his jangled nerves settled. His stumbling progress over the few yards to collect his hat was minor torture. As he approached his pistol he half-fell, half-sat down beside it. If he could just lie back a moment. A minute or two's rest would mend him.

The sky filled his sight. At the horizon clouds gleamed like the pearly inner coating of a moonshell, their edges picked out in light against painted blue gauze. It had the luminous glow of a seventeenth-century landscape painted by the Italian Master. 'A Claudian sky,' he heard himself remark to the peaceful air. A pale insubstantial moth dawdled about a clump of crimson poppies at the edge of his vision. It was pleasant resting there, lulled by the summer drone of the insects and the soft whisper of a breeze in the grasses. With a click of a snapping twig, a rabbit scuttered off in the undergrowth. Jarrett forced himself to sit up, giving an involuntary grunt at the effort. The mail would be near due at Greta Bridge and he must get that letter to the post. Charles must be warned. This tangle was proving more dangerous than anticipated. Loath as he was to admit it, he would welcome Charles's presence. He was beginning to be conscious of his isolation in Woolbridge.

He whistled to his horse. The bay studiously ignored him. He called again. Walcheren barely lifted his head. He even took a casual step away as he browsed. An unexpected fury welled up in Jarrett. It propelled him to stagger towards his mount. 'Here, damn you!' he cursed. 'Stand, you poxy mule!' The horse sidled around, knocking the wind out of him as it slammed into his bad side. Only the strength of his upper body and sheer fury enabled him to swing himself up on to the animal's back. He lay along the neck, dizzy and sick. It was no use losing his temper with the beast. He filled his lungs with cool air. 'I beg pardon,' he said, as calmly as he could, rubbing one soft ear. 'It has been a distressing experience for us both.'

As he pushed himself up straight in the saddle, the animal turned to give his master an accusing look. Then, with a toss of his head and a soft snort, Walcheren condescended to set off once more on the road to Greta Bridge.

CHAPTER FIVE

The kitchen at Longacres, the residence of Mrs Lonsdale and her niece Henrietta, was of cavernous height. The afternoon sun streamed through the tall windows infusing the grey tones of the room with a comfortable, peachy warmth. Mrs Grundy, the long-time cook-housekeeper of the family, stood before the massive central table, the ingredients of a plum cake set out before her.

Over the years Mrs Grundy had grown to suit her kitchen, much as her kitchen had been arranged to suit her. So much so that those acquainted with her would be hard put to imagine her in any situation outside its stone walls. She had a heavy, foursquare body tinted in soft shades from white to grey. The only obvious colour about her was a touch of pink in the veins of her cheeks and the pale blue of her watchful eyes.

Hannah Grundy was never seen to bustle or to be flustered. Her every action spoke of her culinary philosophy summed up in her two favourite maxims. To everything its proper place and proper time; and cleanliness is the first and leading principle of a well-run kitchen. The ingredients of her plum cake were arrayed in a neat semi-circle of bowls before her. The pound of sugar, freshly crushed and sieved by Betsy the scullery maid; the butter pat standing in its cooling dish of water; the glass of brandy to give the fruit that extra zest; the basket of smooth brown eggs, the spices and the almonds, and the flour in her favourite large blue and white mixing bowl. She was concentrated on her task, her steady hands moving about their work with economy. Her chest was bad and her breath wheezed a steady counterpoint to the rustle of the fires in the stoves. She looked up as Black-Eyed Sal walked in from the drying yard carrying a small basket.

'That's my day near done,' the girl said cheerfully. 'Four baskets they left me today, and that overgrown damask cloth that's such a devil to press.' She put the basket on the table and stretched her back, her hands on her hips. She managed to bring a supple sensuality to even that every-day motion. Whether or not she was conscious of this effect was hard to tell. The ill-natured said that Sal never made a movement that was not calculated. Many others (though it had to be admitted, most of these latter were men) swore her natural-ness was a considerable part of her charm.

'And what's that great laundry room for, miss? Must you come dirtying my kitchen table?' asked the cook as Sal took a fine embroidered scarf out of the basket along with a pot of powder and a soft brush. The girl returned an affection-ate, teasing smile.

'Give over, Nan, it's only a little job and there's room enough on this great table. Betsy, girl,' she called across to the little scullery maid who stood near a window chopping vegetables, 'how about a cup of tea? The laundry and me's all wrung out!' Sal got up restlessly and strolled, swinging her hips, to bend over the trays of currants drying before the open ovens.

Mrs Grundy was soon beside her. 'You leave Betsy to her task and those currants alone,' she said, emphasising her words with a brisk slap on Sal's pilfering hands. Nevertheless she fetched the teapot down from the stove and poured a cup for them both. She called the scullery maid to her: 'Pin up that hair, Betsy. I'll not have hairs dripping about my kitchen. Oh, come here, lass.' She turned the girl about and briskly pinned up the straggling strands. The maid, a thin wench of thirteen in a washed-out grey print dress, stood submissively. 'There. Get you to the store room and fetch me a plate of sweetmeats. The third deep drawer by the window – and mind you make sure the paper's covering those left or they'll spoil.'

Mrs Grundy returned to her mixing bowl. She looked under her brows at her lively niece. 'You're telling me all's stowed away in the laundry?'

The girl filched an almond between tapering white fingers. Her long-lashed eyes twinkled in contrast to her assumed air of innocence. 'Tom's cleaning the mangle for me.'

'You're the laundry maid. That's your job, not the gardener's boy's.'

'But he's so willing.'

'That's as may be, but now I'll have the gardener cluttering up my kitchen fretting about how his boy's not at his tasks because he's doing yours.'

'Gardener never frets at me.'

'Aye. I'll be bound. It's a plain miracle how the sight of a pretty ankle can tie up a man's tongue.'

'Yes, Nan.' Sal laid out the scarf she had brought into the kitchen. It was of fine silver lace worked in floss silk. 'Fancy dropping this in the mud,' she commented as she sprinkled an area with fine powdered alum and brushed it clean with delicate dabs. 'Miss Henrietta does have some nice things, for all she's so plain.' Mrs Grundy shot her a disapproving look. 'Well, she is! I'm not saying she weren't fair enough when she were younger but, my, she's well on the shelf by now.'

Sal spoke with the unconscious arrogance of her pristine eighteen years. She smoothed the scarf, then picked it up and draped it over her raven curls with an air. 'I'll have things like this one day. And not by thieving neither.'

Mrs Grundy tut-tutted. 'And who'll be buying them for you? Stop dreaming, girl. We've all a place in life, and yours and mine will never lead us to wear finery like that. Now stop your peacocking and drink your tea before you get that shawl all dirty again.'

A moment of seriousness stilled Sal's mobile face. 'Nan, I'm not stopping here,' she said with conviction. 'I will have things like this of my very own one day. I'll improve myself in life, you'll see.'

'Improve yourself! That's not what folks call it. You'll improve yourself right into the river, my girl. Your wild ways do you no good. Why won't you settle?' Mrs Grundy bit back the words as she said them. She knew it did no good preaching at the likes of Sal, but she feared for her girl. 'You're wilful, Sally Grundy, that's what you are.'

'Aye, I know, and wild...' Sal responded with a cheeky grin. She stretched over deliberately and picked out another almond. She rolled it into her red mouth, her eyes brimming with mischief.

'You!' Mrs Grundy's face warmed with plain affection as she jabbed at the mixture in her bowl. 'Lord knows you'd have no trouble getting any of the unmarried men in the district if you set your mind to it,' she commented briskly.

'Or the married ones...' added Sal. She was deliberately provoking her aunt. Her dark eyes never left the older woman's face.

Hard as she tried, Hannah Grundy's fears could not be concealed. 'God forgive you, Sally Grundy, what mischief are you up to?'

'None that ain't deserved!' Sal softened before the concern on her aunt's face. She put out a hand towards the woman in a gesture of reassurance. 'Never fret, Nan, you know I'd never do nothing very wrong.'

Hannah looked full at her niece. 'You're not fretting after that Will Roberts?' she asked. She dropped her eyes and her voice, striving to sound detached. 'Didn't I always teach you that no man could be depended on out of sight? They're like dogs or cats; they'll go with whoever feeds 'em.'

'I know, Nan. I'd not fret after a man. Not while I've plenty fretting after me,' Sal ended, preening herself in a deliberately comic fashion.

'Well. You have a care, do,' insisted her aunt. 'Not that you ever would,' she continued softly. 'Not even as a little girl. Wild and wilful, that's what you are.' Mrs Grundy gently stroked Sal's porcelain cheek with work-roughened fingers. Then she snatched her hand back. 'Now away!' she said, nodding towards the clock that hung over the door. 'There's scarce an hour and a half to their dinner time and here's me but barely started!'

Sal wrapped her arms about her aunt's solid waist and hugged her. 'I've an early start tomorrow, Nan. I've been recommended, I have – to a Lady that's taken a big grand place near Gainford. A real Lord's Lady. I'm resting at the house, there's so much to do.' The girl was vibrant with anticipation at the prospect.

The cook was suspicious. 'You look mighty excited just for two days in a nobleman's laundry. I know you, Sal. You're not meddling with gentlemen, are you? You'd not be such a fool?'

Sal was not to be drawn. 'Don't fret, Nan,' she repeated, her face shimmering with suppressed mischief. 'I know my own business. I'm not such a little girl any more.' Then she gathered up her goods and danced out, pausing in the open doorway, her face bright with laughter. 'Besides, I've to be back Wednesday night. I've mischief to attend to!' Blowing a graceful kiss to her uneasy aunt, Sal was swallowed up by the bright sunshine.

The George at Greta Bridge was a fine and well-known inn. It stood close beside the elegant bridge that curved grace-fully over the river Greta. To many a traveller it was the last oasis of civilisation before the Roman road launched into the expanse of wild moorland that lay between the prosperity of Yorkshire and the comforts of Carlisle.

It lacked but a few minutes to four o'clock when Jarrett rode into the yard. There was a pallor under his tan and his face bore a set look from his struggle to keep control of the pain in his wounded leg. It took all his concentration to dismount with any semblance of normality. As he regained his breath he took stock of the bustle about him. The yard simmered in anticipation of the arrival of the mailcoach from Carlisle to York.

At the fringes of the crowd a group of postboys lounged in their short blue jackets, leather breeches and top-boots. One stood ready dressed to be called out, booted and spurred with his false leg strapped on to protect him from the carriage pole. Holding his pair of horses negligently with one hand, he looked into middle distance in a world-weary way, detached from the excitement of the onlookers who milled around him. The district was not so rustic that grown men and women would walk any distance to have a sight of the mailcoach passing, but several found their business happened to lie in the way of the George of an afternoon and loitered to witness the spectacle of the Change. Loud, skinny boys, burnt brown from long summer days of mischief, weaved about the sellers preparing themselves for the lightning moment of opportunity to come. A pedlar settled the strap of a tray of ginger nuts more securely about her neck. A foxy-faced boy hugged a basket to his chest as he polished the shine on the apples it contained. An old man in a battered straw hat arranged about himself an armful of nightcaps, pillows and fans to cool the face of the over-heated traveller. The journey by mailcoach was speedy but arduous and the privileged passengers were offered the purchase of an imaginative range of comforts.

Jarrett found the innkeeper putting the finishing touches

to his post list, the mailbags in a heap on the counter beside him.

'I have a letter for York.'

The innkeeper looked up from his lists. 'The mail's near due and my bags are all done up, sir,' he objected.

'It is urgent,' insisted Jarrett. He felt in his pocket and drew out a coin.

The innkeeper looked him up and down. 'You look a mite rough, sir.'

'No matter,' Jarrett brushed his concern aside. 'A misadventure on the road. This letter?'

The innkeeper cocked his head to look out the window and down the empty road. 'Well, I reckon we can squeeze another in. For York, you say?'

'Yes. For the Marquess of Earewith to await collection at the Red Lion.'

'For the Marquess, is it?' The postmaster perked up at the name. 'Well, now, why didn't you say so before – always a pleasure to oblige a lordship.' The innkeeper's shrewd countryman's eyes noted the stiffness with which his customer moved. 'Trouble on the road, you say?'

'Two ruffians attacked me on the way from Woolbridge. After my purse, I dare say, but I saw them off,' replied Jarrett briefly. 'Do you have a pen, ink and sealing wax?'

'You was attacked? Well, sir, that is too bad. We don't get much of that sort of trouble round here. That's bad news, that is.'

'There is a postscript I must add before the mail comes,' prompted Jarrett, urgency giving his words a pronounced edge. He tried to add a conciliatory smile. 'I would be most grateful.'

With a slight sigh at the difficulty of serving the gentry the innkeeper went off to fetch the necessary items.

Jarrett broke open his letter, dashed off a hurried postscript about the attack and his misgivings and resealed it while the innkeeper carefully added the new arrival to the way-bill. The man was just refastening the York mailbag when the sounds of a coach horn were heard in the distance and everyone hurried out to watch the arrival of the mail.

The fresh horses stood prepared under the charge of ostlers. Directly opposite the inn's main entrance, the two leaders fretted, ready harnessed and coupled together. Another blast of the horn and the mail appeared bearing down the straight moor road in the grand style at full gallop. With nice judgement the coachman reined back his horses to bring them to a halt, the red body of his coach settling precisely between the two fresh wheelers lined up on the road. The ostlers leapt up to unthread the buckles and unhitch the four foam-flecked horses. The guard, in his fine scarlet jacket, sprang down from his box, the pedlars surged forward to clamour for the passengers' custom and the innkeeper pressed through the scrum to exchange his bags for the down mail. The George prided itself on performing the Change in less than the five minutes prescribed by the Post Office.

Above the confusion, the coachman sat in a heap on his box, his shape and aspect reminiscent of a comfortable and competent toad. He wore a squat beaver hat with a rakish curl to its brim, and his overflowing chins were supported by a silk handkerchief printed with bilious spots on a chocolate ground. Despite the heat of the day he wore a light over-coat thrown open sufficiently to hint at the several layers of miscellaneous coats underneath. He tied up the reins and stowed his whip in a stately fashion, while the passenger who had won the privilege of sitting by him eagerly wrestled to unbuckle the lead reins.

The guard was a well-made young fellow with curly black hair. He consulted the clock he carried in a sealed case slung over his shoulder.

'You're twelve minutes late,' said the innkeeper, as he checked the timepiece and filled in the guard's way-bill.

'Aye,' replied the guard, 'an affair held us up at the last stage. There's been a murder up on the moor.'

The crowd picked up the sound of the word. 'Murder? What murder?' 'There's been murder done?' The guard looked up to the highest authority present. The coachman prepared to come down from his box.

Despite his formidable bulk the coachman proved surprisingly light on his feet. He descended rapidly from his perch, neatly shifting his feet in turn from footboard to step, to hub, to ground, in one smooth flowing action. He had the timing of the natural-born showman. He paused, gazing mournfully at the crowd, before he spoke.

'Crofter's boy come down from moor all covered with blood,' he announced with relish. 'On Stainmoor, it happened. He's but a speck of a lad but he'd run all the way. A murdering blackguard done in his da. A great tall fellow, a sailor.'

'What would a sailor be doing so far inland?' questioned Jarrett.

The coachman turned to look at the interrupter of his tale. Seeing it was a gentleman, he deigned to explain. 'The boy said his hair were braided up with a tail behind. Dick and me, we told 'em it sounded to be such as sailors wear. Dick has a brother in the navy – that right, Dick?' The guard nodded in studious agreement. 'Justice in Brough told us to hand these about,' continued the coachman, drawing some roughly printed handbills out and handing them to the innkeeper. 'And I took it upon myself to agree. The Post Office may set great store by its timetables, I told him, but His Majesty's Mail is honoured to be a purveyor of Justice's fearsome Wrath.'

Jarrett looked at the handbill being passed around the crowd. It was headed in bold type.

TWENTY POUNDS REWARD –
HORRID MURDER!!

Whereas the dwelling house of Ruben Gates, Crofter of Stainmoor, was entered the morning of this Sunday last between the hours of four and six by a person unknown who did most foully murder the said Ruben Gates.

A tall man, thought to be pock-marked about the face, wearing a blue frock coat torn at the left shoulder seam and having yellow hair, braided and worn in a queue behind, such as is the custom of sailors, was seen bending over the body of the murdered man by his lad who was woken from his sleep.

The Churchwardens, Overseers and Trustees of the Parish of St Clements, Brough, do hereby offer a Reward of TWENTY POUNDS, for the Discovery and Apprehension of the Person, or Persons, who committed such Murder, to be paid on Conviction.

The bill was signed by the vestry clerk and dated that morning, Monday, 29th July, 1811.

'Murder!' exclaimed the innkeeper. 'Why, this gentleman was just set upon on his way here from Woolbridge!' In his excitement he grabbed Jarrett's arm, causing him to wince as he stumbled on to his bad leg. 'See – they hurt him, though he fought them off. Might have been the same crew as fled down from the moor.'

'But there were two who attacked me, and neither fitted the description given here,' objected Jarrett, none too pleased at the attention he was receiving from the crowd.

'Well,' said the coachman, his rubicund features managing to convey the impression that he suspected more than he was saying, 'in your servant's humble opinion the gentleman ought to report the event to the magistrate – and maybe he could give him a copy of this notice, too.'

With these words of advice the coachman reascended to his high seat. He ceremoniously drained the cup of ale offered up for his refreshment, returned it with a stately nod of thanks and collected up his whip. The guard leapt on to his box and blew a fine loud sequence on his horn. With a lightning flash, the coachman cracked the thong of his whip above his leaders' heads. The horses sprang forward in their collars. The pole chains rattled as they took the strain. The black varnished wheels began to roll and the mail was off again.

The crowd spread out as the mailcoach disappeared, reviewing and exclaiming over the news in knots.

'Will you see the magistrate, sir?' the innkeeper asked the gentleman who stood gazing off down the road. Jarrett turned to give him a surprisingly charming smile. He regretted being short with the man who had, after all, done his best to oblige him. 'Yes, I think I will. Can you direct me? I am new to these parts.'

Flattered, the innkeeper gave the question his serious consideration. 'We're blessed with three justices in this district, sir. There's Colonel Ison – he's Chairman of the Bench and Member of Parliament, sir. A much respected gentleman, lives half an hour down the road towards York.' The innkeeper checked himself as he pointed in the general direction and shook his head. 'But there's no use going to him because he's in London at present. No. Then there's the Reverend Prattman at Woolbridge. Likely you've met him, sir?' Jarrett murmured something about having shaken hands with the reverend gentleman that Sunday at church. 'Very likely,' the innkeeper responded comfortably and resumed his contemplation of the problem. 'The Reverend Prattman, however, is not best to be relied upon, being too Christian a gentleman and a scholar to be very handy in such matters. No,' he concluded decisively, 'to my mind, sir, you should visit Justice Raistrick. A professional man, sir. An attorney at law and best suited to murder – failing the Colonel. You'll find him at his chambers in the Horsemarket in Woolbridge.'

*

Justice Raistrick's chambers were easily found. They were located in a narrow house standing in the broadest part of the main street of Woolbridge where the horse markets were held on fair days. The outside was unremarkable. A small plate to the right of the door read: Q. A. Raistrick, Attorney at Law and Justice of the Peace. Beyond the doorway shadows graduated down a narrow passage that splayed out into an open space at the bottom of a staircase. Justice Raistrick was clearly a busy man. There were several working men waiting about the stairhead and Jarrett had the impression there were more in the gloom beyond. He was not sure whether it was his mood, aggravated by the pain in his leg, but he sensed antagonism. The eyes glinting in the shadowed features seemed to watch him with more than casual interest. As he limped up the staircase, two men jostled him. They had the grimy pallor and dress of miners. They took no notice of Jarrett or of their own incivility. He paused to watch them stride out down the passage.

The stairs issued into an antechamber dominated by the imposing oak door that guarded the Justice's chamber. A desk was set at the mouth of the room. The chair behind the desk was at present unoccupied, but before it stood a slight man dressed in black in the fashion of legal clerks. The apparel did not particularly suit him. The black stockings and breeches emphasised the stick-like appearance of his legs and the silver buckles on his shoes drew attention to the considerable size of his feet. The most striking aspect of the clerk's face was the unusually smooth texture of his skin and its waxy, uniform colour. It gave him an oddly fairy cast, an impression reinforced by the impersonality of his eyes. The clerk was in conversation with a woman whose whole appearance spoke of weariness. She had fine bones but her natural advantages were dulled by fatigue. She stood before the clerk submissively, allowing his monologue to flow over her. Other supplicants waited. A farmer stood by his wife. She was speaking to him in a low voice full of suppressed indignation. Jarrett caught a few hissed words.

'You just tell him this time,' she said. 'If you don't, I will.'

The farmer looked about him in a hang-dog sort of way, trying to evade his wife's intensity, twisting his hat in his big hands. Beside them perched a thin, white-faced lad with huge dark eyes. The boy held himself bolt upright, watching everything in the room. The boy's posture alerted Jarrett to some underlying tension. The walls were too thick to allow words to penetrate but there was a voice raised in an adjacent room, querulous, bold and slurred by drink.

The clerk cut short his speech and dismissed the woman to a chair by the wall. Jarrett stepped forward to claim his attention, but the man looked straight past him and slipped through a door set in an alcove to the left. He closed it sharply behind him but not before a barbarian roar demanded: 'Where is he?' There was a muttered response, then another presence entered the room by an internal door. The newcomer spoke evenly, a sense of authority pervading the sound. A harsh noise of some heavy object knocking against another and all of a sudden the drunken bluster subsided. A door closed, then all was quiet. There must be a back staircase, Jarrett thought.

The clerk reappeared, his face a mask. Picking up a paper that had dropped to the floor, he darted to a high writing desk by the far wall where a menial was copying documents. Lifting his eyebrows a little at this behaviour, Jarrett folded his arms and waited. It was quite possible the man might have ignored him longer but that he was forced to return to his desk and there Jarrett firmly waylaid him.

'My name is Jarrett,' he announced. 'I represent His Grace the Duke of Penrith.' For a brief instant he thought his name startled the man, but the impression in the veiled eyes was fleeting. 'I wish to discuss two matters with the Justice – one of which is an attack on my person. If Mr Raistrick is in, perhaps you will be so good as to announce me?'

The clerk's attitude was odd. Jarrett was not normally a man who stood on ceremony, but in most circumstances connection with His Grace the Duke commanded respect. Yet instead of hurrying to announce him the clerk responded with an abrupt question. 'You wish to swear information against robbers?' he asked.

Jarrett had been raised by a woman who taught that a true gentleman had no need to respond to boorishness with anger, so he continued, 'I have also just come from the George. The Carlisle mail brought this handbill from the Justice at Brough. He begged that his fellow Justices should be apprised of it.'

The clerk took the handbill and scanned it without expression.

'Murder, I believe, is a crime a Keeper of His Majesty's Peace would wish to be informed of,' Jarrett prompted dryly.

The waiting supplicants heard him. The farmer looked across and the weary woman's lips mouthed the word, 'Murder?'

'A crofter was murdered on Stainmoor Sunday morning,' Jarrett explained. 'His boy was witness to it.'

A rustle of sympathy ran through the waiting clients. The farmer's wife exclaimed over 'the poor bairn'. The clerk, however, simply looked a trifle annoyed at the fuss. 'I shall apprise the Justice,' he said coldly, keeping hold of the handbill. 'If you will wait a moment – sir,' he added, almost as an afterthought.

As he entered Justice Raistrick's chamber a few minutes later Jarrett was struck by the notion that his host had set a scene for him. The Justice stood by the fire filling a long, slender white clay pipe. A powerful bear of a man, not many years older than Jarrett. The animal impression was reinforced by the noticeable odour of the room. The Justice, apparently, was not much given to soap and water. He bent deliberately to the flames, lighting a taper which he then put to his pipe.

The pause gave Jarrett time to appreciate the full force of his host's presence. He was not an unusually tall man, though broad-shouldered in a way that suggested great physical strength. His face suited his body. It was made up of bold planes, the lower portion shadowed by stubble. He had stringy hair of an indeterminate brown, worn long and swept back over his ears. Perhaps the most surprising feature of his face was a large nose of classical cut which struck a note of civilisation at odds with his square bruiser's chin and sensual mouth.

Mr Raistrick saw his tobacco well lit before he offered to shake hands with his visitor. His powerful energy communicated itself through his grip. To Jarrett it seemed that the ritual gesture served as much as a trial of strength as a greeting.

'You arrived in town this Saturday last, Mr Jarrett, did you not?' The resonant voice matched the man. 'Preparing an audit for the Duke, I understand. A busy man. And now my clerk tells me you've brought us notice of a murder.' He indicated the handbill resting on his desk as he waved Jarrett to a chair. 'How should that be?'

The Justice lolled almost insolently in his great chair, smoking his pipe, his eyes fixed on his visitor's face.

'I happened to be at the George as the Carlisle mail arrived with these handbills. I had occasion to seek out a Justice of the Peace and so agreed to carry the news. My connection is pure chance, that is all.'

'Pure chance.' Raistrick picked up the handbill. 'They arrived at the George, eh? But you've put up at the old manor, I hear?' The Justice sensed his visitor's reaction. 'This is a small district, Mr Jarrett.' The impression of a cynical smile curved about his mouth. 'Any stranger is talked of, and how much more so the Duke's man. You're an important visitor in these parts.'

In their physical components there was nothing remarkable about Mr Raistrick's eyes, but they focused his personality in such a way that his gaze had almost mesmeric force when he chose to apply it. Jarrett had to restrain himself from leaning back to widen the space between them. A strange and unusual fellow to find as a country Justice. Jarrett could not shake the feeling that there was some strategy underlying his host's manner. What his game might be he had no notion but every instinct told him to keep his guard up.

'Pye tells me you were assaulted yourself, sir.' The big man leant over to pick up a little carved ivory stick with which he proceeded to tamp down the tobacco in his pipe-bowl, puffing vigorously to make it burn more smoothly.

'I was jumped by two fellows on my way to the George, on the road from the old abbey. Lead miners, I should have said, by their dress.'

'And you were robbed?'

'No. I fought them off. I always travel armed.'

Again the sense of strategy. Jarrett could have sworn that Mr Raistrick wanted more information from him, but instead the lawyer went off on a different tack.

'You wish to advertise a reward?' he asked. 'To speak the truth,' he continued, looking down dismissively at his pipe, 'it's hardly worth making a noise about such affairs unless you put up a reward.' He offered a sly smile. 'The honest citizen requires a reason to betray his fellow.' He rubbed the forefingers and thumb of his left hand together in a gesture evocative of avarice. 'Like as not you suffered the attention of two fools who had over-indulged.'

If he had been undecided on coming here, the reception he had met with had made up Jarrett's mind. 'Naturally I expect to offer a reward, yes. Would ten pounds be sufficient for information, do you think?'

Raistrick's eyes flickered. They both knew the figure was high. Among poor men a bounty of ten pounds would be hard to resist.

'You are jealous of your person, sir.'

'If it were but a case of that...' Jarrett let the pause hint that he might not have proceeded. 'But I am the Duke's proxy in these parts. I cannot have it bruited abroad that His Grace's interests may be assaulted with impunity. It is my duty to prosecute this matter.' He held Raistrick's stare. There was more than a touch of the barnyard about it. He wished he could identify the source of the antagonism he felt between them.

The Justice broke the stare. He leant back his leonine head to roar: 'Pye!' His clerk appeared at the door. 'Fetch your pen. The Duke's man wishes to swear a complaint.' Mr Pye slid off to carry out this order.

Jarrett found himself looking about the room for some topic of conversation, his host being apparently content to watch him in silence as he refilled his pipe. He noted the internal door revealed behind a hastily drawn curtain. His eyes fell on a piece of material hanging over a chair that stood by the window. It was a woman's stocking. His host's voice recalled his attention.

'You one for the Jezebels, Mr Jarrett?'

The question curled across the room flavoured by the man's sensuality. Raistrick scanned his visitor's reaction with a calculating leer.

'Not as a rule,' responded Jarrett cheerfully. 'I find myself discouraged by the time one must waste with the physic afterwards.'

Raistrick snorted. For the first time in their interview his face lit up with genuine amusement, allowing Jarrett to glimpse a flash of considerable charm. He was unable to take advantage of this opening, as just then Mr Pye returned to copy down the complaint.

Jarrett gave the bare details of what he could remember of his attackers, omitting any mention of the words he had overheard as they fled. He would go through the formalities and have a few handbills posted offering a reward for information. Given the Justice's attitude Jarrett had little expectation of assistance from that quarter. Their leave-taking was polite enough. After pausing to extract directions to the nearest print shop from the clerk, within a few minutes Jarrett was on his way out. As he stepped off the last stair in the lobby below, some instinct made him glance back over his shoulder. He caught sight of a man who stood in a group clustered behind the staircase. As his eyes moved on his mind belatedly registered the man's reaction. He had started as if he knew him. Jarrett turned to look more closely but the man had dropped back into the shadows.

After many years of sketching, he had developed a good eye for detail and as he left the building Jarrett tried to fix the man's face in his mind. It was not immediately familiar, but the more he thought about it the stronger his impression grew that he had seen the fellow somewhere recently – but where? In an abstracted mood he sought out the print shop and ordered the printing up of some handbills offering a ten-pound reward for information of his two attackers. Given the interest the printer and his daughter seemed to find in their contents Jarrett suspected that the fee he paid for the posting up of the bills was misapplied. The news of both incident and reward seemed likely to be spread across town by word of mouth before evening. As he left the shop the printer's daughter was already in an eager huddle with her neighbour, pointing the Duke's new agent out from behind her hand.

He was well out of town, riding up the road to the toll bridge that stood below the old ruined abbey, before he gave up his struggle to place the face of the man he had seen in the Justice's lobby, tucking the puzzle away for later. Before him, at the gate paying the toll, he recognised his reluctant acquaintance from Sir Thomas's tea, Lady Catherine's young friend, Miss Henrietta Lonsdale. She was mounted on a pretty black mare and accompanied by her groom.

'Well met, Miss Lonsdale,' he greeted her. 'I trust I find you in good health?'

'I am very well, I thank you – enjoying the evening air. And you, Mr Jarrett?'

'I have just come from Justice Raistrick's chambers. It is fine weather for a ride.'

She had greeted him with a cautious smile, but now Miss Lonsdale looked distant, as if she were keen to be on her way.

'You are a friend of Justice Raistrick's, sir?' she enquired thinly.

'I never met him before this afternoon. Mine was a professional visit. I fell among thieves,' Jarrett replied, pulling a comic face. 'But not for long,' he continued, 'I do assure you. I came off none the worse but for a sore leg.'

The change in the lady's manner at this story confirmed Jarrett's impression that her momentary coldness had been prompted by the mention of Justice Raistrick. Remembering Mrs Adam's hissed remark at Sir Thomas's tea, he concluded that the Justice was not considered entirely respectable among polite society in the district.

His new character of victim melted some of Miss Lonsdale's ice. As they conversed a younger, gayer self crept out from beneath the elegant poise. He began to wonder what manner of companion she might prove to be if only one could reach beyond her correct reserve. He had even contrived to make her laugh out loud when a boy approached the bridge with a gaggle of geese. As the birds waddled through the tollgate in their absurd, self-important way, one broke free. It poked its reptilian head forward and lifting its wings with a choleric hiss, made a short dash towards Miss Lonsdale's horse. The black mare bucked and skipped back. It was all her rider could do to keep her seat. In a tumble of accelerated emotions Miss Lonsdale was mortified and frightened all at once but uppermost in her mind was how foolish she would appear before Mr Jarrett if she were to be thrown by a goose.

Jarrett read the animal's rolling eye and caught the mare's bridle just as she made to rear. 'Whoa! Easy now! Come help your mistress, man!' he snapped at the groom, who stared open-mouthed. Walcheren was behaving himself like an old trooper but the mare was a couple of hands shorter and Jarrett had to lean at an uncomfortable angle to hold her. The groom bestirred himself and began to coax his own reluctant mount to repel the bird. The boy was roaring and beating his charge back to the flock with his long stick, his face red under his round hat.

Henrietta felt quite faint. She leant forward to stroke the black neck below the agent's firm hand, hoping to disguise her trembling. 'Foolish Felicia,' she said, 'you have never liked large birds.'

'It would seem that Mistress Felicia has reason.' The mare was settling but her ears were still laid back. Jarrett loosened his grip and ran a playful hand over one dark velvet ear. 'You can turn those ears about, Mistress Flighty. The enemy's retreated.'

The agent's hand brushed Miss Lonsdale's as it rested on her horse's neck. In the gap between his glove and cuff she caught sight of something about his wrist. It was a bracelet fashioned from a golden plait of hair.

At that moment Black-Eyed Sal walked up the lane towards town. As she passed through the toll gate she greeted them, resting flirtatious eyes on Jarrett. 'Afternoon, sir ... and Miss Henrietta.'

He could not resist responding to her infectious smile. He tipped his hat, his eyes following the girl's retreating figure as she walked up the lane, swinging her basket. He turned to catch Miss Lonsdale watching him and smiled. 'Who is that wench?' he asked.

'Her name is Sally Grundy. My cook's niece. She is a laundry maid for the houses hereabout.' The lady paused. 'There's none better than Sal at starching a shirt or making good a stained gown,' she added lightly. 'She has quite a reputation.'

'That I can believe.'

Miss Lonsdale gave him a stiff look. 'Well,' she said, 'I must be on my way. Good day to you, Mr Jarrett.'

They exchanged polite bows. As Jarrett looked after her he felt a slight touch of chagrin. Prudishness was the bane of gently born maidens. With a mental shrug he spurred Walcheren on towards home.

CHAPTER SIX

By Wednesday, the last day of July, the fine weather had turned oppressive. Hot air stagnated in the valley and cattle gathered down by the river, mournfully enduring the flies under the dusty trees. The busy life of the streets of Woolbridge dulled as the townspeople clung to shady places. Short-tempered and languid, they exclaimed over the heat and waited for the weather to break. As evening came the atmosphere pressed down on the perspiring town like a lid of cast iron.

In Mrs Munday's rooming house Sal sat at her glass in her shift. Sweat pearled on her bare neck as she lifted the weight of her black hair to cool herself. 'Hark at that, Maggie,' she said to her friend. 'I'd swear that were thunder way off. We're in for a storm tonight.' Her dark eyes sparkled with life and a faint heat flush touched her cheeks with colour, setting off her fine complexion. Too animated to sit still for long, she darted up. 'How I loves a storm on the moor!' She flung out her arms with sheer exuberance, embracing the excitement that welled up in her. She hugged herself and laughed.

Maggie watched her, her pebble eyes entranced and her little round mouth hanging open.

'Now where's that red flannel petticoat o' mine?' Sal tugged the garment from under a pile of clothes and shook out its folds. 'He called me a gypsy once,' she murmured, looking over a smooth, rounded shoulder at her reflection as she tied the tapes at her waist. Her pretty features lit up with an impish smile. 'Let's see what he calls me tonight!' She spun about delighting in the movement of the scarlet cloth.

'Where are you going, Sal?' Maggie asked.

'I'll tell you when I'm back.' Sal spoke in an off-hand manner. Her eyes never left her reflection as she dressed herself. 'If you don't ask no more,' she continued, forestalling Maggie as the other opened her mouth to speak.

A hint of impatience cut up through Sal's merry tone. Maggie was her audience. Audiences applauded or cried, admired or laughed; they grew tedious when they questioned.

'I'm away,' the black-haired girl announced, snatching up a shawl.

'Not all alone, Sal? It's getting dark and storm's coming.' Maggie's concern expressed itself in a whining note.

'The dark and me's good friends. Don't fret me. You go to bed like a good girl and I'll wake you with a tale to tell when I'm back.'

Leaving no time for her friend to respond, Sal skipped off down the wooden staircase. Out in the street she tossed her shawl over one shoulder and headed off out of town in the direction of the abbey toll bridge. She never once looked back and so did not catch sight of the figure that hurried after her in the gathering gloom.

The light was nearly gone. Jarrett stretched and shook himself. He was stiff and his skin felt sanded with grime after the sticky heat of the day. He looked down at the crumpled state of his linen. Loath as he was to admit it, he was beginning to miss Tiplady, his valet. Surely the man ought to be back with him by the end of the week. In the last three days he had ridden many miles about the Duke's estates. He had talked to all the principal tenants. Jarrett ruffled his short hair and yawned. The audit began tomorrow and he had a fair idea what he would find.

Little clouds of the sort millers and sailors call messengers scudded across the lower sky, driven before the winds that heralded the storm. Jarrett leant on his balcony as a rumble of thunder rolled around the circling hills. He looked down at the quickening waters below. Rain must already be falling up on the moors. His mind strayed to Miss Lonsdale and that wench Sally Grundy. What a contrast in womanhood. The one with a countenance of such sensibility, so elegant and correct – the perfect gentlewoman; the other so mischievous, so spirited, so enticing. Together they would make a neat engraving: 'Man's Dilemma'. A whistle came startling clear from the shadows down below the bridge. He leant out over the gloom to see who called him. The whistle came again. With a sudden smile of recognition, Jarrett moved swiftly to gather up some belongings and he slipped out of the folly.

The Queen's Head inn had something of the bustle of a fair day about it that Thursday. The first of the Duke's tenants began arriving around mid-morning. The more prosperous farmers clattered up in traps and gigs; others rode in on solid-haunched ponies and a few even arrived on their own two feet. Many came with family and hands, combining a first view of the Duke's new man with a day in town.

The innkeeper had set out his assembly room on the first floor for the audit. At one end Mrs Bedlington and her maids were furnishing the long table with a fine large leg of boiled mutton, potted shrimps and Whitby polony, muffins and warm oatcakes fresh from the griddle. At the opposite end of the panelled room Jarrett sat behind a heavy oak table, consulting his maps and lists as he interviewed each tenant in turn.

The Duke, who had never shared his generation's passion for farming, had not followed the fashion for improvements. His eldest son, and Jarrett too when he was at home, had often urged him to take better care of his affairs. But His Grace was a stubborn man. He paid scant attention to those estates he liked and the Durham properties he had largely ignored. The sudden death of his steward, Mr Crotter, had forced the Duke to bring his skittish attention to bear. Since he resented taking the trouble it had been a convenient chance that the arrival of the news of Crotter's death had coincided with his Wandering Raif's return to health. Jarrett had no inclination to take up estate management but, exasperating as His Grace could be, neither Charles nor Raif could leave him to deal with this potential scandal alone. As His Grace was fond of telling them when he was in his happier moods, he was a lucky dog to have two such fine young fellows to depend upon.

The greater portion of the Duke's northern estates remained fragmented in small tenancies. Only a handful of his tenants were farmers of substance. These men strode in, their frock coats and confident manner declaring them set above the general run of their neighbours. The smallholders gave way to them, standing back before the inevitable order of things. These substantial men were not just tenants. Jarrett must share a glass of wine with them, exchange small talk and be introduced to their wives decked out in their fresh trimmed bonnets, fine lace caps and gold chains. With such men rent was a matter of subtle barter. Every landlord of sense valued a prosperous farmer with capital and the skill to deploy it on the land, and worked hard to keep him.

As he bowed off the last of a run of three of the Duke's principal tenants Jarrett had to suppress a sigh. This was hardly the kind of work he would have imagined himself doing only a few months before. Fate dealt a man strange cards. Still, it had to be done and Charles had not lingered in York of his own volition. The picture he must make! Raif the Wraith in the guise of a steward, surely the most settled of professions. How his brother officers would laugh if they could see him now. Under the pretext of rearranging his papers he slid a look about the crowded room. There was a convivial hum around the table. The farmers and tenants stood in groups growing gradually more animated under the warming influence of the ale being provided by Mrs Bedlington's minions. A terrier darted out between the forest of sturdy gaitered legs, cheerfully pursued by two lively boys. The gloss of their Sunday best clothing had broken down to a more comfortable condition; bits of shirt hung out from below their waistcoats and their stockings were wrinkled. A chubby little girl in a cherry red bonnet toddled after them on uncertain legs.

A countryman in an ancient surcoat, who had been hanging back by the wall leaning on his thorn stick waiting for a propitious moment, advanced to the table. He was clearly not a quick-witted man. He moved deliberately as if every motion required careful consideration. He settled himself, feet apart, before the table. Jarrett rose to greet him.

'Will you sit down?' he asked courteously.

The invitation upset the train of thought the man had laboriously embarked upon. He looked about him in a startled way seeking the chair that had unaccountably concealed itself behind his broad person. He turned momentarily to face the chair, pondering precisely how to dispose of his staff. He finally settled on the edge of the woven seat, observing Jarrett warily over his stick. He opened his mouth to speak but closed it again with a self-deprecating toss of the head and ferreted in a deep pocket. He drew out a handful of coins and proceeded to stack them in three careful piles on the polished surface. Jarrett looked at him inquiringly.

'Josiah Boyes. How do. Heriot,' the man said. A smile deployed itself across his lumpy face. His front teeth were missing.

Jarrett contemplated the piles, mystified. 'A heriot is not due on the death of a steward,' he said. He pushed the coins towards the man to emphasise his statement. 'The heriot is paid on the death of the Lord of the Manor.' He caught himself articulating the words a mite slowly and lightened his tone. 'And the Duke, I am pleased to inform you, remains in good spirits.'

The information did not appear to penetrate the man's conviction.

'Mr Crotter would always have his heriot,' he persisted, 'and you's taking his place.'

Jarrett paused, light dawning. He pushed the little pile of coins with his finger tips. 'Heriot?' he repeated. Mr Boyes and he shared a conspiratorial smile. Jarrett carefully counted the money and consulted his list. 'Mr Boyes of Marsh Fields, is it not?' He smiled encouragingly, as the man nodded. He read a note on his list. 'It appears you are in arrears, Mr Boyes – and have been from the first in your four years as a tenant of the Duke.'

'That were all arranged with the steward. It's been a bad year,' protested Mr Boyes. 'Mr Crotter agreed – the rabbits, sir, they're mortal bad. Steward said His Grace would rub out arrears on account.' Mr Boyes tailed off and jerked his head meaningfully. Jarrett followed the line of his eyes to the coins.

'The heriot,' Jarrett said.

Mr Boyes nodded with satisfaction. 'Aye. Steward's right.'

Jarrett raised an eyebrow and consulted his papers. 'Mr Crotter has left no account of a waiver. The arrears stand. We shall speak of this again. For now I shall take this on account.' He took up the money and writing out a receipt he handed it to the man. 'I shall be by to visit you in the next week. I must warn you, Mr Boyes, that if we cannot settle this matter His Grace may be forced to evict.'

Mr Boyes's dull features came alive in a look of resentful belligerence. 'It were arranged,' he blustered. 'I paid me heriot. I always pays the steward. You haven't the right.'

'Mr Crotter is no longer with us, Mr Boyes, and in truth I have the right. The time has come for His Grace to reclaim his own – heriot or no.'

Mr Boyes blew himself up like a malevolent toad. He fixed the agent with a killing stare, breathing hard.

'Good day to you, Mr Boyes.'

The force of the glare did not waver. His face bunched up in a caricature of fury, Mr Boyes rose and stumped off.

It was ever a mistake to imagine that simple folk were bound to be endowed with innocence and good humour. Mr Rousseau's theories concerning the nobleness of simple natures merely indicated his lack of experience of the peasantry. Jarrett cursed James Crotter for slipping so easily out of the consequences of his actions by the simple expedient of dying before his comfortable fire, a drink at his side. He watched Boyes elbow his way out down the stairs, muttering explosively for the edification of all those he passed. Charles would need to look about for a new tenant. A man freshly married, perhaps, eager to work hard for himself and his fledgling family, while lacking the capital to start on a bigger farm. Yes, a small tenancy like that at Marsh Fields should be let to a young couple starting out in life, not wasted on some crafty simpleton. He made a note to look out for such a pair. He knew the whole room was watching him. It had to be allowed that agents were not a popular breed but, even so, he could see he was not making a particularly good impression in Woolbridge. He openly returned the stares. He was not one to run from a fight. Besides, he had a fierce dislike of cheats and sneaking fellows. He could feel impatience rising in his veins like bitter sap. He would have to guard his temper if he was to get through these two days without incident.

A new group approached the table. There were three men. The central figure who formed the focus of the group bore himself with the bent posture of age. He had sparse yellow-white locks and pale watery eyes; fine silvery bristles dusted his chin and cheeks giving him an unkempt air. Glancing at the man's hands as he hobbled towards him, Jarrett suspected that his visitor was not carrying his years as well as he might. He was flanked on either side by a couple of tall, sturdy lads, whose meaty figures would have served as an excellent illustration to that popular song about the roast beef of old England. As the older man lowered himself into a chair his two guardians remained standing, observing Jarrett from their heights.

'Samuel Gibbs, at your service,' announced the old man, 'of Fiddler's Croft.' His unorthodox visit to Fiddler's Croft had prompted Jarrett to research that tenancy. One item of information he had gleaned was that Samuel Gibbs was due to turn seventy-five that year. Jarrett would have wagered his horse Walcheren there and then that the man sitting before him was not even sixty years old, despite the hunching up of his shoulders and his quivering hands. The agent leant back to survey the group and addressed himself to the seated man.

'I am, as you know, new to these parts and know not a soul by sight. Is there perhaps some person who can vouch for you?'

The tension in the man's frame was evident about the line of his shoulders, but to give him his due his expression only registered rustic bewilderment.

'Your honour?'

'Vouch for you – some person who can swear that you are who you say.'

'By my word, I am Samuel Gibbs,' he insisted.

The two bullies crowded closer to the table. Jarrett stood up calmly taking account of his position – how far the oak table protected him and how far it trapped him in that corner of the room. 'Since I wish to be certain whose word it is I am taking, I fear I must ask for some independent testimony. Perhaps the parson or his clerk? The vicarage is but a step away; it will be a simple matter to send for the clerk.'

Jarrett snapped his fingers to attract a waiter. As he gestured, his attention shifted from the belligerent figures before him. The whole room full of people was turning towards a commotion that rose up the stairs. He had a glimpse of Jasper Bedlington, the innkeeper, bobbing white-faced, propelled before a wave of newcomers. The crowd parted and Justice Raistrick strode across the room towards him. The lawyer dominated the wedge of onlookers behind him, his solid figure in his mulberry coat marked out against the brown fustian jackets of the farmers. Jarrett stepped forward to greet him. He was not going to find himself trapped to be browbeaten behind a table.

'Mr Raistrick, good day to you.' Jarrett welcomed the man, outwardly unruffled by this unexpected development. 'May I inquire the purpose of this intrusion, sir? This is the Duke's audit and these people, I fancy, are not among his tenants.'

'My compliments, Mr Jarrett, but this audit must be suspended. I have come to request your presence on a matter of urgency. A matter of murder.'

As he heard these words, Jarrett saw that one of the figures standing behind the Justice was the parish constable with his long staff. The man looked ill at ease.

Jarrett rapidly reviewed what he knew, trying to make sense of the tableau. Murder? The man was making such a scene as this because of the handbill he had carried from the George? Jarrett scanned the bold face before him, considering the possibility that the man was mad. Yet there was nothing wild or fanatical about his manner. The magistrate dominated the room with his confident presence. Jarrett sought out Jasper Bedlington in the crowd. What did the innkeeper make of it all? Mr Bedlington was looking from one face to the other, his normally cheerful countenance at a loss.

'I am here in my capacity as Justice of the Peace, Mr Jarrett. My officers and I are on our way to inspect a body that has been discovered.' The magistrate paused to give his next words due emphasis. 'It lies on the Duke's land up at the old manor. I would not wish to trespass without your presence. You have taken that property as your own, I believe?'

'I am lodging there, yes,' agreed Jarrett automatically. He did not like the triumphant way Raistrick looked about the crowd at this admission. He seemed to say Mark that, as if he had just made some material point for the prosecution in a court of law. Jarrett felt his face muscles stiffen in distaste. He was tiring of the fellow's cat and mouse games.

With an open, graceful sweep of the hand, in the manner of a host rather than an interloper, the magistrate resumed. 'I do not take this liberty lightly – but murder cries out for justice. And aware as I am of your interest in the pursuit of justice, Mr Jarrett, I felt sure that the Duke's agent would wish to assist me in this investigation.'

Although he addressed the agent, Raistrick played to the crowd. All eyes were riveted on the lawyer's face. Jarrett sensed he had few supporters in that room. The handful of substantial tenant farmers had left some time earlier. Those who remained were the poorer sort, ill-educated men who were unlikely to have much sympathy for a Duke's steward.

The agent turned to address the room. 'At Justice Raistrick's request, I am suspending this audit. I shall return as speedily as possible to resume our business. In the meantime I hope you will continue to enjoy the Duke's hospitality, so ably provided by Mrs Bedlington. Master Jasper,' he continued with a smile to the innkeeper, 'would you be so kind as to have my horse saddled?'

The publican stepped up, his shoulders well back and his chest pushed forward, his outline reminiscent of an offended pouter pigeon. 'Indeed sir, directly,' he agreed with aplomb. 'And I shall be coming o'long with you, sir. I'm Overseer of the Poor of this parish and as an officer of the vestry it is my duty to go.' He squared up to the Justice as if he expected to be challenged, but Raistrick merely shrugged with a curt, 'So be it.'

As they mounted up in the yard, a gathering crowd pressed about them, murmuring and speculating. Jarrett addressed the magistrate who sat casually on the back of a tall grey. 'Is it necessary that all these people should accompany us, Justice Raistrick?'

The magistrate eyed him sardonically. 'Does the Duke's agent mean to suggest that the peace of their parish is not these people's business?' he asked. 'It is an Englishman's right and duty to defend his neighbours. I would not have justice do her business in the shadows – let them come if they've a mind; I have nothing to hide.'

He let the last statement hang in the air, keeping eye contact to suggest an unspoken question. The dumb show was not wasted on the crowd. Jarrett acknowledged the skill of the man. He was a consummate manipulator.

'Your opponents must tremble when they face you in a court of law, sir,' he murmured as the cavalcade set off.

Raistrick caught his words. 'My enemies do, sir,' came the reply.

As they rode out of Woolbridge by way of the abbey toll bridge, Jarrett turned over in his mind what scene the magistrate was set to spring on him. Whose might the body be? He was certain Raistrick meant trouble for him by it, whosoever the victim. He thought of the poacher. But just then he chanced to look back and caught the welcome sight of Duffin, picked up in the skirts of the crowd of townsfolk that trailed behind them. Their eyes met without acknowledgement. So it was not Ezekiel who lay dead. Who then? Jarrett watched Justice Raistrick as he rode ahead, talking to the man who guided them. The discoverer of the mysterious corpse was a young man who assisted Dickon Pace the gamekeeper – this much he had picked up. Since every question merely provided the Justice with another opportunity to deploy his stratagems, Jarrett was determined not to plead for details. The secret would be unveiled soon enough.

The cavalcade turned down towards the river and approached the bridge by the folly. Jarrett grew uneasy. Was Crotter not the only one to die at the old manor? He had not searched the grounds surrounding the house. Could another body have lain concealed there all this time? The following horses dropped back to make their way across the narrow bridge. The guide stopped abruptly and pointed down into the gorge below the folly.

'There,' he called out, 'down below Lovers' Leap.'

The rain of the night before had buffed up every colour in that beautiful place. Summer foliage of vivid viridian framed the steep gorge. The table of white rock they called Lovers' Leap stood out, brilliant and stark against the green. Beneath the outcrop of rock the rich earth fell away into a wall of stone, terminating in steps of sealskin rock at the water's edge. And there on a ledge, in a pool of shadow amid the intensity of the vibrant colours, lay the corpse that had once been Black-Eyed Sal.

It took a moment for his mind to take account of what his eyes told him; to associate the neat doll laid on the muddy shelf below with the vital, bewitching girl of the churchyard.

''E looks all cut up.'

A busybody and her companion were watching him, their sharp faces brimming with curiosity. Jasper Bedlington moved protectively towards the younger man.

'I reckon we'd best go down, sir,' the innkeeper said in a low voice. He held Walcheren as Jarrett dismounted as if he needed something to do. 'However did the lass end up there? Sally Grundy. Whoever would have thought...' The innkeeper shook his head in disbelief.

The magistrate and his party threaded their way through the woods beyond the bridge to pick a path down to where she lay. The onlookers crowded on to the bridge to watch. Duffin and his dog had somehow attached themselves to the official party. Ezekiel seemed to be on good terms with the parish constable, whom he addressed as Thaddaeus.

Jarrett followed the magistrate and his officers. They moved in silence, concentrating on the uncertain ground beneath their feet. One by one they ducked their heads beneath the web of thin branches that whipped and scratched. His nose caught the pungent, acid smell of wild garlic crushed under foot. As they dropped down into the gorge the noise of the river encompassed them. They stopped and started as broad steps of rock fell away into narrow shelves or dwindled into a bare lip protruding from the flinty wall. At last they found their way to the narrow platform where the corpse lay.

Sal was stretched straight on her back, her delicate arms folded across her body. Her eyes were closed and her blind face turned up to the rock that rose some thirty feet above the river bed. A smooth pool of blood fanned out about her head. The damp material of her heavy skirts had been moulded decently about her legs. The outline of her fine-boned features was no different from when she was alive, but never before had Jarrett been so struck by the meaning of the human spirit. The fine lustre had passed from the skin and the luxuriant tangle of her black hair was reduced to a sodden mess. What lay on that ledge was but the debris of a life. The vibrant, alluring spirit he had hoped to capture one day had evaporated.

'She's been moved – from down that way, I'd reckon.' Ezekiel Duffin pointed to a trail of three red spots that led away from the shelter of the overhang and vanished in the rain-washed stone beyond. The bewildering noise of the river meant his companions read his words in his face more than heard them.

'How can you be sure of that, Ezekiel?' shouted the parish constable over the barrier of sound.

Duffin threw him a scornful look. 'Can't you see? She's been laid out – out of the reach of the river maybe.'

He pointed out the clear line that marked the height of the flood from which the waters had now receded. Crouching down, Duffin gently lifted Sal's head. Blood dripped slowly through the web of her dark hair. The neck was broken. He examined the pale arms, his manner quaintly respectful. 'Joints stiff – she's been gone a few hours.' The settling blood in her body gave the underside of her limbs a purple hue. He pointed out the mud and the scratches on her skin. 'Looks as if she fell,' he said to the men who leant over him to catch his words.

'Or was pushed,' shouted Raistrick.

Duffin ignored him, reading the ground around the body. He leant forward, gesturing to a brown mark on the rock. 'Footmark!'

The poacher uncovered the clear bloody impression of a footprint drying into the porous stone, then sat back on his haunches, his sharp grey eyes searching the ledge. 'He carried her up ...' he muttered to himself. Following the direction of the short trail of blood spots, he climbed from the ledge, taking care to swing himself down, away from the obvious route. Examining the approach to the shelf, he found the remains of another brown stain held in a foothold. 'Looks like he stepped up here, Thaddaeus,' he told the constable. Duffin tried out his theory. He had to stretch his stride to make it. 'If he did it carrying her, he's a tall man,' he said and returned to squat by the footprint next to the body. The parish constable leant over him in rapt attention, blocking the sun. 'A working man's shoe,' Duffin told him. 'Aye, Thaddaeus, that's a straight-lasted shoe, that is.'

The parish constable and his assistants helped Duffin to search some more. The poacher did his best to read the ground ahead of their well-meaning feet, but no one found any further physical details to witness to what had happened in the gorge. At last, when they were all near stupefied by the massive sound of the water, the magistrate laid a hand on the constable's shoulder.

'Take up the corpse,' he ordered, his powerful voice rising above the river's roar. 'We have seen all we are likely to here.'

Raistrick stood back as the parish constable organised two hangers-on to carry the body back up to the road. They sent up for a hurdle and some rope, while Duffin wrapped her dripping head in a cloth in preparation for lifting the body on the stretcher. Jarrett recognised Nat Broom, one of Will Roberts's circle he had overheard drinking at the Queen's Head. The men picked her up, Nat Broom at her head, another man he did not recognise at her feet. They slung her between them with little feeling. Her crimson petticoat, torn and stained with damp, flopped back as they lifted her. The fine white stockings she had taken such care with were smeared with mud.

'You always were after her to lift her skirts, eh, Sam!'

'Show some respect, animal!' Jarrett snarled.

The men flinched at the fury in his tone. The one called Sam looked shamefaced; Nat Broom was sullen and muttered under his breath. They tied her body to the stretcher, her head bundled up in cloth – a trussed up, faceless thing. The two men set off to haul their burden back up the cliff.

Raistrick was watching him from a distance. Jarrett turned away, staring down at the churning brown water flecked with creamy scum. He was well used to death but this one had caught him unawares. As the men struggled to lift the body up the steep wall of rock, one of Sal's shoes worked free. It bounced from rock to stone to come to rest a few paces from where he stood. Jarrett bent to pick it up. The buckle that twinkled in the sunlight hung loose. A flapping motion caught his eye and he looked back up the gorge. A shawl, dyed in the same brown tones as the earth below, was caught in a tree at the edge of the white rock – a tattered banner leading the eye to the site where Sal met her end. The poacher's dog, Bob, was at his side watching him with bright, earnest eyes. With Bob at his heels, he followed the men climbing up the side of the gorge.

Leaving the constable and his helpers to edge their way up the steep bank with the corpse, the rest of the party went ahead to inspect the table of rock. It formed a natural platform from which to view the gorge and the landscape beyond. It was a favourite spot for courting couples which local custom had dubbed Lovers' Leap in tribute to some forgotten legend of blighted love. Up above the deep gorge the noise of the river was dulled to a menacing rumble, as if an unruly god were barely contained below. Perhaps it was the painted colours of nature refreshed by rain or the fine square shape and even surface of the rock, but Jarrett was reminded of a theatre stage with the view beyond as its backdrop. The shawl, fluttering from the twisted tree clinging to the edge of the gorge, bore mute testimony to the tragedy that had taken place. It was here that the magistrate found a cluster of scarlet threads caught in a patch of crushed brambles.

'She fell from here,' he stated with conviction. He laid the tiny scrap of cloth in his huge palm. 'A match for her petticoat – you saw the tear in it.'

Jarrett nodded. Duffin ambled back from a tour of the bushes and undergrowth that circled the rock.

'A mess of footmarks on the path,' he declared, 'but then that's to be expected. Folk often pass this way.'

'Any more of that boot below?' demanded the magistrate.

'None to swear to.' Duffin's manner before the lawyer was courteous enough but evidently independent. 'They're all muddled and mixed,' he explained.

'The bloody print below – it is of a man's boot or shoe, you'd say?'

'Aye,' Duffin confirmed. 'A man's, nailed maybe and

same-sided.' Under cover of bending to call his dog, who had stayed close to Jarrett, Ezekiel gave the agent a significant look. Jarrett glanced towards Raistrick to see if the magistrate had observed them.

The lawyer was looking out diagonally across the gorge towards the balcony and windows of the folly on the opposite bank. The heads of the parish constable and his perspiring assistants appeared among the straggling trees that marked the line of the cliff as they prepared to wrestle the body up on to level ground. Justice Raistrick stood, his powerful figure centre stage on the white rock, waiting for them to arrive. Thaddaeus, the stout constable, reached the clearing. He wiped his pink forehead and straightened his hat as the men lined up behind him carrying Sal's corpse. His little procession organised to his satisfaction, the constable looked expectantly towards the magistrate. Raistrick swung back from his contemplation of the space below. As he turned to his audience Jarrett thought he caught a glint of triumph in the acute eyes.

'Is it not surprising, Mr Jarrett,' he declaimed, 'that this wench should come to lie at your door?'

CHAPTER SEVEN

It was as if a favourite canvas had been ripped. His peaceful retreat was blotted and marred by a surfeit of figures. Jarrett recognised few of the faces. They were those idlers who materialise from any community drawn to the entertainment of unexpected events. The invasion galled him, his mood tainting what he saw. The youths who leant precariously over the parapet seemed to gesture lewdly to the place down by the river where Sal had recently lain. A farmer with a porcine head stood stock in the middle of the bridge staring at him in insolent curiosity. The magistrate led a way through the crowd, never breaking his stride. As he approached the folly he turned.

'A cart must be fetched to carry the body. Mr Jarrett, will you give permission for it to be laid within?'

The whole crowd awaited his answer. He could not refuse. His sense of decency would not allow her to be stretched brazen on the grass before all those prying eyes. He went ahead to open the door. The onlookers rose up and pressed in around the little house. As the men passed him and prepared to lay Sal's trussed body on the table, Jarrett called to the innkeeper who stood by, 'Mr Bedlington, would you be so good as to keep these people from the door?' He had the satisfaction of seeing the crowd fall back a little at his tone of authority.

Mr Raistrick re-emerged from the tiny house. He took up a stance, one arm outstretched at a graceful angle from his solid torso in an antique pose. 'Ah yes, Mr Jarrett, this is your door is, it not? You live here?' he asked in a carrying voice.

'This is where I rest at present,' Jarrett agreed.

The magistrate nodded slowly, his Roman nose in profile to his eager audience. Ostentatiously he contemplated the folly and the river below.

'And you came from here this very morning?' Scarcely waiting for Jarrett's brief nod of assent he continued his public musing. 'Is it not strange, sir, that you did not report this tragedy yourself?'

'I did not know of it, sir,' Jarrett answered, his face expressive of puzzled good humour. It seemed he was caught up in a play for which he had not been rehearsed. He suspected he had been given the part of a villain, or at the very least a fool. He was determined to signal to the audience by his demeanour that he had been miscast. Jarrett was aware that he had potential supporters among the female members of the crowd. Women eyed him up and down, and he caught a whispered comment of 'a bonny lad', followed by a ripple of giggles.

The magistrate gazed at the agent in mock concern. He was a reasonable man, his manner said, a civilised man who only wished to be convinced.

'But your windows overlook this gorge,' he persisted. 'That rock is in plain sight from the window of your cottage. Am I to believe you saw nothing? Heard nothing?'

'As you may see, sir, if you would care to look,' countered Jarrett courteously, 'the river bed cannot be seen from my windows – the gorge is too deep. And as for hearing anything – why, Justice Raistrick, this river was swollen by the rains last night. Nothing could be heard above its roar.'

Amusement flickered in the back of Jarrett's eyes at their cautious public sparring. He had to admire the way the magistrate wrapped himself up so skilfully in a metaphorical toga of Roman judiciousness. The lawyer nodded sagely.

'It was a wild night last night,' he conceded. He paused, the set of his magnificent head both dignified and just in relation to the upper parts of his body. 'And you never looked down from the bridge as you left this morning?'

'I had no occasion to,' Jarrett replied. He was determined the audience should know this comedy for what it was. 'I made an early start. My horse is stabled on this side of the house, away from the river.' He gestured, illustrating the geography of the place. 'My road took me away from the bridge. I had no reason to look down to the water.'

'So you have no answer as to how Sally Grundy came to lie beneath your windows?'

'Indeed I have no notion. I did not know the girl.'

The magistrate nodded, his expression courteous and bland. The tense figure of a dark-haired man separated itself from the crowd.

'So say you!' he exclaimed.

The magistrate swung his gaze to the newcomer.

'And what do you say, Mr – ?'

'Broom. Nat Broom.' The wiry man jabbed a finger at Jarrett. 'He was seen with her, Sal, in the churchyard this very Sunday. Prudence Miller for one can swear to it.'

Jarrett looked down at the man in disbelief. Why should he say such a thing? In his surprise he dropped his part. 'This is absurd. I have laid eyes on the girl, that is true. I passed her on the path amid a clutch of her kind going in to church last Sunday, but that is all.'

'Sal said she had a new gentleman friend!' Nat slid a knowing smile to the magistrate. Around them the onlookers vibrated with the excitement of this revelation.

Off at the back of the throng a man spoke eagerly to his neighbour. 'He has yellow hair! That murderer they're seeking from Stainmoor, he had yellow hair. Murders don't come in twos by accident.'

'That one were done by a tall man, 'tis said,' contributed

a buxom woman. She folded her hands under her apron and nodded meaningfully – although her meaning was not clear.

Duffin gave the man a look of withering disdain. 'Who,' he asked, pointing a solid finger in Jarrett's direction, 'would give him out to be a tall fellow? A dwarf?'

The man was not to be overborne. 'Witness were a boy at that!' he responded resiliently. He was about to repeat his notion to a wider audience when all at once he found himself short of breath. Casually cloaking the motion with his broad back the poacher turned to silence his neighbour with a smart punch in the guts. He held the gasping man up in a companionable way, his interest publicly fixed on the drama in the doorway.

'Mr Raistrick, sir,' Jarrett was protesting to the magistrate, half-laughing, 'you cannot in all honesty imagine that, had I any connection with the girl, I should be such a fool as to leave her corpse so near my own door? Credit me with a little more intelligence, I beg you! Had I known she were there, I would surely have reported the fact.'

'An innocent man would,' taunted Nat.

The crowd murmured in agreement. The space around the doorway seemed to shrink. Jarrett flicked an impatient glance about him, irritated by the absurdity of the scene. Something in Raistrick's face arrested his attention. Behind his public demeanour the lawyer was calculating, waiting.

'If he knew she were there!' Jarrett exclaimed. 'A guilty man would surely have flung the corpse into last night's flood, and let the river sweep away all evidence.'

The magistrate stood aloof, looking between the two. 'It seems it is one man's word against another's.'

Jarrett felt himself bridle. 'I can only give my word as a gentleman,' he responded coldly. 'I did not know the victim and her death is a mystery to me.'

Behind him Nat Broom slid unobserved through the doorway. Darting to the chest by the window he picked up a sheet of paper that lay on it. Before Jarrett could protest he thrust it towards the magistrate, his face triumphant.

'You didn't know Sal, you say? Then how does he explain this, your honour?'

The magistrate looked down at the paper. It was a sketch. A sketch of a girl with an abundance of dark hair.

Jarrett could almost feel the hook's bite as he was reeled in. The bold eyes of the magistrate fixed their heat on him.

'You challenged Samuel Gibbs to prove he was who he claimed; can you do the same, Mr Jarrett?'

Jarrett barely caught himself before he ran a tell-tale hand through his hair. He had not anticipated an assault from that direction. The dreadful pause stretched out as the full folly of behaving as he had done in coming to Woolbridge alone and unattended dawned. The problem of proving his identity had never occurred to him; but then his opponent's audacity was breathtaking. The majority of the faces around him were hostile. The parish constable's nervous eyes were fixed on the magistrate with the awe of a primitive votary who all at once sees his stone god walk. Jasper Bedlington looked plain frightened and Duffin seemed to have disappeared.

Raistrick was enjoying himself. The lawyer made a pantomime of leaning his broad body to look past Jarrett into the bare room.

'Can this be the style of a gentleman?' The golden voice dripped poison into the ears of the eager crowd.

'I have been a soldier most of my life, sir,' answered Jarrett. 'Simple billets are to my taste.'

With a mental shrug he gave himself up to his fate. It would be intriguing to see how far the fellow would dare to go. It would seem that the Justice was gambling deep. Jarrett reviewed what he knew, trying to divine what kind of threat he posed to the lawyer that he was prepared to throw so recklessly against the Duke's man.

'Just a simple soldier, eh?' purred Raistrick. He cast an

insolent look up and down Jarrett's slim figure, willing all eyes to note the agent's creased shirt and rumpled coat. 'And how are we simple country folk to know that this stranger among us is who he claims?'

Jarrett relaxed his face into a half-smile as if this were all in play.

'I have my credentials – does the Justice wish to see them?' He sketched a bow. 'Sir Thomas will vouch for me.'

'Sir Thomas never laid eyes on you before Sunday last.'

'The Duke sent letters of introduction.'

'Pieces of paper can be forged or stolen.'

During this interchange Raistrick had closed the space between them. Now he used his powerful frame to dominate the slighter man. His sour musk of sweat and dirt pervaded the air.

The situation seemed likely to turn physical. Jarrett speculated on the danger he was in. Could the man be playing for mob justice? Surely he could not believe that he could get away with that? Yet – two violent deaths in a week. Might not a distressed people mistakenly turn on a stranger? A stranger who came to disturb the Duke's neglected tenants; tenants many of whom would be glad to remain neglected. He was beginning to convince himself that Raistrick's strategy might be better calculated than he would have hoped.

The big man leaning over him was willing him to offer violence, to defend himself from this insult. Jarrett contemplated his chances were he to accept the challenge. A handful of rough-looking men had moved into the front rank of the crowd. 'What has the soldier and gentleman to say for himself?' drawled the magistrate.

Jarrett deliberately took a large white handkerchief from his pocket with an elegant flourish and held it to his nose. 'I beg pardon, sir,' he said, stepping back a pace. 'I have a delicate nose – a deuced nuisance but a family trait. Forgive me.'

The Justice snatched his arm with an oath. Jarrett's blue-slate eyes held the hot gaze unflinchingly. One edge of the lawyer's sculpted mouth curled and he released his hold as if acknowledging the parry.

'What reason have any of us to trust your word?' he asked. 'You who come among us without servants, without a single person who knows your face?' Raistrick resumed his magisterial manner. 'Constable! Detain this man until some person can be found to vouch for his identity.' He slid the agent a sly look. 'Unless, of course, you have someone who can testify to your whereabouts this last night? No?' He glanced at the sketch of the black-haired girl in his hand. 'It seems we must search this billet of yours, Mr Jarrett. You will understand, as one of His Majesty's Justices, I must be rigorous in my investigations.'

'I am the Duke's representative and a gentleman,' stated Jarrett. 'If you insist on violating my person and my property in this way I cannot prevent you, but I will not give my consent.' He moved to bar the door.

The magistrate gave a small regretful sigh. 'Constable, take this man into custody.'

The parish constable hung back. The expression on his honest face was almost ludicrous. He called to mind a hard-working sheep dog suddenly ordered to rip the throats of his flock. He looked back and forth between the agent and the magistrate, clutching his long staff to his chest with both hands. Behind him the crowd growled.

'Constable!' The magistrate was impatient.

Constable Thaddaeus took an uncertain step towards the agent. 'If you please, sir, if you'd be so kind...' He trailed off, throwing a desperate glance at Jasper Bedlington. The innkeeper stood red-faced and open-mouthed at the turn of events.

'Justice Raistrick, your honour...' Jasper Bedlington began.

The magistrate ignored him. 'You, you and you,' he barked, pointing out Nat Broom and two others, 'assist me in searching this place. And you,' he cast his order contemptuously at the constable, 'see he doesn't wander off.'

Jarrett allowed himself to be shouldered aside. It would not help His Grace's interests in the district if his agent were to receive a public drubbing or worse while a magistrate looked on. A portion of the crowd swept into the folly behind Nat Broom. The magistrate made no attempt to stop them. Jarrett stood just inside the door watching two women as they openly rifled his knapsack and fell to disputing the contents.

Nat Broom hurried up to the magistrate carrying an armful of damp clothes and a pair of long thigh boots, heavy with mud. 'These stood by the fire, Mr Justice; see, the mud's still wet.'

The lawyer picked a coat from the top of the pile.

'Been down by the river in the rain, Mr Jarrett?' He leant back his head to survey his prey. 'I am afraid that you must be searched, Mr Jarrett.' The lawyer flicked a finger and Nat Broom and another bully sprang forward to pin the agent's arms. With an effort Jarrett managed to stay upright. Rough hands felt his coat, found an inner pocket and drew out a leather-bound notebook wrapped around with a thin strap.

'Your notebook, Mr Jarrett?'

'I suppose it is hardly worth mentioning that that is my private property?' enquired the prisoner.

'Hardly,' responded Raistrick, flicking through its pages. They were marked with jottings, interspersed with sketches of views, heads and caricatures. 'You, sir,' continued Raistrick smoothly, 'are held for questioning and I am a magistrate investigating a possible matter of murder.' He waved a hand to his minions. 'Release him. He can stand alone.'

A sturdy couple were walking boldly out of the folly. The man carried a fishing rod and his woman a shirt.

'Law and order,' remarked Jarrett, gazing after them as he smoothed one mangled sleeve.

'Quite so.' The lawyer slid the notebook into his own pocket as he surveyed the devastated room. He shot out an ungentle hand and grasped Nat Broom. 'Pick up those boots – I want them put against that imprint below. Now clear this place!'

The few scavengers who remained scuttled out before the magistrate's roar.

At the rear of the little house a sallow-faced man in a moss-green waistcoat stretched up to snatch a couple of fresh salmon that hung under the eaves. He turned to find himself blocked by a large burly figure.

'What's this?' asked Duffin pleasantly.

'He has no more need of them,' protested the thief. 'Why not put them to use? They'll only rot else.'

Ezekiel detached the man firmly from the fish and pushed him away. 'They'll keep a day or two yet,' he replied. 'And then he may return hungry. Be off with you!' The superior bulk of the poacher won the argument. With an insolent shrug the man slipped away. Slinging the catch over his shoulder, Duffin marched off to join the onlookers.

Jarrett found himself left in the voided room flanked by Jasper Bedlington and the constable.

'The Reverend Prattman, the Justice Prattman, he must be fetched, he must be told; he would never have allowed...' The innkeeper's distress was evident. 'Thaddaeus, what a dreadful thing this is!' he exclaimed helplessly.

The constable stretched his head warily out of the door. The crowd was occupied watching the magistrate as he manoeuvred his way down towards the river bed, followed by Nat Broom who slid after him, burdened by Jarrett's boots.

'In that, Jasper, I would agree with you.' The constable fixed bashful eyes on the gentleman prisoner. 'But Mr Jarrett will agree that Justice Raistrick is the magistrate,' his tone pleaded for understanding, 'while you and I, Jasper, are but officers of the vestry.' Nervously he peeped outside once more. 'A mistake,' he muttered, as if to reassure himself. 'It will be proved a mistake.'

Jarrett gave the man a weary smile. 'Have no fear, Constable Thaddaeus. It takes at least two magistrates to convict on a charge of murder – and, indeed, as the Duke's agent I will be satisfied with no less than a trial at the Durham Quarter Sessions.'

The toll-booth in Woolbridge was a quaint octagonal building set at the mouth of the market. It was a serviceable structure, housing a council chamber above and below an arcade where the dairy women set out their wares on fair days. The open arcade was raised on a dais, reached by a short flight of steps. Behind the dais and sunk below street level was the town lock-up. It was to this place that Raistrick led his prisoner, the crowd of onlookers milling about them. The magistrate stood by while the parish constable, shamefaced, lifted the grate in the stone floor and lowered a wooden ladder into the gloom below.

'Reminds me of a billet I once had in Flanders,' the prisoner remarked.

Some of the crowd liked his humour and laughed. The magistrate stepped forward to reclaim their attention.

'There will be an investigation held into the death of Sally Grundy at this place, in the chamber above, tomorrow at eleven o'clock.' His resonant voice rolled out. 'Let anyone with matter to the purpose come to give evidence before me at that hour.' He sketched an exaggerated bow to Jarrett, indicating the hatch. 'Come, sir, your chamber awaits.'

Jasper Bedlington made one more attempt to intervene.

'Your honour, can I not house Mr Jarrett at my inn? It is just across the way and Constable Thaddaeus may guard him as well there. This is no place for a gentleman.'

'This is where prisoners are held, is it not?' Raistrick spoke deliberately. 'And this man is to be held until I have answers.' He waved a dismissive hand. 'Get him below! This has been thirsty work, lads!' he said to his followers. 'Let's go drink!'

Shepherding several of the front row between his solid arms, the magistrate led the crowd out. Eager at the promise of free ale, few bothered to linger to watch the constable swing the heavy grating shut over the head of the prisoner.

The arcade fell silent as the parish constable retired to seek the comfort of his brazier. The cellar filled the space under the tollbooth. It had a bare earth floor and what light there was came from a small barred window, just above head-height, at street level.

So here he was. Raif the Wraith, the toast of the 16th's Fighting Squadron who had repeatedly eluded capture behind enemy lines, imprisoned by a village demagogue. Some fighting man he. To be manhandled, rolled up so neatly without a peep! He ought to be glad of the darkness to cover his shame. He deserved to be hung, if such a villain could contrive it. Jarrett blew out a slow breath. It was no use berating the shadows. Better harbour up his fury for another occasion when it might do some good.

He examined his cell. He had known worse. The air was fresh enough; he was the sole occupant, so he did not have to suffer the inconvenience of fellow prisoners, and it was a warm night. There was nothing to do but wait. He crouched down, leaning his back against the stone wall. He needed to settle his mind. He thought of the picture he must make cast in his dungeon. A pretty moral piece. He could call it 'The Rewards of Folly'. How would he render the shadows about him, had he his paint box with him? He was glad he had left that behind with Tiplady. The loss of his box would have lacerated his heart more than their theft of his few clothes

– though he would miss his favourite fishing rod. He leant back against the clammy stone and fought against the wave of impotent anger that thrashed through him. It would be a pleasure to tear every one of them limb from limb. Even the women. They were no women, those harpies that sacked his cottage.

It was not the loss of his property that angered him. After all, he had spent a good deal of the last couple of years with little more than his horse, weapons, a change of linen and a pot to boil potatoes and coffee in. It was the indignity of the assault. That this should have happened to him on home soil! He shook himself. Get a grip, man! Those shadows – how would one set about composing them? A pink-brown ground to begin with, then an inky indigo dye, perhaps, for the depths furthest from the light, shading in with grey and Vandyke brown to graduate towards the ochre of the shaft of sunlight. Idly he picked up a twig blown in from the street above and set to sketching in the dirt. He could not see the impressions he made. His physical movements were a mere shadowing of the pictures he constructed in his mind. People and scenes of the last few days mixed in his thoughts.

It all began with James Crotter. All he knew of the man when he first arrived was that he had been the Duke's trusted agent for over ten years. He needed to know more of Crotter. The dead steward was a mystery, a cipher. The most eloquent witness he had encountered as to Crotter's character had been his abandoned home. Jarrett thought of that dreary place. The house of a solitary man. What did it tell of its erstwhile occupant? That he lived alone and drank deep. What of that? He thought of the empty bottles lying in the oblong room and how long it might take him to collect as many, were there no servants to carry them away. No. Crotter's lack of servants was more significant than the solitary drinking. Where had Crotter's money gone? The house was shabby and the deceased was reported to have left few effects. Yet his legitimate pay would have been at least four hundred pounds a year. If the Duke was an inattentive master, he paid well. And then there would be the fruits of those various petty corruptions to swell his income. Even the few he, Jarrett, had come across so far would add up to a tidy sum, and there were likely to be as many more yet uncovered. Could Crotter's whole fortune have been sunk in drink, as Duffin would have it?

The features of Justice Raistrick shaped themselves in the shadows at his feet. He had to be involved somehow, that one. His open hostility could not be explained any other way. It could not arise out of mere pride or misunderstanding. On the basis of his two encounters with the man he was certain that the lawyer was cunning and shrewd. Raistrick was purposefully acting against him to counter some perceived threat. Jarrett straightened his shoulders, his sketching hand idle a moment. At least he knew his enemy – even if he had no clear idea of the reason for their contest.

Who else in Woolbridge might belong to the enemy camp? Could Raistrick be the 'he' behind the two ruffians who attacked him on the road? What if those words he caught by chance referred to the letter he carried to the post? He heard Jasper Bedlington's voice: 'Did you get your letter taken to the post, Mr Jarrett?' And he had drawn it out for the innkeeper to see – had he not? – replying, 'As you see, I have it still.' An absurd suspicion! Jarrett rebuked himself for letting his situation corrode his sense. If he had any skill in judging character, Jasper Bedlington was an honest man.

Then what of this Tallyman? That presence seemed forever lurking in the shadows of this affair. He was an even greater blank than Crotter. Jarrett found his attention drifting back to the face of the man who had seemed to recognise him in Justice Raistrick's lobby. The problem nagged. He was certain it formed a link in the chain of this mystery. He sketched the eyes, the solid bone of the face, the massy neck

– and suddenly he had it. The two boatmen he had followed to the Three Pots. The one with the shirt slung about his neck. That was the man in Raistrick's lobby. A man who must have overheard him ask after the Tallyman.

Sounds came from above. A brisk step was heard, muffled at first, then a penetrating voice. 'I bless my luck that I never married you, Thaddaeus Bone, to share in the shame of this day. To take part with such a scoundrel as that so-called Justice against a sweet-natured gentleman like Mr Jarrett – why, your own dead mother would rise up and cry you shame!'

Mistress Polly, it seemed, had arrived to succour her favourite customer.

'Now, Polly.' The constable's voice elongated the last syllable of her name in a placating whine.

'Never you Polly me!' came the sharp return. 'You let me see him – the poor gentleman!'

Above, the grating began to move. Accompanied by a mumbled litany of self-exoneration from Constable Thaddaeus, the hatch swung open. The homely, hang-dog face of the constable appeared briefly only to be unceremoniously moved aside. Mrs Bedlington peered down into the gloom. As Jarrett moved into the light she exclaimed, 'Oh, Mr Jarrett, to see you so! I'm all overcome!' Gathering up a corner of her apron she dabbed her overflowing eyes.

'Please Mrs B – do not! Not on my account,' Jarrett stammered, disconcerted. 'I am quite well and safe. This whole matter will be cleared up in no time, you will see.'

Mrs Bedlington composed herself with a neat, ladylike sniff. 'I've brought you something to eat, Mr Jarrett. You can't count on that lump there,' she crushed Thaddaeus with a withering look, 'to have the wit to send for nourishment for his poor mistaken prisoners. Fetch the ladder down, Thaddaeus, and let Mr Jarrett come up and eat his supper like the Christian gentleman he is.'

Here Mrs Bedlington met with a check. All her formidable powers of persuasion could not quite overbalance the constable's ingrained terror of Justice Raistrick. Despite all her wiles and scolding, he would not allow his prisoner up from his dungeon. Mrs Bedlington's considerable will battered itself against the rock of Constable Bone's obstinacy while Jarrett found himself growing hungry. At last Mistress Polly gave in with bad grace and allowed her basket of provisions to be lowered down on a string.

Jarrett watched the basket, covered with a snow white napkin that caught the light, drop inch by inch, accompanied by Mrs Bedlington's flowing commentary.

'This is an unlucky night,' she scolded fate. 'The vicar's away till late, preaching for the Bishop – a great compliment, and mighty puffed up he is by it too – and Sir Thomas, they tell me, was seen setting out on the Durham road as if he meant it just yesterday morn. But I've sent my Jasper to seek Captain Adams. He'll know what to do. And you mustn't fret about your horse, neither, sir, for he is safe in our stables. Take heart, Mr Jarrett, all will be well. There are some in Woolbridge still have their wits about them and they'll not let this rest. There!' she pronounced with satisfaction as she watched Jarrett examine the basket's contents. 'You eat hearty. Thaddaeus,' she went on unexpectedly, 'I've brought some of Jasper's best brew. Let us go aside and have a glass and leave Mr Jarrett to eat in peace.'

As the pair retreated Mrs Bedlington fixed her eyes on Jarrett's with a sharp toss of her head that made her curls bounce. He looked behind him puzzled. A bear-like shape formed out of the shadows beyond the street grate and Duffin came to crouch at the bars.

'Now then,' he said.

Jarrett greeted him with pleasure. 'Duffin! Have you come to visit me cast in my dungeon?'

The poacher threw a familiar look around the sunken

room. 'As I recollect, it's damp in there. Gets into your bones, it does. Best keep your coat on,' he advised.

Jarrett grinned. 'I am sturdier than I look. So what news? I had an idea you found something up there on the rock.'

'There's a spot hidden under the trees,' the man answered in a business-like fashion. 'Some person set there a while. I'd not swear it were last night, but marks look fresh. Found an imprint, too – of a woman's clog, or a lad's maybe. Whoever it were, they'd not have been seen from the rock in the dark. I weren't going to tell for *him* to hear,' he finished, scornfully. Duffin, it seemed, shared Jarrett's opinion of the magistrate.

'So now we have two people who might have witnessed Sal's end. The shoe is joined by the clog,' commented Jarrett, intrigued. He smiled up at the man. 'And what of that print? Am I unlucky enough to have feet the size of a murderer's?'

Duffin returned him a lugubrious, deadpan look. 'Good thing you've smallish feet,' he said, then grinned. 'Your boot falt rattled about in that mark. Magistrate would have it that blood had spread soaking into the rock. A print that sharp's never spread, says I. Besides, the shoe that made that mark's straight-lasted – such as common folk wear, the same shoe for left and right. Your boots were made for you. Any fool can see you can tell the left from right. Not that he were listening. He likes you for the deed, that's plain.'

'And did those marks tell you anything?'

'The man who made that stride would be a taller man than you,' Duffin replied confidently. 'A thumb's shy of six foot or near there, I'd swear. And another thing – when he carried her, he got blood on him. It'd have stained his breast and shoulder, the way her head was dripping.'

Jarrett pondered this new information a moment. 'Ah, well. We will see what tomorrow will bring. Raistrick cannot investigate alone. He will have to be joined by a second Justice soon.'

A pallet of boards stood in a corner. Jarrett pulled the bed into the pool of light that fell from the grating. He sat with one leg stretched out and the other crooked up, leaning his chin on his raised knee. The shadows emphasised the vertical creases that marked out his cheeks. Duffin watched him in companionable silence.

'Duffin, you told me the Tallyman was a tall fellow with yellow hair who used to be a sailor, did you not?'

The poacher lifted grizzled eyebrows and grunted. Jarrett's shadowed eyes focused beyond the wall. 'You wouldn't know if he happens to wear a blue coat?'

'Seen him, have you?' asked Duffin.

'No. Have you read the handbill from the Justice at Brough concerning the murder of the crofter up on the moor?'

'Canna read.'

'The witness gave the murderer to be a tall, yellow-haired fellow in a blue coat. A man with hair braided up in a tail like a sailor – and he was thought to be pock-marked. You described the Tallyman as cribbage-faced, I think?'

Silence lay between them.

'How did he die, this crofter?' ventured Duffin at last.

'The bill did not say – though it seems the victim bled freely.'

Duffin pulled back his shoulders with an audible click of his bones. 'Tallyman's mighty fond of his French knife. Likes that chalking trick of carving a man's cheek to make his point – never mind slicing a poor dog's throat,' he added bitterly.

Jarrett got up from the boards. He paced a turn or two between the shadows and the grimy light.

'If we were to say – for the sake of argument – that the description contained in the bill I conveyed to Justice Raistrick brings to mind this Tallyman. If this bully has half the reputation you give him, Ezekiel, the magistrate would know of him – surely?' He stood up on the bed and grasped the bars of the grating, to bring his face closer to the stoic features above him. 'He does know of him, doesn't he?' he asked urgently.

The poacher's bear-like outline was silhouetted against the light. It gave an expressive shrug. Jarrett dropped back and rubbed his hands over his face and up through his fair hair, making it stand up in spikes.

'A pretty pickle my eccentricities have led me into,' he murmured ruefully. Duffin's snort of agreement drifted down with the evening air.

In the arcade above, Mrs Bedlington came to the hatch.

'Mr Jarrett, there are gentlefolk coming down the street!' she hissed in a stage whisper. Jarrett caught a glimpse of Duffin's parting nod before the poacher slid away into the darkness as noiselessly as he had come.

'Well, Thaddaeus, I'd best be off,' Jarrett heard Mrs Bedlington pronounce in a carrying tone. 'If I leave the place for more than half an hour it turns into a bear garden. Enjoy your meal, Mr Jarrett – and sleep sound. Though if he gets any rest in that pit you've thrown him into, Thaddaeus Bone, it'll be a miracle!' she added in a crushing aside.

'Bless you, Mrs B. You are a true friend,' Jarrett called up after her. 'Please present my compliments to Mr B.'

'God keep you, sir. I'll be back in the morning with news and your breakfast,' she responded and departed.

Sleep did not prove easy. The boards were uncomfortable and the earth floor so damp it was no better alternative. The pieces of the puzzle shifted about, unsettling his mind. The magistrate knew more of the Tallyman than he wished to admit. The Tallyman was a likely suspect as the murderer of the crofter. All at once Jarrett recalled the tension of the boy hunched in Justice Raistrick's chamber and the muted roar of the caged presence in that inner room. The Tallyman could have been there in that very building while he, Jarrett, waited, an ignorant dupe, to see his master. His frustration at the thought was leavened by the irony of that juxtaposition. If what he speculated was true, then it must have given the magistrate a devil of a shock to have the Duke's man coming in with that bill in his hand giving the description of his bully as the Stainmoor murderer. Little wonder at his behaviour at their first interview. Jarrett wished he had known at the time how unsettlingly well-informed he must have appeared to the magistrate at that meeting. He would have enjoyed it more.

Gradually he drifted into sleep. The dark figure of the Tallyman dominated his dreams. He saw him at the old manor house standing over Crotter's body. The Tallyman taking the books – an errand boy. He thought of her, Black-Eyed Sal. The tall featureless figure in a blue coat and yellow hair was bending over her lifeless body, a bright red halo spreading out from her black hair.

The sickening thought jolted him awake. Had Sal met her death solely that his enemy might trap him? His blind eyes were wide open in the darkness. Horses' hooves sounded and carriage wheels rolled over cobblestones. The light of flambeaux flickered on the walls of his prison as they passed. The carriages of gentlefolk off to some entertainment. He pictured the town cats exclaiming behind their fans at the scandal of the Duke's agent. He wondered who among his new acquaintance would take his part – if any.

'Tomorrow promises to be an interesting day,' he told himself. He jammed his coat into a more comfortable bundle under his head. 'I can only hope my letter arrived and found Charles.' With that thought he sank into sleep.

Footsteps entered his dreams. He saw Sal's feet walking in those bright buckled shoes and, above, the white stockings. All at once she stopped and looked down annoyed. 'Look at this mud!' she exclaimed. 'How am I to appear before all these folk clarted up so?' She raised her head and her dark eyes fixed him with their mischief.

CHAPTER EIGHT

Mrs Amelia Bedford wriggled a plump shoulder in its socket to relieve the cutting pressure of her long stays. The flat curls of her yellow hair gleamed in the candlelight. She was confident that no one at her Entertainment would be more fashionably dressed than she. She had planned the occasion carefully to fall after the arrival of a certain parcel from the most sought-after dressmaker in York. She stood now, greeting her guests, decked out in its contents, her whole person suffused with the high shine of self-satisfaction.

The Bedford home was the one house of distinction in an unfashionable part of town. It stood in a short avenue that inclined gently down to the river. Its imposing stone front looked across the wide street to the light-catching high windows of weavers' cottages, while the Poor House was a near neighbour, standing only three plots down. Mrs Bedford frequently scolded her husband about the unhealthy situation to which he confined her. He, however, was governed by a superstition that held that the moment he moved out of sight of his mill his fortunes would wither away. At this point in their repetitive argument he was fond of asking her if that was what she wanted; for how else would he pay for her fancies? He would then sugar the jibe with some compliment about how he liked to see her so bonny, before disappearing once more into his office or mill.

Mrs Bedford smoothed the lustrous black satin of her new gown and flicked open her large fan. Tonight she was sure of her desirability. This evening was carefully planned and the object of her preparations could not fail to respond. As objectionable as the location of her house was, within, by candlelight, when she was in a good mood, Amelia Bedford was confident it bore comparison with any in the neighbourhood. Even with Oakdene Hall whose rooms, though large, were, she felt, quite barren. She preferred more detail and crowded her own rooms with a medley of vases, sofas, crystal and candelabra, covering her walls with rich papers and paintings of food in luxuriant colours.

The Reverend Prattman entered and bounded up the hall towards her. He had a youthful air for a bachelor of his age, she thought, as she extended a plump hand to be kissed.

'Mrs Bedford. I am late! I have come direct from the Bishop. He insisted I stay to tea. He invited me to preach, you know. We discussed my text; 1 Corinthians, 33: Evil communications corrupt good manners. Our debate so caught me up I quite forgot the time.'

Mrs Bedford was not disposed to be upstaged by 1 Corinthians, but her eyes fell on new guests. Mrs Lonsdale and her niece were handing their outer garments to the servant. The younger woman's cloak fell back to reveal a dress that made Mrs Bedford's heart burn within her.

'Why, doesn't Miss Lonsdale look well! A veritable forest nymph!' the parson declared enthusiastically, then wondered if he had said the wrong thing.

Dismissing Mr Prattman with a nod Mrs Bedford braced herself to greet the ladies. 'Mrs Lonsdale. So glad you could come. Don't you look fine, Miss Lonsdale! Have you been to York?'

'I am fortunate to have a cousin in London,' Henrietta replied courteously. 'This is her taste you see, and I the lucky beneficiary of it.'

Mrs Bedford's experienced eyes took in every detail. The fine material fell in fluid folds about Miss Lonsdale's slim figure. She wore short sleeves veiled in a drapery that sketched a scimitar sweep along the line of the shoulders, drawing attention to the curve of her neck. From the neat bandeau that confined her soft brown curls to the rounded toes of her little flat-heeled pumps, Miss Henrietta was the picture of elegance. Her skirts were ankle-length, Mrs Bedford noted thankfully, the same as her own. A sea-green crepe Vandyked in points about the petticoat; a pretty colour. She grudgingly admitted that with her height the present fashions suited Miss Lonsdale's figure. Unconsciously, Amelia Bedford smoothed her slimming black. Her own curves were more womanly, any man would say so – he certainly would. Besides, she noticed now that the waist on the sea-green gown was a touch low. She pulled back her shoulders, emphasising the plentiful bosom that jutted out over her own remarkably high waist. Anyone with taste knew that waists were rising this season. Comforted, she ushered the new party in.

Miss Lonsdale was clear-sighted about the world. There was a time, as a poetic girl of seventeen, when she had thrown open her heart and hopes to a young gentleman who had returned her regard. The object of her affections had been sensitive, kind and dutiful. That duty had led him to bow to his family's tradition and join the regiment. The young Henrietta had agreed with her lover on the force of familial duty. She had spent a year contriving how she might find occasion to visit in the neighbourhood of his barracks for the simple joy of watching him at the head of his troop at a public review. The exchange of letters between them had gradually grown infrequent and her dear one's regiment came to be sent abroad. She learnt to give up childish things. The older Henrietta Lonsdale knew herself to be fortunate. The eldest daughter of an improvident father, she had found a comfortable home with her uncle and aunt, a childless couple. In his last years, harried by ill-health, Mr Lonsdale had passed over the management of his affairs to his quick-witted niece. By the time of his death Henrietta was mistress of her own estate in all but name. She ran the household; she dealt with the leases and tenants; the accounts were checked by her hand.

Miss Lonsdale's responsibilities, and the confidence they gave her in her own abilities, set her apart from others of her sex. A shrewd observer of society, she recognised it gave a place only to certain sorts of female. A spinster or widow of property was sure to find a welcome in any neighbourhood as a useful matrimonial resource. A spinster residing with a relative in guise of companion also had her place. But Henrietta laboured under particular disadvantages. She was both handsome and youthful and she managed a considerable property without owning it outright. In such circumstances her reputation was at risk. Since she was not prepared to bury herself in the dowdy obscurity of a spinster companion she chose, taking advantage of a set of elegant features, to adopt a formidable line in reserve. In society she joined the ladies as a sort of honorary matron. In so far as she had to deal with gentlemen in business matters, her habit was to correspond by neatly constructed letter. When a face to face interview was required she combined her native wit with a virginal correctness which left the gentlemen feeling protective, while at the same time kept at a proper distance. In this way Miss Lonsdale was able to create her own place in society and her neighbourhood held her up as a handsome woman of pristine reputation; a model of elegant reserve.

Henrietta Lonsdale gently curled her fan back and forth. The rooms were hot and stuffy with the sickly scent of the rose petals her hostess kept in bowls on the occasional tables. She contemplated the clumsy figure who towered over her. The Reverend Prattman was a man whose middle age had caught him by surprise. His voluble conversation had a tendency to sift down to tales of travels to visit old college friends of his youth (he had been up at Cambridge).

'Dear Squiffy and old Bannister – Daredevil Dick we called him. He came by that name in a most amusing way...'

Henrietta always listened patiently to his stories. She could not help feeling sorry for the parson. He was a man whom equals welcomed with an air of duty. It was not that he ever noticed this – indeed in company he was quite exhaustingly jovial – but she thought he deserved a less lonely life. He told his stories as if relentless repetition would resurrect the good fellow, ready for any lark, from within the careful, fussy man he had become.

'But then in life one never knows what may lie around the corner!' The parson concluded his tale.

'Indeed,' agreed Henrietta. 'Was the fair not only a week ago today and was it not almost at this very hour that they found poor Mr Crotter dead so unexpectedly?'

Mr Prattman looked startled. 'My goodness! Is it only a week since St James's fair? I suppose you are right, Miss Lonsdale.'

'Tell me, Mr Prattman, what do you make of the Duke's new agent?'

Henrietta turned her bright gaze on to the parson's soft moonish features. He looked a trifle uncomfortable.

'A well-mannered man, quite the gentleman – though a little young for so responsible an occupation, perhaps? And what is your opinion, Miss Lonsdale?'

The elegant face was pensive. 'I find him unexpected,' she said at last. 'Even something of a mystery, I think.'

'Really, Miss Lonsdale, a mystery!' The parson threw back his head and laughed loudly. He leant towards her in a playful manner. 'I would not have suspected you of possessing a romantic imagination, Miss Henrietta!' Miss Lonsdale's friendly smile stiffened as he continued in his jocular tone. 'Perhaps he will come here tonight and we shall have the opportunity to learn more of him, eh?'

'Perhaps,' the lady responded a touch curtly. 'I do not see

Mr Raistrick here, yet I believe the Justice is an intimate of this house,' she observed. The Reverend Prattman gulped as if he had swallowed a fly. He emitted a nervous braying laugh, and suddenly recalled that he had promised their hostess that he would help with the musical entertainment.

In his usual company manner of an overgrown puppy the parson threw himself into the task in a way that was at once overbearing and endearingly solicitous of praise. He sat down at the instrument that stood in a corner and unfolded some music from an inner pocket. It was a happy chance, he explained. The sheets had just happened to fall under his attention as he was preparing to come out that evening, a skilful arrangement (for he was a connoisseur) of a popular tune he had written as a boy. Beaming at the assembled company he waited to acknowledge the murmurs of appreciation due to his youthful talent. Bashfully declaring his hope that the little piece might entertain, he drew a deep breath and began.

Mrs Bedford came to share the sofa. She slipped a hand within Henrietta's arm and whispered loudly, 'This is cosy! The Reverend is such a clever man. He reads the music, you know.'

Mr Prattman delivered his arrangement in a fine, forceful baritone, whose only weakness might be said to be a slight uncertainty over the wider tonal intervals. These were approached cautiously at first, the note being squeezed out until a firm footing was found, at which point they were struck upon the air with enthusiasm.

Mrs Bedford's eyes darted continually about the room as she kept up a hissed stream of comments on her guests and acquaintances. Henrietta wished she would stop fidgeting or at least sit a little less close. She was forever pulling her reticule of shot silk through her fingers or twisting the watch that hung on a ribbon from her waist.

'Such pretty pearls.' Her hostess leant so close Henrietta

could smell her breath. 'Mr Bedford prefers to see me in gold and coloured jewels. Pearls can hardly be picked out on my skin, so pretty and white it is – he says.' Mrs Bedford patted the shelf of flesh pushed up under her chin complacently.

Henrietta hid an involuntary smile behind her fan and glanced around the parson's audience. Mr Gilbert, the surgeon, had stretched his legs out before him, and, raising his eyes heavenward, was contemplating a particularly interesting boss on the ceiling. Mrs Bedford's attention focused on the door. A servant was standing there scanning the room. Mrs Bedford snapped her eyes back petulantly to her guests. She nodded towards Mrs Adams. 'Poor Maria. She really has no idea! That fan is far too small.' For a brief moment her sharp blue eyes looked almost placid as she flicked open her own, larger, version of the article. Mrs Adams, a matronly woman, had settled herself foursquare in the middle of a straw brocade sofa to listen to the music. Her head was turned to gaze into the crook of one amply rounded arm, as if it cradled an infant or the germ of a profound idea.

Henrietta pulled her attention back to her hostess. Mrs Bedford's critical faculties had moved on to a fresh victim.

'And so mad keen she is on theatricals, she has taken an actor and his troupe into her household. Imagine!' Mrs Bedford was saying. 'Travelling players,' she emphasised the words as if they were wicked. The servant was picking his way across the room. He came to Captain Adams and leant to speak into his ear. 'So rich and well-born she is, I dare say she believes she can do anything. But I'll say it plain, to my mind it cannot be right. Her husband does not even live in the same house with her!'

Privately Henrietta thought Mrs Bedford's prejudices predictably methodistical – many of the greatest families in the land engaged actors to support their amateur theatricals during the summer recess – however, out loud she merely murmured something about not knowing the lady. Captain Adams was following the servant from the room.

'Lady Yarbrook,' responded her hostess, as if the name were renowned. 'She is the daughter of a Duke, of course, and a peculiar sort of woman. She inherited a fine house by Gainford and has come to live in it, for she cannot abide Ireland. Her husband is Irish. You would have thought that the daughter of a Duke might have done better for herself. Ireland is a dreadful country – don't you think, Miss Lonsdale?'

'I fear I have never visited Ireland, so I cannot say.'

'Oh, neither have I – I would not wish to; I believe it is a wild sort of place.'

Amelia Bedford cast yet another glance towards the empty doorway. The Reverend Prattman embarked upon his tenth verse.

Captain Adams re-entered the room looking flustered. He crossed the carpet and came to hover over the performer. The parson terminated his song hurriedly and acknowledged the ripple of applause, looking a little hurt. Amelia Bedford's whole face and posture sharpened. To Henrietta's amused eyes she almost pointed, like a hunting dog scenting game.

'Oh, I do hope the Captain has not had bad news,' Mrs Bedford exclaimed, rising and stepping out towards the pair at the spinet on the same breath. Her curiosity too great to be denied, Henrietta followed her.

'Ladies, the most disturbing news!' Captain Adams greeted them, his shock overcoming his discretion. 'Justice Raistrick has had Mr Jarrett taken up and confined in the toll booth. It seems some serving girl has been found dead near his house. Jasper Bedlington has just come to tell me of it.'

'Some serving girl? Who?' asked Henrietta, startled.

'The good looking one – what did they call her? Black-Eyed Susan or some such name; you know the one. Was always setting the pigeons fluttering.'

'Not Sally Grundy!' exclaimed Henrietta. 'Oh, poor Mrs Grundy. What a tragedy. Sally Grundy is her only family.'

'You know her, Miss Lonsdale?'

'Sally Grundy is my cook's niece. But, Captain Adams, how could Mr Jarrett possibly be suspected? And how could Mr Raistrick dare do such a thing? Mr Jarrett is a gentleman, not some common vagrant.'

Captain Adams was flushed with concern.

'From my acquaintance with Mr Jarrett, I am as surprised as you, Miss Lonsdale. Jasper Bedlington tells me he denies all knowledge of the victim. Yet Lawyer Raistrick claims he has evidence to the contrary and witnesses who will swear he was seen with her. And they found the poor unfortunate girl beneath the very windows of the folly by the old manor bridge – where, I am told, Mr Jarrett has set up camp, as it were,' the Captain ended haltingly.

'Set up camp in a folly?' interjected Mrs Bedford. 'Why would he not reside in the manor, if he were the gentleman he claims to be?'

'Why, Mrs Bedford, what can you mean? It is surely no business of ours where Mr Jarrett chooses to rest?' Henrietta responded, with an energy that surprised the speaker herself.

Mrs Bedford's sharp eyes scanned the younger woman's face with a knowing expression. She pursed up her lips. 'Well, to my mind it is very odd behaviour. I am not in the least surprised that Justice Raistrick should find it suspicious. The Justice is a very clever man. He would not act without good reason.'

Henrietta appealed to the Reverend Prattman. 'Mr Prattman, you are a Justice of the Peace also – can this be right?'

The parson tried to cover his bewilderment. He composed a judicious face and dropped his voice into a deeper register. 'It is true that Mr Raistrick has a fine legal mind – Colonel

Ison himself says so and he is Chairman of the Bench,' he pronounced. Having delivered himself of this comment he fell silent, gazing at the company owlishly.

'But how could he act so precipitately against His Grace's agent? Sir Thomas himself vouches for him, and he is an old friend of the Duke's,' protested Henrietta.

'And the devil of it is that Sir Thomas is away. A pretty coil,' lamented Captain Adams. 'Mr Prattman, you must prevail on your fellow Justice to have Mr Jarrett released from the black hole. We cannot have the Duke's agent dealt with in such a fashion. By heavens, his treatment so far has been enough to give the Duke the deepest offence.'

The parson's judicial manner abandoned him and he openly shook his head. 'Oh, this is most strange. Most strange. I am all bewildered. And yet Mr Raistrick has a fine legal mind,' he repeated, 'a fine legal mind – the Colonel himself says so. He will have some explanation.'

Mrs Bedford sprang to the absent lawyer's defence, her small features determined and her broad bosom thrust forward. 'Indeed he will,' she declared. 'Captain Adams, did you not yourself say that Justice Raistrick had evidence and witnesses?'

All of a sudden Henrietta saw Mrs Bedford's person soften. She simpered and patted her brazen curls. Henrietta followed the line of her eyes to the doorway. Justice Raistrick himself swaggered towards them. He had not bothered to change for the evening, but trod across the rich carpet in riding dress and boots. He brought with him a taproom whiff of tobacco smoke, sweat and sour ale.

'So you've heard the news, eh?' he asked, without preamble, striding directly up to the group. Picking up his hostess's proffered hand, he pressed his lips briefly to the white flesh. Henrietta watched the look that passed between them. His cavalier treatment seemed no offence to Amelia Bedford. Her whole face was rapt with devotion.

'I came to seek conference with you, Reverend, as a fellow Justice.' Mr Raistrick's manner made it plain that he intended the two of them should go aside.

Henrietta interrupted this intention. 'This all seems very strange to us, Mr Raistrick,' she declared. 'How could the Duke's agent possibly be suspected? He has scarcely been in the district a week. Why – he did not even know Sally Grundy by name...' She trailed off. Justice Raistrick was leaning towards her, his feline face acute.

'And how might you know that, Miss Lonsdale? Did you speak to Mr Jarrett of Sally Grundy? And when might that have been?'

Miss Lonsdale, an honest woman, might later ask herself why she felt so protective of a bare acquaintance. At this moment she was only conscious of her dislike of Mr Raistrick and his bullying ways. She answered his question in a matter of fact tone.

'I met Mr Jarrett by chance at the Abbey Bridge tollgate last Monday evening. Sally Grundy came by on her way into Woolbridge. She said good evening or some such – you know her way.' At this the Captain responded with a short toss of his head and a half-smile. 'She passed and Mr Jarrett enquired who she might be. I told him her name and that she was a laundry maid and my cook's niece. There was no mystery about it.'

'No mystery, Miss Lonsdale, save that Mr Jarrett claimed to me this very afternoon that he had only set eyes on the wench once – in the churchyard last Sunday. And that encounter he only confessed to after a witness had already declared he had seen him there. Why would he lie?' Here Mr Raistrick broke off and waved a hand in a dismissive gesture. 'Why would Mr Jarrett not *mention*,' he conceded with a smile, 'this other encounter?'

'Perhaps because he felt no need,' responded Henrietta tartly.

Amelia Bedford intervened with a little laugh, belied by the spiteful look on her face. 'Why, Miss Lonsdale, I believe your aunt told me you yourself remarked on the agent taking an interest in the girl!'

'That is not what I said.' Henrietta realised she had expressed her annoyance in her tone and she paused. 'I thought he noticed her at church, that is all. What man in this place did not notice her? She was quite the most beautiful girl for miles around,' she ended sadly.

The parson still sat at the instrument. He shook his head helplessly.

'All this is most peculiar and most distressing.'

'Maybe so, Mr Prattman,' Captain Adams pressed him, 'but Mr Jarrett gives his word as a gentleman that he is not involved. Surely he can be lodged at the inn while this investigation is carried further? The lock-up is no place for the Duke's agent, for God's sake! Pardon me, Reverend. Didn't mean to take the Lord's name in vain but this is beyond everything.'

'I must concur in that point, Mr Raistrick.' The parson endeavoured to address the lawyer in a business-like tone, but his eyes were timid. 'Mr Jarrett is the Duke's agent. Surely his word must be respected until he is proven guilty in a court of law?'

Mr Raistrick looked down on the seated man with contempt. Henrietta was struck by the contrast between his physical confidence and the supineness of the parson. The parson's hands were plump and lily-white. Miss Lonsdale glanced at Raistrick's. They were strong, blunt and brown.

'I have my doubts that Mr Jarrett is who he claims. There are enough unanswered questions to warrant holding him. No one in this district knew him by sight before he appeared among us unattended a week ago. Besides, I have a mind to the common people of this town.' The manner in which Mr Raistrick spoke suggested that while the rest of the company could afford to be above such considerations he was a practical man. 'Feelings are running high. This is the second murder in the district in a week. Mr Jarrett is safest in the lock-up over night. He is a young man. He'll come to no harm.'

Amelia Bedford threaded her arm through Mr Raistrick's, her pale bejewelled skin in sharp relief against the mulberry cloth of his coat.

'Justice Raistrick, let me fetch you a glass of wine and you must tell me everything about this dreadful tale. But I warn you! I am easily frightened!' She gave a lilting, girlish laugh and led him off.

Henrietta opened her mouth to protest. Mr Prattman was clearly looking for a pretext to excuse himself. Miss Lonsdale sketched a curtsey to the parson, and taking the Captain's arm she asked to be taken back to her aunt.

'Parson's no match for that rogue,' murmured Captain Adams as they moved out of earshot.

'No, indeed,' agreed Henrietta indignantly. 'I fear Mr Jarrett needs more justice than the two of them may give him. Captain, if I write a note would you take it to Lady Catherine for me – tonight?'

'If you wish it, Miss Lonsdale,' answered the Captain perplexed. 'I cannot see how that may assist Mr Jarrett, but I will take it.'

The screech of protesting iron woke him. Jarrett swung his feet to the floor and opened his eyes to dim dawn light. A ladder was being lowered through the open hatch in the ceiling of his prison.

'Mr Jarrett, sir!' a voice called softly. A cough, then more loudly, 'Mr Jarrett? Captain Adams. I'm coming down.' A pair of riding boots encasing plump calves appeared at the top of the ladder. The boots descended cautiously followed by the well-fed person of Captain Adams.

He removed his hat. 'Mr Jarrett.' He greeted the younger man with a jerky bow. Then, as he seemed at a loss for words, Jarrett stepped forward to shake his hand warmly.

'Captain Adams, so good of you to visit,' he said with a grin. The Captain returned the grip eagerly.

'Ha! Yes! Odd situation, eh? I have come as a member of the vestry, sir, to invite you to come up to the inn. The Reverend's compliments. He hopes you did not sleep too wretchedly. This is a bad affair. Hope to clear it up directly, eh what?'

'Indeed I slept well enough, Captain Adams, but I would be grateful for an opportunity to shave and change my shirt.'

'Of course, absolutely.' The Captain paused and looked at his feet. 'One thing before we go.' He glanced up under stubby lashes. 'Justice Raistrick insists you should not speak of the matter to anyone,' he said in a rush. 'Terms of your going to the inn, as it were. Not to speak to anyone before the investigation.' He gazed anxiously at the prisoner.

'To no-one?' enquired Jarrett. 'Am I allowed to ask for breakfast?'

'Breakfast?' Captain Adams belatedly recognised the joke and laughed. 'Ha, yes of course! Breakfast, hot water, all that sort of thing, but not the umm...' He waved a hand about diplomatically to fill the gap. 'Mr Raistrick has taken measures.'

Jarrett clicked his heels and gave a military bow. 'Captain Adams, I accept your terms. May we go?'

Returning the bow with a relieved look, the Captain settled his hat firmly on his head and waved Jarrett up the ladder before him.

Constable Thaddaeus was waiting for them in the arcade above and the three men set off across the empty market place, flushed pink in the dawn light. Unconsciously, they fell into step. The noise of three pairs of boots striking on stone rang out in the silence. Jarrett broke in on the evocative sound.

'So I am to be allowed to be present during the magistrates' investigation, Captain Adams? This is an unusual courtesy for a suspect.'

'No, sir, no indeed, sir. You are not suspected! A misunderstanding. You are the Duke's agent. If Mr Raistrick wishes the investigation to be held in this public way then the Reverend Prattman insists you be present at the questioning of the witnesses and I concur, sir, I concur.'

Two men, strangers to him, were loitering in the street by the Queen's Head. They had surly, watchful faces. One sketched a half-insolent nod to the constable as the three passed.

The door to the Queen's Head inn was thrown open and the space filled by Mrs Bedlington. For a fearful moment Jarrett thought she was going to embrace him, but her far flung arms stopped short, encompassing the space before him in a fervent welcome.

'Come in, come in, Mr Jarrett.' Emotion clogged her voice. Mistress Polly turned to the consolation of practical matters. 'I have a fresh shirt and linen laid out above, sir, in your old room,' she said, speaking as if she were a family retainer. 'I have a good breakfast waiting for you. You'll feel better once you've food inside you.'

Jasper Bedlington stood behind his wife and by him the slight wiry figure of Nat Broom. Mr Bedlington cast a disgusted look at the sharp-featured man. 'The Justice's man,' he said contemptuously. 'Nat, here, is come to spy on you, Mr Jarrett – make sure no one speaks to you of this affair of Sal's death.' He gave a sour smile as Nat Broom bridled and made as if to speak. 'Don't worry yourself, Nat, I've said my piece,' he told him.

Jarrett reassured the innkeeper. 'Captain Adams has informed me of the terms of my release. I will do my best not to trouble you with unnecessary talk, Mr Broom. Though I would like to say, Mistress Polly, a clean shirt at this moment would be my salvation!'

Mrs Bedlington led him up the stairs followed by her maid bearing hot water in a jug. Mrs Bedlington took the jug and followed Jarrett into the room, only to be stopped by Nat Broom.

'You leave that door open – I'm to hear anything you say,' he warned.

Mrs Bedlington's withering look spoke volumes of her opinion of this officiousness. 'I'm not stopping,' she snapped.

In regal silence the innkeeper's wife walked behind the door and placed the hot water on the stand that stood out of sight there. Feeling slightly sorry for the man, Jarrett gave Nat Broom a rueful smile and got a blank stare for his pains. Mistress Polly, having arranged things to her liking, swept back round the door, displacing the small man with her bulk. She closed the door carefully on her guest, throwing him a meaningful look as she departed, seeming to indicate something behind the door. Jarrett heard her parting shot as she descended the staircase.

'Why don't you just set there and guard his door, Nat Broom, since you've such a mind to become Mr Justice's watch dog?'

As he prepared to shave, Jarrett found to his amusement that Mrs Bedlington had left him a message written in the mist on his shaving mirror. It appeared to read: 'Bee of good hart laddie.' If there had been more it had vanished as the heat of the steam cooled on the glass. It was not a turn of words he had heard in these parts before. Perhaps Mrs Bedlington had Scottish blood as well as a gift for the dramatic. He wandered to the window as he removed his shirt, enjoying the light after his spell in the shadows. He saw two men in the street below watching him. Mr Raistrick was taking great pains to make sure he spoke to no one. He gave an internal shrug. Either Charles or Tiplady had to arrive soon. At the very least Sir Thomas would return to identify him and put an end to this farce. In truth he was intrigued to see how Lawyer Raistrick was going to handle the investigation. Before long his enemy was bound to let slip some further clue as to his interest in the Duke's affairs.

Time soon passed and as eleven o'clock approached Jarrett was escorted once more to the tollbooth. A considerable crowd had gathered about the arcade. As he was led up the winding stone staircase to the council chamber he caught a brief glimpse of a familiar yellow dog. So Duffin was not far away. The thought was strangely comforting.

The octagonal chamber was a muddle of people. A long table stood along the far wall. At one end Raistrick's clerk, Pye, was laying out a familiar bundle of clothes. His escort eased Jarrett through the crowd and Constable Thaddaeus drew him up a chair so that he might sit facing the space where the witnesses would stand. Each of the remaining seven walls was filled with people, standing or sitting on the raked benches that lined the room. Captain Adams left him to join a group of eight or ten men. They looked to be a mixture of the better sort of tradesmen and artisans along with a sprinkling of the lesser sort of gentry. Seeing Jasper Bedlington standing among them, Jarrett surmised that these were the vestrymen.

The two justices walked in together. Mr Prattman made to shake Jarrett's hand but catching sight of Mr Raistrick's fierce expression he veered off at the last minute to hurry head-down to the table. The chamber quietened, attentive with anticipation.

'Pye,' ordered the lawyer, 'open proceedings.'

The pale-faced clerk stood and, reading from a paper, announced in a carrying voice, 'Order! Order in the chamber! In the presence of their honourable Justices, the Reverend

Justice Prattman and Mr Justice Raistrick, this investigation is called to examine the circumstances of the death of Sally Grundy, eighteen years, laundrywoman of this parish of St John's Woolbridge, in the night of Wednesday, the last day of July in the fiftieth year of the reign of His Majesty King George the Third. The corpse being found with neck broken, laid out below the rock they call Lovers' Leap.' The clerk called the first witness. 'Let Mrs Munday come forward.'

A muscular woman with a secretive face detached herself from the front row of the crowd and came to stand before the Justices' table. Her eyes flicked between the two magistrates. She seemed wary rather than in awe of her situation. Justice Raistrick addressed her from his seat behind the table.

'Mrs Munday, you own the house in which Sally Grundy lodged. When did you see her last?'

'I was dipping candles this Wednesday night in my kitchen and I heard her go down the passage. She called out to someone above as she came down the stairs. She lodges with Maggie Walton.'

'What time was that? Had the rain started?'

'I was too busy to watch the weather!' responded Mrs Munday tartly. She considered the question, then relented. 'It seems to me the rain started after dark. There was still light enough as I heard her, but I recall thinking: I'll have to be lighting up soon.'

That appeared to be the sum of Mrs Munday's evidence, yet when Mr Raistrick asked his final question, 'Have you anything more to tell us?' Mrs Munday looked undecided. She glanced across at Maggie Walton who stood waiting to be called with wet cheeks and scared eyes. She closed her lips and folded her hands across her stomach decisively. 'No, your honour. I've said my piece.'

Next the clerk summoned Maggie Walton, Sal's fellow lodger. She came forward with stooped shoulders as if trying to fit herself into the most insignificant compass possible. She was of a similar age to the dead girl. Maggie had protuberant pale blue eyes and a rosy button mouth. Mr Raistrick took some pains to put her at her ease. He favoured her with a friendly smile and asked his questions in an informal, easy way.

'Sally Grundy was your friend?'

'Oh, yes, sir!' Maggie answered fervently, nodding her head. Her friendship with Sal was the sole thing that had made Maggie Walton's existence in any way remarkable.

'And you and your friend talked together, shared secrets – as girls do?'

Maggie's round eyes were eager to please but perplexed. 'We talked, sir,' she agreed eventually.

'And can you tell us where Sal was going on Wednesday night last?'

Maggie looked down at her feet. Her first response was indistinct and the magistrate had to instruct her to speak up.

'Sal wouldn't say,' the girl confessed. 'She said she was off to meet someone and she'd have a tale to tell when she came back. She made a mystery about it and laughed at me.'

'And was it a man she went to meet, do you think?'

Maggie looked quite surprised at the question. Who else would Sal be going to meet if not a man? The lawyer smiled.

'And at what time did she leave for this meeting? Had the rain started, do you think?'

'No, sir. I heard thunder, and I said: Sal, you're not going out? Storm's coming. And she said: Never you fret. I loves a storm on the moor.' The wistful expression on Maggie's face was one of wonder at the exotic mystery of Sal. 'Then she left.' The wonder faded to be replaced by a sad, anxious expression.

'And you never saw her again?'

Maggie glanced nervously towards Mrs Munday. The

landlady's narrowed eyes were fixed on her. When Maggie answered there was a whining note to her reply. 'No! No, sir!'

'And was Sal in the habit of going out at such strange hours? It must have been nine or half past nine o'clock at night.'

Maggie appeared to find such comings and goings usual. She merely commented that Sal liked to go out.

Maggie was dismissed to scuttle thankfully back into the anonymity of the crowd. Turning to his fellow Justice, Mr Raistrick's comment was audible to the chamber.

'So our mystery is who Sally Grundy was going to meet at Lovers' Leap.' He turned the beam of his gaze on to the gentleman seated to the left of the table. 'And thus we come to you, Mr Jarrett.' Ignoring his clerk, the lawyer abandoned formalities. He continued as if addressing his fellow Justice and the members of the vestry sitting beyond.

'Mr Jarrett has told me that he left his cottage – the windows of which look out on to Lovers' Leap – on Thursday morning to conduct His Grace's audit in Woolbridge. He left early and did not look down from the bridge before his door and so did not see the victim, but went directly to the Queen's Head where I and my officers found him. Together we went to inspect the body, which was laid out on its back, with arms folded thus,' the lawyer folded his arms across his breast to illustrate his words, 'on a shelf above the line of the flood that swelled the river on Wednesday night. Laid out by human agency. The victim herself never died that way. A few spots of blood, and two bloody imprints – one complete of a man's boot lying half under the body, and one partial mark in a foothold below – indicate that a man carried the victim, bleeding from a wound in the head, to the shelter of the ledge. Her clothes were damp but not wet through as they would have been had she been out in the heavy rain of last night for any length. This leads to the conclusion that the victim died and was laid on the ledge just before, or soon after, the storm broke. Now Mr Jarrett denies he knew the victim. And yet,' the lawyer got up and went to the pile of items that lay on the table beside his clerk, 'while the body was being laid inside to await the arrival of a cart, this was brought to my attention.'

With a dramatic flourish the lawyer displayed a piece of brownish wrapping paper, perhaps a foot square. The sketch on it was unfinished but unmistakable. Black-Eyed Sal smiled mischievously out at the chamber. Mr Raistrick cocked his head to contemplate the drawing.

'Your work, sir? Accomplished – and detailed. Are we to believe you did not know the subject of it?'

The agent met the lawyer's eyes, his posture relaxed. 'If you would care to produce that personal notebook of mine which you took into your possession yesterday, Justice Raistrick,' Jarrett leant forward to point out the edge of a leather notebook peeping from under the clothes piled on the table, 'you will see that it is my habit to sketch any figures of interest I come across. This Sally Grundy made a striking subject. I laid eyes on her twice, and drew her from memory. As I have sketched many in this town. Anyone may see if they will but examine the book.'

The Reverend Prattman asked to be handed the notebook. Several members of the vestry craned to look over his shoulder as he flicked through its pages. One of the vestrymen gave a snort of surprise and pointed something out to his neighbour with a barely suppressed smile. Jarrett hoped the gods would be kind and prevent the book opening at a particularly successful caricature of the reverend parson depicted as a well-meaning bull in a china shop.

The parson deciphered a phrase or two and coughed. He put the book down hurriedly, a pained expression on his face. 'And how did Mr Raistrick come by this *personal* notebook of yours, Mr Jarrett?'

Jarrett answered the parson evenly, his eyes still fixed on

the lawyer who stood facing him. 'He searched my person and took it from my coat, Mr Prattman. Mr Raistrick carried off several of my possessions. He was not the only one. It was quite a day for it. Thieves carried off several items while the magistrate pursued his investigations.'

Mr Prattman was shocked. 'Can this be true, Mr Raistrick?'

'A crowd had gathered,' replied Raistrick dismissively. 'Crowds attract thieves and pickpockets. The only officers I had with me were the constable and Mr Bedlington, the parish overseer. I was not prepared for a disturbance. Constable,' he demanded, turning his mesmerising gaze on Thaddaeus Bone, 'did you recognise any of the malefactors?'

Constable Thaddaeus stepped forward blushing. Conscious of his boldness, he spoke out a little overloud. 'Indeed I did, Mr Justice, your honours. And saw what they took, too,' he added, daring to throw an accusing look at the lawyer.

Mr Raistrick sneered back. 'Then why did you not do your duty, Constable? What if Mr Jarrett wished to prosecute?'

Jasper Bedlington intervened in support of the flustered constable.

'As the Justice says, I was also present, Reverend your honour. There was but little either Constable Bone or I could do at the time. I am sure I speak for many here when I say all honourable men would wish to support the constable in pursuing the villains. It was a shocking sight, if I may be so bold, your honours.'

Raistrick lost interest in this diversion. He picked up the muddy garments lying on the table.

'As you say, Mr Jarrett, some clothes of yours came to my attention – a coat, a pair of breeches and some long boots.' As he named each garment he held it up for the crowd to see. 'These are yours, are they not? And what is the condition of these items, would you say?'

'I would say that they are soiled with mud, sir.'

'They are soiled with river mud, are they not, Mr Jarrett? I believe it was you yourself, Mr Jarrett,' the voice continued silkily, 'who pointed out to me that Wednesday night was a terrible stormy night. Most of us were glad to be in our beds on such a wild wet night. And yet you, sir, you were not in your bed – you were out in the rain, down by the river – were you not?'

The chamber was hushed. The ordinary, every-day sounds that are made by a hundred human beings confined in one space stilled as every person present bent their attention to the confrontation being played out before them. The Duke's agent was at a disadvantage. He was seated before the imposing figure of his interrogator, his posture stiff. His voice was haughty as he answered.

'Mr Raistrick, I repeat: I did not know the victim. I have no connection with this affair and yet my possessions have been ransacked, my privacy violated and I have been forced to spend a damp and uncomfortable night in your gaol. I see no reason to answer your questions until you can produce a solitary witness who can in all honesty swear that he has seen me exchange even a single word with this poor unfortunate girl.'

Mr Raistrick swept a mocking bow. 'Very well, sir.' He spun dramatically to the crowd, making the skirts of his riding coat fan out around him. 'Bring a chair for Mrs Hannah Grundy!' he ordered.

Hannah Grundy was handed forward, cossetted by murmurs of sympathy from the audience. The cook was in a bad way. Plucked from the familiar surroundings of her kitchen, her bearing was robbed of its authority. Yet despite her confusion grief endowed the solid figure with a certain dignity.

'Mrs Grundy, you are Sally Grundy's aunt?'

The grey woman nodded. 'My only family, since my man died.' The voice was dull as if her personality had been drained by the blow that had fallen on her.

Raistrick's features formed a mask of condolence. He performed a solemn half-bow, his eyes never leaving the blank face. Mrs Grundy blinked. The lawyer's voice was mellifluous, faintly caressing. 'Tell us of the last time you saw your niece, Mrs Grundy.'

'It were at the house – Longacres. I am cook-housekeeper there. My Sal did the laundry. She came Monday as usual. She left an hour before supper. And that's the last time.' Mrs Grundy took a deep gulp of air and stopped.

'Do know what Sal was to do the rest of the week?'

Mrs Grundy answered slowly, as if remembering with care or half in a dream. 'She was to have two days at a big house near Gainford – Lady Yarbrook's, I believe it was. My Sal said she was to be back Wednesday night ...' Mrs Grundy broke off, her breath wheezing in her chest. Her habitual lack of colour had sunk to a dishwater grey and her blue eyes looked lost. The pressed pack of human souls watching her vibrated in sympathy with her emotion.

Mrs Bedlington hurried to the cook's side. She appealed to the parson. 'Reverend Prattman, sir, 'tis plain Mrs Grundy's not well. Cannot others be asked questions in her place?'

'Indeed, Mrs Bedlington, I am sure there is no need to trouble Mrs Grundy further,' agreed the parson, observing the woman's odd colour with concern. 'Might she be taken to your inn? Have you some cordial, perhaps?'

Two helpers joined Mrs Bedlington to assist Mrs Grundy from the room. As they raised the bulky figure her eyes turned to the left of the door. She flung out an arm towards a tall, handsome young man who stood near the back of the chamber. He returned her stare transfixed.

'Him. He was the one she were fretting over.' The old woman spoke her accusation distinctly. Silent tears were running down the grey cheeks. 'He was the one who did her wrong – Will Roberts.'

'Now, now, Hannah, don't you be getting yourself in a

state,' clucked Mrs Bedlington, concerned at the woman's ragged breathing. 'You're not right. You know your chest is bad.'

Mrs Grundy collapsed against her. The onlookers, electrified by this drama, muttered to one other as the bulky figure was carried from the chamber.

Mr Raistrick's face registered annoyance. The sallow-skinned clerk leant to whisper into his master's ear. 'Very well,' the lawyer responded impatiently. 'Call this Prudence Miller.'

Prudence Miller approached the bench swinging her skirts with a confident step. She arranged herself so that she might answer the lawyer three-quarters in profile, over one provocative shoulder. Mr Raistrick weighed Miss Miller up in a long speculative glance, trailing warm eyes over her buxom flesh. When he addressed her an elusive animal quality flickered under his formal manner. It had no distinct expression, but it was almost as if musk perfumed the air between them. The lawyer leant a little towards his witness as he asked his questions. Miss Miller blossomed under this treatment. In no time at all the girl was relating how there had been a rumour for more than a week that Sal had a gentleman friend. Maggie herself would say that Sal had been in the habit of slipping off to see him. Sal's work round about gave her plenty of opportunity to roam.

It was plain for anyone with eyes to see that there had been a rivalry between Miss Miller and the dead girl. The very way she spoke Sal's name was coloured with it. Prudence soon came to the encounter in the churchyard before the Sunday service. She had been there with friends, she told the lawyer (implying that she, Prudence, had many more friends than Sal). Sal herself had told them she had a gentleman friend.

'And then he walked by.' Prudence bobbed her head towards the seated agent.

'And Sal looked straight at him, and they exchanged this look.' Miss Miller tossed her head at Mr Raistrick, as if to say both she and the lawyer appreciated what kind of look she meant 'I knew then it was him – he was her gentleman friend.' Her triumphant conclusion drew a gratifying gasp from the crowd.

Quietly Jarrett turned to address the bench. 'Justice Prattman, sir, may I be permitted to ask this witness a question?'

'No!' Raistrick cut in abruptly. Recognising belatedly that he had given his fellow Justice offence, he checked himself. 'Justice Prattman,' he said, leaning over to speak in the parson's ear, 'as men experienced in the law you and I well know that only a magistrate may question witnesses.'

Emboldened by the security of speaking from among his fellow vestrymen, Captain Adams stood up. 'Mr Raistrick,' he demanded, 'are you accusing the Duke's agent of involvement in this death?'

Raistrick weighed the untimely question. The dice fell on the side of discretion.

'I – ' He restarted more diplomatically, 'We are here to investigate Sally Grundy's death,' he began. His subsequent dramatic pause, however, was overlong and allowed the Captain to riposte.

'We are here to seek justice, Mr Raistrick, are we not?' The Captain appealed to the vestrymen. 'Why should Mr Jarrett not ask a question if he has the mind? I am sure that both the honourable Justices and the gentlemen of the vestry have sense enough to form their own opinion of what is said,' he concluded, with more cunning than might have been expected from a bluff soldier.

The vestry appeared to find this argument reasonable; several of the worthy burghers nodding in agreement. The Captain stared at the parson, fixedly ignoring the lawyer. Mr Prattman hung on to his gaze.

'Mr Jarrett, sir, you may ask your question,' he said in a rush. Raistrick began to speak but thought better of it. With a slightly petulant gesture he conceded defeat.

Jarrett fixed his eyes on Prudence Miller's face and spoke courteously. 'Miss Miller, did you hear Sally Grundy say anything that claimed I was her "gentleman friend"?'

'Didn't have to,' the girl answered pertly. 'I saw what I saw.'

'What were the words Miss Grundy spoke to you?'

'I canna remember every word – Sal said about how she had a fine gentleman friend, one as fine as you. And she looked straight at you and smiled, knowing like. And you tipped your hat!' Prudence gave a brisk nod to the audience as she scored her point.

Jarrett smiled at her in a charming way. 'And did I return the smile?'

'You did! Just like that!' Prudence exclaimed, eagerly.

'Precisely,' agreed Jarrett. He turned to address the chamber. 'When a pretty wench smiles at me I confess I am liable to smile back – and even to tip my hat,' he confided. Several in the crowd smiled with him. 'But that, gentlemen, is all. I did not know the girl – she merely chose to smile at me.'

'That's not all,' cried Prudence, seeing she was losing ground. 'Betsy – she that's scullery maid at Longacres – she heard Mrs Grundy scold Sal for messing with gentlemen. She'll tell you! Who would it be if it weren't you?'

'Then why not ask her,' cried someone.

A slight, half-starved looking girl of thirteen or so, with straggling hair, was pitched forward out of the crowd. Betsy crept into the arena of attention crabwise, her pinched features half-terrified, half-excited.

'Come forward, Betsy,' said the Reverend Prattman, assuming his most fatherly, clerical air. 'Be a good girl and speak the truth and no harm shall come to you.'

'Speak up, Betsy,' prompted Prudence. 'Tell them what Harry told you – of that time at the toll gate.'

After some coaxing it transpired that Betsy was sweet on Harry, Miss Lonsdale's groom. Her Harry, it seemed, had told her of an incident the previous Monday evening, after Sal had finished her work at Longacres.

'Harry said that Miss Henrietta met him,' Betsy pointed to Jarrett, 'at the toll gate and Sal, she walked by and Miss Henrietta was proper put out because of the way the gentleman looked after Sal as she went by.'

This information was received with a few titters from the back of the crowd. The Reverend Prattman was not amused. He scolded Betsy for gossiping about her betters with other servants. 'Everyone knows Miss Lonsdale's reputation is above reproach,' he told her severely. 'You should not repeat such idle gossip.'

This direction was not to Raistrick's liking. 'Perhaps so,' he said, 'but Betsy may know something else to the purpose.' He bent his charm on the girl. 'Betsy, can you describe this gentleman friend of Sal's?'

'No,' came the disappointing reply. But then Betsy suddenly blurted out: 'But he is a fair-haired man like him,' again Betsy pointed to Jarrett, 'for Ned the Carter told Harry that he saw Sal with her gentleman friend in Gainford just this Tuesday. He got a good look at him, too.'

'And is this carter here?' demanded Raistrick, searching the chamber with hawkish eyes.

'Ned Turner, do you mean?' Jasper Bedlington asked Betsy. 'Well, he never saw Mr Jarrett in Gainford last Tuesday,' he scoffed. 'Ned's out Staindrop way today, your honour,' the innkeeper added, 'but he's due to call at my inn five o'clock or thereabouts.'

CHAPTER NINE

Light reflected from a patch of limpid sky warmed his cheek and a sweet breath of air blew in through the open casement above him. The magistrates had suspended the investigation to await the arrival of the mysterious carter and Jarrett found himself once more at the Queen's Head. He uncurled himself from the short window seat of Jasper Bedlington's parlour. He was alone. Spectators had crowded into the Queen's Head from the council chamber to while away the wait with drink. His shadow, Nat Broom, had sat in a corner eyeing him resentfully for a full ten minutes before giving in to his thirst and sidling off with a defiant, 'Never think of moving, for I'll be watching the passage, be sure of that.'

He was glad to be free of the company; it was tedious to be constantly stared at. He was restless. Justice Raistrick clearly had high hopes of this new witness. Where the devil was Tiplady? For a moment all Jarrett's pent-up frustration vented itself towards his absent valet. It was Tiplady's fault that he had arrived in such an unorthodox fashion. If he had only appeared in Woolbridge with a gentleman's servant he might have been treated as a gentleman now. Mr Tiplady was a Character, a family retainer of the old school. He had been part of the Duke's household since Jarrett was eleven. As boys, he and Charles had shared his services as man-servant; then as they grew older Tiplady had made Master Raif his sole charge. When, at the age of twenty, Raif had enlisted, they had parted company.

Enlisted. Such a prosaic word for that desperate action he had taken ten years ago. His thoughts drifted back to that time. He had joined the 68th because that regiment was on the point of sailing for the West Indies, a tour of duty that had meant death for most of them. And not a glorious end but a shivering, retching, convulsing death by fever. Tiplady was part of his first life; the one that had seemed to cease that year he turned twenty and met the private shame that banished him. But then, in truth, no part of a man's life concludes but with death. Raif Jarrett survived the West Indies and returned with the remains of the 68th to barracks in England. In that couple of years Tiplady had resumed his role again whenever Jarrett visited the Duke, as if Ravensworth were still his home. Tiplady was not the kind of servant one took into the field, so he left him behind when he had transferred to the 16th and shipped out for Cadiz. He had engaged a native servant for his service in Spain and Portugal, a cheerful, careless cove who shared his discomforts with little complaint. Joaquin had elected to wait for him in Lisbon rather than travel to England, so during the last few months' convalescence Tiplady had slipped into his old role. Jarrett found the resumption of their relationship uneasy. Tiplady refused to recognise that things had changed; that Jarrett was no longer the Master Raif of the old days.

The abrupt sound of a chair being thrown back on a stone floor came from the next room. Jarrett turned his head to the noise. He was weary of this present farce. What galled him most was the attempt to strip him of his character. In the army a man's rank was assumed on sight, detailed in silver lace and the shape of a coat. Here he found himself shorn of all props – servant, accoutrements, character. He felt the assault at his very core. He could acknowledge the skill of the strategy but in truth the move had shaken him. The audacity of that man! For a Justice of His Majesty's Peace to

cast public doubt on the authority of written credentials. A
gentleman's word should be accepted by a gentleman – how
else could affairs be managed? Then, of course, Raistrick
was no gentleman. And so far the strategy was proving
effective, with Sir Thomas out of town and the parson a
weak fool. He should have known better than to imagine he
could descend alone on such far-flung estates and expect to
restore the Duke's ancient rights without a fight. True, the
extent of the neglect had not been anticipated, but he might
have approached the task with more caution. Jarrett shifted
his weight irritably. The bruising from last Monday's attack
had not yet disappeared and the old wound in his side was
troubling him.

With his usual impeccable sense of timing, Tiplady had
chosen their arrival in York the week before to stage one
of his 'stomachs', as he called them. Jarrett gazed out at the
sky. It was absurd but he could not recall the cause of their
recent quarrel. Some inn servant who had shown Tiplady
insufficient respect? He had forgotten. In any event, Tiplady
had hinted, as he periodically did, that, driven to ill-heath
by his present situation, he was considering better offers of
employment. And Jarrett had been in such a foul mood he
had told the man to take his leave and go plague another
poor fool with his croaking.

Alone under guard in the Queen's Head Jarrett acknowledged his fault. Tiplady had been suffering from a head cold
and they had both been tired from days of travelling. Jarrett
contemplated his slim hands. He missed the old raven. At
least Tiplady knew who he was. The banner of blue sky
beyond the window taunted him. This was a day to be out
on the moors – a good gallop would shake off these frets.
He sighed. Walcheren would be missing him. He wondered
whether he might get permission to visit the stables. He
was about to venture out in search of his hosts when Mrs
Bedlington clumped down the stairs at the end of the passage

to fetch up face to face with her husband as he came from the tap.

'I've had her rest a while in my room, poor soul. She's not well,' Mrs Bedlington shook her mob-capped head at Mrs Grundy's plight. Her husband's face mirrored her own. In that moment they were clearly a pair, as if married life together had given them a common imprint.

'There's a boy just come from Mr Gilbert, Polly. He's finished with his examination and wishes to know where he is to send the corpse, for Mrs Munday says she'll not have it in her house.'

'Well, isn't that just like the man!' exclaimed his wife. 'Fine Mr Gilbert cannot be bothering himself to wait but must be rid of the trouble directly, for all he's known a hundred corpses. Have him send the poor girl here, Jasper. We can lay her decently in the parlour.' Dismissing her spouse with a fond squeeze on the arm, Mrs Bedlington peered into the fug of tobacco smoke that marked out the area of the tap. 'They're getting a mite lively,' she commented. 'Ah, well, so long as they've means to pay. It's an ill wind, as they say.' She turned her broad face to smile at her guest in the parlour. 'Is there anything you might be wanting, Mr Jarrett?'

Her habitual deference in his present circumstances struck Jarrett as at once soothing and so ludicrous he laughed out loud. 'Forgive me, Mrs B. My absurd situation,' he explained apologetically, recognising a tinge of hurt in the kindly face before him.

As he spoke the rowdiness flowing from the tap hushed. Mrs Bedlington swung round to the odd silence behind her. Mrs Grundy stood, a grey phantom at the bottom of the stairs. The innkeeper's wife hurried up to the woman, enveloping her cold, still fingers in warm hands.

'Now, Mrs Grundy, you should be resting. This is no place for you. The tap's all crowded and filled with smoke.'

The grey woman's eyes looked at her, as if from a great

distance. To Jarrett, watching unnoticed, Mrs Grundy did not appear to utter a single word. Mrs Bedlington held a one-sided discussion which ended in her leading Sal's aunt off towards the kitchen in search of a cup of tea.

The hubbub of conversation in the next room was rising in volume. Every now and then more emphatic voices were distinguishable above the din. Jasper Bedlington returned from his errand. His face was creased with two plump worry lines between the eyebrows. He fixed round eyes on his guest.

'That Nat Broom's been stirring again, Mr Jarrett.' He meant the statement to be an exclamation but a touch of doubt crept through. 'And all because you came without a man with you. I told him it was nothing but nonsense. Your valet is to follow any day now – I told him.' The innkeeper's expression appealed for confirmation.

'I am expecting my man Tiplady to follow from York,' replied Jarrett, forcing a smile. 'Indeed, I was in hopes he might arrive today – as you know, I am exhausting my supply of clean linen.'

Relief was clear on the innkeeper's face. 'That's what I told him!' he exclaimed. 'That Nat Broom, he must always be making trouble. Mind you, sir, he's not the only one. I heard Josiah Boyes say you were not yourself – not the Duke's agent at all but a counterfeit.' Mr Bedlington snorted his contempt. 'And who crammed him with that tale? He never thought that up himself. Josiah Boyes has no more fancy in his head than a goose at Christmastide. He'll have learnt his tune from another, I'll be bound.'

More evidence of his enemy's strategy, no doubt, reflected Jarrett as the innkeeper cocked his head to listen to the drinkers in the next room. Surely even Mr Raistrick's audacity could not carry off such a plot. This was England in the nineteenth century, not some melodrama of bandit kings at the Haymarket theatre. And yet, if this tale could be properly worked up he would be well suited to a conviction for murder. The sounds of the crowd next door took on an increasingly ugly note. As if on cue, the nervous features of Constable Thaddaeus appeared in the doorway. Studiously avoiding Jarrett's eyes, he took the innkeeper aside.

'I'm wondering, Jasper, if we'd not best get the gentleman away to the toll booth. He'll be more snug there, for the lads are getting very warm.' He pricked up his ears at the sound of another chair being thrown back. 'Very warm. If the gentleman would follow me up the stairs, quiet like, we could maybe get down the gallery steps into the yard.'

Before this plan could be put into action there was a distraction. A lad appeared at the street door of the Queen's Head. His half-excited, half-solemn air caught the attention and a stillness washed over the sea of voices. The lad walked straight-backed through the tap, his cap held before him. Behind him followed two men carrying a hurdle. The outlines of the body they bore were reduced by the coarse cloth covering it to an indistinct mound the length of a woman: two little peaks for feet at one end and a smooth, rounded lump at the other, where the material stretched taut over the once lively face. The chill thought of death slithered about the room as Sal's remains passed through.

Mrs Bedlington appeared to break the spell. 'You were to bring her through the yard door, Matthew!' she scolded, nearly oversetting the young lad with a smart clip over the ear. 'Have you no decency! Bring her through to the parlour, this way!'

Huffing with indignation Mrs Bedlington led the little procession through the passage. She came to stand beside Jarrett, keeping a sharp eye on the two men, as they laid the body carefully on two tables pushed together.

'Good thing poor Hannah Grundy were not here to see that! She's in the kitchen. Took it in mind to bake me a batch of scones, poor dear.' She lifted the shroud a moment and glanced beneath. 'Well, at least the doctor left her tidy,' she commented to no one in particular. Her plump hands twitched the drape of the cloth here and there, smoothing it. 'It'll do her good to have something to occupy her.' Mrs Bedlington's manner towards the corpse struck Jarrett as remarkably commonplace. She moved as if she were arranging a bed rather than a shroud. In her presence death became almost homely. The innkeeper's wife surveyed her handiwork dispassionately.

'Go fetch some candles from Molly in the kitchen, Jasper my love,' she ordered, then slipping a coin to the two bearers she swept them out. 'You tell them in the tap to stay where they are. She's to have as much peace and decency as I can give her!' She spoke with unexpected fierceness, then turned her back abruptly and began putting up the shutters to darken the room.

'Mrs Grundy says Miss Henrietta has given her permission to fetch Sal to Longacres for the laying out,' Mrs Bedlington confided in a discreet whisper as the room dimmed, casting her rounded features in shadow. 'Miss Lonsdale's gone visiting this morning but she's promised to be by for her this afternoon.' In profile Mrs Bedlington looked sceptical. 'I'll not have a word said against Miss Henrietta for she's a good sort of gentlewoman, but I can't see a lady like her knowing what to do with a corpse.'

Conjuring up Miss Henrietta's composed features, Jarrett reflected that Miss Lonsdale looked likely to prove calmly competent to almost any task.

'I am certain the matter will be easily arranged, Mistress Polly,' he commented as he helped her manoeuvre a particularly awkward shutter into place.

'Why, that is good of you, Mr Jarrett, sir!' Mrs Bedlington responded with unwarranted energy. 'I should have known that you would come to Miss Henrietta's aid, being such a gentleman.' She emphasised her conviction with a congratulatory pat on his coat-sleeve. 'The Longacres household has been short of a proper man since Mr Lonsdale died near two years past now.'

Her confident misinterpretation of his mild commonplace caught him unawares. Jarrett himself hardly imagined that Miss Lonsdale would welcome his assistance. In any event, it began to appear doubtful he would be at liberty to make the offer. He was wondering whether to make an effort to correct this little misunderstanding in case it might grow into some larger embarrassment when his hostess's eyes fixed on something over his shoulder.

'Oh, drat!' she protested mildly.

Mrs Grundy had appeared in the room. Mrs Bedlington eyed her uneasily. The cook's stout figure seemed adrift in a half-conscious world. The sound of her breathing was acute against the ambient silence of the parlour. Listening to the painful wheezing of the old woman's breath through her tired lungs, Jarrett could almost feel a sympathetic pain in his own. Mrs Grundy lowered herself into the chair he drew up for her by the head of the body. She acknowledged no other presence in the room. Carefully, her hands with their purple swollen knuckles reached out. With methodical neatness she folded back the grey shroud to uncover the beautiful face. She smoothed the symmetrical fold she had made and gently patted it.

'Wild and wilful,' she whispered. 'Oh, my bairn, what has your mischief brought you to?' Her body picked up the rhythm of her absent-minded hand and she began to rock, abandoned in her grief.

The investigation was recalled at five o'clock. Constable Thaddaeus was nervous as he escorted Jarrett into the chamber. The drink and the sight of Sal's shrouded body had stoked the fires of righteous anger among the crowd, while the impotence men feel at the whiff of death fuelled bluster to cover the fear. Several men stuck their thumbs in their waistcoats and threw back their heads at him as Jarrett was ushered up the stairs and into the council chamber. He noted the bravado poses, sturdy legs planted out in belligerence, solid bodies set to confront him – the stranger, impostor and even murderer. As the constable struggled to force a way for him through the press, one voice carried above the rest.

'He didn't arrive by post; his luggage came up without him. He said he rode over from York – had business on the way, so he said. Who's to say if he came from York at all?'

Jarrett was puzzled. The man was a stranger to him. The speaker saw the agent through the crowd and he raised his voice a notch.

'The innkeeper knows. He was there. I was in the tap at the time and I heard him.'

Someone jostled Jarrett and he nearly lost his balance. The violence was deliberate. Jarrett swung round to his attacker. Whoever his assailant was, he was not yet confident enough to face him. The encircling figures blended into one corporate identity. The hostile expressions told him they were all against him. He knew only his supposed status as Duke's agent held them back. If Raistrick could but strip that away he was done for.

He was conscious of Constable Thaddaeus shifting from foot to foot at his shoulder, making a nervous mumbling sound. In a brief moment of weakness Jarrett was tired of standing alone. With an effort he straightened his shoulders and picked out the most prominent man in the group. As he held the stare the edge of his vision caught a movement to his right. The man who had spoken, emboldened by the attention brought by his tale, executed a smart shuffle towards him and spat. Jarrett did not flinch. The rest of the chamber was noisy but in the space in which they were locked he could hear the short, excited breathing of the men confronting him. Raistrick strode among them.

'Now, boys, clear a way. We must get started.'

The ring fractured and grudgingly a way opened. The lawyer was back at his table shuffling papers. Jarrett took out his handkerchief and wiped the gob of spittle from his cheek.

'Gentlemen.' With an ironic bow to the company he made his way to his seat. His leg hurt and the chair was hard. He would not give them the pleasure of seeing him slouch. He eased out his damaged leg and tried to appear alert.

The witness, Ned Turner the carter, was not yet in the chamber. The proceedings restarted with the report of Mr Gilbert, the surgeon who had examined the victim. Mr Gilbert was a plain little man. His voice had a trace of Edinburgh precision about it. The faint accent contributed to a general impression that the good doctor valued himself pretty highly in the measure of men and anticipated that others would do him similar justice. Mr Justice Raistrick took up the questioning as before.

'Mr Gilbert, you have examined the deceased?'

'I have, Mr Justice Raistrick. It is my opinion that the victim fell to her death from a height. The scalp covering was split and there was considerable blood lost. That wound, however, was not the likely cause of death. The victim died from her neck being broken – perhaps by striking a stone or some similar object. I remarked a circular discoloration or bruising of the skin about the base of the neck, which mark is consistent with a sharp blow.' Mr Gilbert spoke in a careful, didactic tone. He adjusted his little round glasses on his pointed nose and settled himself more comfortably in his position centre stage. In his discourse he had turned and was now lecturing the vestry as if they were a jury.

'I observed bruises on the side and back of the torso, and scratches on the arms; these, along with mud and scraps of leaves and twigs caught in the hair and a tear in the red petticoat the victim wore – a tear matching some threads Justice Raistrick, I believe, himself recovered from bushes at the edge of the rock they call Lovers' Leap' – the little surgeon bowed in the Justice's direction – 'these are all indications which would lead any reasonable man to conclude that the victim fell to her death.'

'Would Sally Grundy, this poor young woman,' the lawyer underlined this phrase with a graceful gesture somehow evocative of the pathos of the girl's fate, 'have died outright?'

Mr Gilbert inclined his head slightly as he applied his mind to this question. 'No man of science could claim to judge with any certainty. The victim might take a few moments to die from such an injury. In some cases there has been some considerable jerking about of the limbs noted in the shock of the final spasm.'

The watching faces reflected the mood of the chamber as light passing over water. Raistrick stood master of it all, like some pagan god conducting the elements. One could not help but be drawn to the man. Here was a being whose whole power rested in his own form and abilities, without the advantages of birth or connections. Wealth – no doubt he had collected wealth; but watching the lawyer conduct the emotions of the pressed pack of human beings surrounding him Jarrett felt certain that even if he were robbed of all he owned he would, given time, recoup, rebuild and re-emerge strong and powerful once more. With his voice and that one simple gesture Raistrick conjured up for his audience the tragic picture of the beautiful, defenceless young woman cut down by a stranger's deliberate malice.

'The victim would not have been able to turn herself on her back and fold her arms neatly across her breast?'

Mr Gilbert permitted himself a little smile in recognition of this joke. 'Oh, no; dear me, no. That would not be possible.'

'And in your expert judgement, Mr Gilbert, can you suggest the hour that Sally Grundy might have met her death?'

'I fear science cannot instruct us as to the precise time of death. However, I would propose that if the victim was last seen near half past nine on Wednesday evening – as the storm broke near eleven o'clock that night, and the body was found sheltered above the line of the flooded river – simple deductive reasoning would indicate that the victim died between the hours of close to ten and eleven o'clock that night. Rigor mortis was well established when the remains were discovered.' Ever the pedant, Mr Gilbert took off from this statement to wander with pleasure in the byways of qualification. 'It is to be regretted that as the onset of that condition is varied, it is not possible to deduce with any scientific accuracy how long the body might have lain in the gully.' Here the surgeon embarked on a lengthy tale of an instance from his experience when rigor mortis was delayed in the corpse of a child kept warm by a fire for two days by a grieving mother who would not accept that God had gathered her child to Him. The tale was reaching its most affecting part when a commotion was heard outside. The long-awaited carter had arrived.

Jarrett examined the new witness with interest. Ned Turner proved to be a short, muscular man with the air of a choleric dwarf. Collateral arches of creased flesh about his eyes mounted up a high forehead and one of his deep-set eyes wandered, giving him a slightly averted look. He held his broad-brimmed hat in his hand, his expression resentful at the excited attention he was receiving.

'Are you Ned Turner, carter of this place?'

'I am,' the witness answered shortly. 'Folk know me here.' As he threw a belligerent glance about the chamber, several heads nodded in confirmation of this statement.

'And you claim you saw the deceased, Sally Grundy, in Gainford on Tuesday last with a "gentleman"?'

The carter nodded. 'Just Tuesday past.' He watched the lawyer closely. Jarrett could not decide whether he was weighing the man up or looking for instructions.

'Can you describe the man you saw?'

'A fancy sort of man, not a working man.'

'His colour, his hair, his height.'

'A medium-sized man. Fair.'

The economy of the witness's answers was not to the lawyer's liking.

'What do you mean by medium-sized?' The energy with which Raistrick asked the question gave it an edge of impatience. Ostentatiously he swept his eyes about the room, coming to rest on the fair-haired gentleman sitting in his chair to the left of the table. 'Mr Jarrett, might I trouble you to stand a moment?'

The agent complied, his face a mask of polite detachment.

'See this gentleman here, Turner,' continued the lawyer. 'Do you mean medium height as in the stature of this man? I beg your pardon,' Raistrick bowed elaborately to the agent as if recouping an unintentional insult, 'medium height as Mr Jarrett's height might be considered to be of medium height?'

Turner glanced at Jarrett's figure. He gave a graceless jerk of his head. 'About his height.'

Mr Raistrick was too skilful to betray his eagerness to his public, but as he resumed his seat Jarrett could sense the tension under the mask. The Justice stood with one hand negligently hooked in his waistcoat. One had to look closely to notice that the free hand that hung by his side was clenched tight. When he spoke, his tone was almost casual.

'Mr Turner – do you see any man in this chamber who resembles the man you saw in Gainford?'

The carter seemed unsurprised by the question. His eyes detailed a careful circle about the crowded room until they reached Jarrett. There they lingered as he looked full into the agent's face.

'He's like, I reckon.'

Raistrick turned to his audience. 'Mr Jarrett resembles the man you saw talking to the girl in Gainford that day?'

'That's what I said.'

'So you testify that Mr Jarrett looks like the man you saw talking to Sally Grundy last Tuesday in Gainford? Did you know, Mr Turner, that Mr Jarrett has told us he never spoke a word to the girl? And yet you saw him talking to the victim in Gainford just this Tuesday past ...'

'No.' Turner's negative cut into the flow of the lawyer's speech and bobbed there in the arrested tide a moment. 'He's like, but it's not him. I took that fellow for a play-actor – he had this bill in his hand, like the players hand out on fair days. He was asking after a printer.'

An honest witness, by God! In his relief Jarrett almost smiled openly. It seemed that Mr Turner was not the lawyer's man after all. The respite was short-lived. Raistrick's only discernible reaction to this check was to shift his weight a touch, as if planting his feet more securely for the fight. The sense of barely contained energy that always accompanied his presence grew more palpable.

'How well do you see, Mr Turner – in the general run of things?' The lawyer's fingers sketched a little flurry near his face, drawing attention to the cast in the carter's eye.

'As well as any, so far as I know,' Turner responded defensively.

'And how close did you stand, when you saw Sally Grundy in Gainford with this fair-haired gentleman, who resembled Mr Jarrett so closely?'

'I was unloading my wagon across the green from the Blue Boar. She was standing before the door talking to him and then they went in together.'

'The man – he was wearing a hat?'

This gave the carter pause. 'I reckon,' he agreed cautiously.

Raistrick's nimble fingers drew a broad-brimmed hat in the air about his own head. 'A hat.' His tone was patiently scornful. 'A hat throws a man's face in shadow, Mr Turner. You were watching from across the green, you say? That's a fair distance, Mr Turner. How can you be sure? Could this not be the man?'

'Not unless he's been baked in the oven these last few days,' snapped the carter. 'He's a brown-complexioned man. The other was fair-skinned – I could see that, hat or no. Bright red and complaining of the heat he was.' Turner cast dispassionate eyes over the seated agent. 'No, I've not seen him before. The other had golden hair, as bright as a guinea of gold.'

The lawyer darted straight for the weakness. 'How could you see his hair, Turner, if he was wearing a hat?'

'He took it off,' returned Turner, unabashed. 'He took off his hat as he took the chickabiddy into the inn.'

Thank God for true Englishmen, thought Jarrett. Raistrick had finally misjudged. He had offended his witness and roused his independent spirit. With luck this sturdy citizen was digging in for a fight.

'Playing the real gentleman, he was,' elaborated Turner, uncharacteristically warming to his theme. 'What a to-do. I thought to myself: You're not taken in by that dangler are you, Sally Grundy? By the saints, though, but she was a cockish wench,' he added in an unexpectedly regretful tone.

'Spare us your fancies, Turner. We seek only facts here.' Raistrick's confidence was unshaken. He seemed to have no fear of insulting his witness. 'Look again – this man's hair might turn gold where the sun caught it.'

'No, I tell you.' Ned Turner was beginning to sound querulous. 'That one was not a proper gentleman – he was like a play-actor or a beau-trap, I tell you.'

Raistrick surveyed the carter as if he were weighing up some heavy object he had to move from his path. The crowded chamber remained with him. By the occasional exclamation and murmur, the audience indicated it was growing impatient with Mr Turner.

'Mr Turner,' he began.

A disturbance erupted by the door. A path opened between the press of onlookers and a pair of newcomers entered. The leader was a compact gentleman with sparse hair receding off a high domed forehead. The reverend parson sprang to his feet, a rosy blush rising up his neck to his forehead.

'Why, Colonel!' he exclaimed.

Colonel Ison, Member of Parliament and Chairman of the Bench, had arrived.

A glance at Colonel Ison when in repose might lead the casual observer to mistake him for just another prosperous gentleman farmer, but when in motion his face and manner exuded an energy combined with the utter confidence of authority that made him remarkable. At that moment he marched into the room the black brows which gave character to a rounded, almost chubby, face were concentrated in a stern line, and under them his hazel eyes were acute.

'I've come as fast as I was able. Your servant, Reverend. Mr Raistrick.' The Colonel bounced a business-like bow at each. 'I don't believe you know my companion.' Turning to the slight young man who followed him, he said, 'My Lord, may I introduce to you the Reverend Justice Prattman, parson of this parish, and Mr Justice Raistrick. Sirs, Lord Earewith.'

The Duke of Penrith's eldest son executed a polite bow to the two magistrates. The fine cloth of his travelling cloak whispered wealth in every elegant fold, while the sharp, complex creases of his cravat and the silver-topped cane he held so negligently in his gloved hand testified to his sense of fashion. The faintly bored expression with which he acknowledged the introduction gave way to one of charming animation as he walked over to the agent. Jarrett leapt up with hand outstretched.

'Charles!'

The hand was grasped and used to pull Jarrett into an uninhibited embrace.

'Raif, dear fellow! I called on the Colonel here to convey my father's regards as I passed, heard where he was headed and here I am.' Charles turned his closely cropped head to glance around him. 'Might I have a chair?' he asked pleasantly.

The vestryman so addressed stared in confusion. As the gentleman was clearly used to being obeyed there seemed no answer but to start up and offer his own seat. The Marquess watched patiently as the man deposited the chair. With a gracious nod of dismissal, my lord moved the seat to a spot slightly behind Jarrett and made himself comfortable. Resting a careless hand on his friend's shoulder, he surveyed the chamber with a lively expression.

'So, Raif – as I appear to have arrived after the first act – tell me the plot so far.'

The Colonel's arrival revolutionised the universe. As with the appearance of a large planet in a small galaxy, the relation ships in the council chamber switched seamlessly into new orbits. The change in Mr Raistrick was remarkable. One minute the puppet-master, the next he had dampened down all the glowing colours of his presence and retreated – without seeming to retreat – into the role of the lawyer, legal adviser to the bench.

In a tone that was brisk and a touch impatient the Colonel asked for the record of proceedings. The clerk Pye, with no more expression than a mechanical doll, handed over the large book in which he had noted down the testimony of the witnesses. Perching a pair of half-moon spectacles on his nose, the Colonel rapidly scanned the account. He flicked an acute glance under his black brows at the townsfolk crowding the room.

'Odd business. Don't hold with these open sessions myself. Unsettles the public. This affair should have been investigated in private, Prattman. Mr Raistrick, you are our legal man, you should have advised against it.'

He looked over to where Jarrett sat with Lord Earewith. The two men were in conversation, their heads bent close together. The Colonel exchanged a brief nod of acknowledgement with the agent.

'A bad business,' he declared roundly. 'Bad business, badly managed, Prattman!'

'You've not met the Colonel before, Raif, have you?' Charles was asking in a low voice. 'He came to Ravensworth once years back, but you were abroad – on duty in the West Indies, I think. Quite the politician, so I am told.'

Charles's pale skin highlighted his dark eyes which were particularly expressive. He threw a humorous look about the chamber.

'Not a week in the district and you are taken up on suspicion of murder. I see you've made your mark.' The hand resting on Jarrett's shoulder gave it a friendly squeeze. 'And you are well, Raif?' Though his manner was light-hearted, the dark eyes watched his friend closely. Jarrett's smile returned their warmth.

'Well indeed. I have suffered nothing more than a sore leg, a damp night in gaol and bruised pride – which latter no doubt will be to my benefit, for I was careless in this affair.'

'I doubt the foresight of Cassandra could have anticipated this. It is rather splendidly dramatic, though,' responded Charles, looking about the scene in a manner strongly reminiscent of an enthusiastic theatre-goer.

'I hardly think the dead girl would share your enthusiasm, Charles,' Jarrett said dryly.

His companion's open face was fleetingly contrite. 'Forgive me. You know I have no nerves or sensibilities. I hear the

victim was a girl of great beauty. Such a shame.' His agile
mind leapt on to a new tack. 'As to that – it seems you have
made quite an impression among the ladies of this district,
Raif.'

Jarrett, caught off guard, stiffened. 'What can you mean?
I was not acquainted with this Sally Grundy.'

'No need to flare up at me, my boy. I wasn't referring to
the laundry wench, but to another entirely respectable lady.
One to whom you are indebted, it seems, for alerting Lady
Catherine to your plight – now there is a formidable character. Extraordinary woman. One could not have dreamt her
up in one's wildest fancies.'

'Charles, your wanderings have lost me.' Jarrett was finding his friend's humour a trifle tiresome.

'It was Lady Catherine who fetched the Colonel. The
fetching female who fetched her was Miss Lonsdale. I merely
happened to call conveniently on the Colonel as he was setting off. When I received your letter, it occurred to me that
he might be a useful ally.'

'Miss Lonsdale!'

'Your astonishment is wasted on me, Raif. I would take
it as a compliment that a maiden should ride to one's rescue – but then you can be such a strait-laced fellow where
women are concerned.'

Jarrett ignored the jibe. 'You have met Miss Lonsdale?'

'But briefly, to my chagrin.' Charles sat bent forward, resting his chin on his cane and one elegantly clad leg stretched
out, as his dark eyes took in the details of the council chamber. 'At the inn as we arrived. Lady Catherine was assisting
her in making arrangements to convey the cook and her
dead relative. I am, however, in confident hope of pursuing
the interesting acquaintance.' He slid a teasing side look at
his friend. 'I am invited to tea at Oakdene.' Charles laughed
outright at his friend's face as he digested the news. 'And so
are you, Raif – just as soon as we are free of this affair. Lady

Catherine is all agog to hear details of this business and will not be denied.'

Over at the Justices' table the mulberry-coated figure of the lawyer was listening in silence to the Colonel's low-voiced monologue. The friends caught a glimpse of his speculative glance in their direction.

'I presume that is our wild card?' Charles turned away to disguise a faint smile. 'My entrance seems to have floored him.'

'It was a good entrance.'

'Did you like it? I thought perhaps the embrace was a touch overdone – we are after all an undemonstrative tribe, but I thought to reclaim you.'

'I am deeply conscious of your patronage, my lord,' responded Jarrett. Charles buffeted him on the arm and they laughed like boys.

The Colonel completed his assessment of the clerk's record. Assuming a carrying public voice he made for the heart of the matter.

'It would seem that the victim – this Sally Grundy – met her death between half past nine and eleven o'clock on the night of Wednesday last. Is that agreed, gentlemen?'

His fellow Justices acknowledged it was. The Colonel's eyes searched the crowd.

'Which one is Turner the carter?' The sturdy little man stepped forward once more. 'It seems no one has thought to ask you what time you saw this pair in Gainford last Tuesday, Turner. What time was that?'

Smiles were alien to Ned Turner's features, but his expression indicated that he approved of the Colonel. He answered the question with care.

'It was in the afternoon, your honour. I always reach the green at Gainford between half past four and five on a Tuesday afternoon. Mrs Bridey at the Cat and Fiddle, she likes to remark on my punctuality. I was a touch early that day for she remarked to me: You're prompt today, Mr Turner – it is barely half past four. I got down to unload my wagon and I saw them.'

'Thank you, Turner. Well, gentlemen, the matter seems straightforward enough. Mr Jarrett,' the Colonel turned his attention to the agent, 'where were you, sir, at half past four on Tuesday afternoon?'

'I spent the day riding about the Duke's properties, Colonel. As I recollect, I left Mr Peart over at Spinney Top just before four o'clock that afternoon. Around half past the hour I should have been approaching Woolbridge.'

'And did you pass anyone who might confirm this?'

'I might have nodded to an acquaintance or two, but I do not recollect speaking to anyone.'

A voice spoke up. 'I saw him.' A plump woman with a homely face edged out of the crowd. 'Mary Tan, your honour.' She identified herself with a bob curtsey. 'If you please, Mr Justice, sir, I saw the agent ride by. And so did Nathan Binks and Jeremy Fairley, for they were talking before Nathan's shop on the market. You remember, Nathan?' She addressed the watchmaker. 'Jem said he hadn't seen His Grace's new agent and you said, there he is now. That was Tuesday afternoon but I couldn't swear to the time.'

Her uncertainty was soon supplemented by the testimony of the watchmaker. Nathan Binks came forward to declare that it was lacking ten minutes to five o'clock when the agent passed. He was certain of the hour for he was setting a mechanism at the time by the church clock.

The Colonel spread his blunt-fingered hands in a gesture expressive of the simplicity of it all. 'There you are, gentlemen. If Mr Jarrett was in Woolbridge just before five o'clock there is no mortal means he could have been seen by Mr Turner at half past four in Gainford. There is clearly some other man who was consorting with the victim.' The Colonel went on briskly. 'May I suggest that he is the man to seek.

Let us have a description drawn up and posted, offering the usual reward for information.'

'One moment, Colonel.' The lawyer half-rose to claim the Colonel's attention. 'There is still a matter that puzzles me.' He spoke as if the words he used were not his first choice. 'These muddy clothes.' He drew attention to the pile of garments resting on the table. 'Mr Jarrett agrees they are his, yet he will not explain why he was down by the river that night.'

'Is this true, Mr Jarrett? You do not wish to offer an explanation?'

'I beg your pardon, Colonel, but Mr Raistrick's unmannerly inquisition did not incline me to justify my actions as if I were some criminal. I can offer you no witness but I was fishing, sir.'

'Fishing in the middle of a tempest, Mr Jarrett?' Raistrick was scornful.

'The river was rising and so were the salmon,' responded Jarrett coolly.

It was fortunate perhaps that the Colonel, too, was of the angling fraternity. 'Did you have good sport?' he asked with interest.

'It was unusual sport, sir. Exhilarating. I caught a couple of fish of excellent size. I hung them at the back of my cottage, but I suspect they might have been taken.'

Constable Thaddaeus cleared his throat. 'If I may speak, Colonel, Mr Justice, sir. I have the fish in my custody, your honour; a witness brought them to me for safe-keeping, there being many thieving rogues about and Mr Jarrett being from home, as you might say.'

'If I may be permitted, Colonel, I believe there is another fact that points to my innocence, despite Mr Raistrick's suspicions.' Walking to the table, Jarrett picked up his muddy coat and spread it out before the lawyer. It was a wool coat, of a buff colour which the damp had darkened. 'It is agreed,

I think, that the suspect in this crime had to pick the victim up to lay her on the ledge. Those of us who saw the body there can testify that blood was still seeping from the head. As you can see, the coat I wore last night is of a colour that would have been clearly stained, had I held a bloody corpse in my arms.' He could not resist holding out the coat under Raistrick's nose. 'Examine it as closely as you wish, gentlemen. You will find no such stain.'

There was a silence as the chamber digested this. Raistrick sat back in his chair, his bold eyes cold.

'Well, gentlemen,' declared the Colonel, 'it would appear Mr Jarrett is owed an apology.' He addressed the agent in his most public voice. 'Sir, you have been wronged. On behalf of the citizens of Woolbridge, I offer you our deepest regrets for the offence done to you. I hope you may find it possible to forgive the wayward zeal that gave rise to this misunderstanding, in view of the unusual tragedy that has visited here.'

Jarrett stood to return the patrician bow that accompanied the Colonel's words. 'I accept the apology wholeheartedly, Colonel. May I in turn beg a favour from the bench? Conscious as I am of the depth of the desire to penetrate this mystery, I know too that the vestry is not a wealthy one and has not the funds to pursue an active investigation. I would be pleased to offer my services to the parish. For my own honour's sake, I will not be easy until the true author of this crime has been uncovered; for until that moment I cannot consider the shadow of this late suspicion against me entirely removed.'

'A pretty speech!' snorted Raistrick.

The vestrymen however were charmed at the prospect of being saved the expense of raising a reward of perhaps as much as twenty pounds for information. Mr Jarrett's offer put them in excellent humour with the erstwhile suspect and there was a general ripple of comments on the agent's public-spiritedness. The Colonel picked up the mood.

'Your generosity does you credit, sir. I propose that Mr Jarrett be charged with the further investigation of this affair, to report back to an extraordinary petty session – shall we say next Thursday, gentlemen?'

The Colonel was clearly determined that any subsequent examinations would be conducted in private, for only magistrates and invited witnesses or advisers were admitted to such petty sessions. Of his fellow Justices, the Reverend Prattman was eager to agree. The parson was transparently much comforted by the Colonel's arrival to take charge of what had threatened to become a nightmare.

As to Mr Raistrick – the Colonel cast a sharp glance at the heavy-set figure glowering to his right. Given his experience of Mr Justice Raistrick's character, Colonel Ison was confident that the lawyer would swim with the tide – in public at least.

CHAPTER TEN

'Her name is Bronte, though I'd sooner call her Charybdis the way she pulls poor Tansy into her mischief.' Charles jerked the reins impatiently to check the offending mare. He drove a neat pair of Welsh cobs, their glossy chestnut haunches gleaming in the late afternoon sun.

'They are handsome,' commented Jarrett idly.

'Aye, aesthetically pleasing at a stand but their motion as a pair is execrable. It is my own fault. I'm such a shallow fellow – ever drawn by outward appearances in both women and horse-flesh.' Bronte shuddered and skipped a step. 'I thought to school them but this one's an incurable kicker and pulls like the very devil.' Transferring the reins briefly to his whip hand, Charles flexed his gloved fingers to ease the cramp. 'I suppose I shall have to break 'em up and start afresh.'

Jarrett was impatient with this small-talk. 'Don't keep me in suspense, Charles. Why so long in York? May I hope your delay was due to some discovery?'

Charles's face focused as his quick mind came to the fore. He sketched a brisk nod. 'You know I was off to find Dibley, the lawyer, as we parted? Well, old Dibley's papers were quite a mine of information, once his clerk managed to gather it all up. You know I have little head for business...'

On the contrary, Jarrett was well aware that his friend had a sharp eye for a rum deal, a skill honed during a youth enjoyed in a world littered with card-sharps and other rogues determined to regard rich young men as their legitimate prey.

He grinned. 'So what did you stumble across, my simple pigeon?'

'Crotter had been purloining receipts and borrowing against my father's properties. He was in pretty deep.'

'How deep?'

'Deep enough for him – but for us? Perhaps Father will be cutting down on his racing stable and letting out that hunting box in Leicestershire he no longer uses for the next year or so. And what of matters here? I imagine these properties are in a bad way?'

'I have uncovered a number of supposed improvements that exist only on paper, yes. However, I should say that the core of the tenants are perfectly respectable and sound. Have you any idea how long this has been going on?'

'As far as I can tell, only four or five years.'

'So Crotter did not begin a rogue?'

'I think not. Lawyer Dibley values himself as a discreet man but he finally decided it prudent to inform me that there had been a rumour a few years back that Crotter had been tempted to speculate in a bid for a military contract – blankets or some such. The man over-extended himself then lost the business to a local competitor. The most likely explanation is that, finding himself with debts he could not pay, Crotter turned to defrauding the estates to cover them.'

The carriage had left Woolbridge behind and bowled down a pretty lane towards Oakdene Hall. Charles turned to his companion. 'Tell me of your adventures while I have been buried among dusty papers and dustier lawyers. What of this Tallyman you alluded to in your postscript? That scribble gave a touch of melodrama to your epistle. A proper note to be flung by a maiden from a tower!' he teased.

'I am no maiden!' protested Jarrett. 'It is ever a pleasure to see you, Charles, but I am confident I should have extricated myself from this latest incident even had you not arrived as you did. Lawyer Raistrick had no evidence against me. As to my scribble, the postmaster had already done up his bags and I did not want to miss the mail,' he ended defensively.

Charles laughed. 'So tell me – this Tallyman?'

Jarrett sketched the role he suspected the Tallyman of playing, including his suspicion of the man's involvement in the Stainmoor murder. He gave a lively account of his first interview with Justice Raistrick after he was attacked on the road to Greta Bridge, and how his adventures had led him to suspect that most unusual of magistrates of being the Tallyman's sometime employer. Without intending to at the outset, Jarrett found he passed over his acquaintance with Ezekiel Duffin. It was not that he would not personally trust Charles with his life, but he was not confident his friend would show equal diligence for the welfare of a mere poacher. Charles's nature was exuberant and one never knew what he might let slip.

Charles paid close attention to the tale. As his companion fell silent, he paused a moment. 'So, let me sum up,' he began. 'First, we have one dead steward whose account books are missing. Second, the sums taken from our estates are considerable – I cannot believe that they were all sunk into Crotter's debts. Next, this Tallyman is put at the manor at the time of Crotter's death, possibly seen in the act of carrying off those missing account books.' Charles's profile was perhaps his best feature. He had a classical nose and a noble forehead. When he was thoughtful, as now, the pale cast of his skin gave his head the illusion of being carved in marble. He turned to his companion and the illusion shattered. Face to face there was an earthy knowingness about him that was entirely human. 'How certain are you of that tale?'

'Certain enough. I would trust my witness,' Jarrett replied.

Charles threw him a penetrating look but did not press him. 'And finally we suspect that the said Tallyman is in the employ of one of the local magistrates – the same who snatched the opportunity to select you as a likely suspect when this fortuitous corpse turns up at your door. And we conclude?' Charles raised a quizzical eyebrow.

'That Raistrick was in partnership with Crotter in defrauding your father's estates,' responded Jarrett promptly. 'Indeed, I suspect that our lawyer Raistrick had the unfortunate Crotter well under his thumb.'

'And sought Crotter's death perhaps?'

Jarrett took a deep breath, puffing his cheeks as he let it out. 'Why would he kill so productive a goose? It only leads to the expense and trouble of corrupting a new agent. No. I suspect Crotter died as he appeared to die – his heart gave way unexpectedly, leaving his confederate to cover his tracks as best he could.'

'Then you appear. Raistrick must have expected someone to arrive to pick up my father's affairs.'

'But maybe not so soon. By arriving alone at least I arrived in short time.'

Charles grinned. 'Ah-ha! We come to your unconventional appearance in these parts. Am I to understand that that was strategy, not whim?' His manner became half-serious, half-playful. 'I have a lecture for you, sir! Lady Catherine informed me that you asked Sir Thomas not to speak of your true identity. Why, Raif? This whole late affair could not have unfolded as it did if you had only permitted the proper introductions.'

'Anonymity gives greater freedom of movement.' Jarrett shrugged impatiently. 'Besides, if the town cats had once grasped the notion that I might be the Duke's kinsman they would have worried me to death with their picnics and teas until they established the precise nature of my blood, fortune and degree ...' He trailed off with an impatient wave of a hand. 'And all the rest.'

Charles's eyes contemplated his companion with a sympathy at variance with his satirical tone. 'You are such a retiring fellow! You have been a spy too long, Raif.'

'Intelligence officer, I beg you!'

'As you will. But,' there was a sudden note of sincerity in Charles's tone, 'you must shake this habit of concealment. It is unnecessary.'

'Is it?' Jarrett rubbed a hand over his eyes wearily. His cuff fell back to reveal the plait of hair he wore about his wrist.

'You wear it still, I see,' Charles observed quietly.

Jarrett glanced down. 'Aye.' He tucked it out of sight and straightened himself. 'It is the fetter that binds me to the truth of my situation. But you are right. Information-gathering in the field suits my temperament. I seem to have a natural inclination for solitude and concealment.'

'I dispute that it is a true part of your nature.' The words broke out with energy, then Charles continued more quietly. 'It arises rather from the misfortunes you have encountered.' He touched his friend's arm, his voice low and earnest. 'Raif, your family acknowledges and values you. That fact upholds you against any petty gossip.'

Jarrett folded his arms with a wry shrug.

'Forgive me,' Charles said. 'I do not mean to cause you pain.' Dispelling the tension, he moved into a light comic vein. 'I am awaiting word from Ravensworth. I expect to be called back any time. I hear that my father is in another of his blue deeps.'

'How blue?'

'Purple to indigo,' responded Charles in a resigned tone.

Jarrett tossed his head. 'Of course, he is approaching another anniversary, is he not?'

Alexander, fourth Duke of Penrith, had been indulged all his life. From the moment he opened his eyes on the world he had been endowed with money, position, good looks and charm. These attributes, complemented by a naturally hard head for drink and a disarming disregard for expense, had won him a wide circle of friends. He had thus passed his first fifty years without ever giving a thought to his good fortune (His Grace not being much given to thought). Then, at the age of fifty-two, while riding to hounds with his famed recklessness, he had suffered a bad fall. The resulting paralysis of his legs eventually passed, but his spirit never recovered from the shock. Bewildered and indignant that fortune should so suddenly turn her back on him, His Grace took refuge in his bed from the onset of old age. Gradually he assumed the role of an invalid, discovering in that interesting condition the power to make others do as he liked even more effectually than when he charmed them in his prime. Thus His Grace settled comfortably into a premature old age, ruling his family and household from the convenience of his bath-chair. It was his habit to give himself out to be at death's door whenever the supply of amusing visitors temporarily dried up and boredom overtook him. These episodes his family, with weary affection, referred to as his 'blue deeps'.

The left-hand mare shuddered and shook her head, unsettling her pair.

'Step up, Bronte!' commanded Charles in an irritated tone. 'By the bye, I have brought Tiplady to you,' he resumed. 'His story was that you had been seized by a brain fever and gone mad. I suppose you had another quarrel?'

Jarrett moved impatiently on the hard bench, seeking to ease the ache in his leg.

'One of his stomachs,' he said shortly.

Charles shook his head sympathetically. 'Ah me. Family retainers. At times I think we serve them rather than the other way around. But you will have to smooth things over. Poor Tip. He is quite cut up about it all. And another thing. What were you doing camping in a folly? What is the matter with living at the manor?'

'I have no liking for it.'

Charles gave a tut of annoyance. 'Then set about re-arranging it to your taste. The house must be repaired in any case, it has been neglected long enough.' He sat up in sudden animation. 'I could assist you! I have a turn for improvements. I must show you the drawings I made for Thorpe Park – not up to your standards, perhaps, but I confess I am pleased with them.'

Jarrett eyed his kinsman with sardonic affection. Charles had abundant energy but his enthusiasms never made allowance for the time and effort it took others to execute his good ideas.

'Forgive me, but I prefer to stick to my simple folly. Look to your team, man!' he exclaimed, indicating the recalcitrant Bronte who was gathering herself to kick at her companion.

'Your trouble, my lad,' responded Charles tartly, ignoring this attempt to divert him, 'is that you *will* stick to your simple folly – no one has a prayer of talking you out of it!' He reined in his troublesome animal. 'But,' he added, 'ever faithful, I shall try. No, You shall not put me off.' He turned his elegant head to his companion, his features alight with humorous affection. 'I have plans. It shall be like our old days when we lodged together in Half Moon Street, Raif – only in a pastoral setting,' he pronounced obscurely.

The curricle passed through the arched gateway of Oakdene Hall. Charles touched his whip to his hat in acknowledgement of the gatekeeper who hurried out to swing open the sturdy iron gates.

'And what of this dead girl, Raif? Can you make any sense of her death?'

Laughter left Jarrett's lean face, his blue eyes looked away across the green sweep of the park. 'I cannot see how she fits into our affair – and yet, Mr Raistrick's behaviour makes me suspect his motives.'

'Might she have been an intrigue he had grown weary of? Perhaps she died for entirely other reasons and he laid her at your door on a whim? A suitable stranger on whom to lay the blame, as it were?'

'Maybe.'

To those who knew him well, Jarrett's eyes were as expressive as the sea.

'What?' Charles demanded.

'I fear he had the girl killed for no other reason than to entrap me.'

'Nonsense! Use your head!' scoffed Charles. 'Oh, I am no innocent – I believe men capable of such horrors. But this man is a lawyer, a magistrate; he has done well for himself; he must have his wits about him. To entertain murder on the off-chance of snaring you? Only a fool or a madman would risk such a thing. It is not as if you came to this place without ties or connections. He knew you as the Duke's agent.'

Jarrett sat back, his arms folded and his legs stretched out straight, braced against the jolting of the carriage, as he recalled the magistrate's efforts to match his boots to the imprints on the rock.

'Perhaps you are right. Mr Raistrick's behaviour over the last two days has the air of an improvisation. He is a bold opportunist.' Jarrett cocked his head at his companion. 'So what are we to do about Mr Raistrick?'

'Do? We do what is rational. We do nothing.'

Jarrett sighed.

'Raif, what do you expect?'

'I have a mild affection for justice. She makes a more comely mistress than expedience,' Jarrett replied.

'But she is a costly wench,' retorted his prosaic relative. 'Be sensible, Raif. The truth of the matter is that my father is much at fault. It was his neglect that allowed these depredations.'

Jarrett interrupted him. 'In respect of Crotter, I may agree with you; but Raistrick? That man is a villain.'

Charles's lips curved at the energy of Jarrett's words. 'It

may be so.' He spoke soothingly. 'Indeed, very likely so. But it is not in Father's interests for it to be widely known how easily he was bled. Our best course is to resume his rights, let it be known that there is a firm hand at the helm – and that will warn off any predators.'

'And how are we to ensure that Raistrick will not move back into place with the next steward?'

'He would stand very little chance with you.'

All of a sudden Charles's Welsh cobs fell out of their smooth action and conveniently absorbed their driver's full attention. In the middle distance a hawk hovered in the still air.

'Ah,' said Jarrett. 'You have plans for my future, it seems.'

'Raif, it is time you sold out. It would take but a few months – a year maybe – until this magistrate learns his place once more.' Charles was determined to persuade with his conviction. 'Besides, this neighbourhood has many features of interest. You have yourself commented on the splendid subjects there are here for your pen; and my father's possessions in the district are wide. There are not only the farms, but the mines and some other properties further afield in Hartlepool and Durham – plenty to occupy your mind and talents. You would have full control and none better to take up the charge.'

Jarrett gave a short laugh. 'I doubt I am diplomat enough to deal with the likes of Mr Raistrick.'

'Unless there is clear evidence of some crime – what are we to do against Mr Raistrick?' demanded Charles. 'Going to law is a costly business, the courts are sinks to both money and justice. Would you have us apply ourselves to enriching lawyers and clerks for the next decade? Be sensible, Raif; the world is as it is.'

There was a mature awareness in the depths of Charles's sherry-coloured eyes. The Marquess's youthful spirit was that of a child born with a wry consciousness of the sinful ways of the world. The difference between the friends was that where Jarrett regretted, Charles merely shrugged and accepted.

'I am a soldier, Charles. I would make a poor steward.'

'I have put Tip up with Bedlington at the Queen's Head and engaged you your room,' Charles ventured after a pause. 'You will stay, will you, Raif?' he ended on a faintly pleading note.

Jarrett leant back his head and let out a slow breath. He had been restless for some time, his unease predating the wound that had brought him home. For months since, reflecting alone under the stars in the frozen Portuguese hills, the yearning had grown in him for a different life, a life that amounted to something more than a couple of mentions in despatches. Raif Jarrett had discovered that he lacked the true heart of a soldier. A man on active service rises each day to contend with death. His loves are passionate and brief; his friendships vivid in the knowledge they may soon be cut off. The future, like his fate, is something he pays little mind. At the age of twenty the military life had seemed heroic, romantic, a kind of perfect freedom, but as a man grew older he felt the lack of home and the settled ties of affection that give body to existence. He met Charles's eyes with a wry smile.

'I hope to stay to see this affair out. And I promise to play the proper gentleman – at least for now.'

'Good, Tansy! Trot on, Bronte!' Charles registered his satisfaction, having at last managed to coax a smooth action from his pair.

A straight avenue of sycamores opened before them. Down the vista appeared the neat frontage of Oakdene Hall.

'You say Lady Catherine fetched the Colonel,' Jarrett asked. 'How could that be?'

'She has some influence with him, it seems,' Charles replied. 'He mentioned that he had known her since he was a boy. When she summoned him, he came at once.'

'But who is she? I knew of the Duke's friendship with Sir

Thomas but I had never heard of her existence.'

'She's some sort of cousin. A daughter of the second Earl of Shetland. I believe I was told once that her afflictions had her destined for an asylum until Sir Thomas came to her rescue and had her reside with him; that was many years ago now – more than thirty, I should think. But enough of Lady Catherine.' Charles returned to the matter at hand. 'We should consult the Colonel about this Tallyman. He has been an active magistrate in this area for many years, he may know of him.' Charles paused. 'We shall have to tread lightly as to Mr Raistrick.' He slid Raif a cautious look. 'He is after all on the bench and you agree we have no sound evidence to lay against him as yet.'

Jarrett's face was impassive. 'What do we know of the Colonel?' he asked. 'How far can he be trusted?'

'As I said, he is a politician.' Charles let the word hang heavy with a faintly mocking twist of the mouth. 'I dare say he follows his own interest, and who is to know what that may be in any given set of circumstances? However, I trust the Duke's influence carries weight with him – more weight than that of a provincial lawyer,' he ended with a dismissive flourish of his whip as he urged his team about the sweep of the drive at a brisk trot.

'Raistrick is no ordinary rural justice,' warned Jarrett. 'He is something more, I'll wager. Remember, this is a small community.'

'Perhaps so, but the bulk of the Colonel's interests lie outside the immediate district.'

'Well enough.'

They drew up at the door. A travelling carriage was being led away to the stables as Charles brought his horses to a stand.

'In any event, you may form your own opinion of the man. The Colonel has arrived before us, I see.'

*

Lady Catherine sat near Miss Henrietta Lonsdale at a table set in the full light of a window looking out over the park. Her twisted body overhung a piece of muslin tacked on to stiff paper. She was setting the final stitches into an exquisite central design of fruit and flowers worked in white thread. The motions executed by her withered hands were delicate and precise, reinforcing the impression of an unwieldy body kept in check by willpower and rigorous schooling. Colonel Ison hovered by his hostess with the air of a man who had run out of pretty things to say. He greeted the newcomers thankfully. Jarrett took his first opportunity to address the magistrate.

'I was not able to raise this matter earlier, Colonel, but I am anxious to trace a villain who goes by the name of the Tallyman. Have you perhaps heard of him? I understand he is well known in the town, particularly in the river district.'

'The Tallyman, eh?' The Colonel gave an abrupt, humourless laugh. He paused briefly, his speculative gaze on the agent. His eyes were as shallow as bits of glass. 'No. I don't recall any villain coming before me by that name. Why should you ask?'

'I have information that he may have been responsible for a piece of housebreaking at the manor after Mr Crotter's death, Colonel – although I have another interest. You were informed of the recent murder up on Stainmoor, sir? The description I was given of this Tallyman struck me as similar to that reported of the suspect in that affair. I may have been misled but the coincidence seems worth pursuing – in the interests of justice, Colonel Ison,' he added.

'Indeed, Mr Jarrett, indeed. I shall make enquiries.'

'I am at a loss how to frame this, Colonel – but have you perhaps a means of making enquiries without troubling Mr Raistrick?'

'Not trouble Justice Raistrick – what can you mean, Mr Jarrett?'

Lady Catherine was hunched over her white work. 'Stuff and nonsense, Zachary, you know full well what he means,' she said sharply.

The Colonel looked pop-eyed under his black brows. Fierce intelligence peered out from the old woman's crippled body and fixed him with a stare of all-seeing derision. Colonel Ison reddened and dropped his gaze.

'I'll make enquiries, Lady Catherine,' he repeated, with a dignified bow. 'Stap me but where's my head! Mr Jarrett, I must return these to you.'

The Colonel turned away to pick up a couple of items from a side-table. He handed Jarrett the notebook and sketch that Raistrick had taken from him.

Jarrett caught a whiff of scented soap and sensed a warm presence at his elbow. Miss Lonsdale looked over his arm at the portrait of Sally Grundy.

'She was a most beautiful girl. You have caught her very well, Mr Jarrett,' she remarked.

Charles's quick ear picked up the flat, non-committal tone in the cool voice. Miss Lonsdale felt the Marquess watching her and her candid gaze held his a moment.

'So you are an artist, Mr Fredrick Raif Jarrett?' His hostess's thin voice demanded Jarrett's attention. 'You can earn your tea by drawing me a design for me corners. Ye see the size of the piece ' Lady Catherine flicked out the fichu of fine muslin for him to see. 'Something for the corners. Those may inspire.' The old lady waved abruptly to a pair of Sèvres jardinières standing on a gilt table between the tall windows. Jarrett politely examined the porcelain enamelled with garlands of pink and blue flowers curling within elegantly shaped cartouches. Lady Catherine pushed a sheet of stiff paper and a pencil across the table towards him. 'There!' she commanded.

Thus Jarrett found himself fixed by the window at Lady Catherine's side in company with the Colonel, leaving Charles

free to promenade about the length of the room with Miss
Lonsdale. Henrietta Lonsdale was looking very well. Her
grey eyes sparkled with amusement and there was a pretty
colour to her cheeks. Jarrett, preoccupied with his design,
could not help overhearing enough to appreciate that the pair
were getting on famously. It was quite a spectacle to watch
Charles deploying his charm. He put the whole liveliness of
his countenance and supple frame into the performance. Miss
Lonsdale was clearly well entertained. She followed each
graceful gesture of the long-fingered hands, her intelligent
features reflecting the animation of his dark eyes.

'Though this may be counted heresy in these sentimental
times, ma'am, I must confess I cannot share the current mania
for manufactured wildernesses. I appreciate the grandeurs of
nature well enough in Italy or Switzerland – I am as admiring as the next man of the stirring depictions of Salvator
Rosa – but all this counterfeiting wild wastes in a garden,
I cannot like it.' Charles indicated the serene sweep of Sir
Thomas's park framed in the high windows. 'A gentleman's
park should be a well-schooled affair with a decent space
left about both God's and man's best creations, so they may
be properly appreciated. To my mind there is nothing more
exquisite than a well positioned English oak highlighted in a
sunlit park. Would you not agree, Miss Lonsdale?'

'And would the severity of your taste allow a few sheep
perhaps, sir? Or maybe a small herd of deer to add a touch
of interest?' enquired Miss Lonsdale.

My Lord inclined his upper torso in a courtly bow. 'You
have it precisely, ma'am. A small herd of deer, with some
fine sets of antlers. A shade more noble than sheep, would
you not say? I owe it to my lineage – I come from a long line
of huntsmen.'

His eyes twinkled and they laughed out loud together.
Charles caught Jarrett looking in their direction.

'Now I know Raif there will dispute my taste in this, for

he is a full-blown admirer of the picturesque. But then he is an artistic fellow, ma'am, while I have little sensibility.'

'It is true, ma'am,' Jarrett responded, sounding rather less gracious than he intended. 'That poetic countenance of his has misled many a lady as to the depths of Charles's sensibility. In truth he is more inclined to a fine dinner than to a fine view.'

Lady Catherine was watching them like some mischievous imp peeping out from under a rock. Jarrett felt a twinge of impatience. He disliked being treated as a spectacle. Colonel Ison too was irritated. He was unused to having so little attention paid to him. Henrietta took pity on his cross, perplexed look.

'Is it your belief that Sally Grundy was murdered, Colonel?' she asked.

'I am inclined to wonder whether this is all a good deal of fuss over nothing, Miss Lonsdale,' he responded abruptly. 'What was the place called where the piece died – Lovers' Leap? She may have jumped. Sort of overheated thing serving girls do.'

'If that were the case, how should she come to lie as we found her, Colonel?' asked Jarrett, a touch impatiently.

'Maybe some other person passing by found the corpse and tidied it.'

'Without reporting the death, sir?'

'There are plenty of itinerants, Mr Jarrett, who do not like to draw attention to themselves. Gypsies, tramping miners seeking work at the pits up the dale – such folk might go so far as to lay out a corpse safely and decently, leaving it for others to find in time. As indeed it was.'

Jarrett, hawkish after a point of reason, did not seem aware that he was causing the Colonel offence by countering his arguments so briskly. With the age-old diplomacy of womankind Henrietta stepped in to divert the Colonel's attention.

'Indeed Mrs Grundy, her aunt, is convinced that Sal was distressed over a suitor who slighted her to marry another. And yet the little I knew of the girl would not have inclined me to believe that she would so lose her senses. Sally Grundy was spirited certainly, but she was also shrewd and sensible at heart.'

'Do you know the name of the suitor, Miss Lonsdale?' asked the Colonel.

Miss Lonsdale looked uncomfortable.

'Will Roberts is his name, Colonel, but I cannot suspect him of such a crime. He has but recently returned from the militia in Ireland – he volunteered and did his duty with merit. He married his sergeant's daughter while in service and when released he and his father-in-law pooled their bounty to buy an alehouse here in Woolbridge. I have never heard an ill word spoken of Will Roberts. He is a steady, hard-working man.'

The Colonel was unconvinced. 'Begging your pardon, Miss Lonsdale, but you cannot be expected to know these rank and file militiamen as I do. I have considerable experience of the kind, both as officer and magistrate; the most sober of them can behave with utter wretchedness, particularly when the worse for drink or in a passion.'

'I did hear a rumour that Miss Grundy might have sued Roberts for breach of promise,' ventured Jarrett. He kept to himself the means by which he had picked up this rumour. Eavesdropping in a local tavern, although an excellent way to collect intelligence, might not appear entirely well-bred.

'Breach of promise, eh?' barked the Colonel. 'That would put this Roberts on the spot with his new wife and in-laws.'

Miss Lonsdale was not to be shaken in her opinion. 'I cannot believe it of Will,' she said decisively. 'Colonel, I have known Will Roberts from a boy. He used to help his father, a carpenter who worked on my uncle's estates. He was always a gentle lad. Such a character as his could not commit cold-blooded murder.' She cast Jarrett an indignant look. 'Besides, Mrs Grundy, Sal's aunt, is my aunt's cook and speaks to me much of her niece. She never mentioned any such thing as a suit for breach of promise and I feel sure Sal would have confided in her.'

The Colonel looked down at her indulgently. He was fond of well-favoured young women, and Miss Lonsdale had a speaking countenance.

'Sad to say, Miss Lonsdale, boys grow up and even good lads can go bad. But then it is one of the glories of the female sex to think the best of men,' he added gallantly. 'And indeed, Miss Grundy's aunt would have been a likely confidante of any scheme to go to law. It seems then, gentlemen, we must fall back on this play-actor fellow,' he ended jovially.

'A play-actor, sir?' asked Henrietta, intrigued.

'Indeed, Miss Lonsdale,' explained Charles, dropping his voice in a mock dramatic style. 'It seems that Miss Grundy had collected a play-actor among her admirers.'

'But how? There are no players in the area at present – none closer than Richmond at the very least. I feel sure we would have heard of them else, would we not, Lady Catherine?' Henrietta appealed to her hostess.

Lady Catherine pursed up her wizened face as she sucked a thread to refill her needle. She jerked her head in agreement.

'True enough. Fancy always plagues me to let her go gawk whenever there are play-actors about.'

'Miss Grundy was seen to meet with someone whom the witness took for a play-actor at an inn in Gainford last Tuesday,' said Jarrett. 'But surely, Colonel, we cannot lay too much weight on Ned Turner's assumption as to the profession of the man he saw. As I recall, he described him variously as a fancy sort of man and likened him to a beau-trap.'

'A beau-trap?' Miss Lonsdale sought elucidation from

Lord Earewith who leant towards her as if they were old friends.

'I believe, Miss Lonsdale, that the term refers to a type of rogue who haunts inns dressed as a gentleman in order to trick unwary country folk at cards or dice.'

As if ignoring this by-play, Jarrett continued to address the Colonel and Lady Catherine. 'In other words, the carter merely thought the man too well dressed to be a working man and yet not quite convincing as a gentleman. True, he also thought he glimpsed a play-bill in the man's hand and heard him ask after a printer. But as the carter had this beau escorting Miss Grundy into the inn on the green at Gainford in the same breath I dare say we should not put too much reliance on that part of his testimony either.'

'I do not understand what business Sal would have in Gainford, Mr Jarrett.'

Jarrett was startled by Miss Lonsdale's tone. He could not think how, but once again he appeared to have caused the lady offence. He put himself out to be conciliatory.

'I believe, according to her aunt's account, Miss Grundy was employed in some laundry work for a Lady Yardley or some such, a newcomer to Gainford,' he explained politely.

'Lady Yarbrook, perhaps?'

'Why, yes,' replied Jarrett surprised. 'I believe that was the name.'

'Not the fabulous Lady Yarbrook?' exclaimed Charles.

'You know of her?' asked Jarrett.

'Only slightly – she is one of those blue-stockings who hold salons for artists and distinguished men, hoping to harvest glory from their fame. She likes to be thought clever. Not my natural circles, you understand,' he confided to Henrietta. 'I came across her and her entourage in Rome a year or two back. She is an original – one of those persons too extraordinary to like and yet whom it seems beneath one to dislike.'

Miss Lonsdale, while acknowledging Lord Earewith's wit, did not quite like this severe dismissal of a mere acquaintance.

'Well, Lady Yarbrook is also reported to have a passion for theatricals and to have engaged a company of players for the summer!' Henrietta could not help feeling a little gratified at her success in gaining the attention of the company with this piece of information. What was it Amelia Bedford had said? She recalled the stuffiness, the plump flesh encased in tight black satin pressing close, the sickly smell of the rose petals mixed with sweat. 'Mrs Bedford spoke of a Lady Yarbrook – the daughter of a Duke?' She spoke slowly, looking a query to Charles who nodded in encouragement. 'Who is married to an Irish peer – but does not wish to live in Ireland,' she continued, gaining confidence.

'So she don't and he does,' completed Charles. 'Yes, that sounds like the fabulous Lady Yarbrook.'

'And that is the full budget of my intelligence, I fear.' Miss Lonsdale threw an apologetic look towards Jarrett. 'I am not much use as a spy, sir. I only recall that Mrs Bedford was most specific that Lady Yarbrook enjoyed amateur theatricals and had taken her enthusiasm so far that she had adopted a whole company of players into her household. Do you think there could perhaps be a connection, Mr Jarrett?'

'I certainly think it is worth pursuing, Miss Lonsdale.'

'Perhaps you would be so good as to go call on this lady, Mr Jarrett, and make enquiries among her play-actors,' intervened the Colonel, eager to reclaim the initiative due to his rank. 'You'll need to be discreet, though. People of distinction don't like to be associated with a common murder.'

Fortunately, Jarrett was relieved of the need to find a response to such advice by the entrance of a servant.

'A rider has just come with a message for his lordship, my lady.'

Charles broke open the seal and scanned the note

perfunctorily. A faintly cynical look passed over his clear-cut features. He crossed the room to bow gracefully over his hostess's brittle fingers.

'Forgive me, Lady Catherine; I am called away and must take my leave. Raif, I shall have to forgo the pleasure of your company tonight. Lady Catherine, may I beg the use of your writing desk to write a short note?'

His hostess inclined her torso with a stately air, her eyes vibrant with curiosity.

Charles sat down at the neat walnut desk and, pulling out a sheet of pressed paper, began to write. He spoke in a low voice to Jarrett. 'As I expected, it is from Father. I shall go entertain him with this tale. He'll be summoning you next, Raif – you know how he likes to hear of your adventures. I regret I shall not be able to introduce you to Lady Yarbrook in person, but take this letter of introduction. She is a sociable body, addicted to conversation and new company, and I am sure she will receive you.' He pretended to lean back a moment in contemplation of his friend's athletic figure. 'I fancy you will do well enough on your own. Take my advice, go in riding dress – she has a fondness for a well-turned leg in top-boots.'

Having secured a promise of a place in the Colonel's carriage to convey him back to town, Jarrett walked Charles to his curricle. The groom handed over the reins and swung up behind his master. Charles waved as the horses set off.

'Remember! You are to make your peace with Tiplady and I look forward to our reunion in a day or so – I shall bring the drawings I made for Thorpe!' he shouted. With that parting shot he swept out of sight.

When Jarrett returned to the Queen's Head Mr and Mrs Bedlington were nowhere to be seen. He slipped up the stairs and quietly opened the door to his chamber. The first thing he noticed was his silver shaving kit laid out on a fine laundered cloth on the chest of drawers, then, leaning against the wall by the window, his easel and cherished paint box. Amid a freshly created sense of comfort a familiar figure sat by the fire. A pair of spectacles on his nose and an array of coloured silks laid out across his knee, Tiplady was calmly setting stitches in a tambour frame. Unlike Lady Catherine, Tiplady had a preference for coloured work. He was a skilled embroiderer. The housekeeper at Ravensworth much admired the set of chair-seats he had worked for her and gave them pride of place in her parlour. The valet looked up.

'Oh, Mr Jarrett. I did not expect you so soon.' Folding up his materials and setting them neatly in a wooden box, he rose to face his master.

Tiplady was of small stature yet possessed a head that was cast for a greater man. He had craggy features topped by thick grey hair, swept off his brow in a natural wave. His noble nose overhung a slightly petulant mouth, while his majestic eyebrows sheltered pale eyes that were a touch timid. The endowment of such a head on so short a body gave Tiplady a tendency to a haughty look as he always took care to stretch up to his full height and had a habit of surveying the world down his masterful nose even when looking up to taller men.

For a moment master and servant gazed at one another. Tiplady's mouth compressed into a thin line. Master Raif looked run-ragged. It had not taken Tiplady long to draw the account of his master's late adventures from the well of Mrs Bedlington's indignation. Tiplady was intensely loyal to the family he served. His self-respect was intimately bound up with the respect due his master. He was simmering with indignation at the inhabitants of Woolbridge for their late treatment of Mr Jarrett. The very thought of his gentleman being thrown – however briefly – into a common lock-up revolted his passionate attachment to the proper order of things. The fact that this outrage had taken place while he,

Tiplady, was away from his post compounded his shame at the misunderstanding that had taken place in York. The upshot was that he was very nearly not on speaking terms with his Mr Jarrett.

'You've been getting into scrapes, I hear,' he said, looking two inches to the right of his master's face.

Jarrett gave him an endearing smile.

'What do you expect, Tip – my man wasn't with me.' He crossed the room and stretched out an arm. 'Forgiven and forgotten?'

Tiplady wrung the proffered hand with tears in his eyes.

'Oh, Master Raif, I have been in such distress. My stomach has been paining me fit to die. I've not eaten more than a morsel of bread and a sup of tea since Wednesday.'

Jarrett put on a compassionate face and braced himself for the hours of words to come.

As the evening wore on Tiplady talked himself into a calmer frame of mind. He still listed the various mental and physical tortures consequent on his master's inconsiderate behaviour, but the narrative lost its desperate edge, composing itself into a routine account recorded for payment in due time. Jarrett reflected ruefully that he was back in service. He ate the supper that Tiplady had brought to his room with good grace. (Tiplady was not having his gentleman eating in some common parlour.) He was speculating how much longer he would have to endure before he could decently dismiss his valet without causing fresh offence, when there was a knock on the door. Pushing back the table that caged him in his deep winged chair, Jarrett started up. Tiplady set him back in his place with a look and a waggish wave of a finger. With irritating stateliness the valet advanced and opened the door a crack. He held a murmured conversation with someone without. Jarrett leant his head back and deliberately unclenched his teeth. This was his penance. He must take it like a man.

Tiplady closed the door softly. An object caught his eye

and he turned to straighten something on a side table.

'Well?' prompted Jarrett.

'The innkeeper's boy, Master Raif,' the valet responded calmly.

'And what did he want?'

'Some tale about a rough-looking man at the kitchen door asking to see His Grace's agent!' Mr Tiplady scoffed. 'I told him to be off. Foolish scrap! To think of troubling you with such impudence. And after dark too. I've a notion to give the innkeeper a piece of my mind. Fancy allowing beggars to trouble gentlemen guests at his inn!'

The valet gave a start. Master Raif was halfway out of the door.

'Mr Jarrett! Sir!'

'Thank Mrs Bedlington for my fine dinner, Tip,' his departing master called back from the stairs. 'Can't say when I shall return, so don't wait up.'

Jarrett caught up with Jack, the innkeeper's son, on the gallery steps leading to the yard. He was a bright eyed boy with a serious face.

'Master Jack! You have a message for me?'

'Your man said not to trouble you. Said I was foolish. I did try, Mr Jarrett, but he wouldn't let me.' Jack was flushed with indignation. He had formed an admiration for his parents' favourite guest. To a twelve-year-old boy, being a suspect in a murder case adds a certain dash to a man's character, but Jack had privately decided that Mr Tiplady was a poisonous old goose. The Duke's agent patted the lad's shoulder consolingly.

'Never mind, Jack. I'm afraid Mr Tiplady is rather stuck in his ways; you and I just have to put up with them.' Jack exchanged a wise look of sympathy with his hero. 'I thank you for your trouble,' Jarrett continued. 'Now: what was the message?'

'One of the maids told me, sir. A man was asking after you at the kitchen door.'

'A man? It was not a Mr Duffin?'

Jack was cross. He and Mr Duffin were particular friends; he would have been a much better messenger than a silly maid. 'I did ask her.' His round face was creased with irritation. 'But the foolish piece didn't know, Mr Jarrett. She only helps out sometimes and I wasn't there.'

'Was there any message?' Jarrett asked.

'That this man had information for you and you were to meet him by Johanson's tomb in the churchyard.'

'Johanson's tomb? Do you know which one that is?'

'It's the great big one with carvings on it – on the rise at the back of the church, by the door where the choirmen go in.' Jack found this all very thrilling. He eyed Mr Jarrett with attentive respect. Mr Jarrett looked out across the yard to the shadowy street. It was a dark night. The moon was hidden behind clouds and the wind was up, tossing the trees in the darkness of the churchyard beyond. He sent the boy to fetch a lamp and descended the stairs, searching the yard with thoughtful eyes. He spotted a short piece of lead pipe leaning against a wall. He crossed over and picked it up, balancing it in his hand. It had a good weight and was not too unwieldy. He turned to the lad who hurried towards him bearing a lighted lantern.

'Jack, I need you to be my watchman.' He took the lantern from him, speaking decisively. 'Stay here, on this side of the street, and listen out. If you hear any shouts from the churchyard, or if I am not back by the time the church clock strikes the next half hour, you fetch me some help. Will you do that for me?'

Jack drew himself up to his full height, his bright eyes wide. 'You can count on me, Mr Jarrett; I'll not let you down.'

'Good lad. And if help is needed, you fetch your father

– do you understand? I don't want you following me.'

Jack nodded. He was a sensible lad, and besides, he was afraid of the dark. He swallowed hard as he watched Mr Jarrett cross the street and melt into the shadows around the wicket gate.

Moving softly on the grass, the lantern cloaked under his coat and the lead pipe held ready by his side, Jarrett worked carefully around the deserted church. As he came round the back of the building he spotted a large coffin tomb from the last century. Its elaborate carvings of trumpets, skeletons and cherubs were barely discernible at that distance but as he crept closer the moving shadows transformed the carved cherubs into unsettled spirits, half-formed creatures protruding from the stone, striving to break free into the dark. There was a distinct sense of movement to his right. Jarrett searched the shadows half-hoping to see a familiar yellow shape emerge. But there was no sign of the poacher's dog. With a jolt he realised where he was. It was standing on the other side of this same tomb that Sunday that he had first laid eyes on Black-Eyed Sal.

An aggressive figure sprang up on the far side of the tomb. Jarrett caught the glint of light on a blade and stepped back on to the path where he could sense clear space around him. He hoped that the sound of movement on gravel would be distinct enough to give him some warning if an assault was to come from behind. He placed the lantern on the ground and crouched down a little, balancing his weight more evenly, feeling the heavy pipe in his hand.

It was not Duffin but a smaller man, his face in shadow. His shape bobbed from side to side as he shifted his weight nervously. He edged closer around the tomb. Stepping towards the lantern light the man thrust a hand forward, holding out a printed piece of paper.

'This mean money?'

Jarrett did not recognise the voice. He suspected the accent was not local. Taking care to keep out of range of the man's knife, Jarrett advanced a step. The man was holding a copy of the handbill he had had printed concerning the assault on the road to Greta Bridge. Jarrett looked into the face of one of his assailants. It was the smaller of the two; the one Walcheren had winded. Apparently the man could not read.

'The intention was to offer money for information leading to your arrest, and that of your companion,' he explained, trying not to sound amused. 'For your assault on me, you understand.' The miner ignored him.

'But you'd give money for information?'

'What kind of information?' Jarrett was puzzled.

'Word is you've been asking after the Tallyman.'

'You have information about the Tallyman?' Jarrett was sceptical.

The man stepped back from the light. He seemed to be struggling to unwrap something from around his waist. He shook out a bundle of material. Keeping a firm grip on it, he spread it out towards the light. It was a coat. A blue coat, large in size. Too large to fit the man holding it – and there were dark stains on it. Jarrett stretched out a hand to finger the material but the man twitched it out of his reach, pushing the blade towards him to warn him off.

'It's blood,' he stated.

Jarrett straightened up thoughtfully.

'Why should I give you money for this?'

'Not for the coat. This tells you I know what I know. You give me money and I'll tell you more.'

'What can you tell me?'

'I know plenty; about him – the Tallyman.'

'And his master?'

The miner snorted. 'I've no mind to stir him against me. I reckon you know enough about him, and if you don't I'm not the one to tell you more.'

'This coat matches a description of a murderer's coat – a case of the murder of a crofter up on Stainmoor a few days back. There's an offer of twenty pounds for information that leads to the capture of that villain.'

'Twenty pounds!' The man gave a humourless laugh that caught in his throat and made him cough. 'That's a tidy sum. But you have to catch him first.'

'Do you know if this Tallyman killed the crofter?'

The man's face grew cunning. 'I'd say that were his blood.'

'What reason could this Tallyman have to kill some poor wretch of a crofter on Stainmoor?'

'Tallyman was told to disappear for a while, you arriving all of a sudden, asking questions. Tallyman was travelling and he got hungry. Reckon the stupid bastard woke, that's all. It'll be a daft turn if he hangs for that after all he's done,' the man reflected.

'So you're telling me he is back in Woolbridge, this Tallyman?'

'His kind always come back.'

'And you're not afraid of such a man? Why betray him to me?'

'I'm not from here. I'm moving on – and I need travelling money.'

The miner jerked forward, his knife at the ready. Jarrett shifted the lead pipe into the light.

'Maybe your information is worth a coin or two.' Jarrett spoke crisply, as if they were bargaining in a market rather than squaring up to kill one another. 'But there is something else I would pay real money for – if you are a man to get it for me.'

The shape before him stilled. 'Speak on.'

'Books – some half-burnt books. The Tallyman fetched them for his master from the manor house where James Crotter died. If you can bring me news of those, I'd pay you well.'

'How much?'

'Ten pounds?'

The man rubbed a hand over his pallid mouth. 'Books? Tallyman's no reading man. Them books'll be his master's business. I've told you, I've no mind to bring him down on me.'

'Twenty pounds.'

The man stared and licked his lips. 'He has no suspicion of me,' he muttered to himself.

'A man can travel a goodly distance on twenty pounds,' commented Jarrett. 'If you cannot bring me the books themselves I will still be interested in their whereabouts.' He did not believe that the man had any chance of performing such a task. So cunning a manipulator as Raistrick would be unlikely to let such a pawn near any of his secrets. Still, it was worth setting off a ferret or two; it might stir something up.

The man made his decision. 'Done,' he said. 'I'll be here tomorrow night then.'

'That is not convenient – the next night.'

The man was reluctant, but Jarrett was not to be moved. 'If you cannot wait an extra day...' He shrugged and picked up the lantern as if to leave.

'Night after next then,' the man called out. 'I'll be here when the clock strikes midnight – and I'll not linger.'

Jarrett threw a golden coin into the light. 'For good faith,' he said.

The man snatched it up, slipped around the tomb and disappeared as suddenly as he had come.

Jarrett waited a moment, listening to the wind moving about the silent graves. An interesting interview. Picking up his lantern, he pondered the odds that the man would keep their rendezvous. Then, the lead pipe resting jauntily on his shoulder, he marched back to the Queen's Head to relieve his watchman and make for bed.

CHAPTER ELEVEN

'I am advised to sweat, sir. I have a merino gown, a shawl, a wadded cloak and a fur tippet and I perspire, sir, I perspire. It does me no good at all but the doctors wish it.'

Lady Yarbrook was ensconced in a low wicker chaise, her round face flushed and polished with sweat. Her hair was dyed an improbable shade of foxy brown and supplemented by lavish curls of false hair. Instead of the usual carriage bonnet, a Spanish mantilla hung in swags from a silver comb, its airy lace in strange contrast to the bundle of clothes in which she had wrapped her stout frame. She squinted at Jarrett's letter of introduction, held at arm's length between thumb and forefinger.

'Earewith sends you – but how delightful. And how is the sweet boy? You have come just in time to join me on my promenade, Mr Jarrett. Smithers!'

This last proved to be a command to the groom who stood by the head of the plump grey pony snoozing between the shafts. Touching his hat to his mistress, Smithers roused the animal and they set off, Jarrett striding to keep pace with the chaise, while its occupant offered up conversation in a penetrating voice.

'There is a repose, a freedom and a security in a *vie de château*, do you not agree, Mr Jarrett?' she announced, looking about her with a proprietary air. 'When I set out to walk, I feel as if alone in the world — nothing but trees and birds.'

Jarrett tried to look agreeable while he searched his mind

for an appropriate response to this opening gambit. His hostess's head was turned from him, regally contemplating the view while awaiting some apposite riposte. They jogged comfortably past an exquisitely clipped hedge. The hedge terminated and behind it a woman in a gingham dress and a black bonnet appeared on her knees picking up weeds. Nature in Lady Yarbrook's solitary world was remarkably well schooled. His companion was becoming restless. Her fingers drummed a tattoo on the carriage side in the manner of a grand master waiting on a dilatory pupil.

'And add to these retired leisure, That in trim gardens takes his pleasure,' he quoted with as much air as he could muster.

Lady Yarbrook shot him an acute look. 'Milton?' she demanded, swift to congratulate herself on her own erudition. The mood that had looked likely to turn stormy set fair with a playful smile. 'Frederick Jarrett,' she mused. 'As I recall, you are a kinsman of Earewith's, are you not? On the dear Duke's side?'

Jarrett bowed diplomatically. 'I am fortunate to be held as one of the family, ma'am.'

His hostess's shrewd dark eyes weighed him up. 'I believe you are a soldier and a painter, sir,' she stated abruptly. It clearly amused her to see she had taken him aback. Jarrett's intimate circle knew of his hobby but it was not a talent he boasted of. The liquid brown eyes held a note of triumph as well as humour. 'Ha!' the lady exclaimed complacently, settling back once more.

Jarrett recognised the type. One of those capable women born with too much energy and intelligence to suit the confines of society; under-employed souls in whom boredom breeds a passion for ferreting out the secrets of others. He would need to step warily. Her small coup, however, seemed to have assuaged Lady Yarbrook's mischievous curiosity for the moment.

'Well, this is delightful. I was feeling very dull today and now I am sent an unexpected cavalier to improve my constitutional. Fortune smiles indeed!' she announced, bestowing a particularly winsome smile of her own on her guest.

The path before them turned and a brick orangery appeared, set above a lawn. Its high windows were unpegged and removed for the summer, leaving an open cloister. Through the arches the orange trees could be seen, ripening fruit nestling among the dark leaves. Scattered artlessly before the trees was a collection of cherubs with foreshortened legs, posed on speckled marble plinths.

'How do you like my Seasons?' asked Lady Yarbrook as the chaise paused before the arcade. 'That is Winter – the sweet boy.'

The sweet boy was plumply naked. In concession to the cold of his theme he had a sort of fat blanket draped over his head and shoulders. The resigned look of stately piety he wore deflected any sympathy Jarrett might have felt for his predicament. He produced a polite sound of general appreciation while he made a show of inspecting the group. His hostess's rich voice cut short his performance.

'And what brings you to me, Mr Jarrett? I fancy you are not come to admire my statuary.'

He turned to find her contemplating him, her fantastic head cocked to one side. She had a plain face but her countenance was animated by wit and a directness of spirit that was engaging.

'You are not going to try gammoning me that you are in the habit of doing the pretty about the neighbourhood? I would not believe you, you know,' she ended, a roguish lift of an eyebrow robbing the statement of any offence.

He grinned back. 'To tell you the truth, Lady Yarbrook,' he lied, 'I have a fascination with playhouses. I intend to build one of my very own at my house in Lincolnshire,' he elaborated, as if in a rush of enthusiasm. 'Learning of the theatre you have constructed here and finding myself within calling distance, I begged Charles to give me an introduction.'

The lady crowed with delight. 'A fellow Thespian! But I am charmed. My good angel must have sent you, Mr Jarrett. Your visit is perfectly timed. Why, at this very moment my guests and I are getting up a performance of *Volpone* – Jonson's play, you know. You are not familiar with his work? Oh, but Ben Jonson is a great discovery!' She snatched up a leather-bound volume from the seat beside her and began to search through it as she talked. 'I have the part of Celia. A female of great virtue and much beset by perfidious men. The play is most curious. I swear you will be mightily amused. There – you may read Volpone for me while I rehearse my lines; he is a great rogue who wishes to seduce me. Let me begin.' She pointed at the opened page and cleared her throat. '"Oh, God and his good angels! Whither, whither is shame fled human breasts?"'

She had a formidable voice and she threw it with great clarity. At this rate they would be overheard in Gainford, he thought, as he attempted to gather his wits to respond. He scanned the page. Celia's speech was short. Volpone's part appeared to bear the burden of the scene.

It is no simple matter to declaim a passage sight unseen whilst walking alongside a carriage along an unfamiliar path. Somehow he managed to reach the end of his allotted piece without stumbling either vocally or physically. His hostess appeared to approve of his reading. She fastened her eyes on him as he spoke, following every shift of expression, her features rapt with attention. Out of the corner of one eye he saw her swell and gather herself up as he came to his last line.

'"Now art thou welcome!"' he declared.

'"Sir!"' his Celia responded with energy.

'"Nay, fly me not",' Jarrett read on gamely.

His hostess waved a practical hand. 'Aye, aye and all the rest. You may skip the song. Only give me my cue. Come now: "To be taken, to be seen, these have crimes accounted been",' she prompted. 'I think that very fine, do you not agree?'

'Indeed, ma'am, very good,' he responded and repeated the cue obediently.

'"Some serene blast me",' exclaimed Celia, rocking the little chaise as she flung up one massive arm in a classical gesture, '"or dire lightening strike this",' she paused, modulating her rich voice, '"my offending face",' she intoned.

The painted clock over the stables chimed. Smithers slowed the pony and a polite cough drifted up from his stolid back view.

'The clock has struck three, my lady.'

His mistress dropped her part with disarming swiftness.

'Dear me, but you are right, Smithers! When I am with the muse I am quite forgetful of the passing of time! Mr Jarrett, I must return for my rest. The doctor insists upon it. Regular rest and a careful diet – lamb and potatoes with raspberry vinegar and a little light wine. 'Tis the one remedy for biliousness. It is tiresome but I must have a care, I am so easily done up.' She sighed gustily. 'It is an affliction to be born with a fragile constitution but I never complain, for what is the use, say I?' She favoured her guest with a sunny smile. 'You make an elegant Volpone, Mr Jarrett, your voice is excellent. I could hardly believe you did not know the play, you read so well.'

She flung out her hands towards him, her sturdy body swept up by a sudden thought. 'I wonder – might I persuade you to join my little band of players? To be candid, my current Volpone is not up to the task. It is a part that requires a reserve and dry wit he lacks, but you, sir...' Her eyes pleaded with him.

'You flatter me more than I can say, Lady Yarbrook, but

I regret I cannot. Besides, I fear you have formed too high an opinion of my talent. I understood you have some professional players among your troop; I could not hope to rival their skill.'

'Professionals!' she scoffed, then relented. 'I dare say Francis Mulrohney makes a tolerable Mosca but he cannot double up to play Volpone as well, and so for the present my chaplain takes the part. Don't mistake me, my boys are well enough, but they are outward men, entirely unstuffed, not one idea or *qualité* of understanding between them. Will you not take pity on me, Mr Jarrett?'

They were back at the house by the time he managed to convince her that pressing business forced him to forgo the considerable pleasure of performing opposite her Celia.

'If you cannot join my players, Mr Jarrett, will you return to dine with me? The hour is too advanced to be thinking of journeying on today. Why do you not rest at Gainford for tonight? The Blue Boar on the green is the best hostelry. You must go there. But first my man will show you my jewel, my little theatre. It will amuse you.'

He suspected, given the complacent look with which she said this, that Lady Yarbrook would in truth be mightily offended if her theatre did anything less than profoundly impress him. He countered her dazzling smile with one of his most charming and bowed his eager acceptance of her kindness.

'Smithers will see to you. Until five o'clock then.'

He was standing in what had once been an elegant dining room of regular shape on the ground floor. The fine proportions of the room had been stopped up and unbalanced by a proscenium stage that took up a good third of the space. The exterior of the arch was painted in soft blue and white and adorned with cartouches within which Greek gods disported themselves, picked out in gilt. A half-finished backdrop, held within a painting frame, filled the back wall. Before it was slung a painting bridge on which the artist could be winched up and down his canvas. The ghost of his recent presence lingered around a carelessly pushed-aside trestle table, covered with a muddle of pots of paint and long-handled brushes.

Jarrett climbed the miniature flight of gilt steps up on to the boards to take a closer look. The flat depicted a grand Italian interior in which a pair of glass doors opened out on to a sun-baked terrace with a prettily rendered perspective of green countryside beyond. The English view sat oddly beyond the Italian setting. As he inspected the half-finished canvas with professional curiosity he had an odd association. In colour, light and space the scene through the windows somehow recalled to his mind the view from the white rock opposite his folly. He shook off the thought. The matter was so much on his mind it intruded in everything.

He whiled away twenty minutes to give his supposed admiration decent rein, then allowed the bored servant to show him out. As he followed in the wake of the man across the chequered marble hall he heard voices. Through the open door of a library he sensed the presence of a convivial group.

'I don't believe a word of it, Mulrohney! Don't listen to the rogue!' exclaimed an unseen listener.

'Neither do I,' chimed in another. 'But he tells the tale so well I hardly care. Go on, Mulrohney – what happened next?'

Mulrohney resumed his tale in a voice redolent with Irish charm. There was a ripple of laughter and movement in the room as the story-teller repositioned himself. He stood bisected by the half-open door, his back to the hall. He was a medium-sized man, about Jarrett's own height and build. A glancing shaft of sunlight illuminated his bright hair – as bright as a guinea of gold.

*

'Have you come from London, Mr Jarrett? Do you bring news? How fares the Government? I hear His Highness the Prince Regent is to be found dining with the ministers. The wretch! I never thought to see us so betrayed!'

His neighbour was a lively person of a certain age, an actress who had gained some popularity in comic roles at Drury Lane. Although she had a pretty figure, she suffered from a massive nose, the protrusion of which pulled every other feature after it. Rarely had a nose tyrannised so completely over a human face. Since its owner was also good-humoured and in the habit of baring the white teeth beneath it, Jarrett's fixed impression of his dinner companion was dominated by bone and teeth, behind the mass of which lurked a pair of merry eyes.

'You are a Whig, ma'am?'

'And you are not, sir?'

'I am no politician, ma'am.'

'Surely you cannot be so careless of the affairs of the nation as to be content to abandon them to the petty plots and ploys of puny politicians, sir!' A philosopher leant across the table towards him with the staring intensity of a human carp moulded in wax. 'See where that attitude has led us, sir! To sink our prosperity in the mire of Spain and Portugal, that is where, sir!'

'Mr Price, I cannot allow you that!' exclaimed his neighbour, leaping to engage this challenge with obvious relish.

He left the antagonists to bombard each other with verbal salvoes. Lady Yarbrook held court opposite him, seated between an aging poet with a vast appetite and the actor, Francis Mulrohney. The impression of nakedness was startling. Not that the lady of the house displayed a greater proportion of flesh than any of the other females scattered about her board, it was merely that the ampleness of Lady Yarbrook's charms covered a greater acreage. It was as if he faced a mountain of nakedness across the table; a mountain topped by a mercurial countenance about which humour and emotion flashed like a summer storm. There was an undeniable fascination about her. Her vitality was mesmerising. One minute she entranced with her lightning wit, the next she appeared almost clownish in her exuberance and foolish prejudices. She had a habit of folding her vast naked arms across her ample chest when the debate became fierce or the wit too barbed. Jarrett found himself touched by an unexpected hint of vulnerability under the mass of brilliance and clumsy arrogance. To her clients and protégés, however, Lady Yarbrook was clearly a hard mistress.

'This play is too long, Mr Mulrohney. You must cut it again. The business between that dreadful knight and Peregrine – it gives me a headache it is so tedious.'

A full-face view of Mr Mulrohney revealed him to have the even features and colouring of the best actors. They combined to give him a countenance bland enough to be thought unremarkable or handsome according to the light and character he chose to play. His manner towards his patroness was charming and easy; nevertheless Jarrett discerned a weary glaze in the attentive look he wore as he waited for his chance to speak.

'But Lady Yarbrook, Mr Nugent is most skilful as Sir Politic and Mr Nesbitt makes a comely Peregrine – you have said so yourself. He would be mortified to have his part cut, you know he worships you.'

She glanced down the table at the handsome profile of Mr Nesbitt, a youth barely out of his teens, and softened. 'Poor boy!' she exclaimed indulgently. 'Perhaps you are right, but the scene is most dreadfully dull. Can you not find a way to shorten it while leaving poor Perry some place to shine? Of course you can, Francis, you are a clever, clever man. You will do this for me. And perhaps you may also contrive for Celia to be on stage more,' she added as if tacking on some small, inconsequential request. 'The play cannot hang without her and yet she is hardly ever seen! I cannot imagine what Mr Jonson was thinking of.'

Jarrett's sympathy for the unfortunate Mulrohney grew as the dinner wound on its discursive way; it reached a peak when the conversation happened on the topic of the Irish. Mr Price was practically choleric on the subject.

'Make 'em cower, that's what I say. Why, they would treat with Boney at the first opportunity, the mischievous dogs!'

'Mr Price! You insult me. I am Irish!' stated his hostess, her cheeks flushed. Lady Yarbrook might not wish to reside in the country of her husband's birth but she had a strong affection for being contrary to strongly held opinions.

'Dear lady, I do not refer to you, nor to your respected spouse, nor to any of our kind, but to the native paddy. There is a mean spirit about him that cannot be trusted.'

'What think you, Francis?' Lady Yarbrook turned to the actor by her side. 'Do you hate the English?'

It was plain to anyone who paid the least attention to his frozen expression that Mr Mulrohney was finding the conversation painful. Jarrett wondered whether his hostess was being mischievous or merely remarkably dull-witted.

'Ogh, no!' replied Mulrohney in a parody of a pantomime paddy. 'For to be sure England is a wonderful place – plenty of tai and fine craim for breakfast and all the convaniences. I'm fairly out of Ireland, I'll be tellin' you!'

'So you are content among us, Francis?' Lady Yarbrook dipped a flirtatious look under long eyelashes, oblivious to the sharp edge concealed in her neighbour's words.

''Tis like Heaven himself, lady. I might be in the air with the angels, that I might.'

'For shame, sir!' protested Mr Price, sensing what his hostess did not.

Lady Yarbrook flicked a puzzled glance in his direction and back to Mulrohney. 'Is it joking you are, dear joy?' she enquired coyly.

Mulrohney bowed gracefully over her hand. 'No,' he replied in a low voice, 'sure enough, ma'am, I am not joking.'

In the loud pause that followed every observer waited for some outburst, but none came. Lady Yarbrook's smile remained pinned up while a bewildered look flickered in her bright eyes. All at once diversionary conversations started up around the table like birds flushed from a covert.

Jarrett found the remainder of the dinner an endurance. His sympathies were with Francis Mulrohney. The Irishman barely contained himself until the company rose to remove to the drawing room. Jarrett watched him drop back and slip away. Unnoticed he strolled out behind him.

Mulrohney was standing by a stone urn at the edge of the lawn, lighting a cigar from a burning taper. The actor greeted him with a rueful face.

'She will flourish about. All the world praises Will Shakespeare, so my lady critic must discover greater wit in some unknown scribbler. Ben Jonson was better acquainted with the Ancients, says she. That's what comes of teaching your females Greek and Latin! And yet she'll cut him without shame! We'd be better doing a farce, that we would.' He gave a twisted, apologetic smile and held out his case. 'An evil habit, but will you join me, Mr Jarrett?'

'Gladly.' Jarrett took a cigarillo and bent towards the Irishman to accept the proffered light. 'I'll warrant you have an easier time of it in the regular theatre.'

The actor snorted. 'Aye! To think we playing folk call this resting. Her damned cuts! As if we've not already lost one knight, a eunuch and two lawyers. I swear she'd take Celia's part and Volpone's too but for the difficulty of playing a telling seduction with oneself. Pardon me, saire. I'm as bitter as soot tonight,' he ended with angry self-mockery. Jarrett returned a wry smile and they smoked in companionable silence a moment under the broad night sky.

'And where might you have travelled from, Mr Jarrett?'

'I have just come from Woolbridge – do you know it?'

Mulrohney shrugged. 'And what news from Woolbridge?' he asked lightly, his tone at variance with the discontented look he threw out across the shadowy parkland. 'None, I'll warrant, for 'tis plaguey dull in the country, that it is.'

'Oh, it has its native drama, Mr Mulrohney. Why, just before I left there was a tragic death of a young girl in Woolbridge. Some black-haired laundry wench of great beauty, so I was told. It sounded to be a great tragedy – the stuff of ballad singers.'

The twilight robbed his eyes of detail, but Jarrett thought he caught the flicker of a start from the man. The actor straightened up abruptly as he crushed the ember of his cigar under foot.

'I sing ballads,' he said. Someone came to the window and called Mulrohney's name. 'And I am engaged to sing one now. The good lady dotes upon me warblin', so she does,' he elaborated, assuming the comic brogue again. 'It'll not do to keep her waiting.'

'Mr Mulrohney – if you would care to walk with me to my inn afterwards, may I entertain you with some punch? I'll wager you have a store of amusing tales.'

Mulrohney turned, illuminated by the candlelight streaming from the drawing room. 'We players are renowned good company, that we are. I'll accept your hospitality gladly, Mr Jarrett. 'Tis a queer play-actor who can bear to turn down an opportunity to talk of himself.'

A breeze had got up and the moon hid behind a bank of clouds. The dark path was patchily illuminated by the lantern Mulrohney carried aloft.

'The gel you spoke of – the one that died in Woolbridge – her name'd not be Sally Grundy, now, would it?'

Mulrohney had stopped and faced him under the insufficient

lamplight. It swung from his raised hand throwing deceptive shadows that made the vegetation around shift and dart as if alive. Jarrett kept watch for movement from the man's concealed hand, as he sketched a nod of assent. Mulrohney held his eyes a moment. Then, with a jerky gesture of his head, he resumed his progress. 'I knew her. She worked in the laundry up at the house now and then.' There was a plain simplicity in the way he said the words that left Jarrett at a loss how to respond. They walked on in silence. The buildings of Gainford appeared and soon the Blue Boar could be seen across the green, the ruddy light from its windows glowing like a heart beating in the dark emptiness of the night.

Despite the lateness of the hour the dregs of the evening's drinkers still lingered in the tap. The innkeeper settled the two gentlemen in his back parlour. He livened up the small fire in the grate and carried in a tray of ingredients and a bowl. Jarrett occupied himself making punch while his guest stretched himself out in a deep chair by the hearth. He looked up as Jarrett brought him a glass.

'Well, won't you look at me now! Pardon me, Mr Jarrett, I'm not such good company tonight.' He raised his glass with a flourish. 'May this soap me tail for me and let me slip through the rest of this performance. To two more weeks!'

Jarrett lifted his own glass and drank the toast.

'And what after two more weeks?'

'Two more weeks and, praise God, I'm back to Dublin for a season at a proper playhouse with proper actors!'

'So you knew the black-haired girl who died in Woolbridge, Mr Mulrohney?'

For a moment Jarrett regretted the question. A wild look flared up in Mulrohney's eyes and then passed.

'A beautiful creature, so she was,' he said simply. His chin sank down into his neck-tie and he returned to gazing into the fire. 'Ogh, this land o' craim and honey! Sally Grundy – who would have thought? She had a notion to go on the stage.' He looked up, defiant. 'She came to me to teach her. And I did ... some few things. A speech or two; the way to stand and move about the boards. She had the makings of a good little actress.' He sat forward and poked a finger in the air to underline his point. 'She had a voice and the presence for it and she was a worker, so she was.' He slumped back, self-mocking once more. 'With a pretty ankle on her, too.' He took a long gulp of the brandy punch and threw back his head to gaze at the ceiling. 'Sally Grundy – dead.' His mouth twisted on the words and he closed his eyes. A bead of moisture seeped from the corner of one lid, catching the light. He sat up, planting his feet with a growl, as if shaking himself awake. 'I need more punch! Melancholia is but the second stage of an Irishman's inebriation. Help me on me way to the next, Mr Jarrett.'

'Isn't that oblivion, Mr Mulrohney?' Jarrett asked as he poured him another glass.

'Hell, no – you'll be forgetting "fighting merry", Mr Jarrett, that comes well before oblivion.' The Irishman set down his glass and met his host's blue eyes steadily. 'You've precious little interest in the theatre, Mr Jarrett; this is about Sally Grundy. What is it you're after?'

Jarrett rotated the heavy glass in his hand. The dancing flames beyond fired the liquid into a magical ruby red.

'A good fire, a warming punch – they call for a good tale. So why not – tell me how you met this sad girl, Mr Mulrohney.'

'Sad! Sally Grundy was never sad! Not as I knew her, Mr Jarrett. She was the merriest piece!'

'But talk in Woolbridge was that she might have taken her own life.'

Mulrohney's expressive face was frankly astonished.

'Take her own life, Sal? Never!' He was emphatic. 'There are few things certain under God but Sally Grundy would never take her own life. Why, she was on the very eve of a great adventure. Last I saw of her she was full of plans. Full of plans.' He trailed off, mesmerised by the pictures the flames drew for him. 'We had plans.'

'You had plans?'

The actor gave a slight gesture, his hand falling open as if letting go of something.

'We had plans,' he repeated. 'She was coming with me to Dublin, Mr Jarrett, to try her luck on the boards.' He raised his head to meet his companion's curiosity full-face. 'She would have made her mark on the stage. I swear to you, sir, Sally Grundy must have been robbed of her life, for she'd never have thrown it away.'

'How long had you been acquainted with Miss Grundy, Mr Mulrohney?'

The shifting light from the fire deepened the lines on the actor's face, endowing it with gravity and weight. At that moment Francis Mulrohney might have played King Lear.

'A few weeks perhaps.' He dismissed the importance of time. 'But when you are closeted together, as you must be to coin a part or a play, Mr Jarrett, you soon get to know a body. We were of a kind, her and me.'

'And you had no suspicion that anything troubled her?'

'No.' He shook his head as if the motion itself was soothing to his troubled spirits.

Jarrett could not help wondering about the scene they played there in that room, coloured by the red glow of the fire. Had Francis Mulrohney been on stage so long that it had become second nature to perform his emotions, or was he playing a part assumed for the occasion?

'There was an old suitor who'd vexed her,' he was saying. 'Some booby who'd married another. Taken the easier path, I reckon. Sal was not the wifely kind.'

'How vexed was she? Might she have made trouble for the man?'

'How? What could the lass have done? Full sure, she was

affronted, but no more than that. She might have been planning a bit of mischief – she had an impish spirit, my Sal – but she was not the kind to bear grudges. Besides, I tell you, Sally Grundy was about to leave Woolbridge and all its kind behind. Why should she concern herself?'

'She would not have sworn out a breach of promise against this man then, do you think?'

'Sal, go to law? The girl I knew would as soon think of flying!'

'I hope Mr Mulrohney made it back to the big house safe and sound, sir. The Irish, they surely know how to put it away!' The innkeeper had just brought in a fresh pot of coffee. Jarrett had woken with a thick head after the heavy drinking of the night before, and he loitered over his breakfast.

'You are acquainted with Mr Mulrohney, then?'

'He comes by every now and then. Sometimes I reckon he likes a bit of peace and common sense away from all them fancy folk up at the Hall. He's well-liked these parts, is Mr Mulrohney.'

'Has he been here long?'

The innkeeper rocked his considerable weight back on to his heels, straightening his back while he thought about it.

'More than a month it'd be now, I'd say, Mr Jarrett. A week or so back he was coming in pretty regular with a dark-haired lass; pretty as a picture she was. He would hire my back parlour to rehearse.' The big man gave a rumble of belly-laugh. 'My good wife would have it they were up to all sorts of tricks. She slipped about, hoping to catch them at it, if you get my meaning.' He gave a heavy wink. 'And blow me down but they *was* play-acting, just like he said!' The innkeeper laughed good and loud at the memory of his wife's discomfiture. 'He's a good sort of man by my reckoning – for an Irishman.'

Jarrett smiled back. 'I think I agree with you, innkeeper.'

He lingered over the papers, trying to work up the energy to set out once more on the road to Woolbridge. There was a knock on the parlour door and the innkeeper put his head round.

'You have a visitor, Mr Jarrett.'

The innkeeper stepped aside to reveal his companion of the night before. Francis Mulrohney came into the parlour dressed with a careful correctness, marred only by the slightly over-exuberant yellow of his waistcoat. He came forward stiffly. His casual conviviality seemed to have abandoned him in the broad light of day. His sallow skin bore the marks of excess, and there was a chalky look about his red-rimmed eyes. He put together a smile that was but an echo of his old charm.

'You are returning to Woolbridge today, Mr Jarrett?'

'I am. I took my leisure this morning. May I offer you some coffee?'

'No, I thank you. I brought you this.' The Irishman handed him a letter addressed in a florid black hand: '"To whom it may concern". Read it. I'll wait,' he added awkwardly.

Darting the man a puzzled look, Jarrett unfolded the document and read:

I, Margaret, Lady Yarbrook, do solemnly testify that Francis Mulrohney, native of the City of Cork, County Cork, has been a guest in my house, Mannerly, at Gainford these past six weeks. On the night of Wednesday, 31 July past, he formed, as usual, one of the company who dined with me. I am able to swear to his whereabouts for there was a storm that night and my guests and I were occupied conducting certain electrical experiments under the tuition of Mr Wilsbury of Chichester, the renowned scientist, until past 5 o'clock of the following morning.

I and the undersigned, who were also present, vouch for this to be the truth.

The other signatories to this document included an archdeacon, a poet whose name Jarrett recognised and Mr Wilsbury of Chichester himself. He looked up at the Irishman.

'I told her of the matter,' he explained. 'My generous patroness, Lady Yarbrook, has offered to pay my expenses should I be required to travel to Woolbridge to testify before the magistrates,' he added formally.

His face melted into a disarming frankness and the real Francis Mulrohney slipped out, a wry, shrewd Irish adventurer, well acquainted with himself and the world.

'You've no need to say it, Mr Jarrett, and I've no need to ask who you are, but you think Sally Grundy was murdered and there is no reason on this earth why you would trust the word of an unknown Irish vagabond.' He shrugged, indicating the document. 'So I took me precautions.'

'This must put you beyond suspicion.'

Mulrohney nodded. He let out a breath and offered his hand. Jarrett shook it firmly.

'I am glad to make your acquaintance, Mr Mulrohney.'

The actor's face lifted with a roguish smile.

'Would that it had been under happier circumstances,' he agreed. As he reached the door he paused and turned. 'Last I saw of Sally Grundy she was swinging away down the lane, light as a bird. She laughed at me and said she was off to give a performance that night. When I asked her to tell me more, she just called out that she might tell me one day. She was a nice little creature. It'll be many a long day before I forget Sally Grundy.'

CHAPTER TWELVE

Jarrett dawdled his way back towards Woolbridge after the interview with Mulrohney. Somewhere a mile or two beyond Gainford he took a wrong turn. It was not until a blissful sweep of country opened out before him, and he gave Walcheren his head, that it occurred to him the mistake had been deliberate. The big bay's legs stretched out below him and they flew over the ground. They galloped up rises of turf and jumped down steps of moor like mad things. On Walcheren's back he was free of the past; free of the looks, the murmurs and speculations. In those brief, self-sufficient moments there was nothing but sunlight and sky and open ground and two healthy animals moving in harmony.

At last they were both tired. Walcheren's chestnut flanks foamed white and Jarrett's own muscles grew dull. He reined the animal back and turned him for home. The hedgerows were lengthened by shadows as he brought them back to the valley where Woolbridge lay. Lulled by the rhythm of Walcheren's hooves striking the baked earth, he found himself in the lane that led past the gateway to Oakdene Hall. Perhaps Sir Thomas had returned. He should call to present his apologies. The Colonel's petty session now fixed for the next day would prevent him keeping the appointment he had made with the baronet. Besides, he had several hours to fill before his assignation with his informant in the churchyard and he was loath to drag them out at the Queen's Head with Tiplady fussing around him.

The drive forked and he took the left-hand branch that

circled to the rear of the hall. Cresting a gently rising lawn, he saw a rose garden encircled by a set of clipped box hedges. He caught a snatch of the pastel rose of a woman's dress as it flitted past a gap between the dense green blocks. Intrigued, he dismounted and led his horse across the lawn.

The honeyed amber light of the setting sun seemed to encompass him in a dream. Spikes of parched grass snapped under the leather soles of his boots. The long shadows from the rose garden stretched out to draw him near. Wafted through the soft stillness, with the scent of roses, he heard a woman's voice singing. It was an Irish air with a strongly marked beat. The dreamlike quality of the scene was accentuated by an unmistakable pianoforte accompaniment executed with forceful precision.

'Oh, stay! Oh, stay!'

sang the voice gaily.

'Joy so seldom weaves a chain
Like these tonight, that oh 'tis pain
To break its link so soon.'

It was a tuneful voice and it conveyed the words with playful aplomb. Jarrett approached the hedge and paused, concealed, to peep into the magical enclosure of the rose garden.

First he saw Lady Catherine, a large white chip hat forming a pavilion over her eccentric shape. She rested her hunched frame on a high stool while her thin hands jumped about the keys of a decorative little pianoforte. As she struck out the gay melody her body moved from side to side with the lilt of the music. Before he could recover from the astonishment of this sight, he saw the singer. Bound up in the spirit of her song, Henrietta Lonsdale danced in a pale pink dress against the rich backdrop of a profusion of crushed-velvet roses.

An Englishman's upbringing does not excel in preparing him to meet unconventional behaviour with equanimity. Jarrett's first reaction was a sort of smirk that so respectable a pair of ladies should disport themselves in such a fashion. But as he stood at the edge of the garden, peering in on the scene, its charm crept up on him. Henrietta's graceful form embodied the joy of the music completely, uninhibited by the plastic manners that society imposes. He caught himself admiring her honesty and sensed a fleeting melancholy that his own nature would never allow him to experience a similar freedom. As the first flush of embarrassment receded, his artist's eye gradually perceived in Lady Catherine's awkward movements a graceful dancer made clownish by the misfortune of a misshapen body. He watched in rapt silence, the spirit of the rose garden infecting him with a sliver of regret that he should be excluded from the intimacy of the two performers.

The song ended. Henrietta bowed to her pianist, flushed and laughing. Lady Catherine beamed back in a way Jarrett would previously have thought inconceivable. All at once he was aware of his dilemma in lurking behind the hedge. The violent consciousness of his guilt in trespassing on so private a moment rooted him to the spot. Embarrassment piled up on confusion as he overheard Miss Lonsdale speak his name.

'What connection might Mr Jarrett be to the Marquess, do you suppose, Lady Catherine?'

There was a ribald chuckle from the old lady.

'Connection? Connection, Miss Henrietta? It seems to me Mr Jarrett don't wish to acknowledge any connection between them.'

Miss Lonsdale's tone shifted, reflecting curiosity half-reined in by a desire to smooth over a potential *faux pas*.

'I only ask because,' she began slowly, 'I had a notion they might be related. They have a similar ironic glance they give one when something in the company amuses them. And I fancy there is a resemblance about the lower portion of the face – some look about the mouth.' Miss Lonsdale seemed to catch herself and ended with an airy question. 'Is Sir Thomas an intimate friend of the Duke's, Lady Catherine?'

'Intimate enough to be discreet,' responded the old reprobate.

In any normal circumstances Jarrett could exonerate himself of the sin of gossip. Friends and family were in the habit of teasing him for his indifference to the minutiae of acquaintances' emotions and opinions of one another. And yet, although every social instinct told him to slip away, Raif Jarrett lingered behind his bush.

'Do you not find Mr Jarrett a fine artist, ma'am?' asked Miss Lonsdale. 'That portrait he took of Sally Grundy was very like. Of course, she was a strikingly beautiful girl. It is only natural that a man would notice her.'

'And what concern is it to you if Mr Jarrett noticed her, girl?'

Walcheren chose this particular moment to protest at having to stand so long. He tossed his head against the stiff bush with a deafening snort, and nudged his master impatiently. Rudely pushed from concealment, Jarrett was forced out into the garden to face its startled occupants.

'Lady Catherine – I beg your pardon. It was not my intention to intrude. I was passing and – Sir Thomas – I wondered if Sir Thomas had returned? Your servant, ma'am. Miss Lonsdale.'

Miss Lonsdale stood frozen, her left arm stretched out to rest on Lady Catherine's pianoforte.

'Why, Mr Jarrett.' The young woman spoke as if she were quite accustomed to visitors leaping out unannounced from behind bushes. 'I have a message for you...' All at once, a rosy flush suffused Henrietta's skin and she looked away in confusion. The old lady rose from her stool, her face composed into a polite mask that Jarrett found several degrees more unsettling than her habitual look of mischief. Threading her arm through Jarrett's she hurried him to a little bench.

'Come in, come in, Mr Jarrett. You will drink tea with us. Fancy! Take his horse and fetch us some tea.'

The bewildered Mr Jarrett noticed the maid who had been sitting behind her mistress. Fancy had a distinctive face that appeared to have been moulded out of uncooked dough. Two dull button eyes looked him up and down. Returning the compliment he stared back. Lady Catherine's maid was a short woman with a deep bosom that preceded her like the prow of a ship. The weight of carrying this ample endowment gave her a ram-rod bearing, as if nature's humour had been to contrast the curve of the mistress's back with excessive straightness in the servant's. Fancy began to take Walcheren's reins from him.

'Oh, no, Lady Catherine, I cannot stay! As you see,' he pointed out reasonably, 'I have ridden some way today and my horse needs attention. I do not mean to disturb you.'

Reason, however, was as nothing to Lady Catherine.

'Nonsense. Take the animal to Finlay in the stables, Fancy; tell him to have a care of the beast or he'll answer to me. Hurry, girl. We're thirsty. Tea, now!'

Jarrett seldom felt so powerless as in exclusively female company. It was too absurd to begin tussling with a middle-aged maid for possession of the reins, so he let them go. He looked after the woman as she led the big horse away, half hoping that Walcheren would not take kindly to so unconventional a groom. Indeed, a few paces across the lawn, the tall bay stopped and took a hard side-glance at the diminutive figure beside him. Fancy's pugnacious face tilted up, she mouthed some short simple words and the pair resumed their progress. Fancy, it seemed, was to be intimidated by neither man nor beast.

Lady Catherine settled herself on the bench, arranging Jarrett between her and a somewhat reticent Henrietta.

'What news, Mr Jarrett, what news?' she demanded.

'Well, ma'am, I have spoken to Miss Grundy's play-actor friend and I judge him to be out of the running.'

'That is no way to tell a tale, Mr Jarrett. Begin at the beginning. How did this Lady Yarbrook receive you?'

Reconciling himself to his predicament, Jarrett embarked on the tale of Lady Yarbrook's promenade performance and the fashion in which he was press-ganged into her rehearsal. Lady Catherine was particularly tickled by the image of Lady Yarbrook bowling along in her little wicker carriage declaiming the improbable part of a virtuous young wife, and she made him repeat his story until Fancy returned with a procession of footmen bearing tea and a tea table.

The sunset was well established. The amber light deepened and became suffused with violet. The box hedges framing the garden seemed to form a bowl in which the rosy light reflected the decadent glory of the setting sun.

'Will you pour, my dear? You know my wrists. Weak wrists, Mr Jarrett,' Lady Catherine explained. 'Have a need for a good healthy young companion with strong wrists or I'd never get me tea!' She threw her head to one side, as others might throw their heads back, and cackled at her own humour. 'We have not been idle here, Mr Jarrett.' Her bright eyes twinkled. 'No, no. We also have news, do we not, Miss Henrietta?'

After her first moment of discomfiture, Henrietta formed an oasis of serenity in the midst of this extraordinary scene. Her own manner could not be faulted, yet at the same time she managed to treat her companion's behaviour as if it were entirely unremarkable.

'My aunt's cook, Mrs Grundy, would very much like to speak with you, Mr Jarrett,' Miss Lonsdale explained. 'She has had a visit from Mrs Munday, the woman in whose house Sally Grundy lodged, that has distressed her. I do not know what passed between them but she has been most insistent that she must speak with you.'

'Would it be convenient for me to call on Mrs Grundy tomorrow, perhaps?'

'Nonsense. You're a man of action, Mr Jarrett. Grasp the opportunity and escort Miss Lonsdale home tonight.' Lady Catherine did not wait for anyone else's opinion. 'A gentleman escort to see you home,' she informed Henrietta. 'Your aunt would approve.'

'I assume, Lady Catherine, that Sir Thomas has not yet returned?' Jarrett asked, hoping to divert his hostess's attention. Miss Lonsdale hardly seemed to relish the prospect of his escort, while his own mind was increasingly on his forthcoming meeting with his informant. He did not want to be late.

'No. We expect him in the early hours. Zachary Ison sent word to him about this petty session of his.'

'Sir Thomas's business must have been pressing. I imagine it troubles him to be absent when such affairs are afoot in the parish. The magistrates will be regretting the lack of his counsel.'

Lady Catherine snorted. 'Thomas! Poor Thomas has a weakness, Mr Jarrett.'

'Not constitutional, I hope, ma'am?'

'Constitutional! You could say so – to his pocket! For all Thomas likes to fancy his health bad, he's as strong as a mule. He'll outlive us all.' The wizened apple face tilted towards him with sly wisdom. 'Two things you should mark about Thomas, Mr Jarrett. One, Thomas don't like to trouble himself. And two, Thomas's revenues are tied up in mines; lead mines, Mr Jarrett.' The old lady paused for effect. Mischief buzzed, a palpable aura about her. 'Don't know what I'm talking about, eh? Think the old woman's babbling?' She pecked her pointed head at him.

'Lady Catherine, how should I ever dare to suggest such a thing?' he asked in a deliberately satirical fashion. Even allowing for her physical misfortunes, Lady Catherine's behaviour was deplorable. For a moment he watched her debate whether or not to fling into one of her sulks. He judged she enjoyed the game too much to leave it unfinished.

'There is money in mines, Mr Frederick Clever Jarrett. Money; so long as the men go down the workings. In these parts it is our Mr Raistrick who sees that they do – or don't.' The old lady settled her hands over her rounded stomach. Her posture with her hump gave her the look of a leering turtle raised up on its hind legs.

'Can the mine-owners not find another agent, Lady Catherine?'

'Open your eyes, Mr Frederick Raif Jarrett. There is no other agent in this district. If His Grace the Booby has held on to any interest in mines, Mr Raistrick will be his agent, too. He is a cunning fox,' she pronounced, as if she liked Raistrick rather better for it.

'He is a brute, Lady Catherine,' exclaimed Henrietta unexpectedly.

Lady Catherine flicked her a cynical glance, softened with a sort of affection.

'Don't let your nicety cloud your judgement, girl. Brute he may be, but he is mighty clever and determined.'

'I see now how a plain provincial lawyer might find his way on to the bench,' commented Jarrett.

'Not necessarily a quick-witted boy, but he comes round in the end.' Losing interest in her topic, Lady Catherine began to shift restlessly. 'I shall tell Thomas you will meet him at tomorrow's petty session,' she ended petulantly.

Light gave up the struggle and shadows overran the ground. The garden grew cold under a flushed carmine sky. Fancy appeared with a large shawl and began to envelop her mistress in it.

'I've had Miss Henrietta's carriage brought round, my lady.' The maid exchanged a brief glance with Miss Lonsdale. 'Mr Finlay says that, since he has given the gentleman's horse a good rub-down and made him comfortable, he might like to leave him in the stables for tonight. I've taken the liberty of having one of Sir Thomas's saddle mounts readied for the gentleman.'

'She's right. A gentleman always has a care of his horse-flesh, my father used to say. He was a fool but a good horse-man. You take the horse, Mr Frederick Raif Jarrett. Finlay can ride yours over to you tomorrow when it is rested.'

'My horse and I are most grateful for your hospitality, Lady Catherine.'

'Fiddle-faddle! Be off, the pair of you. It's growing dark and I'm chilled.'

Jarrett was calculating how long he had to allow to reach Woolbridge in time for his meeting. He had hoped for the leisure to locate Duffin, thinking that the poacher's local knowledge and brawny frame might be of assistance to him in his next encounter with the miner. As he escorted Miss Lonsdale to her carriage he considered how he might extract himself from his present duty without causing offence.

Henrietta watched the agent's abstracted face. Miss Lonsdale had a secret. She knew that the propriety she assumed in society was a sham; a deceit by which she disguised the shameless, inquisitive person she really was. Henrietta Lonsdale took an infinite interest in people – people of all sorts and degrees. She took pleasure in observing them, learning about their lives, speculating as to their secrets. Her private sense of exile from the person she ought to be was the basis of the affection she held for Lady Catherine. The spirited old woman embodied in her extraordinary exterior the dilemma that Henrietta herself wrestled with inside. Miss Lonsdale examined the tanned features of the man beside

her. He looked tired and drawn. She considered how much
he was likely to have seen of their performance in the rose
garden. In a half-amused way she wondered whether she had
shocked him. A sudden sense of freedom bubbled up inside
her. She did not regret that it was he who had glimpsed the
nature she hid from the general world.

As he was about to hand her into her carriage she turned
to him.

'You have spent so much time on horseback today, Mr
Jarrett, would you care to ride the short distance to Longacres
with me?'

His plans of evasion crumbled before her open-faced
enquiry. So long as he did not linger he would still have
time to make the churchyard before midnight. He cast a
quick look at the coachman. Evidently a family servant.
Surely he would be chaperon enough for country ways. He
bowed acceptance of her invitation and saw the saddle horse
tethered securely behind the carriage before climbing after
her into the cramped interior. They sat side by side. There
was little space between them and Jarrett had to clasp the
window strap to hold himself at a proper distance. Miss
Lonsdale noticed the stiff way her escort pulled one leg into
the carriage after the other and the almost imperceptible
unease with which he settled into his seat.

'Is your leg troubling you?' she enquired kindly. 'You have
been ill, I think.'

Jarrett found her unpredictable character unsettling.
Despite her maidenly status Miss Lonsdale habitually car-
ried herself with the composure of an established matron.
He was at a loss how to behave towards her.

'I am a soldier, ma'am – serving with the 16th Light
Dragoons in Portugal,' he explained. 'I sustained a wound in
February that sent me home on leave, but I am recovered. As
for this,' he cast a light-hearted look at his leg, 'it is merely
bruised and I playing for sympathy.'

He found himself talking to her of his impressions of Portugal and Spain – the landscape, the people, the customs. Her dove-grey irises were flecked with charcoal. They radiated intelligence, blended with a sympathetic interest that solicited confessions.

Henrietta understood why Lady Yarbrook was so taken with Mr Jarrett's reading. His voice was charming of itself; deep with just a touch of a husky catch to it. It had a tone that seemed to reverberate inside her. He was telling her of some friends he had made in Spain. A married couple, charming hosts on whose country estate he had idled one summer.

'Their property lay in the path of the enemy's advance last autumn. Some weeks into that campaign I was in the district and passed by to see what the French had left.' There was a stillness within the carriage. The sounds of the wheels on the road seemed to belong to a separate world. 'It was a dark winter night. I had been scouting in the hills for some days. I had hopes my friends had been absent when the soldiers came. The French are not well-behaved visitors. Through a window, by candlelight, I looked in on a scene of great wreck and destruction. My friends sat on a sabre-torn sofa sharing a meagre picnic laid out on a handkerchief between them. They looked at each other with such clarity...' Jarrett paused, suddenly seeming to recollect his companion's presence. 'They sprang up to welcome me: Come in, friend! Share our good fortune!' He threw up a hand in a Latin gesture.

'Good fortune!' Henrietta exclaimed. 'What did they mean, Mr Jarrett?'

There was a look in his eyes, as if he had grasped the edge of a distant truth. 'They were both well and unharmed, Miss Lonsdale. The enemy had been unable to destroy what they valued most.'

'And will you return to Portugal, Mr Jarrett?'

'I must travel to London to see the army's medical men in a week or so. Once I am pronounced fit ...'

'But you do not wish to go back?'

The seamless way she picked up on something he hardly knew himself astonished him. 'I have spent the last ten years of my life a soldier, Miss Lonsdale. Yet lately I have begun to wonder if I might not try another kind of life.'

'Perhaps you should become a painter of portraits,' she said lightly. She looked away to the country outside the window for a moment. 'That likeness of Sally Grundy was remarkable. Have you painted portraits?'

'Occasionally, but I prefer landscapes – and the army prefers my topography and maps.' As he smiled at her he noticed she was looking at the hand with which he held on to the strap by his head. The bracelet of hair he wore about his wrist was in plain sight. He took his hand down hurriedly.

'Have you been recently bereaved, Mr Jarrett?' she asked quietly.

This was the last thing he wanted to discuss.

'No, ma'am.' He heard the roughness of his tone and cursed his own clumsiness.

Miss Lonsdale privately scolded herself. She had no right to pry and now she had offended him. It was as she suspected. The strange bracelet was a token from an absent love. Mr Jarrett was contemplating selling out so that he might settle down with some flaxen-headed maiden. He had no doubt been pledged to her for years.

The atmosphere in the little vehicle was close, despite the leather flaps being tied back from the windows. He smiled awkwardly at his companion, racking his brains for some way to bridge the silence.

'It is very kind of you to come to speak to Mrs Grundy, Mr Jarrett,' the lady remarked politely.

The gentleman murmured something about it being nothing.

'Mrs Grundy is most unhappy,' Henrietta ventured at

last. The remaining ride to Longacres was not so short as
to be conveniently passed in total silence. 'There are some
dreadful rumours being spread that Sal took her own life,
Mr Jarrett. My cook is a religious woman and the thought
that there might be objection to her niece being buried in
sanctified ground is almost more than she can bear.' Miss
Lonsdale's elegant features took on a determined set. 'I will
do everything in my power to prevent such a terrible thing.
The Reverend Prattman must not pay heed to such malicious gossip.'

He could feel the warmth of her indignation beside him.
He regretted the sense of intimacy that had just evaporated.
She was a woman of passionate concern. A man might consider himself fortunate to be an object of such warmth. He
began to mouth some soothing remark but she interrupted
him almost before he had spoken.

'Just this morning poor Mrs Grundy found dishes of salt
placed about the body!'

'Salt, Miss Lonsdale?'

'The ordinary folk hereabouts believe it stops unquiet
spirits from walking. I suspect it is the work of Betsy, the
scullery maid – she is a simple, deluded child – but someone
will have put the notion into her head. I'd give money to
know the mischief-maker.'

'But who would give this story of suicide any credence,
Miss Lonsdale? The evidence at the inquiry was all against
it.'

'Country gossips hardly care for evidence, Mr Jarrett. It
concerns me. Why should people be conspiring to make
poor Mrs Grundy yet more wretched still? Hardly a handful
of people have come to pay their respects and Mrs Grundy
is generally known to be a good, honest woman. Is the death
of her only family not tragedy enough?'

'I shall do my best to find out, Miss Lonsdale. Have you
no suspicion as to the source of these rumours?'

Henrietta hesitated a moment, an anxious frown between her eyes.

'Mrs Grundy swears they can be traced to Will Roberts's new family. His father-in-law, Sergeant Tolley, is a dreadful man if only half they say is true. I pity Will. I cannot imagine how he managed to saddle himself with such a connection. But I will swear Will Roberts is a good man, Mr Jarrett.' In her conviction Miss Lonsdale laid a gloved hand on his sleeve, willing him to understand her. 'It is easy to see how Mrs Grundy's resentment might pin on him – he did a cowardly thing in letting Sal down so. And yet, is it not understandable that a young man, far from home and seeking to better himself, might make the match he did? Sal being the creature she was, Will had no means of knowing she would wait for his return from Ireland.' Henrietta sighed as she looked out of the carriage window. 'Oh, but this is a sad business.' The falling light had leached the colour from the landscape, rendering every feature in subtle tones of grey. 'We are nearly at the house. I hope perhaps speaking with you may give poor Mrs Grundy some relief.'

As Miss Lonsdale spoke the words a woman's scream ripped through the calm of the night. It wavered and choked, then began again; a dreadful banshee wail that offended the senses of the listeners with its extraordinary note of alarm. Jarrett heard running steps pounding towards them in the night. A dog barked. He thrust open the door of the carriage as it drew to a halt and tumbled out into the arms of Ezekiel Duffin.

'Men!' the poacher cried into his face. 'They've taken the corpse! That way!'

Jarrett had just enough wit about him to detour to the rear of the carriage and snatch a loaded pistol from his saddle bag before dashing off after the receding figure of the poacher. Duffin led him towards the back of the house. The sky had grown overcast and what light there was showed the outline of densely packed trees at the horizon. A cloud passed, allowing the moon to gleam out a moment. It gilded the edges of things with silver, then faded. Perhaps a hundred yards off the moonlight caught the movement of a party of men carrying a glowing light and a bundle. Then the glimpse was obscured among the branches shifting in the warm wind. Reaching the edge of the wood minutes behind the raiders, Duffin and Jarrett plunged into the darkness.

His eyes saw nothing but varying degrees of dark. The lack of light blurred definitions between shades and solids, damaging his perception of space. All nature seemed to conspire to jostle him. A filigree of razor-edged twigs whipped his cheek, then a sturdy branch struck him full chest, robbing his lungs of air. He ran with the cocked pistol held by his side and the other arm up to protect his face, lurching crabwise between the obstacles that crowded about him.

The gentle incline of the wood grew steeper. He sensed a drop in temperature, like the cold breath of danger on his cheek. There was a cavernous space beyond the line of trees that terminated suddenly to his left. His foot slid on leaf mould and propelled a dry stick out into nothing. He heard it drop and bounce down a long way. Shouting a warning to Duffin he veered back into the depths of the wood. It was then that he realised the poacher was following his dog's lead. Bob's yellow form jumped surefooted through the wood, pausing every now and then in his excitement to look back, his eyes reflecting a gleam of light. The tilt of his head and his pricked up ears seemed to urge his master to hurry on, puzzled as to why, all at once, these humans should be rendered so clumsy and uncertain. Jarrett focused his attention on the dog, trying to divine the terrain ahead from the way the yellow shape moved over the ground.

The light Duffin and he followed swung crazily ahead of them through the night. The crashing sounds they made rang out so unnaturally loud, he thought the whole world must hear them and wake. A ditch dropped away, clogged by a fallen tree trunk. The yellow dog scrambled over it and then Duffin's bear-like shape. He half-vaulted, half-rolled after them. They could hear shouts from the men ahead. The voices had a slurred edge of panic. They're drunk, he thought, that and the body should slow them.

His foot sank into a scratchy pillow of moist leaves and ferns and met the root of a tree cloaked within it; a spiny ridge of bone that jarred his ankle. He wrenched himself upright only to step out and trip over another root. Duffin was beside him, his large hand clasping his arm like a band of iron, pulling him up. Together they ran on through the thickening night of the wood.

The longer they ran the more attuned his sharpened ears became to the sounds beyond the vivid noise of their own progress. They seemed to be catching up with the moving life-forms ahead of them. The light they followed dropped suddenly and steadied. Jarrett levelled his pistol and fired. The red flash blinded him briefly to all but its colour. There was a squealing grunt and the slump of a weighty sack flopping down in the undergrowth. Powder smoke filled his nostrils with the rotten tang of sulphur. There was a scrabble up ahead and a confusion of voices. A harsh voice, full of authority, bore over the rest snarling orders. Jarrett could not hear the words but he recognised the tone.

'I'll wager my horse that's a military man,' he said, turning his head to Duffin who panted at his shoulder. As he spoke the words a treacherous dip caught his foot and he was flung full length. Ezekiel's dense bulk landed on top of him, crushing him to the forest floor. For a moment all he could hear was the sounds of their various curses. He had jarred his bad leg, his face felt scratched to pieces and Bob was dancing about them barking with every appearance of frenzied delight.

By the time Jarrett had extricated himself from under the

poacher the sounds of their prey were fading into the distance. The light burnt steady in the darkness. They advanced cautiously towards it. The lantern stood on the floor of the wood throwing changeling shadows about the undergrowth. The yellow flame illuminated a pick and wooden stave. The line of the stake led his eye to a gruesome shape at the watery edge of the light. Sal's husk: a slumped, twisted bundle with a dead white face that glimmered through a net of coarse black hair. He fell to his knees, the hairs rising on the back of his neck. For a moment it seemed as if her eyes were opened and glittered at him from under the ugly web of hair. She smiled at him; a sly ghost of a smile.

He heard Duffin call his dog and the pair returned into the pool of light.

'We'll not catch them now.' The big man was out of breath. He bent his large frame over, resting his hands on his knees. 'How many, would you say? Five or six by my reckoning.'

'Yes, five or six,' Jarrett agreed absently. He turned shocked eyes to the poacher. 'Why in God's name should they take the corpse?'

The older man leant down to pick up the wooden stake. It was roughly carved into a wicked point, the stripped wood gleamed out fresh and white. 'There's a crossroads up ahead a piece. I'd reckon someone fears that Sally Grundy's spirit will walk.' Back-lit in the weird light the man raised the stake and made as if to drive its point into the ground.

Jarrett jerked his face away from the gruesome pantomime. Another light was approaching through the dark from the way they had come. A female form moved through the wood, a lantern held high. Henrietta Lonsdale stepped into the lantern-light, her eyes huge. He scrambled to his feet to shield her from the scene. For some reason she had removed her gloves. He fixed upon the white hand that clutched her shawl to her throat. Ever afterwards he would be able to recall that hand in the most minute detail and the image would conjure up some essence of her to him. Its slender back, the elegant line of the tapering fingers and the twisted gold ring on the third finger with some sort of blue stones woven among its strands. He found himself wondering whether she wore it as a token.

The woman leant to look past him. She saw the body and the stake in Duffin's hands. She met the poacher's eyes with a look of anguish. 'You said there are crossroads ahead.' Her voice rose, seeming to grow younger and more vulnerable with the horror of it. 'What were you at with that dreadful thing?' Jarrett took her lantern from her. He could not find any words to say. Her hands flew to her mouth. 'Oh, sweet Jesus.'

'We had best take her back now, Miss Lonsdale.' Jarrett spoke softly. 'Those villains are gone, but they could return. If Mr Duffin and I carry the body, are you well enough to light our way?'

Henrietta hung on to the kindly sanity of his civilised face. There was a thin trickle of blood oozing from a scratch below his left eye. She put up her hand to wipe it away.

'You are hurt, Mr Jarrett.'

He felt the touch of her skin on his cheek. In an involuntary movement he covered her hand with his. She stood so close he could feel the warm life in her. Gently he moved her hand away.

'It is nothing, Miss Henrietta.'

At the sound of her name Miss Lonsdale started back, shocked at her own behaviour. He must think her mad.

'Forgive me, Mr Jarrett. Of course,' she said, with only a slight tremor in her voice. She bent down and picked up the other lantern. She held out her free hand towards him. 'If you will return my lamp to me, I can manage both.'

The group of servants huddled in a corner of the high-ceilinged kitchen. The older man looked at the wall, but

Betsy the scullery maid and Harry the groom stared at Mrs
Grundy as she sat at the long table, her blank eyes fixed on
her hands. The scullery maid's white face was pinched with
excitement as she whispered to the groom. Henrietta gave
the girl a hard look.

As she entered the kitchen Henrietta Lonsdale was not the
same maiden Jarrett felt so protective of in the wood. She
took charge with a quiet authority that left him feeling useless and overlooked. She dismissed Betsy to sit in her aunt's
room in case she should wake and be concerned.

'But she's sleeping, Miss Henrietta,' the girl assured her,
reluctant to leave the centre of excitement. 'I brought the
mistress her draught and she drank it as usual. I looked in on
her when the screaming started but she was sleeping straight
on her back, like a log.'

'I am glad, Betsy; but you go up to Mrs Lonsdale's room
for a while. You may sit in the big chair by the fire. Go on.
There's a good girl.'

Betsy pulled a sullen face but she went. Henrietta drew up
a chair beside Mrs Grundy and began to talk to her in a low,
gentle voice. The distraction enabled the men to return Sal's
corpse to the large pantry that lay off the kitchen.

The pantry's normal use was as a store for precious table
ware and wine. A bier made of a covered trestle surrounded
by candles stood before the shelves of gleaming silver and
low racks of dusty bottles. They arranged the body as tidily
as they could. It had suffered from its recent indignity. One
foot twisted oddly and the lower left arm had snapped. A
sharp end of bone protruded, straining up sickeningly against
the thin cover of skin. Duffin manoeuvred the ends of bone
into line and tucked the limb back against the body. Jarrett
ran his fingers through the tangle of black hair attempting to
ease it into some sort of shape. It felt reassuringly soft, not
the coarse black fibre it had seemed in the ghastly light of
the lantern in the wood.

'It needs a comb,' he said. The others stared at him and Duffin shrugged.

They spread the shroud over her once more, righting those candles the raiders had overturned in their flight. Mr Saul, the erstwhile coachman, loaded up an old blunderbuss and set the groom to sit on guard before the door. There was a tacit understanding between the men that this measure was purely to reassure the ladies. The raiders were long gone.

Jarrett rejoined Henrietta at the table to listen to Mrs Grundy's story. After her appearance at the investigation he had no high hopes of getting a coherent account from the cook, but Mrs Grundy surprised him. The series of shocks she had suffered appeared to have lit a smouldering resentment in the depths of her stout frame. She gave a lucid account of her ordeal. Earlier that evening she had fallen asleep by the kitchen fire while reading her bible, seeking some words of comfort. She woke to find the kitchen full of men with blackened faces.

'One threw a bit of blanket over my head and growled in my ear that I'd be quiet or it'd be worse for me. I could hear them moving about. Drunken beasts. They stank of it. One of them said they'd come to do for my Sal. Then, quicker than anything, I was knocked to the floor and they all run out. My heart was beating fit to break. I thought I'd never draw breath again.' Her voice, controlled until now, quavered. Henrietta looked into middle distance as the cook rubbed one plump hand over the back of the other laid flat on the table top. 'I pulled the cloth from my head and it were all dark. They'd put the candles out. There were nothing but the light of the fire in the range. I heard the carriage coming and I cried out. I beg pardon, Miss Henrietta, for all the fuss I made. I didn't know what I was at.'

'Did you know any of the men, Mrs Grundy?' Jarrett asked.

'I made out Nat Broom,' interrupted Duffin, 'and one or

two others from the Swan crowd.'

Jarrett gave the poacher a sharp look. He himself had never been close enough to make out any feature of the men they chased.

'I know it was them.' A bitter, corroding resentment infected Mrs Grundy's voice. 'I saw him. He tried to hide his face from me but I saw Will Roberts just before they caught me in that cloth.' She was speaking faster now and two red spots burnt on her cheek bones. 'Had his face all black and covered with soot but I still knew him. The devil – he has no shame. He killed my Sal and now he'll not let her rest. You go to the Swan and ask those heathen devils if they did not do this terrible thing.'

Henrietta laid her hand over the cook's clenched fists. 'There now, Mrs Grundy. Mr Jarrett will see to it. You must be still.' She looked up at the gentleman standing over her. Mr Jarrett had a competent air of authority about him she found reassuring.

'It seems I should speak to Will's father-in-law, Sergeant Tolley,' agreed Jarrett.

'Wait for morning and I'll come along with you,' the poacher said. 'We'll collect some other lads if we're wise. Tolley's not a timid man; you'll not find him alone.'

'Mrs Grundy, I believe you had a visit from a Mrs Munday that you wished to tell me about?' asked Jarrett.

The cook looked puzzled a moment, as if it were hard to recollect a life beyond the trauma of that night.

'She came to see me. Nora Munday's a hard woman but she's honest. She told me – you speak to young Maggie. Maggie knows more than she's telling.'

'Maggie Walton, is that? Miss Grundy's fellow lodger?'

The cook nodded, her face determined. 'Aye; you speak to Maggie.'

'Did Mrs Munday explain why she thought Maggie had something to say?'

The cook just shook her head. 'You talk to Maggie,' she repeated. Mrs Grundy's pale eyes filled up with tears and she crumpled, violent sobs overwhelming her heavy frame.

In face of such emotion, Jarrett retreated. This was women's work. He felt his usefulness at Longacres had expired. With a jolt of irritation he recalled his informant. He pictured the man waiting in the churchyard in vain and cursed the lost opportunity. He consoled himself that the night's work had not been without interest. That someone was desperate enough to initiate an attempt to steal Sally Grundy's corpse increased his confidence that he would ultimately uncover the truth about her death. He reclaimed Miss Lonsdale's attention briefly from her preoccupation with the cook.

'Miss Lonsdale, do you think you might persuade Mrs Grundy and this landlady, Mrs Munday, to come to speak with me tomorrow at the Queen's Head? At noon, say?' he asked in a low voice.

His proximity as he leant towards her recalled the open-hearted way with which he had seemed to confide in her earlier that evening. The contrast between that impression and the impassive face he now wore made Henrietta wonder if she had imagined it. She kept her voice even as she replied. 'I shall do my best, Mr Jarrett.'

Duffin was standing at the door looking stoic as Mrs Grundy's distressing sobs throbbed through the room. Miss Lonsdale bid Mr Jarrett a distracted good night and he left.

Dawn was breaking as he led his horse wearily down the lane beside Ezekiel Duffin. The first light was creeping over the land, giving shape and substance back to the world.

'Tell me, Duffin, how did you happen to appear so sweetly at the hour of need?'

'I've been listening about town since you've been away. If a man keeps his peace, and sits quiet like, and listens to folk, he'll soon grow wise.'

'And you grew wise to what would happen tonight?'

Duffin gave him a reproachful look. He would tell his tale in his own way. His delivery took on a sort of sing-song, with well marked pauses, reminiscent of a fireside tale.

'I heard how salt had made an appearance about the remains. And I heard as how Will Roberts's new wife has been going to the herb woman for draughts to make her man sleep o' nights. Will don't rest easy no more. Whisper is that Sal's spirit has taken to visiting him.'

Jarrett sighed. 'Miss Lonsdale will be sorry. She is convinced Roberts is a good man. But he is also a tall fellow, and I'll wager Roberts wears straight-lasted shoes. By the by, Duffin. How were you ever close enough to say who those men were tonight? It was so devilish dark it could have been Bonaparte himself for all I could make out.'

Duffin snorted. 'Wasn't I drinking at the Swan this night? The lads had just left and the whole tap was talking about how there was going to be trouble up to the Lonsdale house.'

Jarrett laughed. 'So you followed them.'

'There's more,' Ezekiel said. 'Not that it's part of this night's work, but Sergeant Tolley's been getting a crew together. Seems he fancies himself a hard man. Word is there's trouble brewing between him and the landlord of the Three Pots.'

'The Three Pots – that den of thieves?'

'There's always more thieves, though Woolbridge's not like to be big enough for two gangs.'

As Jarrett pondered this new piece of intelligence he realised that Duffin was biding his time. The eyes under the craggy brows were pregnant with anticipation.

'Ezekiel Duffin, you look like a snake that's just swallowed a rabbit. Not more news?'

Duffin grinned as boyishly as Jarrett had ever seen him look. 'When I goes to town I likes to visit this woman. She works out of Fish Lane down by the river, does my biddy. As it happens, she knew you,' he diverted, conversationally. 'Saw you at the lawyer's chambers. Thought you was one of his. Took me time to set her right, it did.'

'And?' Jarrett prompted. He tried to be good-humoured about it, but Duffin's tales were almost as long as that night had been.

'Wouldn't you like to know who's turned up back at the Three Pots wearing a new brown coat?'

All weariness vanished and Jarrett's drawn face came alive. 'The Tallyman!' he exclaimed. 'Now we have the scent, Duffin!'

CHAPTER THIRTEEN

A yellow bird huddled in a wicker cage that rested on a high stool framed at the mouth of the passage leading into the yard. On top of the cage crouched a brindled cat with a tattered ear. With rounded haunches and head held low, the animal watched its frozen prey through the twisted willow shoots. The mauled ear scarcely twitched as Jarrett and Duffin approached.

'We'd have better brought company,' Duffin remarked in a doom-laden voice.

'We have not come for a fight. After the exertions of last night I doubt this Sergeant Tolley wishes to draw the further attentions of the magistrates.'

The poacher gave a sceptical grunt and brushed the cat from the bird cage as he passed. The animal skittered off with a furious look.

'Daft bugger,' he commented. 'I'll bide here.' Duffin stopped in the penumbra of the doorway. Jarrett glanced back. It was mildly surprising how successfully one of the poacher's bulk managed to blend into the grey of the passage. Duffin had a curious gift of immobility that made him easy to overlook when he wished it so. Jarrett stepped out into the bright morning.

Sergeant Tolley sat sunning himself in the yard overlooking the busy river, a pack of young men lolling about him. Jarrett judged Duffin's concern unwarranted. These lads looked in no condition to pose a threat to anyone. Grimy-faced and befuddled they slumped, blinking in the bright sunshine. He recognised several faces he had first glimpsed in Will Roberts's company at the Queen's Head soon after his arrival in Woolbridge. Will himself was missing. From a distance Roberts's father-in-law had the benign look of a prosperous family man – mutton-chop whiskers and a receding hairline; a solid frame, spread firmly between two trunk-like thighs. He was talking and did not choose to be interrupted. His eyes, like pieces of boiled meat leached of all goodness, slithered over the newcomer. The sergeant's was a homely face with no one at home.

It appeared that something had offended the proprietor of the Swan Inn. He sent a stalking look about his followers. For all the marks of exhaustion there was a wariness about the lads in the yard. A skittish note of tension permeated the movements of even those competing to look most at ease in this hard man's company.

'I'll take no disrespect – not from any man alive, high or low.' The sergeant's voice, like his stare, was a tool of his trade. He built it up with skill and careful timing into a bellow that had the semblance of a gale, conveying a similar threat of destruction. 'I'd soon as wring the neck of any man that crossed me. Know what I'd do? Do you?' Sergeant Tolley stood up. He swaggered a few steps to snatch up a chicken scratching in a corner of the yard in surprisingly swift hands. 'I'd sooner bite his head off than have any man disrespect me,' he declared.

The tableau was absurd yet Sergeant Tolley had a quality of ingrained menace about him that gripped the attention. The bird struggled with all its puny vitality against the ring of muscle and bone that imprisoned it. A ridiculous, clumsy, feathered, straining thing. The sergeant opened his vast mouth and stuffed in the jerking head. With a snap and a wrench and a soft ripping sound, there was a spurting wound where the head had been. Red, red blood seeped between yellow teeth and dribbled over the pasty chin. The sergeant spat the head on to the table. Slowly, deliberately, he leant over to pull a handkerchief from about Joe Walton's neck. The youth drew back from him then braced himself, his fair skin flushing with shame. He stared out of round fascinated eyes as the hard man wiped the gore from his lips. Tolley, his eyes full of contempt, lifted up his head and laughed. And with the staccato start of a line of muskets, his lads began to laugh with him.

A small-boned young woman with the face of a guarded child appeared carrying a tray of drink. She kept her eyes down as she distributed the mugs, weaving a pattern among the tables that seemed to draw her inexorably towards the man who was the centre of this universe. As she paused in profile to him, Jarrett saw the high bulge she carried under her heavy skirts. He heard again Nat Broom's malicious voice back at the Queen's Head: 'whatever the skirt's condition.' The baby looked to be due soon. If this was Will's new wife, as he assumed she was, Roberts's impending fatherhood put a new complexion on things. Jarrett examined the girl who had secured Will Roberts's affections in spite of all Sal's charms. He doubted it was her physical attractions that had got the lad to the altar – terror of her father, more like. And yet there was a wan vulnerability about the girl's underfed frame that solicited protection. Her face wore the unnaturally blank expression of the abused. Lack of visible emotion is the best defence the defenceless can hope for. As his daughter laid a mug by him, the sergeant flung the mangled corpse on to her tray. A few drops of blood settled on her thin hand.

'That's for the pot,' he declared. The chorus of laughter punctuated his words.

Jarrett caught a glimpse of doe eyes framed by long lashes. A spurt of anger caught him off guard. He was tired of men like Tolley. The army had taught the sergeant well. Jarrett would wager no line had ever broken under fire with Tolley at its heels. He had all the tricks – the sneer, the hard stares, the random eruptions of viciousness – all the bully and show by which petty tyrants force their inconsequential wills on less determined men. Tolley's kind were the backbone of military discipline. Discipline of the kind that had tethered two thousand men of the 68th to their indefensible post in the West Indies until disease shattered the regiment and fewer than two hundred remained to be shipped home. That same discipline which, three years later, had mired hundreds of fresh recruits to the 68th in the Walcheren marshes to rot away with swamp fever. Blind, unreasoning, brutal wilfulness.

With the lordly air of a pasha in his court of infidels, Sergeant Tolley deigned to acknowledge Jarrett's presence.

'You, stranger! What do you want here?'

He stowed the anger away and surveyed the man.

'It does not concern you, innkeeper. I have come in search of Mr Roberts, Will Roberts. I understand he dwells here?'

Mrs Roberts darted a bird-like glance up at a window. He followed its path. There was a face at a window. It was a brief glimpse, but now he understood the talk of Sal's ghost walking. Will Roberts had the face of a haunted man.

Sergeant Tolley spread himself at ease. Secure in the yard of his inn he was free of the army now. Jonah Tolley had no more need to bow and scrape to officers and gentlemen.

'I make it my concern. You'll not see him,' he said flatly. 'My son-in-law's poorly. A weakly man is young Will.'

A familiar voice piped up. 'Might be something he ate, sergeant!' Jarrett recognised the narrow features of Nat Broom.

The sergeant belched theatrically. 'More than likely. Has a tender stomach, does our Will.'

The lads laughed again. They were perking up at the prospect of a common victim to taunt.

'Are you here too, Mr Broom?' commented Jarrett mildly. 'I must congratulate you on a wide acquaintance.'

The sergeant cast his sycophant a look that made Nat shift uneasily. Out of the corner of his eye Jarrett saw the young woman take a step towards him, as if seeking his protection against the expression on her father's face. He had a strong impulse to vent some of the anger he had bottled up over the years. All those times he had stood by in the name of order to watch ruthlessness ride roughshod over humanity. His irritation spread to encompass Roberts. He was a fine tall young man. Was he too much of a coward to protect her from all this? He searched the sergeant's pebble eyes. Compared to Roberts's grieving face they were the windows to a soul that reflected no trace of feeling. Maybe Miss Lonsdale's assessment of the lad was right. After all, Will had married the girl. Perhaps Roberts had done all he could and his all had simply not proved enough.

The church clock across the river chimed the hour. He was late for the Colonel's session. It would serve no one's purpose but Tolley's if he were to get into a fight with the man. Jarrett placed his words clearly in the tense air of the courtyard for all to hear.

'Please inform Mr Roberts that Mr Jarrett called to see him. The Woolbridge magistrates are now meeting at the Queen's Head and wish to speak to him in connection with the recent death at Lovers' Leap.'

For all his conviction of his own strength, Tolley's years with the army had not taught him how to counter the effortless superiority of the officer class.

'You have no business with Will,' he blustered. 'That mad trollop killed herself. Will has nothing to say to any of you – away with you now! I'm sick of the sight of you.'

It had been many a long year since Raif Jarrett had flinched before a sergeant's roar. 'See that Roberts receives my message. Tell him it will be better for him if he comes himself. It would be a pity if the soldiers have to be sent.' He bowed to Mrs Roberts with a polite smile. 'Good-day.'

Colonel Ison's petty session met in Mr Bedlington's upper assembly room. The Reverend Prattman was sitting close to the Colonel's elbow, wearing the solemn Sunday face of a well-behaved child. The Chairman of the Bench looked up as Jarrett entered.

'Ah, Mr Jarrett! You are late. We can start. Mr Raistrick has sent word he will be delayed – some affair of a man's face cut in an alehouse brawl. You know Sir Thomas, I believe, and the parson, of course. Now, what news, Mr Jarrett? I have had no luck in tracing this Tallyman fellow of yours.'

Colonel Ison was at his most brisk. He vibrated with the bottled energy of a highly schooled thoroughbred fretting to be off. Sir Thomas of Oakdene Hall, after greeting Jarrett with a soft smile, appeared at a loss how to behave towards him. His anxious eyes drifted about the room until he settled into an exquisitely polite contemplation of a spot just before the end of the Colonel's nose which avoided the necessity of acknowledging the agent's presence.

'As to that, Colonel, I have intelligence that the villain has been seen again at the tavern called the Three Pots down on the river. If some men may be sent down there with due despatch, I have hopes he might be apprehended.'

As he spoke, Jarrett's mind calculated the impact of this fresh information. A man's face cut in an alehouse brawl? Duffin had told him that the Tallyman had a liking for that 'chalking trick of cutting a man's face to make his point'. And Raistrick was there to deal with the problem before him. Jarrett tensed against the thought. Whatever progress he made, it seemed as if the lawyer was always ahead of him.

'You think this Tallyman will give us answers, Mr Jarrett?' The Colonel's question recalled his attention.

'I believe him responsible for the murder of the Stainmoor crofter, yes. And I would be glad to examine him about circumstances surrounding James Crotter's death.'

'But James Crotter was not murdered!' The parson was shocked.

'No, I think not, Mr Prattman, but certain papers were taken from the manor at the time of his death and I have reason to believe that this Tallyman knows what took place there.'

Colonel Ison expelled a heavy breath that puffed out his cheeks.

'Well then, gentlemen, it seems we should send for Captain Adams. He can take a party of militia down to the river district – the Three Pots, you say?'

'Yes, sir. The murder bill from the churchwardens at Brough carries a description of the felon.'

'As I recall, there was a witness to that murder, was there not? The victim's son? It is inconvenient for me to be away from London at this time. Let us expedite this matter. I propose we send Constable Bone over to Stainmoor to fetch this boy. If he can identify our man we will have a murderer.'

Sir Thomas surfaced from his dreamy distraction.

'Poyston goes at quite eight miles the hour – even on the moor roads,' he announced. 'So much more expeditious. Constable Bone may sit with Poyston on the box.' The baronet's vague face clouded a moment, then cleared. 'Boys are slight enough, I dare say. The boy may sit between them.'

Eyeing the vacuous face with some wonder, Jarrett realised that Sir Thomas was offering his carriage and personal escort to the constable.

'That is a gracious offer, Sir Thomas, and timely,' Colonel Ison responded smoothly. 'Most timely. You are able to start at once?'

Sir Thomas agreed he was. Parson Prattman appeared to have been rendered speechless by this extreme generosity. He bobbed his head several times in the baronet's direction, a repressed smirk of approval on his rosy features. Sir Thomas basked, blinking, amid the congratulations.

Jarrett's brusque cough made him start. 'I should report, sirs, that Miss Grundy's actor friend proves to be a dead end.' Drawing out Lady Yarbrook's letter, he gave a brief account of his trip to Gainford.

'A pity,' sighed Colonel Ison, removing the spectacles from his nose and casting the letter aside. 'Ah well! To work, gentlemen. Let us set the hunt after this Tallyman fellow, eh?'

The meeting dispersed – Sir Thomas to his carriage, the Colonel to summon Captain Adams and the constable, and the parson to hurry to his vicarage to exclaim over the whole affair with his clerk. Jarrett descended the stairs alone. There was still no sign of Raistrick. He had the uneasy sense that this game was already lost. He gathered himself up. The Colonel had at least set an official pursuit in motion. There was still a faint hope that the Tallyman might be apprehended before the lawyer magistrate got wind of it. Once the villain was in custody then at last he might have the chance to unravel this mystery.

Mrs Bedlington's jolly face peered up at him from the foot of the stairs.

'You have visitors, Mr Jarrett.' To his astonishment she winked, adding a little tap on his forearm. 'In the parlour – Miss Lonsdale.' Curiosity crept into her voice. 'She's brought Mrs Munday and that Maggie Walton with her.'

Miss Lonsdale stood in the light of the parlour window, her elegant face determined. She laid a slim hand on Mrs Munday's sleeve to emphasise some words as she spoke. The contrast between Miss Lonsdale's refinement and the landlady's shorter, coarser outlines had elements of a caricature about it. 'The Maiden and the Fishwife' was the title that occurred to him. He dragged his errant thoughts back to the matter at hand.

'I'll say my piece here but I'll not repeat it. 'Tis Hannah

Grundy weighs on my mind. She deserves better.' Mrs Munday swung round to the miserable figure who sat concealed in the window seat. 'And you're no connection of mine, Maggie Walton.' Nora Munday addressed Jarrett. 'I'll speak out this once and you can make of it what you will,' she declared with every show of one determined to perform a distasteful duty.

Miss Lonsdale greeted him with seamless reserve.

'Good-day, Mr Jarrett. Mrs Grundy was unwell, so I bid her stay home and rest but, as you see, Mrs Munday has come to talk with you – and Maggie too. Come, Maggie, stand up and make your curtsey to the gentleman.'

Miss Lonsdale was at her most distant and capable. Her manner contrasted so strangely with his glimpse of the nymph of the rose garden that he found himself momentarily confused. He subdued the brief twinge of offence at her blithe neglect of his part in calling the meeting. He told himself he should be grateful for Miss Lonsdale's presence. He could claim little familiarity with the ways of serving maids and female domestics.

'Now you may sit down again, Maggie. There is no need to be afraid. No one here means you harm. Why do we not all sit down, Mrs Munday? We will be more comfortable. There. Now, you told me you were wakened that night Sally Grundy died – the night of the storm?' Miss Lonsdale prompted.

The landlady nodded brusquely. 'I rose up thinking a shutter had blown loose. The wind was howling about and carrying on. I found no shutter.' Mrs Munday narrowed her eyes at Maggie and Jarrett was swept back to the inquiry in the tollbooth chamber. The landlady had cast the very twin of that look at her lodger when Maggie first gave her evidence. 'But the stairs were wet,' Mrs Munday was saying. 'And the next day she' – she poked a sturdy forefinger at Maggie – 'went out in her best petticoat, for all it was a Thursday.'

Although he had wit enough to realise there was some significance in this piece of sartorial information Jarrett was not sure what it was.

'Her best petticoat, Mrs Munday?'

'Her crimson petticoat!' the woman repeated with emphasis.

He looked to Miss Lonsdale for assistance.

'Her best petticoat – the one kept for Sundays and holidays, Mrs Munday?' Henrietta suggested.

'Aye,' came the impatient reply. 'Her Sunday wear. And what's more it set me thinking. So I goes up to her room and there was her everyday one spread out over the chair. Fresh washed and wet through it were.'

Maggie hunched in the farthest corner of the window seat staring down, her face blank, as if she heard nothing. Her scrawny ankles protruded pathetically white above the wooden clogs that dangled an inch off the floor. She was a pitiful specimen.

'You tell them, Maggie Walton, where you were that night.' Mrs Munday's tone expressed her resentment at being drawn into such a public affair. Her patience with her lodger was fast running out. The girl's plain features registered no response. Jarrett moved to squat on his haunches before the window seat so that he might look up into the closed face. He concentrated his full charm on that charmless creature. His deep voice reached out to her, detached and lilting as if he were narrating a child's story.

'I know where you went that night. You followed Sally Grundy to Lovers' Leap in these very clogs here,' he brushed one shoe with a careless finger, 'and hid by the white rock, in a bush out of sight. What did you see?'

Maggie gave a hiccup and twitched. He caught a glimpse of blue pop-eyes watery with tears. He cocked his head closer to catch the mumbled words.

'What was that?'

'I didn't mean wrong! I didn't!' she wailed, suddenly animated and loud. 'Sal was took. The spirits took her. I never
should have gone. I never should!'

Jarrett ran a perplexed hand through his hair. God preserve
him from hysterical females. Henrietta Lonsdale was fussing
over the wench. She shot him an accusing look as if he were
Torquemada himself. Was it his fault the girl was soft in the
head? With a combination of bullying, measured sympathy
and a glass of strong spirit supplied by Mrs Bedlington, the
women gradually coaxed Maggie into coherence. The girl
fixed her reddened eyes on Jarrett's face like a timid mongrel, eager to please but fearful of cuffs. Cautious in case she
might fragment into another storm of emotion, Jarrett began
with a slightly lopsided smile.

'What did you see that night up on the rock, Miss
Walton?'

'Maggie,' prompted Henrietta, conscious that formality
was more likely to oppress than impress the girl.

'Maggie,' repeated Jarrett dutifully.

'I didn't see – not much. It were dark and I was frightened.
I didn't think Sal would go so far and the storm started. And
I was afraid of the ghosts – them spirits that walk out on
stormy nights.'

'But Sal went to meet someone at Lovers' Leap?'

Maggie nodded hard, like some wooden toy. Now that
she had begun her confession she seemed eager to unburden
herself, as if the gentleman held the hope of her absolution.

'And you could see Sal – just a little, through the
branches?'

Maggie bobbed her head again.

'And what did you hear?'

'The wind was blowing and the trees made such a noise
– and the river was rushing and roaring.'

'What else did you hear?'

The girl squirmed in her seat and began to gabble again.

'Sal was possessed. She was talking and crying out. She cried out to the good Lord and his angels and cried him shame and flung her arms about.' Maggie flung out her own thin arms in imitation. 'And the good Lord sent down a lightning bolt and threw her into the river for doing wrong!' Tears overflowed the pink eyes and she ended in a convulsive gulp.

'Not again, girl!' Jarrett exclaimed. 'Steady now,' he resumed in a more measured tone. 'You said Sally Grundy was speaking – who was she speaking to? Who did you see there on the rock with her?'

'No one! I saw no one. There were demons on the rock that night. Only Sal saw them!'

The fear the girl had suffered that night appeared to have driven the last remaining particles of sense from her brain. She was convinced that Sal had been tumbled from the rock by supernatural agency in punishment for a sinful life. While biddable in other ways, Maggie was utterly determined on this tale. Her face assumed the stubborn, cunning look of the foolish who know what they know. She could not be talked out of her belief by reason, sense or scolding.

'If you don't believe me, ask him!' she cried out. 'He'll tell you!'

Jarrett spun round in the direction of her pointing finger. Will Roberts filled the doorway. The perfect apparition to illustrate such a gothic tale.

'Will Roberts – were you there?' Jarrett heard himself ask. Henrietta glanced at him, astonished at the agent's composure.

'Not at the rock, but after,' insisted Maggie, stamping her foot in frustration. She sprang up and ran to Will, grasping his coat in her conviction. 'You tell them! You know. Will, you know I'm telling the truth!'

Save for his obvious physical solidity, Will Roberts might as well have been an apparition for all the reaction he gave. His bemused eyes stared out over the head of the girl who hung on his coat. There was a moment of silence, then both Mrs Bedlington and Mrs Munday bore down on the unfortunate Maggie; two ample, bustling figures, determined on confining the rising tide of hysterics.

'There's no sense to be had from this one,' Mrs Bedlington pronounced flatly. 'We'll be in the kitchen if we're needed. You'll be wanting a bit of peace.' Casting a shrewd look at young Will as she passed, she ushered Mrs Munday and her weeping lodger from the room.

Will rubbed a big hand over his face. The pale skin clung to hollows and plains, accentuating its gaunt beauty. The mournful eyes seemed to notice Miss Lonsdale for the first time.

'Miss Henrietta. You were always good to me.' His voice was soft and slow. He trailed off and hung his head. Henrietta stepped towards the towering youth, her face full of compassion.

'Oh, Will.' The quality of her voice made Jarrett's heart jump. The emotion set up a counter-twinge of annoyance. He might have little skill with hysterical kitchen-maids but Captain Jarrett was well versed in the ways of men. Such feminine sympathy would only unman the lad further.

'Perhaps you should leave us, Miss Lonsdale?' he suggested quietly.

Roberts raised his head. A weary child in a six-foot frame.

'No, Miss – will you stay?'

'Of course I shall stay, Will,' Henrietta responded at once. There were tears in her eyes as she led him to the window seat. 'You shall sit here and tell me what you have come to say – and Mr Jarrett shall listen. You went to meet Sally Grundy that night, did you not?'

The young giant nodded. He gave her a side look and a half-smile, struggling to hold back the tears that welled up in his averted eyes. She smiled back in encouragement.

'Why would you meet so late?' she asked brightly.

He swallowed and began to answer by rote, nodding his great head as if to mark time. 'Had to slip away so my father-in-law wouldn't know. Drink's usually got the sergeant by ten or so.'

Jarrett watched Sal's lover encourage himself with another dip of his head, then the sad eyes came up to fix on Miss Lonsdale's face with a simple directness.

'When I got there it was well dark and the storm was blowing up. It was a daft night to be out. Sal was there before me. We'd often met there. She was not in her right mind. She was speaking strangely. Didn't understand the half of it. She kept flinging up her arms and moving about. She cried on about shame and men putting off their honours and how she was withering and I'd exiled her for money. I tell you, she was raving. She was as one possessed. She'd have never spoken those words in her right mind.'

Will's story was carried on by its own momentum. Jarrett could imagine the young man rehearsing it to himself again and again, evolving it into a ritual that contained the pain.

'I saw she was too close to the edge. I said: Don't be daft, lass, step back from there. But she wouldn't hear me. There was a flash of lighting and she must have slipped – it all happened so quick. She just fell. It was black as pitch. I couldn't find my way down. I near fell after her. She was on the rocks, all twisted. I sat by her such a long time, then the breath came out of her and I knew she was gone.'

'And you lifted her up?' Jarrett asked.

The great head with its melting eyes turned to him. 'The rain had started. River was rising. I couldn't let the river take her. Sal was always afeared of drowning. I couldn't carry her up.' A sudden note of hysteria sprang up in Will's voice. He braced his muscles against it, then settled back once more. 'It was too steep. So I laid her on a piece of rock where it was dry. I closed her eyes and I left her there.' He appealed to Miss Lonsdale who sat silent at his side. 'There was no one to ask for help. No light anywhere.'

Jarrett drew his attention back. 'So you made your way back to town and you met Maggie Walton?'

'What was she doing out that night? It was madness. She gave me such a start – leaping out at me and gabbling on about demons and Sal being taken.'

A spark of annoyance flared out from beneath the numbness and for a moment the confidence of youth reasserted itself. 'I thought she'd seen the blood on my coat, but it was dark and the silly baggage thought the ghosts had taken Sal. She hadn't seen me at all. So I let her think it. I told her to go home and stay safe in her bed and tell no one – for who would believe her? I got back to the Swan and he was up. Just my luck. Drink hadn't taken that night.' Unconsciously Roberts wiped a grimy hand against his breast as if to clean it. 'He saw the blood on my coat. He made me tell him. He said: You're nothing. You're a little bit of a man.' Jarrett could hear the sergeant's sneering intonation faithfully represented by his brow-beaten son-in-law. 'Where'd your wife and your new baby be if they hang you for that whore? You hold your tongue and say nought. But I canna hold my tongue, Mr Jarrett. I have no peace. I must speak though they hang me. I'd be dead soon any road if I'm to go on like this.'

The lad was utterly weary. Jarrett's blue-grey eyes were keen as they watched him.

'Did you kill Sally Grundy, Will?'

'She died because of me.'

'You caused her to fall?'

'No, I never! I'd have given my life for Sal. I would – even though I sent her out of her mind by marrying another.' His voice broke on an edge between reproach and shattering bewilderment. 'Oh, Sal! What did you do it for? You weren't that kind. If I'd have thought it, I never would have gone out that night.'

The agent stood up and walked away to leave Roberts to compose himself. Behind him Miss Lonsdale was murmuring to the boy about how it could not have been his fault; he was foolish to speak so. He had a new wife and a baby on the way. His family needed him. What kind of man would he be if he let this tragedy pull him down and them with him? Jarrett rubbed the back of his neck and stretched out his shoulder blades trying to release the tightness there. Miss Lonsdale clearly believed the boy. He watched the posture and the desperate way the lad tried to listen to the woman by his side. Jarrett sighed. The story was plain foolish, and tragic enough to be true.

There were sounds of bustle outside in the yard. Duffin's laconic head appeared at the open window. The grey eyes under the brim of his disreputable hat were lively and he moved with a spring in his step.

'Here's Captain Adams back,' he announced. 'He's mustering some lads in the yard. There's a bit of bother between the Three Pots and the Swan – he'd appreciate some help, if you're free.'

Will Roberts was at his side. 'Trouble at the Swan? Mr Jarrett – I must go,' he pleaded. 'I swear on my life I'll come back and face the magistrates but I must see my Mary safe, sir. She's got no one but me.'

Miss Lonsdale added her voice. 'Let him go, Mr Jarrett. I'll vouch for Will's character. I know you can trust him to return.'

He met the force of her conviction, acknowledging it by a half-smile. With a gesture of his hand he let the boy go.

'I'll keep an eye on him,' Duffin said. Jarrett watched the increasingly familiar shape of the poacher swing off at a smart pace out of the yard and down the hill.

'Hurry on, lad,' he heard him urge as Will raced out after him. 'Things were getting a touch hot last I saw.'

The yard had filled with people. Captain Adams, supported

by a couple of grim-faced burghers, was drawing up a company of six militia men in red coats. There was the ordered confusion of assembling men and gun-barrels and powder being checked. An excited boy dashed up.

'Captain Adams's compliments, sir. He says there is a riot started down in the river quarter and he asks whether Captain Jarrett would be so good as to lend him his assistance, sir.'

Exchanging a grin with a remarkably cheerful looking Captain Adams who stood some thirty feet away from him across the yard, Jarrett replied, 'My compliments to Captain Adams. Tell him I shall join him directly.' As the boy raced off he added, 'And saddle my horse!'

He felt a touch on his sleeve and turned to Miss Lonsdale at his side.

'You do not believe Will killed her?' she asked. The grey eyes were startlingly passionate in such a refined face.

'No, Miss Lonsdale, I do not.'

'So you will not permit the magistrates to charge him with her death?'

'I promise,' he replied soberly, 'to do my utmost to persuade Colonel Ison that Sally Grundy fell to her death by accident.' He laid his gloved hand over hers a moment. His sincerity appeared to satisfy her.

'Thank you.'

'Your horse, Mr Jarrett.' The stableboy had brought Walcheren. He swung up on to the bay's back.

'Could you do something for me, Miss Henrietta?'

Her first name had just slipped out. For a still moment he waited for her to recoil, but the dove-grey eyes held his gaze.

'I am ready to do anything I can to assist you in this matter, Mr Jarrett.'

'I am grateful, Miss Lonsdale. Will you ask Lady Catherine whether Sir Thomas has a copy of *Volpone*, an old play by Ben Jonson? I believe Sir Thomas is a collector of rare volumes.'

'The play Lady Yarbrook was rehearsing, Mr Jarrett?' Henrietta was puzzled. 'What interest could there be in that?'

He smiled. She was a quick-witted woman, but there was no time to elaborate. Captain Adams called over to him. The party of militia were setting off at a jog-trot down the hill. Jarrett gathered up his reins and kicked Walcheren on.

'Borrow me a copy, if you can, Miss Henrietta,' he called back over the melee. 'I shall explain at our next meeting.'

CHAPTER FOURTEEN

Walcheren led the way down the steep hillside. High buildings closed in overhead and the big bay stepped into a
triangle of deep shadow. The swift transition from light to
shade momentarily blinded Jarrett. Hairs rose at the back of
his neck as he found himself in another place. Here was that
immediate stillness into which sounds drop like coins; every
sense straining to decipher distant noises channelled down
alleyways and reflected over rooftops. His body tensed with
that half-sick, half-exhilarated feeling, the anticipation of
ambush. Behind him, Captain Adams slowed his men to a
cautious pace. Jarrett's eyes adjusted and he caught movement beyond a stall protruding across the mouth of a courtyard. A walnut-faced crone was putting up her shutters. She
was bent and slow but determined. She huffed and puffed
and muttered to herself as she fixed her defences into place.

'You get to your work!' she scolded, turning her back.
'Racketing about on a Tuesday! Eeee! Lazy, no-good
buggers.'

The old witch dispelled the tension. His memory was
playing tricks on him. Up ahead erupted the sounds of heavy
shoes pounding on packed earth. A couple of young louts
issued out of an opening, bodies as dense as young calves
and features pinned up in an irreverent grin of excitement.
They saw the rider and the red coats behind him and skipped
back to dodge down a ginnel. Jarrett had the vivid sense of
arriving after an action. He picked up the pace, curious to
see what evidence it had left by its passing.

Two streets came together at the river bridge. It seemed as if the whole human life of the quarter had gathered there. Skiffs and barges huddled at viewing points on the river. Spectators crowded about doorways and leant out of windows. Scanning the scene, it occurred to Jarrett, as it had before, that physical type does not necessarily distinguish a fighting man. Some of the burliest bargees floated in mid-river, encouraging or deprecating from the safety of their craft, while on shore wiry little scrappers threw punches and gouged and kicked as indomitable as bantam cocks. Here and there knots of girls concentrated on a particular contest, glee distorting their faces with something vicious and primitive. Down at the river edge an old man was batting a broom furiously at two golden-haired urchins who rolled in the mud fighting like rats.

This was not an ill-natured skirmish. No knives, just hard heads, fists and feet, with the occasional assistance of moveable objects picked up in passing – a bottle, a stick, a window shutter. Assessing the action with a professional eye, Jarrett judged it largely leaderless. This was a display of the conquering instinct of man, that same spirit on which kings build the armies with which they pursue their interests. Armies, however, employ a vast machinery of training and discipline to bind men into some sort of order and direct their violence. The brawl on the bridge was chaotic.

The mere sight of the clump of red coats drained the heart from the fight. Its seething centre began to diffuse. Captain Adams lined up his little party of soldiers to block the street down which they had come. As the tide of the press of bodies ebbed down the other street that ran parallel to the river, Jarrett urged Walcheren on to the stone pavement of the bridge. Beside him, Duffin shouldered his way against the flow of the crowd.

'These lads aren't in a mind to give real trouble,' he observed comfortably, heaving a red-faced little man out of his path. The drunk staggered against the parapet of the bridge and reached towards the rider to drag him off his mount. The rider's boot sent him reeling back with a smart kick to the chest.

'I agree,' Jarrett replied retrieving his stirrup. 'Something's amiss here.'

He was not sure that Duffin heard him. The poacher was moving with a brisk rhythm, clearing a little semi-circle before him by dint of roaring and the occasional sharp jab of a large fist.

'This is lively,' he called back. 'Haven't seen as good a barney as this since that time Old Pointer thought to lose Lumpin' Jack his licence by wrecking the docks.'

Jarrett was hardly listening. Where was Raistrick? The timing of this outburst in the river quarter worried him.

A distant figure caught his eye on the other side of the bridge – something about the shape and the way it moved. He was almost certain he recognised his erstwhile informant, the miner of the churchyard. He stood up in his stirrups, straining to get a better view. A man was thrown violently against him. Walcheren fretted against the reins, stamping his front feet. At the edge of his vision he saw Duffin square up to a quick lad with a compact body. The poacher easily broke the left-handed jab, but his opponent followed it with a swift hammer right that caught the older man on the side of his grizzled head. Duffin rocked and began to fall. Jarrett's attention was rudely claimed by a tall man with lashless eyes who clawed up at him, striving to get a grip on his coat. He jabbed him hard in the forehead with an elbow and shoved him away.

He strained up again, searching over the sea of heads for that one distant figure. No sight of him. Duffin was up, hunched and growling like a bear. His opponent lowered his own head and tried again. Moving with more speed than might be expected from a man of his years, Duffin blocked the feint in passing and kicked the weight-bearing leg from under the youth, just as his right fist was picking up speed. With a grunt of surprise the lad toppled past him into the arms of Will Roberts. The young giant swung him up and over the parapet. The splash from his fall nearly reached the bridge. Duffin and Will gazed over the wall.

'He'll do,' Duffin said after a moment. Below, a boatman was pulling a bedraggled figure from the water.

They passed the crest of the bridge and the dense pack of human flesh eased. Jarrett's keen eyes quartered the crowd, examining every movement and shape. The hope that had flared with his brief glimpse of the miner dissolved into barely caged frustration. He had an acute sense that he was falling behind in this race. They found themselves at the door of the Swan. Leaving Walcheren in the charge of an honest-looking old man who stood apart from the fray, Jarrett followed Duffin into the inn. As they crossed the threshold the purpose of the riot became clear. The flags of the narrow passage were awash with aromatic liquid. A vast vat of beer had been emptied and rolled, blocking the doorway into the yard. They heaved it aside to reveal a cat crushed beneath its iron hoops, slimy coils of intestine bellying out from the wet fur. Duffin kicked the foul mess aside.

A figure staggered out of the sun towards them. It was the sergeant, one eye opaque and rimmed with blood. The skin of his head puffed out, blue and mottled; brown rivulets of blood marked trails from his nostrils. His voice issued vitriol from a mouth of broken teeth.

'You're a nothing, Will Roberts – you're a worm, a puling, crawling, little man. Where have you been hiding?'

Will stood his ground. 'Where's Mary?' he demanded.

There was a crash and across the yard a man leapt from an attic window on to the low roof of an outbuilding. Jarrett caught an impression of basalt eyes glittering in a grimy face. The figure scrabbled over the river wall and was gone. A muffled explosion, smoke billowed and red tongues of flame began to slither in the recesses of the window. Tolley threw himself at his son-in-law.

'You come with me,' he snarled. 'They'll not burn me out.'

He fastened on to the youth's shirt and tried to haul him into the inn. The dead weight of Will's six-foot frame defeated his battered strength.

'You leave me be,' Roberts spat out.

Swearing terrible oaths the sergeant pushed him aside. 'They'll not burn me out.' He repeated the words like a bitter prayer as he clawed his way up the stairs. The yard resonated with the snap of glass giving way before heat and in the depths of the building the fire roared. Jarrett moved as if to follow the man up the stairs but Roberts barred his way. The handsome face was fixed with a new determination.

'Leave him be. Let his fate have him.'

Across the bar room there was a window cut into the thick wall overlooking the river. Jarrett caught the movement of a head. It bobbed as if its owner dragged his feet or rocked on unsteady legs. He pushed past Will, leaving Duffin standing amazed. Outside, he ran up towards the bridge. A steep stone staircase dropped beside the riverside wall of the Swan. Narrow and ancient, it curved down to the secretive shadows under the bridge. He leant over the parapet straining to see into the well below. He could hear the sounds of a man hurrying down the steps. The hidden presence dragged against the stone in passing as if in panic or injured. Jarrett reached the first curve of the stair. He saw a back view foreshortened. A long coat like many travelling men wore. The outline of the shoulders was a possible match. Turn, man, turn!

Down below him the man was almost at the landing. A boat waited under the shadow of the arch. The figure paused and turned, his face raised awkwardly. It was a mask, marred as if the maker had thought to begin again, one side all livid and swollen about a gash that ran from eye socket to chin. It was the miner of the churchyard. Jarrett opened his mouth to shout. As he heard his own voice he knew it to be useless. The man's eyes recorded something that could not be reversed. For a moment he stood on the quay and they looked at one another, then the connection broke. The miner turned away and stepped into the boat.

A larger craft drew up at the landing disgorging a party of brawny men carrying buckets. Faces determined, they piled up the narrow staircase. The first one shouted to Jarrett, who blocked their path.

'Get away, man! That fire needs tending or it'll spread.'

Reluctantly Jarrett backed up the steps. People were everywhere, blocking him, jostling him as he fought his way from side to side of the bridge. The river was dotted with boats but he could not make out his man. The miner had disappeared.

Jarrett sensed an urgent figure bearing down on him from behind. He turned a split second before Duffin grabbed his arm.

'Reckon you've lost your chance to have a word about them books of yorn. They've found the Tallyman.'

The Tallyman lay in a few inches of stinking water, his huge frame stretched out like the waxen effigy of a Viking. Dirty skeins of yellow hair floated on either side of the brutal, pock-marked face, an unwholesome weed on the surface of the oily water. A passer-by on his way to the Three Pots had stopped to relieve himself in the dry sluice of Bedford's Mill and found him there. Now Captain Adams stood up on the road in urgent discussion with a couple of vestrymen, while the red coats kept the crowd at bay.

'Well, it's clear what did him,' Duffin remarked. A broad slash had severed the throat nearly to the spine.

Jarrett touched the clammy skin. 'He's not been dead long.'

For a moment he was sealed in a humming sense of an ending. So the chase finished here. All the days he had spent pursuing this malignant, ghostly Tallyman – perhaps it was only fitting that when at last he looked upon the infamous features he should find the bogeyman nothing but the dumb shell of a corpse. He lifted the body experimentally as if he hoped life might still linger. The weight of death impressed its finality on him. Had the miner killed this man in revenge for the marks on his face? The notion had a neat symmetry to it.

The Tallyman wore a blue coat, torn at the left shoulder seam, the front creased and stiff with blood. Duffin fingered its texture. 'You see what I see?' he asked.

'Your whore said she'd seen him wearing a new brown coat.'

'Aye.'

'And I have seen this coat before, two nights back in the possession of another man. I suppose there would be a lot of blood – a man's throat being cut like that.' Jarrett grimaced. 'But this garment looks as if it's been used to swab up a floor of blood.' Grasping the filthy hair he lifted the head forward, and picked back the coat collar. Underneath the coarse shirt was saturated with blood. It stuck to the waxy skin of the neck, but the wool cloth on the inner side of the coat collar, where the hair had protected it from the outer mud, was merely smudged.

'This is not the coat he died in, Duffin,' he said.

If the miner had killed this bully, why change his coat? To mark him as the murderer of the crofter? The miner's character was not so subtle. That touch had to belong to another. There was a splash of colour. Like a sudden clap of thunder that underlines the lightning as it fades, Raistrick stood framed against a patch of sky up on the road above the ditch, watching him.

Captain Adams called out. Colonel Ison had arrived and behind him Constable Bone stood with his hand on the shoulder of a boy. Raistrick swung himself down into the drain. He moved jauntily as if he had been recently refreshed. He greeted the agent with a carved smile and a bow.

'Mr Jarrett.'

Behind him, the Colonel followed more cautiously. Producing a copy of the Brough murder bill from his pocket, the Chairman of the Bench examined the corpse at a distance, checking off details as if from a list.

'Tear at the left shoulder seam. Yellow hair, braided and worn in a tail behind in the custom of sailors – this would appear to be your man, Mr Jarrett. Constable! Bring the boy.'

The boy of the murdered crofter, the witness fetched from Stainmoor, was barely eight or nine years old, with a head too big for his thin body. Next to him the gory corpse of the Tallyman was like some slain monster of fable. Jarrett moved to interpose himself.

'For God's sake, sir, he is but a child,' he protested.

The Colonel lifted his eyebrows at such tender sensibility. He did not even bother to make a show of speaking privately.

'These peasants are raised in a hard school, Mr Jarrett. It does no good to coddle them. Now, lad, there is nothing to fear. This man has gone to account for his sins. Is this the fellow you saw the night Crofter Gates died?'

Constable Bone patted the boy, as if to encourage him, his face pursed up in disapproval. Ruben Gates's son stared at his father's murderer with primitive curiosity. ''Tis him,' he said and spat.

Constable Bone shuffled awkwardly into the silence. 'Well, Mr Justice Ison, sir, if that's done – might I take the little lad up to Mrs Bedlington? He could do with a good meal.'

The Colonel waved them off. He nodded briskly to his

fellow magistrate in a pleased way. 'A most satisfactory day. We have our murderer, gentlemen.'

Raistrick bent over the body, nonchalantly turning over its clothes. He wiped blood from his fingers on a cleanish piece of the blue coat.

'What's this here?'

He held a package wrapped in a red silk handkerchief in his brown palm. He shook out the material to reveal a shiny silver disc on a long chain. A watch.

'Fancy thing from foreign parts,' Jarrett murmured to himself.

Raistrick met the steel-blue eyes unflinchingly. He wound the watch and pressed it to his ear.

'Broken,' he said and held it out.

Jarrett turned over James Crotter's fine German pocket watch in his hand. The golden deluding voice rolled past him.

'Colonel, I believe that some days back Mr Jarrett was asking after just such a watch; it was missing, I understand, from the effects of the unfortunate Mr Crotter – the Duke's previous agent.'

'Is that so, Mr Raistrick?' exclaimed the Colonel. 'That is strangely interesting. Two birds with one stone, eh, gentlemen?'

'I wish I could agree, Colonel.'

'What now, Mr Jarrett?'

'Surely this death raises more questions than it answers, sir. Who killed this man? How comes he to be found so conveniently just as Captain Adams is sent to bring him in for questioning? And what was his connection to James Crotter?'

'Mr Jarrett, I sympathise. It is indeed inconvenient to be denied the opportunity to question the felon – but in truth what mystery is there? A thief happened upon a house where he discovered the sole inhabitant had recently succumbed to a weak heart.' Colonel Ison shrugged. 'What should a thief do but carry off whatever he could find?' Scarcely pausing for effect, the Chairman of the Bench sailed on, determined to dispel all objections with his reason. 'And as for the manner of his death, I have not been a Justice for near twenty years in this district without recognising the signs of a river brawl.' The Colonel was comfortable in his superior wisdom. 'Why, you know yourself, Mr Raistrick here was just called this very morning to investigate reports of a knife attack during some taproom brawl. Perhaps this fellow here is one party to that encounter – the one who got the worst of it.' He raised a hand to arrest Mr Jarrett's protest. 'This was a villain, Mr Jarrett. We are not in Hartlepool or Newcastle here. We have our rogues but murder is a serious matter in a quiet district such as this. It is a kind of justice – not one I might support officially,' the Colonel gave a brisk shrug, 'but a murderer is despatched. Let us bless our good fortune!'

'So you will not pursue the author of this death, sir?'

The Colonel was scornful. 'A river-rat, Mr Jarrett? He'll be long gone. Unless his wounds fester and kill him,' he added as a pleasant afterthought.

The more Jarrett argued, the more the Colonel's impatience grew. He began to sigh heavily, his eyes wandering over the river and the crowded road. 'We may review these objections more thoroughly in private another time, Mr Jarrett,' he cut in. 'But now we must let Adams remove this corpse and have the people disperse. We want no more unrest.'

Raistrick took no part in the exchange. He stood apart, watching the fire-fighters at the Swan Inn across the river. At the Colonel's last words he turned expectantly. His point won, Colonel Ison's manner relaxed.

'I understand from Captain Adams that you are to be congratulated on clarifying our other little mystery, Mr Jarrett.' Ever the politician, he clapped the agent on the back. 'An accident eh? Always thought the wench jumped.'

*

It took three men to sling the massive form of the Tallyman into the open cart. It slumped there uncovered for all to see, and many came. They pressed five or six deep about the cart and at first were strangely silent. They gazed and pointed to the blood that dripped between the boards and the distorted face and the gory coat. Then someone began to rock the cart. Captain Adams hurried his men, bayonets fixed, to clear a way. A howl went up and a handful of mud was thrown. Then more mud, and stones and vegetable matter began to rain down as they hastened away the remains of the notorious Tallyman.

Jarrett watched the procession move off, the howls and jeers receding down the narrow street. He rubbed his head wearily.

'Could do with a dram myself,' a familiar voice said. The poacher was crossing the empty street towards him leading his tall bay. Jarrett's face broke in to a slow grin. He was opening his mouth to make Duffin some wry response when he felt a tug on his coat sleeve. He looked down at the diminutive errand boy from the Three Pots. The urchin handed him a note and scuttled off. Straightening out the crumpled sheet he deciphered a flamboyant scrawl.

'Mr Raistrick desires that Mr Jarrett will favour him with a visit,' he announced. 'He claims to have some items of interest to me. He is waiting at the Three Pots.'

'And you're going?' The poacher eyed him with a dour face as he rubbed Walcheren's ears.

'How can I resist, Duffin?'

It was a plain room; bare lime-washed walls and sufficient light from a window overlooking the river. Raistrick sat by a table to the left of the light, a bottle and a couple of glasses by his elbow. The man's presence was such he could make the most elaborate room his frame, but this rough, bare setting struck

Jarrett as particularly eloquent. The scene which seemed stark at first sight was full of incident and detail. The river view beyond the window was not a mere stretch of water at sunset. The oily surface reflected the moving colours of the flames as the Swan Inn burned. The sounds of the fire-fighters and the crackle of the fire seeped into the room, a disturbing counterpoint to the regular lapping of the water outside.

'You must forgive these poor surroundings, Mr Jarrett. This tavern happened to be convenient and I wanted to waste no time in showing you these. A scavenger came upon them at the river's edge and brought them to me.'

The lawyer tapped a muddy parcel lying on the table beside him. 'They are sadly damaged, but I believe they will interest you.' He wiped carelessly at the muddy coating with a bit of cloth and pushed the object towards Jarrett with a little gesture of invitation. The agent approached the table. It was the remains of a pair of leather-bound books. They were burnt and charred and pulpy with mud. Inside there was scarcely anything left that could be called pages, but on the cover of one it was still possible to make out the embossed crest of the Duke of Penrith.

'We must suppose that someone – this Tallyman, perhaps – took them from the manor in the hope that they would prove of value, then, finding they had none, discarded them.' Raistrick leant back in his chair, his posture relaxed, a faint sense of elation shimmering about him. 'Now, what else would you seek, Mr Jarrett?'

Jarrett's previous encounters with both the Three Pots and Raistrick's own chambers had not led him to expect excessive cleanliness in either. And yet this room had been recently scrubbed, and a patch of wall appeared to be freshly limed.

'It is an Englishman's right and duty to protect his neighbours – your words, Mr Raistrick. I would add: and to seek justice for them all. Is that not the aim of all just laws?' the agent responded.

The lawyer laughed out loud. 'Just laws! A truly radical fancy, Mr Jarrett! The law has little to do with justice. It is about maintaining the order of things. And the law has been satisfied in this case. But why not sit down and join me in a glass? Come, draw up a chair,' he invited. He poured the wine with a flourish and pushed a glass towards his guest, leaning forward to rest an arm on the table.

'Let us review some practicalities, Mr Jarrett. You asked the Colonel earlier: Who killed this Tallyman?' Raistrick boomed the question in mock-dramatic style and shrugged, both hands spread with palms up. 'We have no witnesses. But then, why should we good citizens complain? The villainous murderer of an honest man is dead. Had we caught him alive we would have hanged him. Now we are saved the expense and trouble. Perhaps we should rather send up a little prayer of thanks to the good Lord that we are relieved of the necessity.'

Jarrett took a sip of wine, heady with a touch of spice. The aura of confidence was palpable. The magistrate knew he had won, yet it seemed he needed his opponent to know more so that he might appreciate the full quality of his victory.

'It was my impression, sir, that the law does not distinguish between the relative virtues of victims. Under the law murder is murder, is it not, Mr Justice Raistrick?'

'You are a philosopher, Mr Jarrett. You are interested in hypotheses. I, on the other hand, am a lawyer and a practical man. I deal in cases.'

'Then let us discuss cases, by all means. I find it extraordinary, sir, that a Justice of your abilities and experience should not have known of this Tallyman.'

'Did I say I did not know of him?' The magistrate leant back in his chair. 'But you never mentioned a previous interest in this Tallyman to me, Mr Jarrett. Had you done so I could have told you he was a petty thief and bully sometimes hired to collect debts.'

'Collect debts?'

'Debts, Mr Jarrett, or rents. Among the rougher sort of people due rent is not rendered up on a pretty please. It is necessary to put a little more salt behind the request. This Tallyman was the kind employed on such errands.'

Jarrett's lean figure sat at ease, his bruised leg extended. He was close enough to take in every detail of the eyes facing him across the table. Smoky irises defined by a darker outer ring and pupils as black and sharp as sin. He searched them for any glimmer of conscience or guilt.

'I was informed, Mr Raistrick, that this Tallyman was seen at the old manor, while Crotter's body still sat by the fire – seen taking these very books.' If he had hoped to trip his opponent he was disappointed. The magistrate expressed genial astonishment.

'You had a witness! But, Mr Jarrett, why ever did you not say so before?' he chided. 'Had you only spoken up we might have caught this fellow before he went to meet his maker.'

Jarrett gave a slight bow as he sat. 'I fear, sir, I was distracted – a certain misunderstanding about a girl's murder, as you might recall.'

'Ah.' Raistrick acknowledged the point with a salute of his glass.

'But let us discuss,' Jarrett paused, 'a hypothesis, if you will. Say that this Tallyman had a reason other than robbery to visit the manor. Might Crotter himself have hired him? To collect debts, say?'

'It is possible.'

'Then, you will allow, it is also possible that the villain came to collect debts from Crotter himself?'

'Perhaps.'

Jarrett seemed absorbed by the lights reflected in his wine. 'Crotter, by all accounts, died a pauper.'

'Where is the mystery in that? A debtor is a pauper.'

Raistrick stretched over to refill his guest's glass.

'The mystery lies in the extent of the depredations made against the Duke's estates. Considerable sums were passing through Crotter's hands. Were they all swallowed in debts? What sort of debts?'

'Now that is a puzzle. You can find no paper evidence of a connection?' The eyes, predatory for a moment, grew faintly amused. It was Jarrett's turn to acknowledge a point. He sketched a faint imitation of his host's salute with his glass.

'A pity.' Raistrick brought a french knife out of his pocket, all freshly oiled and shining, and began to clean his nails. Little reddish crescents of dirt fell on to his coat as he talked. 'This district is small, Mr Jarrett, I have considerable interests here and am generally thought well-informed. A few years back, it is true, Mr Crotter made an unlucky commercial speculation. I was able to be of some assistance in extricating him from that affair. I warned him then that he had no head for business. I never heard of him dabbling in the same way again. He must have gone fishing further afield and come to grief.'

'So you think this Tallyman was a collector for some person from outside the district?' Jarrett suggested. He nodded slowly. 'Ah, but then...'

The magistrate looked up from his manicure. 'Now that is the pause of a man who is about to reveal a winning card, Mr Jarrett.'

'My witness also saw this Tallyman attempting to burn the books,' Jarrett confessed with an apologetic smile. 'Now that puzzles me. The attempt to destroy the books makes them appear valuable, or incriminating; but to whom? To the Tallyman – who, by all accounts, could not read – or his employer? You see the source of my bewilderment?'

The carved face assumed a mask of sympathy. 'Irrational behaviour to men such as you or I, Mr Jarrett. But this Tallyman was a petty rogue. Such creatures spend their lives drowning what little reason they have in liquor.' The Justice met Jarrett's sceptical look and his eyes slid off a moment. 'Or perhaps he was merely discontented with his employer and sought to spite him,' he concluded.

'By destroying something of value to him?'

The magistrate shrugged.

'And then he found the books would not burn up and changed his mind?'

'And discarded them in the river, where they were found and brought to me.' Raistrick threw off the matter. 'Who is to know now?' He shifted his ground. 'So, Mr Jarrett. Does His Grace the Duke share your passion for justice? If so, he must indeed be a pearl among his kind.'

According to Charles, Jarrett was born with an oak face; at that moment he hoped it was serving him well. There was the nub of it. Charles was a practical man, too, and Charles, in the end, spoke for His Grace. Crotter had died of natural causes. He had defrauded his master the Duke, but he was beyond retribution now. Any paper linking the lawyer to his depredations appeared to be destroyed. The Tallyman might have been a witness but he, too, would be forever silent. And the miner who likely killed him? Even if he had done so at the lawyer's instigation, he would never talk about a deed that would hang him if he were caught. And even if this lawyer himself had wielded the knife that took the Tallyman's life – perhaps the very knife that pared the nails on the blunt-fingered hands before his eyes – was the law to hang a Justice of the Peace for the death of a certified murderer? In his heart Jarrett knew the idea was preposterous.

'So your quest is complete, Mr Jarrett; you have your books. Or should I say Captain Jarrett? For you are a soldier, I believe. I might have guessed. You have been diligent in this affair; the very soul of honour. For King and Country!' Raistrick flung up a hand, inclining his head in mocking acknowledgement. 'Most noble, Captain Jarrett.'

'You sneer at a soldier's honour, Lawyer Raistrick?'

'Please don't mistake me. I have great respect for a fighting man. No. I merely imply that a soldier may hold a different, higher view of the proper order of things. In battle it is simple to be heroic. In civil life – well, it is more complex. One must be content with sufficient order.' Raistrick drained his glass and belched. 'Murder, now. Murder, Mr Jarrett, is a messy business. Speaking hypothetically, of course, as a military man you will no doubt agree that as an act of conquest it has its transitory excitement. I am open-minded on the subject, but in civilian life the consequences of murder are in general cumbersome. Still, in this case...' He made a dismissive gesture, his voice bored. 'This Tallyman was born to hang. I dare say his despatch was convenient to the public interest.'

'And sudden death puts a useful seal on mysteries,' Jarrett suggested.

'Perhaps.'

'And the same wax, in turn, veils the murderer of this Tallyman himself.'

'Why, Mr Jarrett, you have another hypothesis!' the lawyer exclaimed, almost gaily. 'Have you identified a killer?'

'I have a notion as to the instrument. I merely wonder how he was contrived to be used.'

'Are you suggesting one man might use another to commit murder, Mr Jarrett?' The magistrate made an elegant pass with his knife with a thoughtful air. 'I suppose it might be said that sovereign princes use their soldiers for just such purposes.'

Jarrett ignored the jibe. 'You compare yourself to a sovereign prince, Mr Raistrick?'

'Mr Jarrett,' he chided, 'we are discussing hypotheses, not cases.' Ever the genial host he refilled the glasses. 'You still look puzzled, Mr Jarrett.'

'It is only a small matter, sir, but I was told this Tallyman had a devil of a reputation. How come he allowed his throat to be cut so neatly? There were no signs of struggle on the corpse. It is almost as if he were caught unawares, somewhere he thought he was safe.'

Raistrick picked up the gleaming knife and returned to his nails. 'A wide reputation is a dangerous thing, sir. It can lull a man into believing himself invulnerable – it can make him careless. In my opinion' – the bold eyes rose to meet Jarrett's – 'based on my inspection of the wound, you understand, the man's throat was cut while he slept – in a chair, say. A sleep perhaps deepened by drink.'

Putting down his knife, Raistrick picked up the bottle. He cast the dregs into his glass until it brimmed over and wine slopped on to the table. 'Speaking of which ...' He made a play of holding the empty bottle up to the light. 'We are in need of fresh supplies.'

He leant his broad-shouldered frame over and fetched up another bottle from under the table. Jarrett's eyes fixed on the patch of wall behind his chair. There was the shadow of a stain underneath the new white-wash. It mapped some dark liquid that had splashed, perhaps from the height of a seated man, and dripped in trails down to the floor. Every sound and smell came sharp and thin through his senses. With a certain click Jarrett knew he was present at the site of the Tallyman's death. His host's figure reclaimed the space, his knowing eyes dancing with amusement.

'After all,' he continued smoothly, 'what was the substance of this bully's reputation? A hard head and a viciousness of temper that overawed little people. A flea who dreamt he was a tiger!' The Justice fluttered a scornful hand. 'It bites and in its last moments awakens to the truth!'

To Jarrett's heightened senses the lawyer's personality seemed an expression of some primal force of human nature, unadulterated by morality, custom or guilt. The man clearly

relished displaying himself to one he judged able to appreciate his talents. Jarrett was amused, and faintly honoured,
that he had been considered worthy to witness such a display. The lawyer sensed the ebb of power between them.

'You have high-born friends, Mr Jarrett, but I guess that
you yourself lack their material means? It is a misfortune
to be born without the property to support natural talents.
Now, I have made my own fortune – but then I am no gentleman.'

Jarrett acknowledged a certain pride in the virtues he
believed to belong to the condition of gentleman. He felt the
sting of the other's scorn.

'This world is no kind place to impecunious gentlemen
of honour.' The insinuating voice curled about him. 'It is a
sad fact that however fond our noble friends may be of us,
distinctions in property do tend to make a client of a man.
You keep to your soldiering, Mr Jarrett – it is the profession
for heroic gentlemen without property. Maybe you are the
sort who needs a coat and badge. Some men seek a more
bounded, disciplined life; it relieves us of the burden of re-
sponsibility for taking the larger decisions. It takes an odd
kind of man to stand alone in this world.'

'Are you insulting me, Mr Raistrick?'

'Am I?' The lawyer's expression portrayed enquiry without malice. 'Most men are petty creatures. They huddle for
comfort in the stinking proximity and warmth of the herd,
blowing down each other's snouts so they may not have to
listen to the harsh truth in the wind. I have no such weakness.
I am who I choose to be, Mr Jarrett. Can you say the same?'

Could he? Jarrett faced the stark question.

'In some ways we could almost be alike, you and I, Mr
Jarrett,' the animalist voice flowed on. 'We live off our wits.
Independent men who must make our own fortunes – and
judgements.'

This man was a knave; a Justice-embezzler; a lawyer who

mocked the law and perverted even sacred codes to his pure advantage, and yet Jarrett was half-shocked to discover he felt no revulsion. To have no loyalties but to the self; no ties of love or duty to call you to self-sacrifice; to know no guilt. In the darker corner of his soul he envied the man his total freedom.

'You mistake me, sir.' Jarrett reclaimed his own integrity. 'There are some principles I will not give up.'

Raistrick nodded slowly. 'And there, Mr Jarrett, there lies the difference between us.' He gave a little stretch of his body, a contented predator, resting at high noon. 'Well – you have solved your mystery; you have your books and we return to the status quo.'

Jarrett stood up and snapped a military bow. His features relaxed a little into a crooked smile. 'Until our next engagement, Mr Raistrick.'

The lawyer inclined his pagan head. 'Until our next, Mr Jarrett.'

He swung his legs up on to the table, straight and strong, and cocked his profile to look out of the window. The fire at the Swan glowed red in the heart of its blackened shell as the smoke curled across the surface of the river, stained ox-blood in the setting sun.

'In the words of our Colonel Ison – a most satisfactory day,' the lawyer magistrate remarked. And there Jarrett left him; framed in that room, whittling the blood from under his nails, the charred remains of James Crotter's books forgotten beside him.

A light breeze lifted the petals strewn over the simple coffin as the choirmen bore the earthly remains of Black-Eyed Sal to her grave. The Reverend Prattman had been persuaded to ignore the gossip of ignorant folk and had granted her a spot by railings at the bottom of the churchyard where the air murmured restfully in the tall trees.

The burial was well-attended. The Woolbridge maidens lined the path. Prudence Miller, a fetching ribbon twisted in her hair, wept loudly within the arms of two stiff-faced lads who exchanged uncomfortable glances over her glossy head. The young people bunched together, averting their eyes from Mrs Grundy's grieving figure, supported between Jasper and Polly Bedlington. The cook huddled within the warm earth tones of Sal's shawl, which Ezekiel Duffin had retrieved from the place where she fell. Her restless hands moved constantly, smoothing the rough wool.

Even Mrs Munday came to pay her respects, standing, hatchet-faced, beside a shrunken Maggie Walton. The Duke's agent arrived late and walked over to join Captain Adams who escorted Miss Lonsdale, her aunt being indisposed. The Woolbridge maidens cast knowing glances at the trio. They bent their heads together, exchanging speculations. There was an added frisson when Will and Mary Roberts were seen approaching and stopped at a respectful distance among the trees. For a moment all eyes fixed on Mrs Grundy, but wrapped up in her sorrow the old woman made no sign.

'Man that is born of woman hath but a short time to live.'

As the Reverend Prattman boomed out the service for the dead, Jarrett found his gaze drifting up to the crest of the path and the elaborate coffin tomb where he first laid eyes on the once vital creature they came to bury. A stir amid the outer ring of mourners reclaimed him from his thoughts. It fluttered among the maidens and spread to the lads who looked to each other perplexed for a moment. An elegant figure was descending the path.

The mysterious newcomer seemed oblivious of the attention. Two rows of gold buttons gleamed on his lavender coat and the travelling cloak that brushed the ground was loaded with numerous capes. He swept off a broad-brimmed beaver hat and stood with head bowed, the breeze stirring the curls of his guinea-gold hair.

The coffin was lowered and the Reverend Prattman finished the service at a brisk pace. The principal mourners turned away from the grave. The mysterious gentleman threw up an arm in a peremptory gesture, arresting the grave-diggers as they began to shovel the earth on to the coffin. Flicking his cloak behind him, he sank gracefully to one knee. The maidens noted his poetic countenance and the piece of heather he clasped in his gloved hand. He pressed the spray to his lips. Dividing it into two, he dropped one purple sprig on to the coffin below. Eyes downcast, his melancholy lips appeared to frame Sal's name as he held the remaining sprig to his heart.

Francis Mulrohney rose with an air and paced solemnly away from Sal's grave. The Woolbridge maidens would tell of Sally Grundy's mysterious gentleman friend for many a year.

The actor stopped to shake hands with Mr Jarrett.

'So what did you think of me performance, now?' he asked with a lift of one eyebrow.

'Touching,' Jarrett replied.

'Was it not? I fancy my Sal would have liked it.' The Irishman held the sprig of heather to his nose, running a quick glance over the gaggle of maidens who exclaimed over him at a distance. 'From what she let drop now and then, they did not treat her kindly.' He brought out a bill-fold and tucked the heather into it. He paused as he replaced the wallet in his breast pocket. 'A useful piece of business that,' he reflected, giving his breast a brief pat. 'I might use it next time I play "The Stranger" – not merely a ring, but a flower. Aye.' He gave Jarrett an engaging smile. 'Well, I'm for Dublin. My gracious patroness has lent me a chaise for the first stage; it'll not do to keep the coachman waiting any longer. The occasion apart, it has been a pleasure, Mr Jarrett.'

'Mine also, Mr Mulrohney. I hope I may one day have the opportunity to see one of your complete performances. You give me a high opinion of your talent.'

They shook hands heartily and, drawing himself back into his part, Francis Mulrohney made his exit through a clutter of admiring maidens.

Miss Lonsdale left a conversation with Mrs Bedlington and joined the Duke's agent.

'Was that Sally Grundy's gentleman friend, Mr Jarrett?' She sounded unconvinced.

'Yes, Miss Lonsdale. The actor, Mr Mulrohney, with whom she became acquainted while working at Lady Yarbrook's.'

'Ah, of course. He is an actor.'

Jarrett smiled at her tone. 'I believe he was putting on a performance for the benefit of Miss Miller and her kind, Miss Lonsdale.'

The grey eyes were suddenly full of warmth. 'Was that it? But how very kind of him.'

Mrs Grundy was labouring her way up the hill. By Johanson's tomb she stopped. Will Roberts stood in her path. The tall youth held his ground, pinned by the blank look. With a stiff nod the grey woman acknowledged him. Will Roberts dipped his head and stepped aside and Mrs Grundy passed by.

'Mr Jarrett, will you escort me?' Jarrett started at Henrietta Lonsdale's brisk voice. She linked arms with him in a determined fashion and steered him towards Will and his wife.

The young man greeted the pair with a shy smile.

'I wish to thank you, Mr Jarrett, sir.' He bent in an awkward bow. 'Miss Henrietta told me you spoke for me before the magistrates.'

'It was only justice, Will. I believe you would have prevented Sally Grundy's death if you could,' Jarrett responded.

'That I would, sir.' Will slid a shamefaced look at his silent wife. 'She was never a bad lass, just wild,' he mumbled.

It seemed as if her release from the sergeant's tyranny had begun to allow a personality to form in Mary Roberts's anonymous face. Jarrett discerned a genuine flicker of annoyance at her husband's mention of Sal.

'What news of your father, Mrs Roberts?' the agent asked gently.

The child-woman looked to Will.

'Should have known even fire couldn't take the sergeant,' Will commented.

'Devil didn't want company,' muttered little Mrs Roberts.

Will clasped her hand more firmly over his arm. 'He'll not rise from his bed again, Mr Jarrett.' Will spoke with a new found assurance. 'But we'll see he's looked after, Miss Lonsdale. I still know how to behave like a man, even after what he made of me.'

'Are you to stay in Woolbridge, Will?' Miss Lonsdale asked. The Swan Inn was hardly more than a shell after the fire. In Henrietta's opinion neither Will nor his wife had the character for an alehouse life.

'Smithy up Barningham way says he's getting old. Ours is a good corner for business,' the youth replied. 'We'll build a shop, he and I, and a decent dwelling. He's a single man – he'll come live with Mary and me and teach me the trade. He says I've the shoulders for it.'

'You were right, Miss Lonsdale,' Mr Jarrett remarked as they walked off together in search of Captain Adams. 'Will Roberts is a good man. He has a sensible head on his shoulders. I wish him and his little wife well.'

'As do I, Mr Jarrett. At least something good comes out of this sad business. I do not wish to sound devoid of human feeling,' she reflected, 'but I cannot help wishing that they had waited a little longer to pull the sergeant from the fire.'

'Miss Lonsdale!' Mr Jarrett exclaimed in mock reproof.

'Mr Jarrett, I dislike hypocrites,' the lady stated firmly. 'I will say it plain. To my mind such sinful men as the sergeant, who prey on good men such as Will, are much better left to their Maker.'

More than two weeks had passed since the riot in the river quarter. Jarrett knelt before his campaigning trunk while Charles sat in the window seat watching him as he folded his blue regimental jacket.

'Could Tiplady not do that?'

'I sent him off on an errand. I had a fancy to do it myself,' Raif replied.

He had just returned from a journey to London to see the army's medical men. They had pronounced him fit for service. He spread the coat in the trunk. The high collar stood up, its scarlet facings set off within silver lace. The 16th was not a swaggering regiment but he and his fellow officers wore the uniform with pride. Their service in the Peninsula could match that of any of the units fighting with Lord Wellington. He arranged the few books around the edges of the space, spines upmost. Dulles's *Mathematics,* Percy's *Ancient Ballads, The Spanish Duty* – Cocks had given him that volume the time they travelled together into southern Spain in the winter of 1810, a pleasure tour that had ended abruptly with Victor's advance across the Sierra Morena. They had been caught out by that one. Sight-seeing had turned into scouting along the lines of the enemy's march. Lying concealed to count troop movements in the distant dust and moving by night to avoid straggling parties of French dragoons.

Charles handed him his telescope. 'Fine instrument,' he commented.

'It is the one you procured from Dolland for me a couple of years ago – you always have had an eye for quality.'

'Thought I recognised it.'

'You sent it out at the same time as this old friend.' Jarrett drew his sabre from its scabbard.

'That I remember! Roomy in the handle and not too heavy at the point.'

Jarrett chimed in and they spoke together. 'And take care that the handle is not roughened with fish skin!'

'You were most specific.'

'And you procured me a very fine sword.' It balanced sweetly in his hand, a deadly extension to the arm. Its very grip transmitted an echo of the sensation of battle; that flow of spirits when the mind is animated, the body exercised and all faculties fully employed in the simple, vital contest of staying alive or being conquered.

There was a pair of sketch books on the floor, bound in Russian leather and each fastened with a metal clasp. Jarrett had no need to turn the pages to see their contents. He remembered every line and daub. His insufficient attempts to record colour and atmosphere and place wherever the army had taken him. The West Indies, the Walcheren swamps, the elegant cities of Spain and the stark mountains of Portugal. He placed the books in the trunk. The battered little travelling case containing his water colours and dwarf brushes he slipped into a pocket.

He looked about the room.

'What else? Ah, the map.' Jarrett rested the canvas folding map of Spain and Portugal on top of the trunk. 'All stowed away.'

Charles leant forward and pointed to the bracelet of hair about Jarrett's wrist.

'And what about that?'

'This?' Raif traced the golden strands with a gentle finger, a half-smile warming his features. 'No. Her I shall keep. That tie can never be severed. But she can go.' He picked up his sketch of Black-Eyed Sal and threw it into the trunk, closing the lid smartly after it. He pulled the straps tight over the gold-leaf lettering: Capt. Jarrett 16th LD. He paused, resting a hand upon the trunk.

'Have I done right, I wonder?'

'I believe so.' Charles was emphatic. 'I know it is no simple path, but, as I have said before, your family supports you.'

'A man cannot live solely within the ramparts of his family, Charles. To live a life one must face the world alone.'

'Better face the world, then, than stand aside, measuring out your years in exile. Besides, who asks you to pay this price?'

'It is the way of the world, as you well know. "The sins of the fathers …" and the mothers too.' Jarrett fell silent, turning the bracelet of hair about his wrist, recalling the revelations that had made a bastard of him that year he turned twenty. 'Knowledge changes us, Charles,' he said in a low voice.

'Not materially.' His cousin's conviction broke into his isolation. 'Knowledge cannot alter the quality of an honest man.'

Jarrett's eyes were affectionate as he searched his cousin's face. 'A man asked me the other day if I had the courage to live in this world.'

'Courage? You? You are the soul of courage! Whoever this man was he was a knave and a fool!' Charles was indignant.

'A knave he is assuredly, but no fool. And he was wise in this. It takes one kind of courage to ride to face death in the enemy's fire but another sort entirely to take on the world.'

'And you have sufficient courage of both sorts.'

'Do you think? Well, I have done the deed now. I have sold out. It is farewell to the uniform and farewell to fighting King George's battles!' Raif Jarrett gave his bound trunk a smart tap and rose to face his cousin with a wry smile. 'Time to come home and fight some of my own.'

'About time, indeed!' Charles responded. 'I have missed you these last years.'

EPILOGUE

It was one of those grand days when the light seems to keep the observer at a distance, displaying the landscape as some exquisite masterpiece to be wondered at and admired. In between the rich, golden sweep of the harvested fields the decadent green of the late summer trees was powdered with russet – that first precursor of autumn. A collection of carriages and somnolent horses clustered under an oak in view of the old manor house, their coachmen and attendants sitting about them in the burnished grass. The manor, crouching within the rosy circle of its brick wall, was under siege. The century had come to strip away the clutter of the past. The five yew trees were felled and their roots grubbed up. The new light poured in on carpenters, plasterers and masons, busy banishing the house James Crotter had left.

'I designed the staircase myself – drawing inspiration from some notions I came upon in Rome.'

The Marquess spread his plans on a trestle table between the fluted columns of the new entrance hall, Mr Jarrett's guests gathering around him. There was Colonel Ison, supporting Lady Catherine who lurked under a frivolous bonnet. Sir Thomas waved a lorgnette above a finely penned detail of an arch, while Mrs Lonsdale fixed her mournful eyes on the young Marquess with dog-like devotion. Jarrett caught Miss Lonsdale surreptitiously dabbing a handkerchief to her eye beside him.

'It is just the dust, Mr Jarrett,' she whispered, blinking at him.

'May I escort you outside?' he murmured back. 'Perhaps you find this rather dull work – I do myself.'

'I should like that, Mr Jarrett.'

They slipped away without advertising their departure, like guilty children. As they stepped outside Miss Lonsdale paused to despatch her groom on an errand. Jarrett took her arm, and they strolled about the carriage circle while they waited for the man to return.

The house was seething with works. There were men on their knees tearing up weeds, men in aprons wheeling barrows and others up scaffolding wielding hammers and chisels, all filling the air with bustle and noise. Henrietta contemplated the confusion.

'Lord Earewith has enthusiasm,' she remarked.

'Indeed.'

She slid her companion a quizzical side glance and he grinned.

'I have to confess I feel the charm of my little cottage.' Jarrett held himself up in gentle parody. 'As Charles would have it, I will ever stick to my simple folly. But,' he expelled an exaggerated sigh, 'now that I have exchanged my regimentals for the garb of a man of affairs – a Duke's agent must live like a gentleman; one owes it to the neighbourhood.'

Her calm face grew serious. 'You do not find your folly a melancholy place, Mr Jarrett?'

He glanced down at her with a half-smile. 'I have no fear of ghosts, Miss Lonsdale.' He looked out across the bow of land leading down towards the river and the trees that hid the bridge. 'Even ghosts can have their charm.'

She wondered at his wistful tone. Her grey eyes watched him with a tinge of sadness. 'She was a vividly beautiful girl.'

'Vivid!' He was startled. 'Yes, vivid.' He confirmed his words with a thoughtful nod. 'Sally Grundy was a vivid sort of creature.'

'Whenever I laid eyes on her,' Henrietta began, 'I found

myself thinking – there is a girl who loves life. It is painful to think of her end.'

The groom approached and handed his mistress a book bound in red morocco.

'I have brought something for you, Mr Jarrett.' She laid the book in his hand. 'Your *Volpone*. Do you recall, you promised to explain?'

'So I did, Miss Lonsdale – and I shall.'

He turned the volume over in his hands. She watched a private look close over his face like a shutter. She felt as if she were present at an intimate moment and wondered if she was trespassing.

'This is to do with Sally Grundy's end,' he said. His keen eyes met hers almost shyly. The recognition made her heart jump. Suddenly he resumed their walk so she had to give a little skip to catch up.

'It seemed so incomprehensible.' He was utterly focused on his thoughts. 'The tale Miss Walton and Will Roberts told – I do not mean to suggest they lied. I simply could not believe in the notion of Sally Grundy out of her mind with misery and passion on the rock that night.'

He opened the book and began to search out a passage. 'Something bothered me when listening to their testimony and then I recalled a passage Lady Yarbrook rehearsed in my hearing. Listen to this.

> Oh God, and his good angels! Whither, whither,
> Is shame fled human breasts? That with such ease
> Men dare put off your honours, and their own?
> Is that, which ever was a cause of life,
> Now placed beneath the basest circumstance,
> And modesty an exile made, for money?'

'"Oh God, and his good angels!"' she repeated. In her eagerness she grasped his arm. 'Maggie heard her speak those very words!'

Delighted with her quick understanding he laid his own hand over her hands.

'And Will said she cried about shame and men putting off their honours. They were both so sure she was possessed. Do you recall – Will even said she was not speaking her own words.'

Miss Lonsdale glanced down at her hand. The fresh air became her. There was a pretty flush to her cheeks. Jarrett took a brief step back and continued as if there had been no pause.

'Then there was an odd thing the actor Mulrohney said. He told me that the last he saw of Sal that Wednesday, before the night of the storm, she called to him that she was off to give a performance.' For a brief moment he saw again those dark eyes full of mischief under the brim of her gypsy hat. 'His words were: she was swinging away down the lane, as light as a bird. How could that be a picture of a woman sent mad by grief and shame? I believe Sally Grundy was playing a scene that night. A piece of mischief, if you like. She wanted to frighten her old suitor a little – a good-humoured game in revenge for Robert's jilting her.'

He stole a glance at his companion's elegant face. It puzzled him that he should be able to talk so freely to her. Could a man become friends with a woman? Miss Lonsdale was watching him with a studying look.

'It is just a notion, of course. I barely encountered the wench but she seemed to have – how can I put it – a theatrical quality about her.'

Henrietta hesitated. 'I suppose ... Indeed I have wondered more than once whether Sal was sincere or play-acting! Although there was not a particle of malice in the girl that I could see,' she added hurriedly, not wishing to be misunderstood. A little frown pleated her forehead as she turned the idea over in her mind. 'It seems absurd that the girl should go to such lengths – and yet ... mischief ...' She paused.

'What are you thinking of, Miss Lonsdale?'

'Something I overheard Mrs Grundy say while she was grieving by Sal's body. I fancied I heard her ask: What has your mischief brought you to?'

They stopped side by side, contemplating the view towards the river gorge where the white rock lay screened by trees.

'Sal's last performance in Woolbridge before she left for a new life.'

'And she just slipped and fell to her death.' Henrietta was indignant. 'What an absurd waste, Mr Jarrett! To die play-acting. What a tragic little fool!'

'No. No, Miss Lonsdale,' he protested. 'I cannot think of Sally Grundy as tragic. Her death was, certainly; but she – to me she remains a vivid girl. Her death cannot rob her of that.'

The living woman at his side drew a deep breath.

'You should paint her, Mr Jarrett. Work up that sketch you did. I thought it very fine.'

He wondered what had caused her change of tone. Perhaps she did not approve of artists.

'We should go back,' she said almost briskly. 'I believe Lord Earewith's tour has finished.'

They turned away from the river.

Across the bowl of the valley pink puffs of cloud decorated the margins of a limpid blue sky. The soft sweep of land was green and old gold: everything as it should be under a perfect English heaven. It made the heart ache with the impossibility of ever achieving anything half so glorious. Jarrett saw his guests scattered before the house, diminutive figures in a toy theatre. There was Lady Catherine, her eccentric shape peeping up at Charles, who bowed over her with one hand behind him, flirting as if she were sweet and twenty. And in the doorway, Sir Thomas in his white straw hat and spectacles, the very parody of an antiquarian, clutching a dusty plan and soliloquising about knot gardens to the Colonel and Mrs Lonsdale.

'We are all actors in one way or another, Miss Lonsdale, are we not? Save perhaps for Mr Raistrick.' The last was an afterthought he had not meant to speak aloud. The energy of his companion's response made him start.

'Mr Raistrick,' Miss Lonsdale stated firmly, 'is a black-guard, full of deceit. You of all people must know that, Mr Jarrett.'

Caught off-guard by the force of her disgust he tried to explain himself.

'Yes, indeed, of course Mr Raistrick is a deceiver. But I mean – in one respect he is so to others and not to himself.' He was sounding absurd. He smiled meekly, mocking his own confusion. 'Forgive me. I hardly know what I mean.'

'I beg pardon, but I do not find deceit a quality to admire in a man,' she replied severely.

He suppressed a smile at the sight of her prim expression. He doubted Miss Henrietta Lonsdale could ever be brought to appreciate the qualities of a man of Raistrick's stamp. He bowed with a conciliating face. 'Indeed not, ma'am.'

In a honey-coloured field of mown grass Tiplady, his repentant valet, fussed and ordered his little company of slaves around a table set under a silk canopy, hung with flowers and vines. Tiplady had always had the gift of fash-ioning civilisation in the midst of nature. A pretty picnic was laid out with cool wine, rich coloured fruit and crystal glasses that threw out diamond sparkles in the afternoon sun.

Charles walked up to meet them. 'So, Raif, have you been showing off your new domain to Miss Lonsdale?' The Marquess picked up the lady's free hand and linked her arm in his with easy familiarity. A gentleman on either side, the three crossed the brazen field toward the others who sat under the billowing silk awning.

'Now that the family has bullied and brow-beaten poor

Raif into selling-out, do you not think that the neighbour-hood will benefit from such a fine accession to the ranks of its bachelors?' Charles threw a mischievous look over Miss Henrietta's charming bonnet. Raif was wearing his oak face again. 'I intend to keep Raif company as much as I can.' Charles's dark eyes contemplated the works in progress with a satisfied air, his brain clearly teeming with new possibilities. 'This project will amuse me for many a month.'

Jarrett eyed him with sardonic affection and sighed.

'Now, Miss Henrietta,' the Marquess confided, 'Raif always made out he was a wanderer by birth. But do you know, I begin to see quite a settled look about our Mr Jarrett.'